BALANCING ON AIR

Balancing on Air

KATE FENTON

MICHAEL JOSEPH
LONDON

MICHAEL JOSEPH LTD

Published by the Penguin Group
27 Wrights Lane, London w8 5tz
Viking Penguin Inc., 375 Hudson Street, New York, New York 10014, USA
Penguin Books Australia Ltd, Ringwood, Victoria, Australia
Penguin Books Canada Ltd, 10 Alcorn Avenue, Toronto, Ontario, Canada m4v 3b2
Penguin Books (NZ) Ltd, 182–190 Wairau Road, Auckland 10, New Zealand

Penguin Books Ltd, Registered Offices: Harmondsworth, Middlesex, England

First published 1996
1 3 5 7 9 10 8 6 4 2

Copyright © Kate Fenton 1996

Set in 11/13pt Monotype Garamond
Typeset by Datix International Limited, Bungay, Suffolk
Printed in England by Clays Ltd, St Ives plc

A CIP catalogue record for this book is available from the British Library

ISBN 0 7181 3946 1

The moral right of the author has been asserted

To my friend Dilly

Acknowledgements

Many people answered hours of inane questioning and let me clutter up their studios, outside broadcasts, telephone lines and fax machines. Anything I've got right is courtesy of them; everything I've got wrong is my own fault. My grateful thanks are thus owed to: Geoff Sargieson and colleagues at BBC Radio York, and Ivan Howlett and colleagues at BBC Radio Suffolk; also to Nick Beeson, Teleri Bevan, Dr Stuart Calder, Tom Chadwick, Angela Cook, Bob Doran, Nick Evans, Margaret Garbett, Graham Henderson, Peter Hoare, Martin Leeburn, Mark Owen, Dave Sheasby and Alastair Wilson. Finally, heartfelt thanks as ever to my editor, Richenda Todd.

1 Mid-morning with Rose Shawe

Tune into the show which reflects and celebrates life in
this corner of Yorkshire. Regular features include the
Good Neighbours' phone-in, **Book of the Week** and
Consumer Soapbox – along with the music you like and
a host of surprises every weekday morning between ten
and one.

I

Is *hubris* the word I'm after?

Sorry, but it's a good few years since I left university and, let's face it, the conventions of Greek drama don't feature much on your average local radio chat show. Still, if memory serves me right, hubris is that condition of elated pride and inflated ambition in a mortal which is positively guaranteed to make the Gods stick the boot in. And the downfall of the poor hubristic pillock is all the more painful because he never sees it coming. Or rather, in my case, *she* doesn't.

True to the convention, when this story begins, I was on top of the world. Great job, beautiful house, teeming diary – you name it. Plus there was a prospect of nuptials sufficiently hopeful for me already to have tried on several hats (surreptitiously, to be sure) in Wakeborough's smartest store. I'd fancied a dashing chocolate-brown number the size of a dustbin lid with a wisp of spotty veil – and a price-tag to make you wonder whether the freehold of the shop was being thrown in. No matter. Those marriage plans (and the hat) were to be an early casualty. And, my job being what it is, I can tell you *exactly* when the long, slow slide began. Picture me, if you will, bright-eyed and neatly coiffed in a radio studio on a rainy Monday morning last October.

'It's 11.49 here on BBC Radio Ridings and this is Rose Shawe,' I was carolling, shoes kicked off, headphones clamped over my ears and the microphone winking matily up at me. 'Good Neighbours' phone-in coming up after the news, but now it's time for us arm-chair hikers to put our feet up, as Jim Rumbelow leads our weekly ramble into the countryside . . .' I stabbed the 'play' button on the tape-deck and jumped because there was a sneeze in my headphones.

'Hear that snuffling?' whispered 'Rambling' Jim Rumbelow.

'That's Mr Badger, a-rootling in the woods . . .' Chomp, slurp, snort from Mr Badger. A contented sigh from me as I shut my mike. I was back in my studio, Jim was in his hedgerow and all was well with this wonderful world. That's hubris for you. 'Now then, young Brock,' Jim was chuckling, in a voice which my friend George rightly declares to be as comfortingly redolent of Yorkshire as a slab of treacle toffee, 'enjoying that tasty worm, are we?'

'Yuck city,' muttered the midday headline-reader, slipping into the chair opposite mine. 'Isn't it time they pensioned the old bugger off?'

Which is exactly the kind of cheap crack you expect from a news boy. 'Never trust a mike's dead when the studio's live,' I retorted priggishly. 'Don't say anything in here you're not prepared to broadcast.'

Pete gave a dimpled, pimpled grin. 'Pardon me for breathing.'

'Jim's a great old guy, and the punters love him. When he had his coronary last year, he got more flowers than the Queen Mother.' I felt obliged to to say all this, but I knew it was a waste of breath. Far as the hacks are concerned, my whole three-hour show of chat, advice, music and entertainment is not so much a rich tapestry of Yorkshire life as any old wallpaper to fill the gaps between the real business of the station. Which is, you guessed it, the news pro-grammes and bulletins. And, yes, I do realize we're all supposed to be news animals in today's revised, improved, washes-brighter-cheaper-sharper BBC local radio, but frankly some animals are more news-fixated than others. Not to say more animal-like. Al-though as hacks go (which isn't far) Pimply Pete wasn't bad. Still too young to have developed the full characteristics of the adult of the species. 'You're early,' I remarked. The hold-the-front-page ethic generally has them exploding into studio with seconds to spare, regardless of content. These guys can gasp the latest on bus passes like it was a serial killing.

'Wondered if you'd heard.'

'Heard what?'

'Our new arrival?'

Now, if this were a movie, that would be the cue for music: the big doom-and-destiny theme. This being real life (mine) no helpful orchestra warned me what was in store. I wasn't even paying atten-tion. I was shuffling my running order with an eye on the clock.

You'd be surprised how fast a five-minute tape can vanish if you take your ear off the output. 'Rival?' I said vaguely. 'A bidder for the new commercial station?'

'*Arrival*, dimbo. Arriving here in the near future. Surely old Stainless spilled you a few tasty beans?'

I glared. 'Why should Stephen confide in me?' Just in case Pete could suggest exactly why, however, I hurried on: 'Besides, in case you haven't noticed, I've been away for a week. Bridging muddy ponds with splintering planks and dredging the murky corners of my psyche.'

'Come again?'

'He whom the Gods wish to destroy,' I said, innocently quoting my friend George's parting shot, 'they first send on a management course.'

Pete grinned. 'Serving your stretch, eh? Then you won't have heard, because it's only just gone up on the board. Our new Assistant Editor.'

Since Assistant Editor is only the latest fancy title for News Ed, this didn't excite me nearly as much as it should. 'Didn't even know it'd been advertised.'

'Hasn't. Seems we've got some bloke coming up on a six-month attachment.' He scowled. 'From *London*.' London, you must understand, is a value-laden term in these far-flung outposts of the Corporation. 'Television Current Affairs, no less.'

That at least made me look up from my running order. 'Blimey. What's he doing coming here?'

'From what I hear on the grapevine . . .' Pete glanced round and lowered his voice to a conspiratorial croak. Typical. Our hacks might exhibit the swiftness and perception of hearing-impaired tortoises on, say, bonking-councillor scandals, but they are second to none in the gathering and propagation of in-house gossip. 'The guy's leaving telly under a cloud. It was a one-way ticket to Wakeborough or his P 45.'

I actually laughed. Blithe as a canary who can't smell gas. 'Nice to know we work in the media equivalent of Siberia. What's he called then, this television – ?'

But a flicker of red tape caught my eye and – did I but know it – yanked me back, temporarily, from the precipice. I had to break off in mid-question to open my mike, backlink Rambling Jim and cue traffic reports. Once Pete had read the noon headlines, I could only nod a distracted farewell as I embarked on the phone-in.

'And our first call today . . .' I scanned the computer screen in front of me, 'comes from a village just down the road from me, Lower Mill. Maudie's calling about . . .' WALKING TREES said the screen. With many a gleeful exclamation mark, because, as my friend George says, a phone-in without nutters is like chips without salt. 'About trees,' I said carefully. Rule One for dealing with nutters: leave the loony bits to them. 'Hello, Maudie?'

'Hello to you too, young woman,' hooted a voice as tart and tartanned as Miss Jean Brodie's. 'And for your information, it's just the one tree, and a poor weedy specimen it is, too. Two fat sparrows on a branch, and I dare say it'd be flat on its face. If a tree can be said to have a face, which I *pairsonally* doubt, although your trendy tree-huggers would probably disagree. Pantheist prats.'

It was the word 'pantheist' that alerted me. Like 'hubris', it's not much heard on local radio. All at once, this sprightly soprano Scot began to sound . . . familiar?

'A mountain ash, I believe, although the deformed hillock to which it clings is by no means a mountain.' Oh God, *horribly* familiar. 'Och no, as any fool can see, it's nothing but an auld slag heap, for all some optimist has scattered a few grass seeds and christened the result a nature park, if you please. Myself, I've seen lusher growth on a billiard ball. I beg your pardon?'

I hadn't spoken. I'd choked and was glaring through the glass into the cubicle where sat Amanda, my Goth-haired, twenty-year-old assistant, who fields the calls and plugs them through. With a phone clamped to her triple-ringed ear, she was too busy to notice.

'But this miserable shrub has always stood in a direct line between my little abode and the third pillar from the left of the Victoria Viaduct. I live in The Willows, the old people's bungalows, you know.' I knew all right. Except 'Maudie' more commonly described this desirable little close as Death Row. Alzheimer's Alley. Shunting Yard for the Crem. 'However, I glance out of my window this morning and what do I see? The tree is mysteriously standing in front of the *fifth* pillar. Now what are we to make of that?'

'You think the tree has moved?' I asked the question poker-straight. Not that I was tempted to laugh, believe me, but Rule Two for dealing with nutters is that you never laugh at them. They tell you Hitler has moved in next door with his General Staff and you ask politely what makes them think so. Mirth may be rocking nine-tenths of the county, but the minute you join in, you can bet your life you'll offend the remainder, who suspect Adolf always did have his eye on a nice little end-terrace in Wakeborough. 'Well, thanks for calling –'

'Now, as I say, the tree stands on a defunct slag-heap, so I'm wondering, could this be a wee landslip? Remember Aberfan?'

'I –'

'And it's not just any old coal slag, gracious me, no.' Getting faster so I can't interrupt. 'Long after the mine closed, this heap became a common-or-garden rubbish tip, and I'm wondering whether some noxious cocktail of chemicals might not be a-brewing and a-bubbling underground? I canna help but notice the stream is an interesting shade of khaki this morning.'

'Well, there's been a lot of rain, so –'

'With a perfume curiously reminscent of putrid kippers –'

Bang. Everyone has to breathe eventually and I slammed the phone line shut. 'Dear me,' I sighed, 'we seem to have lost the line.' I even squeezed a smile into my voice as I thanked Maudie for her *interesting* call and invited listeners to offer explanations. Ho blooming ho. Having set a disc playing, I spun myself round and glowered at the cubicle window. Which (wouldn't you just know?) was crammed with laughing faces as I stabbed the talkback: Pete, Amanda, the lunchtime news producer . . .

'Maudie, my foot,' I snarled. 'Otherwise known as Mac Bag-shawe. Otherwise known as my bloody father. If the old bastard pulls a stunt like this again, I swear –' I broke off. Not just because of the consternation in the faces behind the glass, but because I realized I could still hear my voice in my headphones along with the music. Ergo, my mike was open. Ergo, I had bellowed these words to the world. I shut the microphone. And my eyes.

'Nice one, Rose,' crackled Pete's voice smugly in my ear on talkback. 'Never trust a dead mike in a live studio, eh?'

I raised two mutely eloquent fingers. Then, more to silence the cheeky pup than anything else, pressed my own talkback switch. 'I say, Pete . . .' Before continuing, though, I checked my mike really was shut. I flattered myself I was a byword round the station for scrupulous efficiency and at that moment, poor sap, I couldn't imagine any worse catastrophe than making a double fool of myself on air. I glanced at the disc player. Two minutes left to run on the music and – as it was to prove – five seconds on my old, carefree life. 'This new Assistant Editor?' I enquired. 'You never told me what he was called.'

He did now.

A tip. Avoid emotional turmoil when presenting live radio programmes. This job, according to my friend George, is like juggling live ferrets while singing a calypso and riding a unicycle. Only more so. God knows how I got through the rest of the show. Some kind of autopilot kept me chatting to callers, sliding the faders, rattling out the timechecks and zapping in the jingles; all I remember thinking about was our Assistant Editor-to-be. Who was called Tom Wilkes.

I was feverishly telling myself this wouldn't be the same Tom Wilkes, that it could be any old Tom Wilkes. I knew for a fact there were plenty around because, over the years, the name had jumped out of newsprint at me as though lined with fluorescent text-marker. There was Thomas Wilkes, manufacturer of tweeds in Perthshire (with a nice line to the Italian couture market); a Professor Tom Wilkes, brain-drained to California. Heavens, there was even a T. Wilkes Esq., solicitor, in nearby Harrogate. A-tremble with nerves after reading his name on the the seating plan at a charity dinner, I'd found only a tubby, balding stranger who assured me my programme was never missed in his house. By his char lady. Lord, there were probably hundreds of Tom Wilkeses. And, yes, one of them was employed on BBC 2's current affairs flagship, *Fulcrum*. I'd long since spotted his credit scudding down the screen and wondered . . .

'Well, that's about it for today,' I finally gasped, gladder than I've ever been to see the minute hand edge up to the hour. 'I'll be with you again tomorrow at ten, until then, it's good bye from me, um . . .' Only then did I stumble.

'Sounded like you'd forgotten your own name,' chortled Pete as I emerged from studio. Little did he know. 'Who is he then?'

'What?'

'This Tom Wilkes, of course. You went white as a sheet when I told you. He an old flame of yours or something?'

That was all I needed. But having survived this far, I wasn't about to crumble now. 'God, no,' I said, with a flinty titter. 'Ten to one it isn't even the same guy. Anyhow – anyhow, it wasn't even me knew him. It was, oh, someone I used to know. Hundred and fifty years ago . . .'

2

One good sound effect, according to my friend George, is worth a thousand words, 'Add a few together, old love,' says George, 'and you're building yourself a technicolour film set, right there in your listener's head.'

So, are we sitting comfortably? Then first of all you should be hearing a Hammond organ playing 'Strangers in the Night' at a gentle bossa nova. Not absolutely accurately. The odd chord's adrift. Also the drummer has been on the Newcastle Brown all night and it shows in some dodgy cymbal shots. Not that this matters because the music is nearly drowned by a buzz of people; a fat, raucous, beery buzz which will ooze smoke and cheap after-shave out of your stereo speakers. Got the picture?

Right, now you hear a popping and a tapping from a tinny PA system. 'Hello, hello, mission to earth control, are you receiving me?' It's a sweaty, tight-cummerbunded wheeze of a voice. 'Thank you, boys, thank you.' The dynamic duo on Hammond and drums drizzles into silence. The crowd does not. 'Gentlemen, friends, brother comrades and what have you' – this raises a few desultory cheers – 'welcome to Blackpool, famous for fresh air and you-know-what, and I promise we've plenty of that tonight, oh yes indeedy. So now, gents, a bit of hush *if* you please, because it's cabaret time here in the Flaming Flamingo.' Voice lowers to a (still breathily amplified) whisper. 'Is she ready out there or what? Champion. Right then, folks. Let's be having a big warm Flaming Flamingo welcome for the very lovely' – the voice crescendoes along with the play-on riff from the Hammond – 'the rip-roaring, ritzy *Rita*!'

And threading between the cramped tables, there's this girl I used to know. Very well.

With a smile as unwaveringly bright as a neon strip light, she kicks and elbows her way across to the dance floor. The slumped lumps of lard blocking her path gape round vacantly, long past recognizing an *artiste* when they see one. She's not daunted. Our Rita's handled many a more dangerous crowd than this bunch. She seizes the mike and, because her play-on music has all the pep of a funeral march, snaps her fingers – *five-six-seven-eight!* – and blasts into her opening medley. Offhand, I can't remember which number she began with that September night fifteen, no, *sixteen* long years ago, but you can bet your life it was up-tempo and loud. Very loud. Definitely more your con-belto than your bel-canto is Rita. She uses this medley like a volley of stun grenades to soften the place up for the main assault.

Actually, I suppose if this were a radio play you might imagine from her lusty contralto voice that she's six foot tall and gorgeously black. So I'll cheat and tell you she's disappointingly pale (Blackpool's climate has not been kind for suntans this summer) and barely tops five foot in her stockinged feet. However, she's rarely shoeless because her calves give her terrible gyp if she abandons her stilettoes. The ankle-wrenchers are gold tonight, and still more inches are added to her height up top by a fiery cascade of lacquered auburn curls, at least half of which are her own.

'Thank you,' she murmurs huskily into the microphone. '"Scuse us a sec, while I slips into summat a bit more comfortable.' There's a cymbal crash and whistles as she shrugs off a feathered wrap. This she places beside the organist with care. Not only did the feathers cost enough to make her ask the shop whether they were plucked from the wings of the Angel sodding Gabriel, she doesn't want some smart-arse hiding it before her Big Exit. Which has happened before.

Now she's revealed in a shimmer of white sequins, so slinky the bodice might have been applied with a spray gun. Her pneumatically packed cleavage and a black-stockinged leg kicking through a slash in the skirt hypnotize a hundred drunken faces into eye-popping hush and she keeps 'em slavering as she struts and sashays and pouts and croons through half a dozen ballads. By the time she's mopping up the applause after what she pretends was her final number, they're baying like famished wolves. You might think, as she bows and smiles round the room, she's just basking in the applause. Is she hell. She's trying to locate the stag party. And her appointed victim.

'Now a little bird tells me we've gorra very important delegation with us tonight,' she whispers into the microphone, *à la* Marilyn Monroe. If Marilyn can be imagined lisping in a ripe Barnsley accent. 'And I hope they're *gentlemen*' – a chorus of whoops and whistles – 'because they're the, um, North-Eastern branch, Allied Union of' – she flutters caterpillar lashes and giggles fruitily – '*Tool* Fitters!'

And that flushes them out. A quarter of the heaving floor erupts into cheers, and, snatching up the microphone cable, she prowls across. 'Well, I hope you fellas keep your tools in working order.' Delighted laughter. 'Because one of your lads is getting himself wed, come next Saturday. Am I right, gents?'

And finally she has her prey in her sights. This one's got to be him. Twenty years younger than his mates, she was told. On the outskirts of the group, he's hunched on a stool which is too small for his great gangly legs. Holy Mother, the poor lad hardly looks old enough to walk to school by himself, let alone to tramp down the aisle. No wonder he daren't look at her. His head's buried in a mug of orange juice, with only a tangle of fair curls emerging. He's all long bones and knobbly joints, all clumsy hands and feet, re-minding her of nothing so much as a Great Dane puppy. Unlike his roaring union colleagues who, by and large, are pompously suited, bristling with pens and badges, he's clad in the tattiest of jeans and sweatshirt.

Rita's nearly swallowing the mike as she moves in for the kill. 'Well, hello, stranger,' she breathes in a whisper which froths round the whole club. 'Come here often?'

The youth starts, as though someone has kicked him, and raises his head, bewildered. All at once she thinks: I'm going to enjoy this. Not just because the boy is plainly harmless as a newborn babe – the routine she's about to perform has health hazards when prac-tised on jokers keen to prove their virility – but because he's so achingly pretty. His eyes are pale hazel-green. At least, let's be honest, she couldn't have made out the colour of his eyes in the smoky twilight of that club, but hazel-green they were. They looked almost golden in certain lights. What she can see is that, while he has the square jaw of a man with raw spikings of beard, he hasn't yet lost the creamy, downy cheeks of a choirboy. And he's blushing bright as a fresh-boiled crab.

It's not surprising he's embarrassed, because Rita is bending so low and so close that his choirboy cheeks are buried in her bosom as she slips off a long, black, satin glove ... Ah yes, I forgot to mention the gloves. Rita is sporting the up-to-the-armpit variety peculiar to Royalty and strippers. Although Rita is not a stripper, goodness me no. She is an *artiste*. Who twines the glove lovingly round her victim's neck even as she instructs him to cop hold of her zip. And she can feel the tension in his wide, bony shoulders. Hell, she could almost twang the tendons.

The dynamic duo, who've backed this routine so often they can play it in their sleep (and often do), are vamping till ready. And Rita is nearly ready to vamp.

She has to help him with the zip, but the dress eventually falls away in a puddle of white sequins (which she expertly kicks out of harm's way) as there's a belated crash from the cymbals and the inevitable roar from the crowd. But Rita is *not* a stripper. She's a singer who, well, sheds a few garments by way of enhancing her finale. Besides, our Rita is a good Catholic girl who has her stand-ards, and those include keeping the relevant bits covered. With two tiny spangled hearts up top (she finds eyelash adhesive adequate) and a titchy (and itchy) feathered G-string below. Plus a diamanté collar, black stockings and a red garter. Of which more later. Much more, God help me.

'I need to sit down for this song,' she announces, and the floor quakes with the scraping of proffered chairs, but she stems the rush. 'On a friendly knee'. She grins and perches herself upon the trembling thighs of her golden boy. 'Is that a gun in your pocket?' she drawls into the mike. Naturally, the audience is chortling before she reaches the punchline, which the organist knows is the cue for hitting the vocals: 'Or are you just pleased to see me, honey?'

Except – and this is the startler – she really has felt something stir against her thigh. And the boy's face is scarlet with mortifica-tion. Real anguish there. She thrusts the microphone away and whispers swiftly into his ear (he smells antiseptically sweet of dan-druff shampoo): 'Don't worry, pet. Just do what I tell you.'

No time for more. '*You're my Mr Adorable*,' she crooned, all those years ago, gazing into his tawny, terrified eyes, '*I just adore you, Mr Adorable . . .*'

3

'I could murder you,' I hissed into the telephone. The programme had finished and I was back at my desk with a low-calorie sandwich and a high-blood-pressure list of jobs for the afternoon. Item One: *Ring Dad*.

I was keeping my voice low because it's a big communal office and I reckoned my family rows had supplied enough entertainment today. Anyway, my colleagues would probably side with Mac. The general opinion seemed to be that they hadn't had such a good laugh since the wife of a notoriously randy disc jockey rang in live, demanding an explanation of the crotchless knickers in her duvet cover.

Mind you, this wasn't the first of Dad's own exploits on the air. A few months back, posing as 'Honest Mac, Turf Accountant to the Gentry', he'd presented the tame vicar on our Sunday-morning slot with a solution to the cash crisis in the Church of England: 'Parish lottery's yer answer, innit, padre? Fixed stake in the old collection plate, guess the hymn numbers and Bob's your Archbishop.' Nor was anyone likely to forget 'Colonel Bagley's' modest proposal that the pigeons fouling the town hall should be shot and casseroled in soup kitchens for the homeless. Killing, as it were, two birds with one cartridge. Old chap. My friend George thinks he's hilarious. Says we should put him on contract.

'But Maudie's walking tree was a gag too far, Dad,' I said grimly, scribbling a star by Item Two: *Check Stephen re T. Wilkes*. 'I've had your number pinned up on the studio blacklist. No calls to be accepted under any circs. Far as these airwaves go, you're grounded, sunshine.'

'Oh aye?' If you didn't know Mac, you'd never believe this tar-soaked Gorbals growl could be disguised as Maudie's mincing Morningside. 'And what, oh golden-tongued viper in my bosom, if

I have a heart attack? What if the grim reaper comes a-knocking between the hours of ten and one when Rose Shawe is giving her all to a breathless world?'

'Tough.' My pen, of its own volition, had inscribed a voluptuous heart beside T. Wilkes. With a huge question mark.

'You know, I sometimes wonder how I came to beget a child so lacking in the milk of human compassion.' I could hear him sucking his fag, and the philosophical sigh as he blew the smoke away. 'Not to say the healing balm of humour.'

With a guilty glance round, I scribbled out the heart, T. Wilkes, and then, for good measure, Stephen too. 'Considering the amount of time you didn't spend with my poor mother,' I muttered, 'I wonder myself how you begot me.'

'Begat.'

'Pedant.'

My parents had separated before I could remember. They lived apart without ever actually divorcing. Mum was Catholic; Dad couldn't be bothered. No point, he said, since he wasn't going to be fooled into the parson's mousetrap twice. So while my mother laboured on alone in her corner shop, Mac hurried back to the boards. He was a comic and, unless you happened to have caught that particular edition of *Opportunity Knocks* circa 1965, you're un-likely to have run across him. Short and fat, with piercing blue eyes and skimpy red hair, he would bounce round the stage in those days like an enraged Scottish leprechaun.

I come from a theatrical clan, indeed I do. My Pappy did a vanishing act when the rent was due, and the auld woman chucked knives at him when he came back. I won't say we were poor, but my idea of a square meal was a cream cracker . . .

No, the audiences didn't laugh much either. Over the years, his act progressed from this sort of kilted variety turn, through oc-casional pantomime damery and comedy magic, to a mohair-suited, cool-on-a-barstool monologue, whisky in hand.

Regrets, I've had a few. Being born for one, meeting the wife for another. It was love at first sight. Then I put my specs on. Still, I did what I had to do. Got married. I won't say the bloom faded fast but it ran the wedding bouquet a close second . . .

Not so much comedy, he used to say, as bleeding chunks of autobiography.

> I went to the doctor; I said, 'Doc, I've a wee drink problem. My hand shakes so much it won't stay in the glass . . .'

Like he said, autobiography. As far as my childhood was concerned, Maxwell 'Mr MacMisery' Bagshawe was a noisy stranger in shiny suits who breezed by once in an infrequent while, scattering fag-ash, jokes and (depending on the horses) largesse. Mum disapproved of gambling. Also of drinking, smoking and – he once shouted – any other pastime designed to alleviate the tedium of man's existence. He must have been very drunk, and I must have been very young because I thought he meant watching the telly.

I can see Mum now, glancing at the bead curtain which divided living room from shop, imploring him to keep his voice down. Mac, reared in a tenement where rows were shared like community theatre, was unhushable. For God's sake, she would whisper. God, he would roar, *God?* Her God, according to Mac, was Respectability. To be worshipped behind net curtains and privet hedges in a shrine so refined there were crocheted covers on the bog rolls.

Poor Mum. Her God, I'd since had plenty of cause to realize, was a cruel one. And if He knew what He was about when he let her fall for this feckless, drunken heretic, twenty years her senior, then He knew more than I did.

'Must we drag your poor dear mother into everything?' said Mac now, with the wounded dignity he's come to affect ever since he learned he was safely widowed. 'You know you grow more like her by the day.'

Deliberate provocation. I refused to be side-tracked. 'Listen, Mac, this station is my career. I've worked damned hard to get where I am and –'

'Och, where's my violin?'

'I love this job.'

'I was fond of my own. God's sake, Rosie, you know me, I need an audience.'

'Well, I'm sorry, but I won't have you chucking spanners into my life just because you're bored with your own.'

'Sweet Jesus, you call this a life?' Indignation erupted in a racking, tar-thick cough. Oh, how I hated that cough. A Wurlitzer organ of wheezy pipes.

'You should stop smoking.'

'Why prolong the agony?' His sigh gusted miserably along the telephone line. Typical. Mac never hesitates to play the pathos card. Two years ago he smashed his Cortina into a tree, losing his legs and, since he was tanked up to the eyeballs at the time, his licence. The blessing was that no one else was involved; the only terminal casualties were his dwindling career and my hard-won peace of mind. All at once his voice dropped. 'You know what really gives me the shivers in the small hours, lass? I lie here pondering whether maybe I didna actually perish out on that road. I think to myself, maybe I'm dead, who's to tell? Maybe The Willows – this gentrified, geriatric zoo in which you've seen fit to incarcerate me – is in fact Hell, custom-designed for yours truly. If so . . .' He laughed bitterly. 'If so, I hand it to your mammy's old friend. The Great Joker in the Sky certainly knows how to bring a sinner to his knees. That's if He'd seen fit to leave me any.'

For an unwary moment, I softened. I could see my dad, hunched in his wheelchair like a mangy old owl, snapping at anyone fool-hardy enough to be kind to him, and getting even madder when they didn't snap back. Compassion-fatigue, he was fond of declaring, is experienced chiefly at the receiving end. Then I remembered exactly what it was costing me to keep him cossetted in the sheltered groves of The Willows, not just in service charges but in grovelling politeness to exasperated neighbours, and that fatigued my own compassion.

'Stop moaning, Dad. You've got yourself a lovely bungalow there, warm, peaceful –'

'Peaceful? By three in the morning, the bloody birds are auditioning for *Tosca*. Anyway, I'm an urban creature, my ears crave the rattle of traffic, my soul thirsts for pavements . . .'

I stopped listening and shoved a scribbled note across to Amanda: *Anything in the post?* There's no stopping Dad in purple vein.

'I dream of a city skyline, etched on sooty, crepuscular clouds . . .'

Yes, *crepuscular*. One of the long-suffering District Nurses was unwise enough to observe recently that Mr Bagshawe displayed an extraordinary vocabulary for a man who left school at fourteen. He promptly told her he must have absorbed it from the complete works of Shakespeare in the communal lavatory of his childhood. 'And you read it all?' she marvelled indulgently. His smile was angelic. 'My dear madam, I said "absorbed". I assure you the book wasn't placed there to be *read* . . .'

It's no use asking him to behave. Although I always do, and I can hear my late mother's pleas echoing in my own. 'You might at least think about your neighbours,' I said now. 'Your performance this morning probably scared some poor old lady witless.'

'Had she but wits to lose.'

'Listen, Dad, walking trees might be a good joke but toxic waste isn't. People get seriously worried.'

'Indeed they do. Barely a knicker remains untwisted in The Willows today.'

'Dad, how dare you sit there and –'

'But I cannot, alas, claim credit for the uproar,' he continued and, too late, I recognized the smugness in the old villain's voice. '*Au contraire*, it is my neighbours who have put the fear of God into me.'

All my life I've ended up playing stooge to his comedian. I gritted my teeth. 'Oh yeah?'

'In the past week, while you have been disporting yourself –'

'I've been on a bloody management course.'

'To manage what, pray? My God, your passion for self-improvement knows no bounds. If they offered a diploma in farting you'd be first to sign up. *However*, in your absence, rainfall breaking all records for October has been stripping the paltry skin of soil from our so-called nature park and revealing its ugly past. So much so that some of my neighbours, poor dears, have banded themselves into an environmental action committee. Maudie was my small contribution to the cause – unauthorized, I admit, by the blue-rinsed executive of COSH.'

At that very moment Amanda shoved a sheet of paper across to my desk. The only press release I've ever seen typed on blue Basildon Bond. 'Is that C-O-S-H?' I demanded. 'As in: Clear Our Stream and Hill?'

'I take no responsibility for the clumsy acronym. My own suggestion to the good ladies was Clean Up Nasty Tips. Whereupon, I was asked to leave. I believe it was Polly suggested COSH.'

'*Polly?* Where's she come into it?'

I might have guessed. Polly had been staying with her grandpa while I was away. If there was an environmental bandwagon rolling, it was inevitable my daughter would have leaped aboard. With, according to Mac, a platoon of her bean-eating, planet-saving chums. 'As you would know,' he concluded sanctimoniously, 'if you'd been at home, where you belong. A fifteen-year-old girl needs . . .'

'Sorry?' But I was addressing this to Amanda who had mouthed something at me which seemed to include the word 'Stephen'. 'Hang on, Dad.' I clamped my hand over the receiver.

'Stainless Steve rang earlier on,' repeated Amanda, miming a yawn. (The Lamb is not appreciated as he deserves round this office.) 'Wanted a word some time.'

'I suppose I'd better go and see him,' I even managed to sound quite convincingly exasperated. I took my hand off the mouthpiece. 'Look, Dad,' I said, drawing question marks beside the crossed-out names and doing some fast thinking. If Steve were free after work . . . 'I might be, um, a bit late picking Polly up this evening.' With luck.

'I beg your pardon?'

'Lot to catch up on.' Chiefly, the full story on this Tom Wilkes geezer. Not to say my love life.

'And what about your poor daughter? You've already abandoned her for a whole week.'

'You're a fine one to talk about abandoning daughters.'

'And look what became of you,' he said triumphantly. 'Now if you'll excuse me, I think I hear my Meal on Wheels at the door. *Ciao.*'

4

There's a tentative knock on the door.

Rita, this girl I used to know, is peeling the sequinned hearts off her nipples with many a wince and curse. She takes the fag out of her mouth and bellows: 'Keep your hair on.'

Not that they usually bother to knock. Which is why, being as how there's no bolt, she's stacked three crates of Guinness against the door. The Flaming Flamingo does not run to such refinements as dressing rooms; Rita is changing in the beery gloom of the drinks cellar under the bar. It was a choice of here or the Ladies. Cellars might be chilly, but experience has taught her that shivering alone is preferable to struggling with a long skirt in the heaving, pee-swilling maelstrom of your average club lav. Anyway, she always arrives for this sort of gig lipsticked, lashed and lacquered. Now, after a fast and feather-swathed exit, she's about to re-clad herself in something more appropriate to those famously fresh breezes along the Blackpool front. But there's no time to waste if that's Big Al knocking at the door – she wants to be paid. 'OK, sonny boy,' she yells, pulling on her fur coat and shoving the crates aside. 'Come in if you're good-looking.'

Nothing. Has the skunk pissed off already? She flings open the door. But it is not the ruddy face of the compère confronting her. Instead, alone here in the grimy corridor with a naked light bulb blazing above his curls, stands the golden choirboy, the blushing bridegroom himself, all towering six feet-odd of him, bashfully holding out a scarlet frilly garter. The selfsame garter which, minutes earlier, she made him remove from her thigh. With his teeth.

'You forgot this,' he mumbles. So quietly she can hardly make out the words with the disco beat pounding down from over-head. Even so, she hears the cadence of his voice and it's all wrong for this place. Soft and pure-vowelled as a sodding bishop. 'I thought I'd, um, better bring it back for you.'

'Don't talk daft,' she retorts, wrapping the fur more closely round herself. Christ, it's cold down here. 'You're meant to keep the garter. It's your –'

Wedding present, is what she is about to say. A little souvenir of your stag night, courtesy of the mates who set you up for tonight's fun and games. But she's broken off because Big Al, genial compère of the Flaming Flamingo, is at last following his bouncing belly along the corridor. He casts a contemptuous glance up at the boy and then turns to Rita. 'It weren't him, you silly cow,' he wheezes. 'T'lad what's getting wed were sat over by the bar.'

Rita looks at the boy and, all at once, laughs. 'Good for you, chuck. Stay fancy-free, eh?' She's smiling up at him in a way which makes him flush even brighter.

'I could dock your pay for this by rights,' adds Al.

'Not likely,' she snaps, her attention sharply recalled. 'I'm paid to do my thirty-five minutes and thirty-five minutes I did. You should've pointed your bloke out better. Any road, I went down a bomb, didn't I?' This is shot at the youth, who seems to be trying to melt himself into the sweaty corridor wall.

'Yes,' he stutters. 'Gosh, yes. You were first class. Excellent.'

She winks at him, and thrusts a crimson-clawed hand at her paymaster. Who, with much grunting and scowling, draws out a wad of crumpled fivers and counts them over. 'Just gerrit right next time.'

'You should be so lucky,' retorts Rita, riffling through the notes with the skill of a bank teller as he huffs and puffs off down the corridor. She raises her voice. 'That there'll be a next time, I mean. I've better things to do with my life than sing in dumps like this. Are you coming in or what?'

'Sorry?' The boy is amazed. 'You mean me?'

'No one else, is there? Bloody draughty in the corridor. Mind,' she adds, leading the way, 'it's like a fucking fridge in here. Here, hold this for us, will you, pet?' And she hands him the money as, with a swing of her hindquarters, she slams the door behind them, then kicks a beer crate back into position. 'Ta. Cigarette?'

The boy pats his pockets helplessly. 'I'm sorry.'

'I meant, d'you want one?' She thrusts her open packet towards him.

'Oh, I see. That is, no. No, thanks very much. I don't. Smoke. But please feel free.'

'Oh, I will,' says Rita, and bursts into laughter again. This lad is too much. Politely inviting her to smoke in her own dressing room. She lights a fag and draws deeply, watching him. He, in turn, is staring back at her, although evidently trying not to. His face is a proper picture. Like a kid at a tropical fish tank, she thinks. Gawping at some improbably gaudy specimen and wondering if might not be plastic. 'Cat got your tongue?'

His eyes fall at once.

She tries again. 'So what's your game?'

'Sorry?'

'Put it another way. What's a nice boy like you doing in a dump like this? As the song goes.'

'D-does it?'

'No, but never mind. What I'm saying is, if you're a comrade of the Allied Tool Shunters or whatever they call themselves, I'm the Queen of bloody Sheba.'

This makes him laugh. Nervously. 'She was supposed to be fantastically beautiful,' he says, all in a rush. He doesn't quite add 'like you', but that's what his face is saying and Rita grins, flattered. That accent is something again. She remembers a poor sod of an English teacher at school who talked just like him. Dropped out after half a term with a nervous breakdown. 'So what're you up to here, kid?'

He flushes. 'I'm not a kid.' And very indignant he sounds. She wants to pat his tousled head. He is, she will learn, nineteen. She is twenty-four, which means there are a mere five years dividing them. Or five hundred, depending on how literal you want to be. She shivers. 'I'll perish if I don't get some gear on.'

He's been perching on the rim of a steel barrel, but now he catapults up. 'I'll go.'

'Stay where you are. At least, plonk yourself on that crate in front of the door, will you? Just in case the animals upstairs get any clever ideas.'

'I'll shut my eyes,' he promises.

'I bet you will and all,' she says drily. And he does. She stands for a minute, watching the struggle he's having with his conscience. He laces his fingers across his brow, as though he can't quite trust himself. His forearm glints with pale-gold hairs. There's an ink blot on his thumb. 'I'm, um, a student, actually,' he announces, speaking more loudly, as people do when they're temporarily blinded.

'Ah,' says Rita, chucking the fur on to a chair. 'Hoxford, I hassume.' She's only taking the piss out of his accent, but it surprises him into opening his eyes. And at once clamping the hands back into place. 'Help, sorry. But I mean, how'd you know?'

'Clairvoyant, that's me.' Rita can't be bothered with a bra, just wriggles into a T-shirt, yanks on a minuscule leather skirt – embroidered, embossed and interestingly perforated – and swaps the gold stilettoes for a pair of white mules scarcely less precipitous. 'And what are you studying?'

'Greats.'

'Pardon?'

'Classics. You know, Latin, Greek, Ancient History. All pretty boring stuff.'

Rita zips up the skirt and adjusts her T-shirt. 'OK, I'm decent now.' Although the way he looks at her suggests decent isn't the word he would choose. She is amused. Rather, I imagine, in the way one is beguiled by a prettily precocious toddler. Only this is a six-foot-three-tall and really rather handsome infant. 'Is it?' she demands.

'What?'

'Boring. What you're doing.'

He shrugs. His face, all at once, squares with purpose, reminding her – not at all pleasantly – of a fledgling priest. 'Oh, you know. It doesn't exactly have much relevance to life, does it?'

Life? Whose life? And what the fuck do the likes of him know about *life* anyway? Some such retort tingles on Rita's tongue, but she doesn't utter it. Now, I'd like to think a kindly impulse checked her, because it's clear she could have crushed this shy and sensitive youth. However, knowing Rita as I do – you might almost call her an older sister – I fear it was the contemplation of his arms. He's folded them across his chest. Call her kinky, but Rita is a connoisseur of men's forearms. As it happens, I know how she feels and, I agree, his are amazingly sexy. I can see them now. Tennis-playing

23

limbs, strong without being lumpily muscular, warm-tanned and dusted with those glinting, wheat-blond hairs. So she's silent because, almost as a game with herself, she's asking whether it might not be time this college boy learned something about life. Real life.

She sucks a last drag from her cigarette, chucks it down and grinds it into the lino. 'Always sounded quite fruity to me, all that ancient times stuff,' she murmurs, flaunting her own classical education (three weeks' glamour-work in and out of a transparent toga in a show called *Roman Nights*). 'Randy Gods screwing the peasants, orgies in the forum. Peel me a grape and what have you.'

'*What?*' His voice strangles to a froggy thread. 'I mean, no, hardly. Except, well, possibly up to a . . . But that's not, exactly, um, real life? Is it?'

And this is when Rita makes the most momentous decision of her merrily heedless career. There are no excuses. She's not stupid, our lass. She knows exactly what she's doing and she damn well knows she shouldn't. For a whole host of reasons. 'No?' she says softly. And she leans over and pats his cheek. 'Fancy a drink, do you?'

He glances round. After all, they're in a cavern of alcohol. Lager, lager everywhere and never a drop . . .

'Not here,' says Rita. She snaps shut her vanity case and tucks it into his unprotesting hand. 'I was thinking we could go back to my place, my little Adonis.'

'*Adonis?*'

'He's Latin isn't he?'

'Uh . . . Greek.'

Rita giggles. 'All Greek to me, chuck. You coming or what?'

5

'Ah, Rose, come in,' called Stephen. I'd drawn back because all I wanted was a quiet word and his office was like Grand Central Station.

As Managing Editor of Radio Ridings Stephen rates a Scandinavian-pined and rubber-planted chamber big enough to double as a conference room. Today, he'd evidently been hosting a buffet lunch for what I recognized as our Advisory Council. The Bishop's purple shirt-front was a dead giveaway. And here was Her Worship the Florence, Mayor of Wakeborough, vast and splendid in emerald check. She winked at me. 'Young Stephen's showing off his new computer system. Boggling us with technology.'

'We're talking radio for the twenty-first century here, Florence,' protested my brave Lamb. 'To meet the challenges of today's multi-media, multi-cultural market place we have to target our audience. Look.' He stabbed a button.

'Abraca-bloody-dabra,' murmured Florence in my ear. 'Eh, Rose, I wanted a word about your show this morning.'

'Three-colour pie-chart,' declared Stephen, standing back to display the full glory of the screen, 'showing a graphic breakdown, percentage-wise, of gender balance of contributors. Still weighted 60–40, male to female, but improving. And then our audience profiling facility . . .'

I'm sorry about the gobbledegook. Don't hold it against the Lamb. It's compulsory in management circles these days, like aprons at a Masonic banquet. And he was sweet, really. Reminded me of a kid with a new Meccano set. Besides, he looked lovely in his Italian suit, so clean and wholesome. Surely, I said firmly to myself, no sensible grown-up woman could ask for more in a relationship?

Well, except perhaps the freedom to acknowledge that relationship publicly. Call me unreasonable, but I felt I'd be happier if Stephen and I could share dinner invitations as well as clandestine take-aways, Saturday mornings in the local supermarket as well as the odd Saturday night in a distant hotel. Dammit, I wanted us to *make* the bed together on a daily basis, instead of just wrecking it once in a furtive while. I was beginning to think an extra-marital affair would be less of a strain. Oh, sorry, were you assuming this actually was good old-fashioned adultery? If only it were that simple.

'Excuse me, Stephen,' interrupted a bosomy female. Our Advisory Council is a sort of local board of governors, appointed to keep a watchful ear on our doings. 'But what've all these statistics got to do with making good programmes?' I eyed her narrowly. Had some subversive spirit in the building set her up to ask this?

'Hear, hear,' Florence grunted, with the belligerence of an old-timer used to having these lunches alleviated with a splash of booze. The new squeaky-clean BBC runs on Perrier.

'Key issue,' responded Stephen promptly. 'Of course, programming of quality and distinction is central to our ethos.' Her eyes were already glazing. I wondered how I could tactfully suggest to the Lamb that one-syllable words delivered in fifteen-second bursts, preferably with a few gags, might go down better. 'But we have to constantly monitor and review our performance as we go . . .'

Stephen Sharpe had arrived at Radio Ridings – what? – nine months ago, when our previous boss had finally been shovelled into early retirement. And let's get one thing straight, something which my colleagues seem only too ready to forget in the mellowing haze of Donald's leaving orgies: that man was a menace. One of the crusty, curmudgeonly diehards who gave the old BBC a bad name, he'd run Radio Ridings since it was launched and, over the ensuing twenty years, had refined the job to a point where the whisky bottle could emerge at noon and none of us was daft enough to approach him thereafter unless we wanted an expenses form signing. Amazing he survived as long as he did. Still, out he finally went, and in came Stephen: a knight in grey Honda to the rescue of our beleaguered outpost.

Don't ask why we were beleaguered; local stations are *always* in peril. Never mind that a commercial rival would soon be rearing its ugly transmitter outside our very gates, the current threat was amalgamation with our sister station in Harrogate, and amalgamation is only a managerial euphemism for our total extinction. Even under Donald's *laissez-faire* regime, we'd sacrificed a pack of virgins to the accountancy dragons. It wasn't Stephen's fault we'd had to chop a few more. As I was forever pointing out – and, whatever my friend George claimed, I most certainly was not blinded by lust – we *needed* someone like Stephen to sort us out. OK, perhaps 'knight' is pushing it a bit. Even I couldn't claim Steve was built in swashbuckling-champion mould. In fact, I've sometimes thought he arrived here more like a lone missionary despatched to a particularly lewd and libidinous shanty town of the Wild West, armed only with a bag of Bibles. Or, in Stephen's case, a stack of management textbooks.

Poor Lamb. I remember being summoned to his office the day he arrived and my first bizarre impression was that this flat-voiced, spectacled stranger reminded me of Thomas. Heaven knows why. Rarely were two men less alike than thirty-four-year-old Stephen Sharpe and nineteen-year-old Thomas Wilkes. Steve was nearly a foot shorter; and where Thomas was all golden curls, a tawny, shaggy lioncub, Stephen was close-clipped, premature grey, a shy, neatly shorn lamb. I recall thinking the guy was a symphony of toning greys: hair, suit, shirt, eyes, steel-rimmed specs – even his jaw had a rather sexy greyish shadow which shaving never eradicated. Probably it was just his boyish enthusiasm as he jumped forward to shake my hand that made me think of Thomas. 'Good to meet you, Rose,' he said. 'I've heard a whole lot about you.'

'We've heard a whole lot about you, too,' I replied carefully. I did not add that, in the eyes of my colleagues, none of it was good. Well, the hacks despise on principle anyone who hasn't served their time before a newspaper masthead, and it was unfortunate Stephen's last job had been (so the grapevine buzzed) Controller Paperclips, Television Centre. For which read a successful stint in administration. Add to that our Yorkshire suspicion of anyone born south of Sheffield and a professional resentment of television, of *London* . . . Oh, the knives were glinting before ever he flaunted a five-point news rationalization plan.

'I'm the latest recruit to the team,' he said, with endearing modesty considering he was here to run the joint, 'and I'm counting on you, because Head of Centre says if I want to get up to speed, you know the station and the patch better than anyone.'

I can resist everything except flattery. Besides, as far as Stephen Sharpe was concerned, resistance was never on my agenda.

'Rose, my dear,' said the Bishop now, sailing across as Stephen got enmeshed in megabytes. 'You were missed at the school last week.'

I was explaining my absence to this fellow governor of St Catharine's when we were interrupted by a member of the Arts Festival committee, enquiring about the draft schedule for next year. Tricky, I sighed, my eye still on Stephen, what with the Dale Preservation Society, not to mention my family and the small matter of a daily programme here, but . . .

Maybe this was what Head of Centre had had in mind when he told Stephen I knew the patch. After eight years, I felt I was knitted into the very fabric of Wakeborough. My diary read like a gazette of local life and, make no mistake, that's how I liked it. Normally, there was nothing I'd have relished more than sharing coffee and pleasantries with His Reverence and assorted Wakeborough grandees. Just now, though, I was wondering whether my precious and intricately woven corner of that fabric was about to be shredded by the arrival of one Tom Wilkes. I mean, if he proved to be *Thomas* . . .

'Rosie,' said Her Worship the Florence, cruising over and picking up where she'd left off, 'like I said, I was listening to the show, with your dad and all. By, we were laughing that much we nearly pranged t'official Rover.'

I winced, glancing at Stephen, hoping he hadn't been tuned in. If I couldn't sneak a word with him soon, I'd scream.

'A character and a half, isn't he? Still' – Flo sobered into civic mode with startling abruptness – 'he was right, summat's got to be done. You can't make a blooming great rubbish tip vanish just by dumping a bit of soil and calling it a nature park. I've been saying for years it's a disgrace.'

'Sorry?' With difficulty, I wrenched my gaze away from Steve. 'Surely that's up to your lot? If a tip needs clearing?'

She shook her head. 'Wouldn't be t'Town Council, not up the Dale. Besides, it's not public property, never was, and it's part of The Willows now. Deal was, the company that built them fancy old folks' bungalows got their planning on condition they sorted the tip. Now then, what's their name?'

'Lime Holdings,' I said. I should know, I paid a hefty cheque to them monthly. That had been the deal between me and Dad, struck, he claimed, when he was imprisoned in hospital with a brain softened by anaesthetics. He would buy the bungalow if I chipped in the service charges. Still, as I used to remind myself, the monthly cheque was a small price not to have Mac living a mile up the road with me.

'That's them,' Florence said, with satisfaction. 'I knew it were one of Trevor's outfits.'

That finally diverted my attention away from Stephen. 'Trevor?' I wasn't asking whom she meant, because everyone in Wakeborough knows who *Trevor* is. The new wing of the art gallery is named after him. So is the stuffed crocodile in my friend George's drawing room. 'I never noticed his name on the letter heading.'

'Surprise, surprise,' said Florence with the natural scorn of a Labour stalwart for a nouveau capitalist property developer. 'Probably channelled through some mud-shack in the Cayman Islands with a fax machine, but it's his outfit right enough. Why'd you think nowt's been done ever since that estate were built? Half the blinking council works for him; t'others are scared stiff. I tell you, Rose, that man's dealings stink to high heaven and the day is fast coming when . . .'

But I'd heard Florence on this tack before. Besides, at that moment, clear as a fire alarm, I caught the name 'Wilkes' nearby. 'Sorry, Flo,' I stammered rudely. And hopped sideways.

'Well, I'm glad we've an Oxford man coming in,' the Bishop was observing to Stephen. 'Wilkes, you say?'

'Oxford?' I gasped. But Oxford is a very large university. Vast. Much bigger than, say, Guildford, where Stephen got his degree. Or York, my own alma mater.

'Yup,' said Stephen, a touch grittily. 'Seems the old Oxbridge mafia hasn't lost its stranglehold round this organization yet.'

'Pooh, nonsense,' boomed the Bish, who's a jolly cove. He used to disc jockey the odd hymn programme before his episcopal diary grew too crowded. Or maybe it was when Steve decided our Sunday programming needed to broaden its cultural base. 'Which college?'

I held my breath, but Stephen only shrugged. 'What's he like?' I burst out. 'I mean, well, how old is he?'

Stephen frowned. You could almost see the personnel file scrolling behind his specs. 'Much the same as us, say –'

'Never reveal a lady's age,' chipped in the Bishop gallantly.

'I don't mind owning up,' I chirrupped, even as my heart thudded like a lead pendulum. 'Thirty-five then, if he's the same age as me.' I turned back to Stephen. 'You've not met him?' He shook his head. No point asking what he looked like. 'Married?'

'Well, no,' he began. 'And that's –'

'Funny way to run a business,' interrupted the Bishop, who was rather deaf. 'Appointing a chap as your number two without clapping eyes on him.'

'Too right,' snapped Stephen with evident annoyance, although he cloaked it at once behind his most sphinx-like smile. 'The buck doesn't stop with me on this one, Bishop. Head of Centre's pushing the guy our way. Compassionate resettlement.'

'I'm glad to hear the modern BBC is still capable of compassion,' said the Bishop and, with a pretty sphinxy smile of his own, he purpled away.

'What's compassionate about it?' I whispered, now I had Stephen's ear at last. 'I'd heard this geezer was threatened with the sack in London.'

Stephen looked pained. 'Well, I guess it's common knowledge consensual termination was on the agenda.' That's manager-speak for 'yes'.

'So when's he arriving?'

'God only knows. Honestly, Rose –'

But then, so help me, Florence homed in again and – anything to get rid of her – I found myself promising we would follow up the Willows story, that Trevor or his cohorts would be hearing from me . . .

'Trevor Green?' echoed Stephen, as Florence sailed off. He might well look perturbed. Trev had recently expanded from boring old million-pound property deals into media ownership by buying the *Wakeborough Gazette*, a journal with which Radio Ridings has always had a love–hate relationship: They love to hate us.

'It's nothing,' I said hastily. 'Not the paper, a property company. Non-story, if you ask me, but I'll check it out. Um, look, Steve . . .'

I braced myself. Sure, I know feminine diffidence went out with cross-your-heart bras, but our newly hatched affair was still at that delicate stage when a girl doesn't like to seem pushy. 'You're not free after work by any chance? I rather need to talk.'

'Squash tournament. Tomorrow?'

'Polly's parents' evening, but –'

This was hopeless. People were closing in and Steve raised his voice. 'As you know, Rose, I leave Wednesday night for a three-day working party in Durham, brainstorming options for the future. Should be very stimulating.' But then, without so much as a twitch of the lips, the clever Lamb murmured: 'Back Sunday morning, free all day. My flat, twelve thirty?'

6

They are walking back to the flat. This is itself remarkable because Rita never walks further than her front door if she can help it. But her regular cab firm's swamped round pub-closing time and although the lad offered a lift, his car's in a multi-storey miles away. Besides, she's retained enough sense to be chary of parking a strange vehicle in the numbered forecourt of the Bella Plaza.

They are buffeted along the promenade by a September gale as warm as a hair-drier. The air is sweet with candy-floss and boiled onions. The famous illuminations jangle and jump above as the ocean softly slaps and tickles the beach. 'Slow down a bit, will you?' she pants. 'Not far now.'

Never mind that he is burdened with all her gear, the boy is striding along like a guardsman, while Rita wobbles behind on her silly mules. The wind snatches away half their words, and they are continually separated by drunken sightseers, gawping up at the lights and screaming with laughter. Nevertheless, she has learned that he's called Thomas Wilkes, that he lives forty-odd miles northeast of the town, and that he did not drive down to view the lights – although he gazes round from time to time in comical wonderment. Nor did he plan to visit the Flaming Flamingo Nite Spot. He'd thought it might be educative to spend a day at some trades-union conference which is also (Rita learns without interest) taking place in Blackpool. It seems a friend in the University Labour Club put him in touch with some delegates who kindly secured him an observer's pass and, this evening, insisted on sweeping him along with the lads for a convivial spot of *après*-TUC.

'Dead educative,' quips Rita.

'Absolutely. Until you've actually watched a debate starting to rip, you can't imagine –' He breaks off and laughs uncertainly. 'Sorry. I, um, see what you mean.'

'Your face when I sat on your knee . . . Here, don't go marching off. We're nearly there. See that red sign: 'The Westways'?' She almost laughs again because he looks so horror-struck.

'You mean that hotel?' What does the soft ha'porth think she's going to do? March him up to reception and insist he sign the register as Mr and Mrs Smith?

'Building next door, the block of flats. We're the top floor, the penthouse.' There's a smugness in the way she says this. And by the time she's unlocked the flat door, flipped on the lights and heard a gasp from Thomas, she's every inch the proud proprietress: 'Well, this is the pad. Dump the bags anywhere you like.'

Oh Rita, sweetheart, I blush for you still.

Mind you, it's here we find ourselves frustrated by the confines of radio drama. I have argued this very instance with my friend George: how could one do justice to such a palace in mere sound? That flat, I'd said, is one film set even you couldn't create in your listeners' heads. We need a camera, tracking lasciviously around every lurid detail.

'A wash of Mantovani?' had suggested this artist of the airwaves. George, you understand, never saw the penthouse, but had been much entertained by my description one drunken evening.

'Too tame.'

'Hawaiian guitars perhaps? Or a James Last arrangement of . . . "Big Spender". A go-go, naturally.'

'Naturally.'

'With a faint, chilly tinkle of cocktail ice-cubes?'

'Plus a glooping from the fountain,' I said thoughtfully.

The fountain was in the hallway, as it happened. A spouting mermaid with fat goldfish nibbling round her plastic tail. Overhead, a thousand stars, seemingly, were buried in the velvety purple ceiling. It was when they twinkled into life that Thomas gasped. And if you walk through to the lounge – as Rita does now, kicking off her shoes and flexing her toes appreciatively in the shag pile – you're met with infinite acres of real sky because one wall of this exotic chamber is sheet glass, huge sliding doors opening on to a narrow balcony. The illuminations glitter below, threaded with the caterpillar crawl of traffic, but we don't hear that. Double glazing seals us from the real world. The carpet furs cosily over the split-level floor and the walls are heavy with mock suede.

It must have had an extraordinary acoustic, that chamber, what with the bounce from the glass meeting the deadness of the plush. But Rita is unlikely to notice as she twiddles a knob and – *voilà* – soft music oozes from concealed speakers. She walks over to the bar to supply (all unknowing) our essential spot effect. The rattle of ice. 'What's your poison then, Thomas?' Funny that. Right from the start, she calls him by his full name. Shortening it to Tom never occurs to her. He *looks* like a Thomas.

'Uh, thing is, if I've got to drive home . . .'

'Mummy and Daddy waiting up for you?' There's an edge of irritation in her voice.

'They're away,' he replies eagerly. 'But, well, it's Ma's car.'

'Mustn't take any risks with that, must we?' agrees Rita, satisfied. Concealed behind the bar, she selects two tall thin glasses, stacks them with ice and ladles in the Bacardi. Topped up, scantily, with cola. For good measure, she spears a green cherry on a parasol and plops that in too.

'Thank you,' says Thomas, accepting his glass. He's standing in the middle of the carpet, looking as lost and gawky as a giant sunflower on a football pitch. 'This is, um, a pretty amazing place. Have you had it long?'

Rita, patting the huge television with fond pride, feels obliged to admit that she does not actually own the penthouse. She is just staying here for a while. Looking after it for – a friend.

'Some friend,' murmurs Thomas. Some friend, thinks Rita, with a stab of disquiet. She smothers it immediately. Frank is away on the Costa Brava. And while the cat's away – or, in Frankie's case, the bloody ferret . . .

'What are you laughing at now?' asks Thomas shyly.

'Nothing. No, not at you, pillock. Sit down, make yourself at home.' She pats the sofa beside her, but he sinks to the floor on the spot with the gangly grace of a young giraffe. There's a crack across the sole of one of his desert boots, grey sock visible within. She's surprised Mummy and Daddy don't spruce up their son a bit. She does not for a moment suspect poverty, not with an accent like his. He takes a swig of his drink, and then sniffs it. 'Is there something else in here? Apart from Coke?'

'Don't you like it?' Rita is casting around for an ashtray.

'Sure, yes, it's terrific but . . .' He essays another taste, and then squares his shoulders. 'Well, it's a long drive home, and Ma only lets me use her car in the vac on condition I don't drink and drive. Anyway . . .' He daren't meet her eyes, but finishes defiantly: 'Anyway, I don't actually believe in drinking and driving either.'

'Good on you. So?' She's tormenting him.

'So, I'd better not drink this. If – if I'm driving home. Tonight.' There, he's said it. And looks scared out of his wits.

'Fine.' She stands up. He nearly drops his drink. ''Scuse us a sec,' she says cheerfully.

The boy's clear as glass. When she returns from the bathroom where she's taken some measures which, while they might imperil her eternal soul, preserve her mortal career prospects, he manages to look both relieved and disappointed. Maybe he was expecting her to waft back in a black negligée or something. Or nothing at all. Rita, enjoying herself, lights her fag and sprawls across the armchair beside him. 'Do you think I could have a plain Coke?' he asks in a very small voice. 'Or – or anything soft?'

'Suit yourself. But . . .' She blows a perfect column of smoke up at the ceiling. 'You don't have to drive home if you don't want.' Oh, the mingled hope and apprehension in his so-transparent face, but she can't resist adding: 'It's a big flat. Sleep an army in here.'

He turns away from her, shoulders hunched, his chagrin hilariously evident. 'Sure,' he mutters. Then remembers his manners. 'I mean, thanks. I can crash out on the floor, if you like.' He downs nearly the whole of his drink in one swig. Consolation prize. 'I can sleep anywhere.'

Oh no you can't, Rita is thinking. Not tonight, you can't, sunshine. Because at this moment she is feeling randier than she has ever done in her entire life. Her body is leaping with lust so fierce she's surprised at herself.

Years later, she will call up the picture of this shabby, shaggy boy hunched away from her on that god-awful carpet. His hair's flopping over his face, and his inky fingers are clenched round the glass. There's a rip in the knee of his jeans, and a faint golden line of down on the back of his neck. She will even be able to conjure up the scent of his shampoo. For years, the smell of coal tar will bring a lump to her throat.

Sometimes, when she replays the scene and reaches this point, she will tell herself Rita should have marched him to a spare room with a sleeping bag and a mug of Horlicks. Fat chance. What she actually does is stub out her cigarette and lean stealthily towards him. She rests her hands on his shoulders and she traces, with her tongue, that faint golden line of down on his neck.

This is the moment. The moment which, years later, she'll remember with excruciatingly sweet clarity. He twists round to look at her, with those wondering, golden, lioncub eyes – and it's as though the world stops spinning, pivoted on that magical instant.

Mind, what follows is as inept as it's predictable. Painful, too, because she bashes her thigh on the coffee table when they topple over the split-level. No time to get to a bed. Hell, there's no time for anything because it's all over in minutes. She will retain only one clear picture: of his face above hers, transfigured with astonished joy as somehow (well might he look surprised) she contrives to ram herself on to his plunging erection. Whereupon, instantly, he explodes. And the great idiot, when he's recovered himself enough to speak – which takes rather longer than the act itself – gasps with painstaking politeness: 'I'm sorry. Was that rather, um, quick? For you, I mean?'

'Broke all land-speed records, I should think,' mutters Rita, glancing round for her fag packet. But she relents when she sees the distress in his face. 'Cheer up, I came.' Which, after a fashion and much to her surprise, she did. Says everything for how revved-up she was beforehand.

'Wow,' he sighs. And then: 'I mean – *wow*.' He kisses her forehead. Then her nose and her fingers. Damp, grateful little kisses like the snuffles of a puppy. 'Thing is, I don't know quite how to say this . . .'

She brushes the curls out of his eyes and grunts. 'You're breaking my ribs.'

'God, sorry. That better? It's just . . .'

'You were fine.' Rita lights her fag and sighs deeply. 'Terrific.'

'I was? Only, well, as a matter of fact . . .' She can feel his heart thumping in his chest. 'I've never done it before. This.'

'You don't say.' Yet she no longer feels inclined to laugh at the kid. For a weird instant, she almost wants to weep.

The golden eyes are steady on hers. Clear and honest as sunshine. 'But I guess that was obvious.'

The easy lie is ready on her tongue. But she can't utter it. Suddenly, it feels – cheap. So she pulls a comical grimace and, slowly, his face splits into a matching grin. He even begins to chuckle.

'What's the big joke?'

'Sorry, mad. Just, oh God, I nearly found myself saying, you know, thank you for . . . for having me.'

Rita giggles. 'Pillock.'

'No wonder Ma always claimed it was' – he can hardly splutter the words out – 'a singularly vulgar expression.'

She hoots. 'Well, my mum always said I should thank people nicely for coming.' They're laughing helplessly, the silly pair. Post-coital hysteria.

'I was terrible, wasn't I?'

'Bloody awful.'

'D'you think I'll ever get the hang of it?'

'Another thing my mum always says' – Rita wonders if she's taken leave of her senses – 'if at first you don't succeed . . .'

7

'Did the earth move for you last weekend?'

Careful, Rose, careful: this is a family show.

'As they say. Don't get me wrong, I'm talking about a curious report we heard on Monday's show about a tree which seemed to have, well, *moved*. Since then, we've had any number of calls . . .'

Eleven. Anything over ten is a lot; twenty, and we've been inundated. I sketched in the geography – a dozen retirement bungalows in a valley, with a former tip across a little stream – then whipped through listeners' concerns: murky water, mangy vegetation, persecution of poodle by dive-bombing seagulls (no, honestly). 'And I'm joined this morning by a spokeswoman from COSH, the group which is pressing for action on the site . . .'

Do you detect a lack of conviction in that link? I hope not, but it was certainly there. Or rather, not there. When I'd called in on Mac at crack of dawn this morning, the stream looked no dirtier than you'd expect after prolonged rain. The so-called roving tree was just a sapling which I reckoned had keeled over in the wind. All in all, I felt I'd been conned into running this item, what with Dad and Her Worship the Florence. Not to mention the listeners. Their calls did not prove there was anything worth phoning about; an April Fool spoof about flying teacups over Hog's Moor (to go with the all those flying saucers) had immediately produced a rash of sympathetic sightings.

Anyway, this story's off my beat. Yes, I cover environmental issues, but strictly of the home-and-hearth variety. Never mind the surveys which insist our audience is three-quarters geriatric – sorry, of mature years – I know the listener I'm talking to on this kind of item. Not just do I know her, I used to *be* her. She's a young and struggling mother with too much to do and too little to spend, but she's grittily determined to do right by family, home and self. Thus, what she cares about is what directly affects her. Pesticides on carrots, fine. Rainforests (sorry, Polly), forget it. Likewise (sorry, Stephen), she doesn't give a twopenny écu about grain subsidies. And, unless it's on her doorstep, she's not too bothered about some old tip. Besides, I reckoned if there'd really been anything amiss, the hacks would have grabbed it for news. They'd scoffed at the Basildon Bond press release, however, confirming my suspicion it was a dead duck.

Nevertheless, here I was on Thursday morning, live in studio, coaxing the aims of COSH out of its Honorary Secretary. Dorothy was a silver-permed widow who lived two bungalows up from Mac and who, he swore, was forever after seducing him with her iced fancies. Dream on, Dad. Bracelets a-jingle with nerves, she managed to quaver through her campaign manifesto, but only thanks to some tactful prompting from our very own Jim Rumbelow. Yes, for an impartial green perspective (and twenty-two-carat articulacy), we'd had the bright notion of balancing the opponents in this discussion by sticking Rambling Jim in the middle.

Actually, to be accurate, it was me who'd had the notion, and had to fight for it. Amanda, like most of our youthful staff, sees Jim as a bit of a joke ('The answer lies in the soil, my dearios . . .'), but I won't hear a word against him. George talent-spotted him years ago, when he was still gardening for the council. A widower, he lives in a tiny cottage up on the moors and you couldn't meet a kindlier old codger. When Polly was doing her ten-year-old best to turn my elegant garden into an animal hospital (lost pigeon, three-legged hedgehog, assorted cat-damaged fledglings), Uncle Jim was her chief consultant, helping her patch, feed and, when necessary, inter her charges. One of nature's all-round Good Eggs, as George puts it.

'. . . The trouble as I understand it,' he rumbled in again now, rescuing Dorothy, 'is that no one seems to know what was put on that there tip in the first place.' Jim looks *exactly* like he sounds – not everyone does, as you know. You often get radio actresses playing fluffy ingénues who look like Godzilla's mother-in-law. Jim's ruddy, bearded face, however, is as genially bucolic as his voice, and he dresses to match, in hairy tweed and balding corduroy, with a fat game-keeper's bag permanently by his boots. 'What they want is a few facts.'

'Thanks, Jim,' I said. 'Well, the nature park is part of The Willows, which is administered by Lime Holdings. Their spokesman's also with us, Mr Mike Smithson.'

Trevor Green, chairman of Lime Holdings, prefers omnipotent invisibility and, like God, speaks through his minions. This minion was one half of a Leeds-based public-relations firm. 'And a very good morning to you, Rose.' Your typical coiffed and cologned rent-a-gob, the guy proceeded to be as ear-numbingly garrulous as you'd expect on the prestigious name of Lime Holdings, blah-blah, their concern for the community, blah-blah, their environmentally sensitive planting . . .

'One tree,' interrupted Dorothy indignantly. 'And it's shifted, like there's been a landslip.'

'Those mountain bikes,' Mike Smithson tutted. 'Kids will be kids, eh? They even knock over the sign saying biking's not allowed.'

'Nevertheless,' I cut in hastily (because my daughter had once been pack leader of the said Hell's Cherubs), 'it used to be a tip.'

'A landfill site,' he conceded.

'And do we know what was actually dumped there?'

His smile oozed sincerity. 'Low-grade – I stress, low-grade – industrial waste. Chiefly building rubble, and although tipping finished before Lime Holdings bought the site, we naturally commissioned in-depth investigations. I've copies here –'

'A number of our callers, however,' I ploughed on, 'are worried about the stream.' I can't claim I'm built in the Rottweiler mould of interviewer (more, according to my friend George, a well-trained Yorkshire terrier), but I know my job. 'It's been a peculiar colour recently.'

'Hardly surprising, with all this rain.' Smithson began spreading glossily bound documents across the table without (the guy was a pro) thumping the mike. 'But I'm glad you mentioned it, Rose, because, as I said, I have here our site reports from the time of purchase, which show the water quality was excellent, and since there's been no further tipping . . .' Another oily grin, 'I hope I've managed to set minds at rest.'

He'd managed to set my teeth on edge, for sure, but before I could wind up this flabby debate, Jim leaned forward. 'Building rubble, eh? So what do you make of this?' Now there was a mighty thump on mike, because Jim had plonked his keeper's bag on the table. He flipped back the lid and ripped open a polythene sack. We all reeled. The stench was stereophonic. 'Dead frog,' he explained for the benefit of listeners as he brandished a bloated corpse. 'There's plenty more where that poor little beggar came from. Fish belly-up and all.' He plunged his hand back into the bag. 'See these rushes? Well, that's not pond mud, it's some oily muck, thick as plum pudding. And what about this, Mr Smithson? Plug from a steel barrel, if I'm not mistaken. No, don't touch it. I did, and I've still got the stain here on my thumb. Rubble, you say? Don't make me laugh.'

I was as dumbstruck as everyone else. It was as if a jolly chuckling Father Christmas had suddenly whipped a Kalashnikov out of his sack. *Ho, ho, ho, boys and girls, have I got a surprise for you . . .* Rent-a-gob, suspecting a set-up, glowered at me as he gabbled that a few bits of debris proved nothing and, besides, the tipping had all happened before Lime Holdings bought –

'Give over with your excuses,' roared Jim, before I could get a word in. 'Never mind who did the dumping, the point is that tip's rotten to the core, and the rain's just brought it oozing up. The only living things I could see thriving in your so-called nature park were some damn great rats. I'm telling you straight, Mr Smithson, something's got to be done about that tip, and I intend to see it will be.'

'Blimey,' said Amanda, when we were finally off air and alone in studio (although the aroma lingered on). 'You were dead right about this one, Rose, I admit it. Good old Jim, eh? He really hammered that smarmy PR git.'

'Good old Jim,' I snapped, unimpressed by her handsome apology, 'was supposed to be balancing in the middle of the see-saw, not jumping on Dorothy's end and launching the opposition into bloody orbit. As I told him afterwards, in no uncertain terms.' I'd wound up the debate as even-handedly as I could. Which wasn't very. Even my friend George has never coined a maxim for dealing live with dead frogs.

'This story should run and run,' beamed Amanda. 'Here, second post came in. Card for you.'

'We're handing the Willows story to news,' I said, taking the postcard. 'Lock, frog and dodgy barrel. At least Jim's outburst should find COSH a place on the news agenda. Although, as I said to him ...' My voice tailed away, because I was studying the postcard.

'What's it all about then, eh?' enquired Amanda. And winked at me encouragingly. 'Long-lost boyfriend?'

I slammed the card down as though it had burned my fingers. ''Course not.'

'Oh, come on. I'd read it before I twigged it was a bit personal. I thought, being as it was from a very old friend, you might bend the rules and play the record he's on about.' She pulled a face. 'But I asked Delia, and even she's never heard of it.'

Delia had been in Radio Ridings longer than anyone except the Chief Engineer and kept a proprietorial eye on what was still, quaintly, called Grams Library. Never mind that we play compact discs, mixed and matched weekly by computer. Yes, I'm afraid so. You feed in your music policy and it spews out your tracks, carefully balanced by mood, tempo, sex of vocalist, colour of socks and Lord knows what else. Gone are the days of a cosy browse through the record pile.

'Can't quite place the song myself,' I said with a flinty smile. 'And I've no idea who wrote this postcard. Some nutter, I guess.' And, ignoring Amanda's muttered 'Puh-*lease* ...', I swept on to discuss the next day's programme.

Only when I was locked into the loo (the one place in Radio Ridings where you can guarantee privacy), did I fish the card out of my handbag and study it again.

A picture of Blackpool Tower, that's what had caught my eye, although the postmark was indecipherable and it was addressed to me personally, care of Radio Ridings. I read the postscript first, as Amanda obviously had, because it was sprawled across the top.

REMEMBER OUR SONG? GO ON — PLAY IT ON THE SHOW FOR OLD TIMES' SAKE

Under that, in capitals inscribed so hard the biro had carved grooves in the card:

WELL, STONE THE CROWS. AFTER ALL THESE YEARS, HERE SHE IS IN SUNNY (HA HA) WAKEBORO'! SMALL WORLD

BECAUSE, I KID YOU NOT, YOURS TRULY IS COMING UP THERE
TOO, FOR A LITTLE PADDLE IN THE LOCAL AIRWAVES! I'LL BE
STRAIGHT ROUND, PROMISE. IN THE MEANTIME,

LOADSA LUV & KISSES FROM YR VERY OWN

'MR ADORABLE'

8

'You're my Mr Adorable,' croons Rita absent-mindedly. 'I just adore you, Mr Adorable . . .' She's naked in the middle of a huge bed. Circular, wouldn't you just know, in a flat like that. There's even a mirror overhead, much to Thomas's amusement.

'Is he, um, kinky?' he'd asked a week ago, when he first saw his own face goggling down. 'Chap who owns this place?'

'Not to my knowledge,' replied Rita, with perfect truth. 'He said it was like this when he bought it. I think the geezer did the block up was a mate of his.'

The penthouse is pretty comprehensively wrecked now, however, with that pair in occupation for a week. I dare say Thomas is as impervious to squalor as any boy his age, but Rita's no better. Her acquaintance with the vacuum cleaner was ever slight, and her labour-saving approach to washing up involves pillaging cupboards until no cup or spoon remains unused. Bottles litter the tables, ashtrays spill over the shag pile and a warm September sun bakes smears of takeaway Chinese into days of discarded plates. '"Busy old fool, unruly sun,"' exclaims Thomas in a sudden, exulting burst.

Rita stops singing. 'Come again?'

'"Who dost", no, "*Why* dost thou . . ."' Shit, I can't remember the next line.'

'Good,' she mutters, unimpressed by Thomas's taste for declaiming poetry in bed. Only yesterday, he was wondering, by his troth, 'what thou and I did till we loved? Were we not weaned till then? But sucked on country pleasures . . .'

'Don't be disgusting,' she'd said, giggling.

'It's amazing,' he declares now, kissing her breast. 'I did Donne for A level, but I never realized how brilliant the guy was. He really understands sex.'

'Oh yeah? Since when were you an expert?'

He grins. 'You tell me.'

'Cocky bugger.'

'Come on, Rita, admit it. You like it, don't you? With me?'

Rita pretends to yawn. 'I can put up with it once in a while. Gerroff, you great hairy maniac. Look, if you think just because . . . Oh blimey.'

She does like it with Thomas, no two ways about it, although she's as sparing with her praise as any teacher might be, coping with such exuberant precocity. So she wouldn't dream of telling Thomas that she never before enjoyed sex as much, or as often, as she has these past seven days.

Matter of fact, Rita doesn't as a rule reckon overmuch to sex. Don't get her wrong, she isn't lezzie or anything. She knows an orgasm when it shakes her, and fakes one when it doesn't. She's never disliked the act – she just hasn't seen much point in all the fuss, once the novelty of a new partner has gone flat. Which generally happens within a few days. Or, in Frank's case, before reaching the end of her first post-coital fag. After that, screwing has always seemed more a painless means to desirable ends than an end desirable in itself. And there's the puzzle. Because there is no end beyond Thomas Wilkes. No promised jobs, fancy dinners, borrowed penthouses or slinky fox furs lure Rita on now. There is just – Thomas. She must be mad. He *definitely* is. Know what she found him doing yesterday? She was just flipping through a magazine in the lounge when she heard him call . . .

'Out here!' Dressed only in his knickers, he was prancing along the parapet of the balcony. Six inches wide that wall, five storeys up. But, arms flapping, he was grinning and balancing – oh, holy Mother – balancing on one naked foot, stretching the other leg behind him. 'Guess who?'

She couldn't speak. Couldn't even breathe. She was seeing those long golden limbs smashed to jelly on the tarmac below. 'Eros, you idiot,' he yelled springing down to safety. 'Boy-god of love.'

He thought it was hilarious when she flew at him. And this afternoon, when he eventually dredges himself out of bed and into the bath, he inspects with interest the faint bruise on his jaw.

'Child-batterer,' he says, before resuming a piercing whistling of what might possibly be a hornpipe.

'Anyone ever told you you're tone-deaf?' She's in there with him. Given the rest of the penthouse, you will not be surprised to learn that the bath is a sunken whirlpool big enough, Thomas observed on first seeing it, to house an orgy on Caligulan scale.

'I'll have you know I used to sing in the school choir.'

'Only because you looked the part.' She herself is looking a complete Charlie with her hair knotted up in a laddered stocking and wearing not a smudge of make-up. This has nothing to do with Thomas's opinion that she doesn't need make-up. She's well acquainted with the mating-babble of the lust-blinded male. Probably she can't be bothered to paint up because, well, Thomas doesn't count. As a man. She can't fit him into her scheme of things at all. Not into Real Life, as she knows it. He's a one-off. Sweet-natured, funny, dead brainy – and dead thick. Like he had to get her to operate the pay machine at the car park when they eventually retrieved Mama's bloody Morris Minor. Like he can't add up figures to save his life. Like he's never even heard of Frank Henderson – can you believe it?

'Frankie and Ferdy?' Rita said incredulously.

He shrugged. 'I, um, don't watch much television.'

'So what do you do of an evening?' she enquired, cheesed off he wasn't dazzled to learn he was staying in the famous Frankie's flat. 'If you don't watch telly and you never screwed?' And that was when he got on to wondering, by his troth, what they did till they loved . . .

Oh, he's a one-off all right. It's not just that she's never fucked so much, she's never laughed so much neither. Yes, *laughed*. It puzzles me to this day, because I've always assumed a shared sense of humour rests on a certain communality of culture, and she and Thomas might have been reared on different planets. Nevertheless, they seem to find infinite amusement in one another, and they never stop talking. Lord knows about what. I don't see Rita entering into political debate, but she seemed to end up knowing plenty about Thomas's starry-eyed brand of left-wingery. However, I suppose everything is fascinating to lovers, from the speed a fingernail grows to comparative flavours of potato crisps. Plus, they have autobiographies to swap which, since their lives have so little in common, take some explaining. Thomas pours out everything but Rita is, shall we say, economical with the mundane detail of her past. She prefers to dwell on the glittering triumphs of the present. Like her two days as an extra in *Coronation Street*. Like her recent interview *on the BBC*. She doesn't add the word 'radio'. Rita doesn't reckon much to the wireless.

'God,' says Thomas, 'my life's so boring compared with yours.' But Rita doesn't find it so. She is deliciously appalled by the privations of his distinguished school. This is nevertheless the kind of joint, once she's made her pile and should she ever get round to having any, she quite fancies for her offspring. Well, maybe not Eton exactly, but somewhere almost as fancy. Thomas is equally shocked by her tales from the comprehensive – although it is, you may be sure, the sort of school he intends for his heirs. Except not, God, never, a *Catholic* outfit like hers. None of that superstitious brain-warping for him, thank you very much. Rita tuts. Sure, she may not have been to Mass for years, but she never fails to have a quick word with Our Lady before she goes on, by way of insurance. She says she'd better offer up a few prayers for him. After all, just supposing Thomas is hit by a bus tomorrow?

'I'm in Heaven already.'

'On the fast track to Hell more like, you heathen pillock.'

They argue as splendidly as they fuck. Maybe this is why the novelty of Thomas is taking so long to wear off. Although she knows it will – indeed it must – because she can't fool around like this for too long. She's got her career to think of, and Rita – if this is not already evident – is ambitious. She never doubts she's destined for fame and fortune. Yes, she's still doing the odd gig of an evening while he's here, but goodness only knows what other opportunities are slipping away in the world far below. She says something of the sort to Thomas now, as she soaps his back. 'You should go to London,' he agrees promptly.

'Very hard scene, clubs down there.'

'Why clubs? You could be on the stage.'

'I'd kill to get in a musical. Know any friendly producers?'

'Didn't you ever want to do any serious music?'

'Sad songs?'

'Idiot. I meant, I dunno, more operatic kind of stuff?'

She drops the soap, and snorts with laughter. 'Get real, baby.

Maria Callas didn't play the Flaming Flamingo. *Trra, la-la-la la!* This is an arpeggio, trilled in the style taught by the Edna Broadbuck Academy of the Musical and Dramatic Arts, where Rita long ago tap-danced through the tulips.

'See? Your voice's amazing.'

'Me in opera wouldn't be amazing, it'd be a fucking miracle.'

'I didn't mean opera exactly, but you're such a natural performer . . .'

'More, more, I love it.'

'And funny and intelligent and –'

'And you need your head examining. Know how many O levels I got? One. For woodwork. Eighteen boys and me in the class, God did I have a ball.'

'Intelligence is nothing to do with passing exams,' stoutly claims this laurel-laden scholar of Magdalen College, Oxford. 'Your brain's as good as mine any day. Quicker.'

'At least I can work out ten per cent of a hundred quid without a calculator.'

'You understand things. People.'

'You reckon?'

He grins. 'Maybe you should write novels. I mean, your life'd be a good starting point, wouldn't it?'

She eyes him narrowly. There's no denying certain of her auto-biographical embroiderings (for instance, her renegade heir-to-the-troubled-mill Dad who, you guessed it, put Mama up the duff and turned them into the blizzard) have owed rather a lot to her pre-ferred brand of fiction. Maybe Thomas isn't as daft as all that. She has the grace to blush. 'Give over. Tell you what, we'll make a deal. When I'm starring at the Palladium, you can bring a gang of boys up from your school and I'll give you all – oh – pink champagne in my dressing room.'

'What school?'

'What else d'you do with Latin? You're going to be a teacher, aren't you?'

'God, no,' he says, as if she'd suggested smack-dealing. 'I'm going to do something that matters. Something to change this lousy world.'

'Better change your hair-do first,' says Rita.

*

She cuts it herself that very morning, still wet from the bath. She would have preferred to wheel him into a trendy hairdresser, but Thomas recoiled with horror. So ('Just call me Delilah, honey') she snips away, and is so impressed by the result that she sneaks out while he's dozing and buys him some decent clothes to match. Her idea of what constitutes decent clothing. I cringe as I try to remember what was in that bundle of carrier bags. Thomas is appalled, too, but that's only because of the money she has spent, which he cannot possibly repay. 'It's a present,' she interrupts impatiently. I'll say one thing for Rita, she was always generous to a fault.

I seem to recall she repackaged him in white jeans, sharp-cut shirt and suede loafers of a lurid blue. Whatever, the transformation enchants her. In fact, it's so startling, it alarms her. Thomas is no longer a scruffy boy, he's a golden youth, heart-stoppingly handsome. He could, she marvels, model aftershave in a magazine. She can think of no more dazzling compliment. He grimaces at the mirror and says the jeans are castrating him.

'Shows off your bum,' she says, patting her handiwork.

He laughs. 'Do I drive you wild with desire?'

'Aye. For a quick fag before I get my face on. I'm working tonight.'

He catches her to him. 'I'm a totally different person, Rita. You've changed everything.'

'Don't talk daft,' she protests, because for a moment she's wondering whether she wants him to be so very different after all. 'A pair of jeans and –'

'I'm not talking about clothes. It's you – us. I look back, and it's as though I was only half alive until now. Until this.'

Now she understands. 'Sex, you mean.'

And he blushes. Looking, for all the cropped hair and natty outfit, just like Thomas again. 'I mean love,' says the kid fiercely. 'Making love.'

Rita also has to make money, however, so she abandons him that evening and departs, glued, glittering and gorgeous, for her gig. Thomas always wants to accompany her, but she's not going to perform her garter routine with him gnashing uxorial teeth in the wings. Having settled him in front of the telly with instructions to fetch in a curry later, she's surprised, on her return, to find him staring out at the sea in the dark. 'Who owns this block, Rita?' he demands.

'No idea. Why?'

'I was talking to the Pattersons, the old couple in the flat below.'

Her voice jumps an octave. 'You were *what*?'

'Their cat was stuck on a windowsill at the back. I went down to lend a hand. Nice people. D'you know them?'

''Course not,' snaps Rita, telling herself that it's unlikely Frankie does either. 'Get the curry, did you? I'm starving.'

'Lord, sorry, I forgot. You see, they insisted on giving me supper and we got talking –'

'Terrific,' she hisses. And she wonders how, discreetly, she can suggest he should not make too public his presence in this flat. A brighter lad would have twigged when she insisted on parking Ma's precious motor down a side road, rather than in the courtyard below.

'But it's awful, Rita,' he's saying. 'They might have to move out of their flat, after saving up for years to retire here . . .'

Rita hears no more because she's disappeared into the kitchen, where she's inspecting, without enthusiasm, a lump of cheddar. 'Here, did you finish that loaf?'

He appears in the kitchen doorway, and she realizes he looks quite angry. She's never seen Thomas angry before. 'It's the maintenance bills in this block. Hasn't your friend told you?'

'What friend? Oh, you mean Frankie?'

'They're absolutely outrageous. Mr Patterson was showing me the bills. It's ever since a new company bought the block and did it up. Thousands of pounds for new lifts, fancy doors, all kinds of stuff. People like the Pattersons don't want the ritzy trimmings, and they jolly well can't afford them.'

'So why don't they *jolly well* move?' she mocks.

He doesn't notice. 'Why should they? Anyway, they tell me the place is practically unsellable with these bills coming in every year. They reckon they'll be forced into flogging it cheap, back to the property company which owns the freehold. That's what everyone else's done, apparently. And the bloody fat-cat company's now renting them out for a king's ransom as luxury holiday . . . Rita? Rita, this isn't a joke. Don't you care?'

She's too tired to be amused for long by his little tantrum. 'Nothing to do with us.'

'And the company's trying to pressure them out, Mr Patterson told me. Water suddenly being cut off, silent phone calls. It was the same with an old lady downstairs who didn't want to go. And you'll never believe what happened to her.'

'Give it a rest, will you?'

'They killed her budgie,' he shouts. 'Oh, for Christ's sake, don't laugh . . .' Although even he has to smile. Nevertheless, he won't give up. 'OK, very funny, but just imagine. Some poor old biddy thinking her precious bird's escaped, and a day later it comes through the letter box in a padded envelope. With an offer to buy the flat in the same bloody post. She's –' He breaks off. 'Rita? Where are you going?'

'Bed,' she says. 'I've done a hard night's work, and I'm too tired for sodding lectures.'

He stomps away in a sulk. Which he maintains for a full ten minutes before joining her, and falling on her as hungrily as if they'd been apart ten years.

Afterwards, she lies awake in the darkness, stroking his shorn head as he sleeps. Staring at the mirror above and feeling about a hundred and two. Wondering if this novelty is finally beginning to wear off.

9

'Whither idealism?' demanded my friend George the instant I opened the door. 'Whither *ideas*, come to that, in today's grubby and grovelling Corporation. Oh, Reith, where is thy sting? Good to see you, old love. You've arrived in the very nick. Start that tape, would you, when I give you the cue? And . . .'

Typical. I'd tottered round to George's house after work in search of a little drink and comfort. The doorbell had clanged unanswered but since the key, as ever, was under the bust of Churchill in the porch, I'd let myself in, only to find her in full creative spate in what had once been a rather splendid dining room and was now fondly dubbed by her Studio One. A cluttered elephants' graveyard of obsolete BBC equipment.

I scuttled across and poised my hands over tape-reel and fader. These old machines are temperamental beasts. One false move and they cough, wow or even, if seriously affronted, spew tape at you like spaghetti. You need the finger-sensitivity of a hardened safe-breaker. George started a disc and, as a piano concerto flooded out of the speakers, leaned over the makeshift control desk and closed her eyes ecstatically. 'Wait for the swell, and . . . *go*!'

On my tape, some old buffer remembered the first time he clapped eyes on his wife, across the deck of an ocean liner. The orchestra billowed beneath like the Pacific.

'OK?' I said, once the musical tide was safely ebbed.

George slowly lifted her hand off the fader. 'Orgasmic.'

'Thing is, if you're busy . . .'

'Forty seconds to the end of this insert and I'm all yours. Gin's in the usual place. By the look of it, you need a stiffy.'

There's no easy way to sum up my friend Georgiana Penistone. Six feet tall, beak-nosed, wire-haired and baritone-voiced, she takes a size-nine brogue, has an extravagant passion for hats – and fits into a modern BBC local radio station like a brontosaurus into a rabbit hutch. Nearly half a century ago, fresh from finishing school ('Ma's last attempt to bludgeon a few husband-trapping skills into me, poor sausage'), George sneaked off to London with a typing certificate and entered the magnificent bronze portals of Broadcasting House. 'The pearly gates to me, darling, because what lay beyond was certainly Heaven.'

In those days, of course, radio was the Wireless and undisputed ruler of the airwaves. Television mewed in the corner, a mere delinquent infant. Installed in the legendary Features Department, George typed scripts for Louis MacNeice, decanted Dylan Thomas into taxis, booked third-class rail tickets from Stratford for Richard Burton ('Only an *actor* then') and wielded stop-watches for the likes of Reggie Smith and Lawrence Gilliam. She worked and drank with all the mythical giants; listened, learned and within a decade or more (opportunities in those days being distinctly unequalized) was herself a features producer. Unfortunately, by then, the brash infant with pictures was growing up. Anything the wireless could do, telly reckoned it could do better. Soon, one-off radio programmes of the sort she crafted with such artistry were no longer the prized jewels in the Corporate crown. 'More like Great Aunt Maud's whopping silver epergne, as far as the nouveaux telly-crats were concerned,' she'd explained to me. 'Expensive, hand-wrought, handsome (if you like that kind of thing), but honestly, in this day and age . . .'

Did that deter George? Does an artist stop painting if his work falls out of fashion? Her masterpieces still sang across the evening airwaves, never mind that, come six o'clock, ninety-nine per cent of the Great British Public riveted themselves to the box. Given the choice. 'But I used to get the sweetest letters from long-distance lorry drivers,' she once told me. 'So appreciative. I would lie in my bath imagining these chaps, all tattoos and biceps, blinking away a manly tear as they juggernauted along the M4.' She guffawed. 'If I'd had more sense and a less inhibited upbringing, I'd have invited some up to explore my archives.'

Yes, George has led a robustly heterosexual life, although you can perhaps see why people tend to assume otherwise. Notably Stephen, when he first arrived at Radio Ridings. George hooted and said I shouldn't have disillusioned the poor fool. With luck, he might have put her back on salary as Sexual Minorities Consultant. George, if this is not already obvious, is very dear to me. I'm one of the few people she's told about the love of her life, an immensely distinguished and famously indecisive radio-drama producer. Married, inevitably, and twice her age when they met, he promised divorce for twenty years and was promising it still when he suffered his final heart attack – in her bed. George said it was consoling to know he'd died so happy. She wore bright-red to his funeral and was conspicuously ignored by his family. The lot of a non-widow is not a happy one. 'But he was a genius,' she explained briskly to me. 'One has to make allowances. I loved the old bugger to distraction. And, without being maudlin, I dare say I always will.'

From him, she claimed, she had learned not to give a damn what anyone thought about her. 'He said I was never going to be beautiful, so I might as well be *different*.' She was certainly that. I like to think she was appreciated in London. BBC Radio, after all, employed a famous crew of eccentrics on the staff in the old days. Or infamous, depending on your perspective. But Wakeborough is not London, and the second tragedy in George's life was that she'd had to move back here. She might have been sublimely unconventional, but there was no evading the duty of an only daughter with ailing parents. She was thus transferred to Radio Ridings, and installed herself in a basement flat in the family mansion.

I say 'mansion' because the place is vast. Built during Wakeborough's glory days, hers is now the only house in a toweringly solid granite crescent which has not been split into offices and flats, and she occasionally has to supplement a pension too small to cover her heating bills by taking in an attaché from work or visiting actor from the Grand. ('Like every theatrical landlady, dearie, I only does it to get a nicer class of company.' And considering the care, food and booze she lavished on her homeless ducklings, company was all she did get out of it.) Called Brook House, the place is known by George, inevitably, as BH. And only a hearse will move her from it now.

In my more fanciful moments, I see the that huge chilly house as a Tower of Babel, clamorous with ghostly voices. Every programme George ever created is stacked in here somewhere. So many hundreds – thousands? – of souls have spilled incoherently over her tape, had their truths dissected by George's tender blade, and been glued back together into miraculous articulacy. There are prime minsters and terrorists, bishops and witches, dukes and rat-catchers. There is even, echoing faintly somewhere, the brassy laughter of a long-vanished cabaret artiste called Rita . . .

Yes, getting on for twenty years ago, while making a witty little documentary called *Arts and Clubs*, George once interviewed the Barnsley Bombshell. I've listened to the tape and I suppose I can understand why George remembers her fondly. Rita's account of her famous garter routine is a high point in a gem of a programme. Even I laughed when, in vowels so thick you could cut them with a plastic fork, she tells of the time some poor old geezer's dentures clattered out on to her stockinged thigh. In fact, it was precisely because George had met Rita that I'd felt impelled to come round this evening. As I curled up in one of the elephantine armchairs in her drawing room with my drink, I handed over the postcard which had arrived that morning. George eyed the picture of Blackpool Tower at arm's length, turned it over, tutted, and pottered off to find her specs.

The hunt took some time. That drawing room, as my daughter Polly wittily observed, made Miss Haversham's domain look like Delia Smith's kitchen. George's parents had been dead for years, but you'd never guess it. Her mother's magazines, patience cards and embroideries were still mixed higgledy-piggledy with Papa's pipes, hearing aids and legal books; there were newspapers golden with age alongside yesterday's *Wakeborough Gazette*, seaweed drifts of gash recording tape, stacks of old cassettes and a cornucopia of bric-à-brac which had tickled George's wayward fancy, from Trevor the crocodile to a red-spangled piano accordian. The wallpaper was patched with damp, the curtains made my fingers itch to beat the dust out of them – and I felt totally and utterly at home.

'Good heavens,' said George at length, having located the glasses and studied the text. 'Addressed to you, too. Rose Shawe.'

'Yup.'

'Are we to assume a long-lost admirer?'

'Looks like it, doesn't it?'

'Some poor errant knight, searching the length and breadth of the kingdom for umpteen years, with a red garter fluttering from his lance? Come, confess all.'

I laughed, but I didn't answer. George was echoing my first, breathless conclusion in the loo earlier on. Only I'd been able to put a name to that long-lost admirer. *Paddle in the local airwaves*; *old times' sake*; *Mr Adorable*: who else but Thomas? Just as immediately, however, I'd dismissed the idea. This card surely couldn't have been penned by the Thomas Wilkes Rita knew. Never mind that (as she would undoubtedly have put it) she never got a sodding letter from the sodding bastard in all her sodding life, this didn't *read* like Thomas. The turn of phrase, the stilted print, the arch humour . . .

'George,' I said tentatively, 'changing the subject for a moment, I don't suppose you ever ran across a producer called, um, Tom Wilkes?'

George, whose knowledge of BBC staff lists, past and present, was encyclopaedic, smiled enquiringly. 'Producer, you say?'

'Telly. Current affairs.'

She shuddered. 'Darling, *hardly*.' George dates the demise of the BBC from the day it fell into the hands of a) television and b) journalists. And as for the accountants and management consultants . . . 'Why? Could Mr Wilkes be Mr Adorable?' George's ears are too acute. Forty-odd years of editing tape means she hears what is left unsaid as clearly as the spoken word. Even as I denied any possible connection between the postcard and our Assistant Editor-designate, I knew this was spooling past her as so much gash. She had returned to studying the text. 'Can't recognize a fist from capitals,' she mused. 'How thrilling. I wish I were in receipt of mysterious postcards. It would make a refreshing change from gas bills. Not to mention the memoranda of stone from your beloved chief.'

'What's the Lamb been writing about to you now?' I enquired – but cautiously, for Stephen Sharpe was one of the few subjects on which, sadly, George and I had yet to find common ground.

'Oh, expenses claim returned because I'd failed to dot the i's in triplicate; new rules on works cars, usage thereof by non-staff personnel; *counselling* for recently retired employees . . . Since I've technically been retired for seven years, I wondered if that was a hint. I tell you, I daily expect delivery of the Black Spot.'

'Nonsense.'

She smiled faintly. 'What worries me more is the discovery that I care so much about retaining a toe-hold in Radio tin-pot Ridings. Pitiful, isn't it?'

George, after all, was hardly cut out for local broadcasting. Accustomed to creating, on average, some thirty exquisitely crafted minutes of output a month, she had found herself committed at Radio Ridings to three solid hours daily. Plus the odd weekend and evening filler. The culture shock alone would have wrecked a lesser personality, but George had winced and adapted. She was now officially retired, however, and had carved a highly congenial niche as a freelance. She retained the weekly arts slot; stocked holes at the weekends with whatever took her fancy; invented taped series for shows like mine – oh, wherever you looked in the schedules you could find George. 'Radio Ridings couldn't run without you,' I said stoutly, 'and Stephen knows it.'

'Which brings me to this morning's *billet doux*,' she sighed, as though I hadn't spoken. 'I have it here. All ten pages, snappily entitled: "ARTS COVERAGE: a discussion document exploring diversification and redefinition of current cultural ouput". Read it?'

'Not yet,' I said weakly.

George beamed. 'Guess what? Stephen's new market research suggests we want more wimmin, more kids, more ethnics, and probably more disabled, although I don't think that's actually spelled out. Oh, and here's a surprise, more poetry because apparently *pomes* are cool with *yoof*.'

I braced myself. 'Well, why not?'

'Darling, had Stainless ever bothered to listen, my presenters are all female, including your talented self, we ran a rap series for months, we've done House and Jungle and God knows what other music, and we even spear-headed the damn campaign for ramps in the Grand.' George tossed the report aside. 'It isn't the content that sinks my aged heart, it's the philosophy. Radio by numbers. Sixty per cent of this, forty of that. Call me Neanderthal, but my aim has always been to broadcast what is *good*, not good *for* ... I'm an entertainer. At best, I trust an informative and even an educative entertainer. What I am not is a social bleeding engineer.'

I'd heard it all before. I sympathized, of course I did, but let's face it: every ex-staffer the Beeb's ever had is convinced the place went to pot the day they drew their first pension cheque. 'Be fair, George. I know there are one or two teething problems –'

'While Stephen sharpens his?'

'But we were in a terrible mess before he arrived.'

'At least it was a creative mess. The only thing that's creative now is the bloody accounting.'

'Don't you start, please. I can't hear myself think in the office these days, with the mutterings from the hacks.'

'He's certainly reformed the news coverage,' agreed George cordially. 'Once it was just incompetent. Now it's unlistenable as well. Not that I claim to know anything about news, but I do know about the kind of programmes people like, without paying bloody market researchers.'

I told myself I wouldn't be swayed by her prejudices. Creators loathe managers on principle, don't they? Have done, I dare say, since a tribal chief told the first cave-dauber he was splashing the paint a bit freely. 'Times change, George. Steve has to define targets for the station, set parameters –'

She guffawed. 'Targets? *Parameters?* Oh, Gawd help us, I'd forgotten he sent you away for brain-washing. Did you learn the lingo on your management course?'

I flinched. 'If you don't mind, I'd rather forget that course. You were right. I shouldn't have gone.'

'Ho, ho,' said George. 'That bad, eh?'

I stirred the ice-cubes in my glass with a pensive finger. We can all of us swap horror stories from the training front these days, but George alone of my colleagues would understand the particular nature of my battle scars. 'Put it this way,' I said. 'Like anyone else, I don't enjoy falling into muddy ponds because a bunch of wallies from Enterprises can't hold a plank straight, but I'll suffer it. I can even cope with devising marketing strategies for the Lego garage we . . . Don't laugh, George, it's not that funny.'

'More, more, I need cheering up.'

'. . . the Lego garage we had collectively constructed. My team won that round, by the way.'

'Does one clap or weep?'

'But when it comes to the psychometric testing and –'

'Psycho-what?'

'– and personal-development workshops, well' – I let out a shuddering sigh – 'that's when I realized the course might have been a mistake. George, we were locked nightly into encounter groups, with the brief of sharing our life histories in every last intimate detail.'

Her eyebrows flew up. 'Every detail?'

'From first memory onwards. First day at school, first period, first job, first love. How did we feel about our parents, partners, children, bosses? You name it, we were supposed to spill our all. Our *truthful* all. You may laugh, but I nearly had a nervous break-down. And if you dare utter one word about tangled webs, I'll fucking well scream.'

'But, my poor darling, I raise my glass to you,' said George in tones of awe. 'The first person ever known to be inspired by a management course to a feat of truly *fabulous* creativity.'

IO

Maybe I'll tell him my mam's been took ill, thinks Rita as she steps into the lift and stabs the top button. She's been collecting from the cleaner's her frock, over which some joker sloshed brown ale. 'Say I've got to go home pronto.' This wouldn't be a total fib, because she's had stuffed into her handbag for weeks Mam's rose-patterned notelet (sold in aid of Our Lady of Somewhere-or-other), telling how she's been 'under the doctor'.

> ... but not to worry, lovey, I know how busy you are with your Shows and Lessons. The neighbours are a Tower Of Strength in the shop although, as you know, I hate to Impose, and Father Michael was saying we haven't seen much of our Little Ballerina recently ...

Well, Rita has to dislodge Thomas somehow. She'd cheerily assumed he'd be due back at his college any day, and now he tells her term doesn't start until halfway into blinking October. Frank will definitely be back before then. And, to tell the truth (which she hasn't to Thomas), the stingy pig only said she could stay on for a few days. That was over a month back. She finds Thomas in the bathroom cleaning his teeth. He mumbles something, and she's just leaving him to it when she catches the words: '. . . he was, standing in the sitting room.'

'What?' she squawks, dropping her dry-cleaning as she leaps to the lounge door. But, no, the room's empty. 'Frankie? He's come back?'

Thomas is drying his face on a towel. 'Don't think so. It's all right, he's gone.'

'Who?' She snatches the towel and hauls him into the bedroom. 'What did he want? Did you let him in?'

'No,' he protests, 'that was the bizarre thing. I just walked through and found this guy by the bar. He looked pretty stunned, too, but then I'd only just got up. I mean, I hadn't got any clothes on. Felt a bit of a fool, actually.'

'Oh, Mother,' groans Rita. 'What'd he look like?'

There are times when she could strangle Thomas. Such as now, when he gazes into mid-air and shrugs. 'Oldish.' This means nothing. Anything over twenty-five is geriatric in his eyes. 'Big, dark-haired, going a bit grey.' She relaxes a little. Frank Henderson is five feet two, with a corn-blond Beatle cut. 'Not the kind of face you'd forget, though, thuggish like a prize-fighter, with –'

'Never mind. What'd he say?'

Thomas looks indignant. 'Asked me what I was . . . No, hang on. First of all, he said the place was a tip, that he'd have to throw an army in.'

'What?'

'Well, quite. Frankly, I thought I'd got some kind of nutter on my hands, so I told him pretty sharply I was staying with you and just what the hell did he think *he* was doing here? And then, believe it or not, he told me he owned the joint.'

'It's got to be Frankie,' wails Rita, groping for a fag, telling herself not to panic. So, Frankie finds out she's stayed on. With a friend. A friend who prances round starkers. Well, so what? Frankie's tantrums wouldn't frighten a flea.

'No, honestly,' protests Thomas. 'This guy's called Lincoln.'

'Lincoln? What's his first name?'

'Search me, he just said Lincoln. Don't you know him?'

Rita puffs frantically as she racks her memory, but finally shakes her head. 'Maybe I left the door on the latch. Maybe that's how he got in.'

'Well, he obviously knows your friend Frank, because he said he'd rung him in Spain and –'

'He *what*?'

Thomas, maddeningly, begins to laugh. 'I say, this might sound weird, but does Frank keep ferrets? Thing is, the guy said Frank and his damn ferret were . . . Rita? Rita, what are you doing?'

'What does it bloody look like? Packing up, aren't I? And you're going to help.'

Thomas blinks. 'Why?'

'Give me strength,' mutters Rita into her open suitcase. Then, turning to face Thomas: 'Frank said, um, come the end of September, he'd got some friends arriving for their holidays . . .' Pure fantasy. It's Frank who'll be hot-footing home if this Lincoln tips him off. 'So that'll be who it was. Frank, um, probably sent him a key. I promised I'd clear out, OK?'

'But this geezer didn't say he was *borrowing* the flat. He definitely said –'

'The flat belongs to Frank,' hisses Rita between clenched teeth. 'Get my stuff off the hangers, will you?'

He takes exactly two steps towards the wardrobe, and halts. 'God, d'you think he could have meant he owned the block? Because, if so, that's the bastard who's putting the screws on the Pattersons. He looked the type.'

'How would you know?' she snaps, sweeping bottles and jars off the dressing table.

'No, honestly, Rita. He stank of scent, with great gold cufflinks and –'

'For Christ's sake, what does it matter?'

'It matters one hell of a lot,' he shouts back. 'Characters like that are scum, trampling over everyone.'

She flings a sweatshirt at him. 'Shut up and pack up. We're going.'

He looks amazed. 'Going where?'

'Fuck knows,' she screams.

And thus, gentle reader, does our heroine come to Ashburtley Hall.

Well, eventually. Reluctantly. To be honest, Rita can't believe her ears when Thomas proposes taking her home, to Ashburtley sodding Hall, no less. They are, at the time, chucking the last armful of her possessions into his car. 'Meet the family?' she jeers, slamming the boot and capsizing thankfully into the passenger seat.

'I'd have loved them to meet you,' he says. Truly, Thomas Edward Featherington Wilkes uttered those words. And with no hint of irony, because he added: 'But they won't be back. They were breaking the journey down from Scotland with some friends near Carlisle.'

'If it's all the same to you,' says Rita, 'I'd sooner go home. My home, I mean.'

'Fine. I'll take you.'

Oh no. No way is Rita going to wheel Thomas home to meet her parents. Or rather, *parent*. Heaven knows what he might blurt out. Mam thinks her little girl is tap-dancing through the tulips nightly. Teaching – don't laugh – teaching ballet of a morning. Besides, Rita's portrayal to Thomas of her swashbuckling life didn't encompass a mundanely respectable corner shop in Barnsley. She prefers to leave him with the vision of herself rising, phoenix-like, from the cobbles and clogs of an unspecified Northern slum, *à la* Catherine Cookson. 'Don't bother. Just give us a lift to the station.'

'Honestly, it's no trouble. Where exactly – ?'

'I'll catch a train, OK?' To anywhere but home. She hasn't yet worked out where, but she doesn't feel quite up to Barnsley and Mam. Not to mention Father sodding Michael with his flinty Irish eyes and peck-peck-pecking questions.

'You'll never manage all this lot.' Thomas gestures at the clutter on the back seat. 'At least come back for the night and get your gear sorted out.'

Rita eyes him suspiciously. 'Look, are you certain your mum and dad are away?'

'Can't I tempt you to a tomato?' enquires Sir Philip Wilkes. 'Our gardener's rather proud of them this year.' The tomato looks deformed to Rita: lumpy with scabby cracks. And the cheese is mouldy, the cold beef oozes blood and the opening soup reminded her of nothing so much as dishwater. No, I think we can fairly conclude Rita is not enjoying this lunch party. She certainly wasn't expecting it.

Thomas and she arrived at Ashburtley Hall yesterday afternoon to find the place empty as he'd promised, echoingly, creakingly empty, with only age-crackled ancestors staring snottily down from their gilt frames. 'Do you show folks round?' she'd asked, jumping as her voice echoed across the vaulted hall. 'Visitors, like?'

Thomas laughed. 'Gosh, no. A little place like this?'

'Oh, titchy-tiny,' said Rita, overdoing the sarcasm. 'Hardly room to swing a bloody tiger.'

That made him blush. 'I just meant, well, it only used to be a shooting lodge. We're not in guide books or anything. Besides, who'd be mad enough to pay to see this dump?'

Rita did not immediately see through this typically English

modesty. Dump, as far as she was concerned, was the right word. Sure, it had looked OK from the outside, except for a slithering jungle of creepers. But inside . . . It was cold as a tomb and every gleaming floorboard shrieked. There wasn't one decent fitted carpet, only mangy rugs, faded as hell, and she'd never seen an uglier bunch of furniture in her life. She's not daft, she knew it must be antique and all, but she thought they might have made some attempt to match the bits up. No way. Every chair was a different dreary colour from the sofa; some of the tables were black and lumpy, others so spindly you'd hardly dare breathe on them, with curly gold trimmings like a fairground ride. Downright vulgar, in our Rita's view. She was lighting a fag and groping for something polite to say when the phone had rung . . .

'Home for lunch tomorrow?' she'd been horrified to hear Thomas exclaim. 'Brilliant. You'll be able to meet Rita. Sure, don't worry, I'll warn Simmy.'

Simmy, she learned, was Mrs Simpson, 'our daily, well, sort-of housekeeper'. It was on account of 'dear old Simmy' that Thomas made up a bed for her last night in what he called the Blue Room. And then been mad as hell when she'd clambered into it. 'You don't have to sleep here,' he'd expostulated. 'We'll just ruffle the sheets a bit, so when Simmy arrives in the morning –'

'And where were you thinking I'd kip?'

'In my room, of course. It's only a single bed, but –'

'Forget it. I want a decent night's sleep for once. I'm knackered.' She was also drunk, from the large quantity of (disgusting) red wine Thomas had unearthed in cobwebby bottles from the cellar, and cross, because a survey of her belongings showed that, among many less vital items, she'd forgotten to pack her precious white-sequinned stage dress. She could see it now in the bedroom at the flat, still in its dry-cleaner's bag. Naturally she blamed this on Thomas. He'd slunk away, miserable as a kicked puppy; she'd knocked back two of her pink pills with a large brandy and, as a result, snored until noon. She was still putting her face on when a car crunched round the gravel drive below and Thomas was summoning her. To meet the family.

Rita, who never has much time for her own sex anyway, expected to dislike Mama. She did so on first sight, and this interminable lunch is not mellowing her. The woman is almost as tall as Thomas, with a hand like a bunch of dried twigs and a reedy voice like the Queen's. Over the opening sherries she couldn't meet Rita's eye. Kept fiddling with her wedding ring as she blathered on about rabbits in her flower beds. Fortunately she's now half a mile away at the other end of the table, having her ear bent by a camp old priest. Sorry, vicar. Sorry – *canon*.

I try and recreate that lunch now, sixteen years on, and I still can't help flinching. I long to shake the silly girl. Tell her to sit up straight and mind her manners. I could forgive her if she were nervous, unsure of herself. But oh no, not our Rita. She couldn't give a toss. Plate pushed aside, she's studying a chip in her nail polish, as arrogantly, contemptuously, *patronizingly* bored as any Brit stranded in a funny foreign land.

'More wine, ah, Rita?' murmurs Thomas's dad, who's at her end of the table. She assents, although it seems to be much the same red muck as last night. Still, with a hangover like she's suffering, she'd accept meths. 'And we must find you an ashtray,' he adds, earning a grateful wink from her and a laser flash from her ladyship down t'other end.

Sir Philip, Rita is graciously prepared to admit, is not as bad as his wife. He's just – old. Old enough to be Thomas's grandfather. His hair is white and, for all he's tall, he's a real bag of bones. Still, at least he looks at her when he's talking to her. Smiles, too. Not in a dirty-old-man way, though, for all she's bloody-mindedly donned her leather mini and a T-shirt so skimpy even Thomas blinked. But Papa just expressed his courteous hope that she wouldn't find the dining room draughty. Tell the truth, she doesn't know what to make of him. He asks sensible questions and, even if his understanding of the Northern club scene is sketchy, listens intelligently to her answers. Laughs, too, when the wine and a couple of fags mellow her into recounting the odd anecdote. I seem to remember she served up the false-teeth tale. Although, in deference to the Canon on her right, she cleaned up the language. Rita has respect for the cloth, even when it's the wrong colour.

'But I mustn't forget Lucy's a musician, too,' he says, turning to the girl at his other side to whom, thus far, Rita has paid no heed whatsoever. A droopy shadow, in a dish-raggy dress, she arrived with Thomas's parents. Niece? God-daughter? Something like that.

Afterwards, Rita will remember only her staring eyes, bulging from a thin, chalky face, and her twitchiness. She puts Rita in mind of a racehorse. If only she could have learned the trick, the lass'd surely be swatting flies with that long frizzy plait. She jumps now, because her host has spoken to her.

'Musician?' she stammers. 'Gosh, hardly, Uncle Philip. Although I –' She breaks off, because her name is being spoken loudly at the other end of the table.

'. . . Lucinda has to sit a college exam on Wednesday,' Lady Wilkes is telling Thomas.

'But I don't need to go up yet,' he protests. 'I don't actually have to be back in Oxford until a week on Thursday.'

'Darling, I promised the Flints I would drive Lucinda down with us tomorrow.'

'I'm frightfully sorry, Tom,' chips in Lucinda. Something in her voice catches Rita's attention. Hello, hello, she thinks, amused. Does the twitchy horse fancy my little Thomas, then? Just look at her fiddling with her plait and blushing . . . Oh aye. She fancies him something rotten. And does Thomas know? Does he heckers-like. Although his scowl lightens when she says eagerly: 'I'm sure I could catch a train.'

'Absolutely not,' says Mama crisply. 'Thomas told me he planned to go up early this term.'

'Sorry, Ma, but I've changed my plans.'

'Don't worry about me,' stammers Lucinda.

'I'm quite sure Thomas has a great deal of studying to catch up on – after the past fortnight,' declares Mama. With meaning. Rita catches the steely flash of claw, the yowl of Mother Lion protecting her golden cub. This really gets up her nose. Is the woman dumb enough to think Rita wants to hang on to her son?

There's a screech of chair legs. Thomas is on his feet. 'I've got commitments of my own,' he's saying. He sounds very young; not endearingly young, just schoolboy sulky. 'I've invited Rita to stay here.'

The silence quivers electrically. The Canon buries his nose in his napkin.

'Fuck this for a lark,' breathes Rita. Very quietly, I am glad to say, but perhaps not quietly enough because she notices Thomas's papa smiling at her. And, to her great surprise, in that old and lined face, she suddenly recognizes Thomas's grin. As though Thomas himself, half a century on, is sharing a joke. Hell of a shock.

'I'm sure we can find a solution,' he begins. 'Darling, if you drive Lucinda down, I could take Thomas back when –'

'Listen here, will you?' interrupts Rita, loudly because Mama is already bleating protests. 'There's no problem on my account, because I'm off after dinner – *lunch* – like, I'm leaving now, OK?'

Thomas skews round. 'Rita?'

'My mum's ill,' she says with the composure of one producing a little story she prepared earlier. 'I've got to get home. Mind, I've left some stuff in the flat, so if you'd just run us back to Blackpool, Thomas? And,' she adds, hoping fervently that if Frankie's returned she can square things and this won't be necessary, 'I'll get a train home from there. That suit you?'

It doesn't, of course, but Thomas can hardly say so. 'Well – well, if that's what you want . . .'

As they are leaving, he's still thunder-faced but his dad very pointedly thanks Rita. And, shaking her hand, he murmurs something so softly she can hardly hear. It sounds remarkably like 'Be kind to my boy.' Which seems unlikely on the face of it, but she smiles kindly enough on him. A twenty-two-carat, old-fashioned gentleman, she thinks, a real sweetie. Unlike his wife, who appears on the steps only to hustle Thomas aside for a whispered exchange which turns him even redder about the gills. He snatches something from her and stuffs it into his pocket before stumping down to the car. Lady Muck remains on the steps, with dogs weaving round her legs and the droopy girl twitching beside her. As they drive away, she raises a skeletal hand. Goodbye and good riddance is written all over her face.

'Up yours and all,' mutters Rita.

For several miles, they don't speak. Thomas has put a tape into the machine: some violins diddle-diddling, all trills and no tune. Rita smokes furiously. 'What was all that about then?' she demands at length.

'Sorry?'

'Turn that racket down, can't you? Your mum, I'm talking about. On the steps, just now.'

'Oh that.' He snaps the tape off. 'I'd, um, forgotten something, that's all. Mrs Simpson found it in my bed.'

'Your teddy bear?'

'Your garter, if you must know,' he bursts out. 'You wouldn't sleep with me and I – well, it may sound stupid but I had it under my pillow. Simmy found it when she was making the bed and gave it to Ma, who promptly assumed –'

'Bloody cheek,' cries Rita.

'I know. Why'd she have to go running to Mama?'

This, however, is not what is inflaming Rita. 'They don't think I'd wear a tarty bit of tat like that, do they?'

'Sorry?'

'Not *offstage*. What do they think I am?' Suddenly, in spite of this affront to her taste, Rita begins to laugh. It's the vision of Thomas's mother being handed that tarty garter by the house-keeper, *found in the young master's bed, m' lady . . .*

'It's not funny,' yells Thomas.

Tears prick her eyes and she chokes on her fag. 'Keep your eyes on the road.'

'I've told her I don't care. I'm not going back to college with them tomorrow, whatever she says, and I'm not going home.'

If she weren't laughing so hard, Rita might have noticed that Thomas is working himself up into a dangerously angry state. 'Oh aye? Then where are you off to?'

'Wherever you're going.' He glances round, looking quite unchar-acteristically sure of himself. 'I knew you were making up the stuff about your mother. Where shall we go? Back to the flat?'

That kills any lingering mirth. 'Don't talk daft.'

'No, look, if Frankie's friends have turned up, we –'

'What friends?' she says exasperatedly, and then remembers the yarn she spun to get Thomas out. She sighs. 'There's no friends coming for their holidays.'

'There aren't? Then why – ?'

'Christ, do I have to spell it out? Point is, Frankie himself's due home any day.'

'So?'

For a clever boy, he's amazingly thick. Or acting thick. 'So,' says Rita tightly, 'maybe I can go back to the flat. If I play my cards right. But you can't.'

'Surely, if you explained, Frankie wouldn't mind my staying a few more days? I mean, it's a huge place and –'

'It's a huge fucking bed,' snarls Rita, reaching the end of her patience, 'but I don't suppose he wants three of us in it.'

Whereupon Thomas drives straight into the path of a lorry. And they're on a motorway. The lorry manages to swerve, blasting its horn furiously. Thomas ignores it, roaring on to the hard shoulder where he pulls up, chest heaving. 'You mean,' he gasps, 'you actually *sleep* with this – this Frank?'

'What do you think?' snaps Rita, all the more sharply because the anguish in the kid's face stings her.

'But he's – old.'

'Bollocks. His kid's still in nappies.'

'He's got *children*? He's married?'

'He's left her now, hasn't he?'

'And that makes it better?' he shouts. 'Oh, my God, you mean in that bed, the bath, those mirrors – everything . . .' He collapses over the steering wheel, shoulders flapping, dashing off Rita's hand when she tries to stroke his head. 'Don't touch me. I can't bear it, thinking of you making –'

Making love? Rita wouldn't call what she and Frankie got up to love-making. They hardly got up to anything most of the time: Frankie lacked the sex drive to match his king-size bed, thank God. He had to be half-cut to fancy it, and one drink too many meant he couldn't manage it anyway. 'Grow up,' she sighs. 'Look, I'm sorry if you got the wrong end of the stick, OK?'

'You *lied* to me.'

'I bloody didn't.' This is no place to have a row. The car is rocking every few seconds in the slipstream of juggernauts, and they've both been drinking. 'It was dead obvious, that I was living with Frankie, I mean. How else d'you reckon I got to live in a flat like that?'

'That's why you were doing it?' he howls. 'For what he gave you? My *God*.' He grabs the shirt he's wearing, the selfsame shirt she gave him a few days back, nearly ripping it off his arm. 'Was it his money paid for this?'

This is straight out of a bloody novel, thinks Rita. 'What d'you want me to say, you daft pillock? That I'm crazy about Frankie?'

'Whore,' he spits at her. 'Slag.'

Rita hits him, only the steering wheel gets in the way and catches her elbow such a crack she cries aloud.

'Rita? Rita, are – ?'

'Out,' she shrieks. 'Get out of the car.'

'What do you mean? You can't dump me here, in the middle of the motorway!'

'We're getting off the sodding motorway before some lorry makes jam of us, and I'm driving. You're in no fit state. Go on. Give us the keys. *Now!*'

She drives like a maniac; the pair of them are seething, the air inside the car is hot with anger. At length, she squeals to a halt on the forecourt of the Bella Plaza. 'You can't go back in there,' he bursts out. 'Not in there, not with him.'

'Watch me.'

'If – if you get out of the car now,' he shouts, 'and go up to that flat, I'm driving straight off.'

'That's the idea,' she retorts, hopping out of the car and briskly chucking bag after bag on to the tarmac. 'You just toddle off home and back to college. Like a good little boy.'

'I'll leave. For good. You'll never see me again.'

In another mood, she might have laughed. Or maybe cried, because even though he's shouting, he sounds unbearably miserable. *Be kind to my boy*, she remembers. She grasps her last suitcase and manages a smile. 'Tarra, Thomas. Take care. Been nice knowing you.'

The car has vanished down the promenade even before she reaches the door of the flats.

A bicycle crashed against the wall outside. I winced and hoped she'd missed the climbing hydrangea. 'Lunch's in half an hour,' I called as the front door banged shut. 'Victoria in, was she?' But there was only a thunder of boots up the stairs.

It was Saturday morning and I was curled on my sofa with the newspapers round me. I wasn't reading, however. To be honest, I was just basking in the pleasures of my beautiful sitting room. I apologize for the immodesty. Number Two, Weavers' Row, may not be your idea of heaven, but it is certainly mine. This house is my haven, my creation, my definition, my *reward*. I personally exposed, sanded and waxed these golden floorboards; I lined and interlined the curtains crumpling thereon; I raided auction rooms for the age-mellowed rugs, the interesting bits of furniture . . . No, of course they don't match. I flatter myself they mingle harmoniously but, even as I chose them, I was amused and reassured to reflect how Rita would have loathed the whole damn room. Dad isn't keen, either, come to that. Says the faded pinky-gold effect reminds him of the telly when the colour's on the blink. No matter. I also commissioned the bookcases from a local joiner – such a pleasing shape, the pediment, don't you think?

Sorry, I'm being a house bore. There was a time, during the thick of the restoration, when even George refused to see me unless I promised to shut up about it. So I will just tell you this is a 200-odd-year-old terraced stone cottage, three-storeyed because in earliest days a weaver would work at home in the airy attic which is now my bedroom. The back garden, as is the way in so many of these Yorkshire mill villages, sheers straight up to the moors where fat, grey sheep rub themselves against my drystone wall. To the front, views stretch for dappled miles across the valley, and a reservoir winks below.

Not surprisingly, Top Mill has become fashionable. I bought just in time. The mill which gave the village its name has been rescued from dereliction and converted into flats and studios. We have a couple of artists, a wrought-iron worker, several potters and even, much to my daughter's horror, a taxidermist. The surrounding cottages were built by a philanthropic capitalist to house his workers, and, to this day, a few are occupied by hardy survivors of the industrial past. You can spot them by the aluminium window-frames and the ghastly frosted-glass doors. Don't bother telling me I'm a snob. Polly already has, frequently. But I'm also a founder member of the Dale Preservation Society and, as I point out to her, we're very *proud* the village still has some of the original inhabitants. We'd just like them to be prouder of their own heritage, that's all. In the meantime, we buy up their cast-iron ranges and curly-legged bathtubs as fast as they chuck 'em out. Our village post office now stocks fresh pasta; the former Temperance Hall is, ironically enough, a wine merchant; and the recobbled alleys are thick with BMWs. Yes, this village is recognizably a preserved preserve of the upwardly mobile middle class of Wakeborough. Which is why, wouldn't you know, Polly despises it.

I could hear her thumping down the stairs again now and, with a sigh, stood up. The door crashed open. She stood upon the threshold like an avenging angel brandishing, in place of a sword, a cassette tape. 'Mother,' she said, 'how *could* you?'

Truly it is said that in every apple there has to be a worm. This is the worm in mine. Don't get me wrong. You can take it as read that I love my daughter Polly with every fibre of my being. Just now, though, she was at a stage when liking her was an uphill struggle. Without hesitation I would lay down my life for her. Living with her was another matter. 'How could I what?'

'You'd have let him walk all over you.'

'Who?' I enquired. Sweetly.

'Mike thingy. Trevor Green's pathetic sidekick on your show on Thursday. I borrowed the tape off one of the COSH committee.'

'Oh *that*.' I re-adjusted my mind into work focus and tried to think back two days. 'What do you mean? That PR guy was fried alive.'

'No thanks to you. You were lapping up all that stuff about building rubble. You were really *polite* to him.'

'Strange to say, I'm not paid to abuse the guests on my show.'

'Don't you *care*?' Polly did. Oh, how she cared. About whales, calves, seals, ozone layers and now The Willows' nature park. However, she did condescend to ask what was for lunch.

'Cheese omelettes?'

'Yuck. Got any mushrooms? And I hope the eggs are proper free-range.'

I sighed as I cracked the correctly muck-spattered eggs into a bowl. It seemed that, almost until yesterday, this angry Amazon had been a pigtailed, talc-perfumed bundle of hugs, never happier than when helping Mum strip a skirting board. And, apart from her youthful attempts to turn my garden into a zoo and the odd conflict of opinion over the desirability of piano lessons, we had co-existed in delightful harmony.

Was it puberty that was responsible? Had the same hormones which made those chubby limbs suddenly shoot fast and straight as bamboo also transformed her nature? By now, at fifteen, she was a good four inches taller than her mother, and wishing she was a changeling. I think I'd have minded less if the teenage rebellion had taken the obvious form. If Polly had started locking her innermost dreams in a diary and herself in the bathroom for hours on scented end, I'd have been exasperated, but I would at least have understood.

But no. Frankly, I don't think Polly had so much as discovered what mirrors were for. And as for boys ... 'Oh, *Mother*,' she'd sighed when I'd recently been crass enough to ask if she was being escorted to the school dance. Not only was she not inviting a friend to the St Catharine's hop, she wouldn't dream of wasting her own time at such a moronic wake. And what really made me want to tear my hair was that she was *gorgeous*. You needn't make allowances for fond-mother speak. Polly might only be fifteen, but she already had the leggy, busty figure of a Barbie doll. And the even more precocious development of her brain showed in a face as lively as it was lovely. But did she care? Did she make anything of herself?

Look, I know it's a middle-aged cliché to moan about youngsters' taste in clothes, and I am *not* middle-aged. Besides, it wasn't just that her gear was the usual depressing mix of droopy black and clumpy boots, she simply wasn't interested. As for her hair . . . I reckoned there was a hundred quid's worth of artistry in the streaky shadings of that silky mop, except the whole golden kaleidoscope was natural, a blessing from heaven, a priceless, peerless crowning glory. And what did she do? Wash it every ten days under duress, and yank it back in rubber bands. Still, you don't want to hear the cluckings of this despairing mother hen.

'Good thing I went round to Victoria's this morning,' she informed me, selecting a biscuit to plug any gap left by the omelette. (And that's another irritating thing. No matter how much Polly eats, she stays lean as a whippet.) 'It's all beginning to happen.'

'Are we, um, talking about The Willows again?'

'Sure, COSH.' She chuckled happily. 'The wrinklies on the committee won't know what's hit them, once us lot get the campaign moving.'

'Are you sure you've got time for all this?' I enquired unwisely. 'With your homework and everything?'

'God, Mother, why are you so hung up on homework?'

'Because you're clever, and I want you to do well.'

'Should've sent me to a decent school then.'

Deliberate provocation. St Catharine's College is one of the best independent girls' schools in the country. I'd have scrubbed floors at night to pay the fees if my clever girl hadn't won herself a scholarship. At the time, she'd been as thrilled as I was. Well, almost. And when I was myself invited to become a school governor, truly, my cup ranneth right over. 'I only want you to have the choice to do whatever you like with your life.' I said this with the studious disinterest of one who has long since fixed on Oxbridge as her daughter's destination. 'I admit, I'd always rather hoped you might go to, um, university.'

'And get myself pregnant in my first year like you did?'

I didn't lose my temper. No, I even managed a laugh. 'You'd have more bloody sense.'

And she grinned at me – quite the old grin. Polly wasn't a full-time monster. She ricocheted disconcertingly between teenage misfit and lovable scamp. 'Don't worry, Mum, it's half-term a week from now. We're saving our big moves till then.'

'Who's we?'

'Me and the rest of COSH. Oh, and Uncle Jim's helping, too. You did well, getting him on the show. He was dead good, wasn't he?'

'Dead lucky, more like. I've told him regular contributors can't use the station as a soapbox. He could've got himself sacked, only Steve's away at the moment, on a working party.'

'Is he? I wondered why you'd been so ratty.' She rolled her eyes. 'Are you missing him *terribly*?'

'We're all missing him,' I said tartly. 'Without a proper Assistant Editor either, the place's been like bedlam.'

Even Helen, who was deputizing and whose ambition made Tina Brown look like Mrs Tiggywinkle, had hissed she'd be glad when the new Assistant Editor showed up. 'Tom Wilkes?' I'd said swiftly. 'Do we know when he's arriving?'

'Possibly never, from what I hear,' she snapped. 'But not soon enough, anyhow.'

'*Never*?' I'd croaked, knowing I should be relieved and wondering why I felt numb. Sipping my coffee now, I tried to decipher these murky feelings. I failed.

'You're not listening, Mum,' said Polly.

'Sorry? I mean, yes, I am.'

'I said Grandpa's not speaking to you.'

'If only. Why?'

'He was looking forward to his Sunday dinner tomorrow.'

'Pete's sake, what is it with men and Sunday dinner? I've promised I'll leave it ready. I've got to go out tomorrow. Um, work.'

There are times, not often I admit, when I see Mac's malevolent twinkle in his granddaughter's eyes. 'Stephen back from his working party by any chance?'

'And what if he is?'

She shrugged. 'It's your funeral. Anyway, doesn't matter to me. We're all going round to Kevin's tomorrow.'

'Kevin?' I said. In the way a mother does when an unidentified male name wanders into her daughter's conversation. But Polly's little toss of the head gave me no clues.

'I've *told* you about him, Mum. Lives in Lower Mill, not far from Grandpa's. In the Sixth Form at the Hollands.'

'Oh,' I said. A name like Kevin and a school like the Hollands –

the toughest comprehensive in Wakeborough – are not a combination to warm maternal cockles.

'And you needn't look like that,' she said instantly. 'He's pretty clever actually. Applying for Cambridge. Medicine.'

That sounded a whole lot more promising. 'Is he, um, nice?'

'Bit of a nerd. But he can drive, that's the main thing.'

I concentrated on infusing my voice with light-hearted nonchalance. 'Invite him round some time,' I said. 'If you like.'

'What, to this dump?' she said. And vanished upstairs.

'Look at it,' called my father. 'Cast aside your blade, raise your blinkered suburban eyes, and actually *look* at it.'

The 'it' in question was the view from his lounge window. Which, OK, on this Sunday morning featured horizontal rain and clouds like granite boulders. But in fairer conditions, I promise, the prospect was charming. Mac's bungalow, jutting out on a corner of the close, commanded by far the best view of the valley and viaduct, with the stream meandering prettily between his garden and the hill – well, slagheap, if you must. Even this, as I shouted through to Mac while peeling his veg, could only become greener.

'D'ye realize how far it is to a pub?' He did a sharp spin-turn in his wheelchair and shot through the kitchen door towards me. Having pronounced himself too old to learn stilt-walking (for which read mastering artificial limbs), he had nevertheless begun immediately to ride his chair with the perilous panache of a trick-cyclist.

'To the Cock? Half a mile?'

'Up a pot-holed one-in-five precipice.'

'You seem to manage to get there.'

'And I don't know why I bother.' Dad glared up at me, hunched in his chair like a malevolent garden gnome. 'The bar rumbles to the snores of bucolic bumpkins. Suffice to say, they recently outlawed dominoes on grounds of unseemly rowdiness. No, I've made up my mind, Rose. I'm going.'

'To the pub?' I glanced at my watch. 'Will it be open?'

'I meant I'm leaving,' he snapped. 'Escaping for good this lonely, stagnant backwater. I want to sell up and move.'

That stopped my chopping mid-carrot. 'You mean . . . come and live with me?'

'How kind. But you jest, I feel sure.'

'Am I laughing?' I promise you I wasn't. Horror at the prospect of my haven being invaded by Mac warred with guilt that I should feel this way about an elderly, disabled parent. Who was eyeing me with cynical amusement as, very slowly, he shook his head.

'Thank you, but I intend to return to the land of the living, not swap my fine and private coffin here for your wondrously tasteful mausoleum up the hill.'

In case relief shone too plain in my face, I turned to scrape the carrots into the boiling pan. 'Oh yeah? Which means where precisely?'

'Somewhere – anywhere – where dwell kindred spirits with whom I can converse,' he said promptly. 'Friendly pavements along which I can bowl my trusty chariot to take my pick of jostling, clamorous hostelries.'

'Dad, you couldn't possibly cope on your own.'

'I envision a bustling high street with a convivial local bookie, a genial tobacconist, a picture palace . . .' He heaved a longing sigh. 'I even dream of an iron-railed park whose sternly regimented geraniums will salute my senile progress when I'm beyond taking any pleasure but the air itself. Smoggy, vibrant, *city* air. Anything but that wild and weedy wasteland out there. Not to say polluted, unstable –'

'Give me strength.' I adjusted the gas and turned to face him. 'Look, don't wind me up, Dad. I know you get pissed off on your own, and I'm sorry I'm not here for lunch. I'm, um, seeing Stephen, OK?'

'Stephen Sharpe, is this?'

'Who else? I haven't had a chance to talk to him all week.'

'Some of us have not had a chance to so much as clap eyes on the gentleman. A regular Scarlet Pimpernel. Although if my granddaughter is to be believed, this is no great deprivation.'

'Oh, for God's sake. Has Polly ever liked *anyone* I've been out with?'

'Can you blame her?' he enquired sweetly.

'I'm warning you, Mac . . .'

'And I'm telling you, I've had enough of being buried alive. What d'you think this place would fetch?'

*

There was no point arguing. A fight, after all, was exactly what Mac wanted. Rows to Mac are like bones to a dog: to be worried down to the last tasty morsel, then buried for later retrieval and further fun. So I arranged his precious Sunday dinner, gravy and all, on a plate to be warmed up at the appointed hour, then made myself a coffee and carried it through to the lounge to apply my make-up.

He deigned to glance up from his crossword. His second of the morning. He always warms up on the *Express* ('filthy fascist rag'), proceeds through the *Observer* ('bleeding conscience of the bourgeoisie') and concludes with the *Sunday Times*, which he generously admits has a halfway decent puzzle. Even if it's contained in a journal whose thickets of trendy twaddle epitomize, for him — let me get this right — 'the truly monstrous vacuity of modern capitalism'. Have I mentioned that Mac professes himself a communist? Well, no matter. It never affected his mode of living in any way I could discern, save for enriching the arsenal of insults he could hurl at the world. 'Aren't you getting changed then?' he enquired. 'To visit your fancy man?'

My mascara wand didn't even quiver. 'Funnily enough, I'm going just as I am. Why, don't you like the outfit?' Even Mac, I thought, could find no fault with these perfectly cut trousers, this criminally expensive silk shirt, plus my best — well, OK, my only — Hermès scarf. All of them chosen in the mossy shades which I happen to think flatter my hair, which remains, with a little help from my hairdresser, a quiet, russety-brown.

'Charming,' agreed Mac, 'if you like compost heaps.'

And still the wand remained steady as I laughed good-naturedly.

'Time was,' he mused, 'when you dressed brighter than a bird of paradise.'

'Times change. I —' But then I broke off. I saw a familiar anorak scrambling down the hill towards the stream. 'Is that Polly over on the tip? Honestly, she'll catch her death in this weather.'

'Fanatics fear neither cold nor heat,' he murmured, not glancing up from the page. 'In another age, I've no doubt Polly would have sung hymns all the way to the blazing stake for whatever God was fashionable at the time. What's a little rain in the service of the great green deity? She told me she was planning some fieldwork.'

I scowled into my mirror. 'She only told me she was going round to Kevin's.'

'Kevin, you say?' Mac abruptly dropped his paper and bowled himself over to the window. 'Indeed, yes, there he is. Gallantly holding the jam jars while our heroine shovels in the mud.' I twisted round too. But, what with the driving rain and Kevin's hooded anorak, I could see only two long thin legs, with jeans flapping wetly in the breeze. 'Don't strain your eyes,' said Mac. 'He's no matinée idol, but at least he doesn't favour his father.'

'You know the family, then? Apparently he's applying to Cambridge, so –'

'So he hasn't inherited his father's brains either. Or total lack of same. Yes, of course I know the Marlowes. A harmless, if tediously respectable couple. They run the newsagent's in Harrogate Road and the boy helps out sometimes.' He looked at me most peculiarly. 'You seem to be taking it very calmly.'

'Sorry?'

'Aha. So Polly didn't tell you.'

'Tell me what?' I was back to the make-up again, flattening my lips over my teeth and loading the lip-brush.

'She only mentioned it in passing to me. No doubt because, in her kindly if misguided view, we were once employed in a similar line of business. I suppose it wouldn't occur to her that you might be even more interested than I.'

'Stop being elliptical, Mac. Interested in what?'

But, of course, he didn't enlighten me at once. Like a conjurer, he always spins out his routine before, finally, yanking the rabbit from the hat. 'I'm just trusting there's nothing more serious binding those two children than the future of the planet.'

'Probably isn't,' I hissed through a lipsticky grimace. Damn, I'd missed a bit in the corner. 'Polly seems to be a late developer as far as boys are concerned.'

'Unlike her mother,' he couldn't resist murmuring. '*Deo gratias.*'

I scowled but let it pass. 'The best she could tell me about this Kevin was that he'd got a driving licence. Hardly sounds like a girl in love.'

'Let us hope so indeed.'

I blinked round at him. 'Why the voice of doom? Shit, it's nearly quarter to twelve. I'm going to be late.'

'I assume she didn't mention Kevin's surname, either. To be sure, his mother is Mrs Marlowe now, has been for many a long year, but Kevin's kept his pappy's name.'

I should have known. Should have picked up the danger signals. But no. I was anxious to get to Stephen's and I kept right on tracing the Cupid's bow. In deep blood-red.

'Henderson,' he said. So flatly, however, I didn't immediately recognize this as his precious rabbit. Generally he managed more of a flourish. 'Kevin Henderson,' he said. 'Son, if not heir, of the more famous Frank . . . Dear me, did your hand slip? I hope that delightful ensemble is washable.'

12

Amazing how a good row clears the head.

By the time she's carted her bags into the lobby of the Bella Plaza, Rita has her story worked out. She knows Frank is home because the bedroom window's open up there. OK, she stayed on in Blackpool because she was offered a load of gigs. And Thomas is her cousin, right? Her kid cousin who came to stay for a couple of nights. She knew Frankie wouldn't mind. He's a nice, well-behaved lad . . .

For an instant she gazes back at the prom. She finds herself wishing the business hadn't ended quite so messily. Thomas is probably howling his baby heart out. Well, just so long as he's not driving under lorries. She never meant to hurt him. She'll – she'll send him a postcard or summat. A comic postcard with a rude picture, yeah, that'll cheer him up. Next thing you know, he'll be out on the town, chasing all the Oxford girls . . .

For some unaccountable reason, this vision doesn't comfort her. Silly cow. She thrusts all thought of Thomas aside and kicks her luggage up against the lobby wall. If Frankie swallows her tale, he can help her shift this lot upstairs. If he wants to take the hump, well, she's ready to move on. In fact the thought of Frank in that great circular bed more than half inclines her towards moving on anyway. But she's going nowhere without her white dress. And that's up in the flat.

Once in the lift, she flits a comb through her curls and experiments in the mirrored wall with a few cheesy welcome-home-lover-boy smiles. Unconvincing. She looks a wreck and, after that row and all the plonk at lunchtime, her head's beginning to pound. So she's not pleased, as the lift doors slide open, to hear disco music throbbing from the penthouse. It doesn't even occur to her that Frankie's never been much of a disco man. More your Herb Alpert and Perry dopey Como. She stabs in her key and opens the door. 'What the hell . . .?'

The hall is deserted and dim, but her gaze is fixed on the sun-flooded, open doorway of the lounge. Framed wherein, to her goggling astonishment, she's seeing a fat, white-haired man, standing with his back to her, legs akimbo. Save for a mortar-board cocked on the side of his head and a striped tie knotted round his thick neck, this geezer's pinkly, plumply naked. And he's – flexing a cane? She doesn't know whether to laugh or puke. Just what does this ugly lump of blubber think he's playing at?

'Who's been a naughty girl?' he sniggers, and then she sees the girl up-ended beyond his hairy thighs. Gym-slipped, black-suspendered and knickerless, she shrieks blue murder when he thwacks her one. There are guffaws and whistles and flashes from a camera. 'Give it to her, mate,' a beery voice bellows.

Rita hears laughter echoing from the bathroom, too. How many people are there in the place? Suddenly she remembers Thomas, grinning bemusedly in that tub, saying it was big enough for an orgy. Little did he know . . .

Dis-bleeding-gusting, she thinks. Is Frankie in on this? Is this kinky carry-on what he needs to get it up? Twisted little perv. He might be a creep, but she'd never have suspected *this*.

'Time for a speedy exit, Rita, my girl,' she says to herself. 'Grab the dress and get the hell out.' The dry-cleaner's bag, she knows, was lying on a chair just inside the bedroom. After a second's hesitation, she nudges open the door. And immediately shuts it again. There's a viper's nest of limbs writhing on the bed. Two black girls and some elderly gent trussed up in handcuffs. She couldn't see what they were tying on his willy, but he was gasping he'd double their money if only . . .

Sod the frock. She's not hanging round here. She's halfway across the twilit hall, cursing as she trips over a glass, when the lounge door slams and a thin figure catapults into her, grabbing her. 'Gerroff,' yelps Rita, outraged.

It's the gym-slipped tart, shirt half ripped out, lipstick smeared all over her chin. 'Where's the bog?' Her voice is slurred. Dead drunk, probably, because her skinny arms are still clutching Rita for dear life.

'That's the bathroom,' she hisses. Then pulls a face. 'Except, by the sound of it, your mates are at it in there too. Toilet, by the front door. Now leave off, will you?'

'Sorry,' grunts the girl and paws Rita's shoulder.

Rita looks down. There's a dark smudge on her T-shirt where the girl fell against her. Even in this dim light, she can see it's not lipstick. 'Holy Mary, your face is bleeding.'

'Bit my fucking mouth,' she mumbles. 'Bastard really hurt me.'

Rita suddenly realizes it's tears, not booze, thickening her voice. 'Here,' she finds herself asking, 'how old are you?'

The girl springs away, scowling. She barely looks into her teens, never mind legal. 'What's it to you? You working for Lincoln too?'

Rita's just hissing that she's never clapped eyes on this Lincoln when the implications of the question sink in. 'You mean . . .' Rita might be pint-sized, but so is the Queen and I promise even Her Majesty never managed a more toweringly regal glower. 'Do I look like I'm on your filthy game?' With her studded leather hemline hoicked so high and and her neckline bulging so low that the distance between one and t'other can be measured in handspans? Perhaps the girl can be forgiven for just shrugging as she refastens one of her suspenders. But not by our Rita, whose cheeks blaze fierier than her hair. 'I'll have you know I'm Frankie Henderson's girlfriend,' she snarls – and then remembers Thomas's furious wail: *whore, slag* . . . This only makes her madder. 'Was, anyway. Not any more.' She jerks her head towards the lounge door. 'He in there?'

The girl looks up. 'Who?'

'Mine flaming host, of course.'

'You kidding? Linc never shows his –'

'*Frankie* . . . Oh, forget it. I'm off. For good and all.'

'Suit yourself.' The girl sniffs thickly. 'That the bog? I've gorra have a piss before Whacko there gets back on the job.'

Rita's already flinging open the front door but, in spite of herself, she turns back and grabs the girl by her skinny wrist. 'You're never going back for more?'

'Pardon?'

'He's hurt you.'

The kid glares at the lounge door. 'He'll pay. Fat pig.'

'Look, love, I'm calling a cab, outside,' she hears herself gabbling. What in the name of all the saints is she playing at? 'To the station. I'll give you a lift.'

'You what?'

'What are you? Fourteen? Jesus, thugs like him should be locked up for –'

'Fuck off.' The girl twists out of Rita's grasp and slams into the loo.

There's a blinding flash of sunlight. Someone's emerging from the lounge. Rita doesn't see who. She's out of that flat and pelting down the back stairs like all the devils in hell are after her.

13

'Oh, darlin',' moaned Stephen, plunging even harder. 'That feel good?'

'Mmm,' I managed. Although it wasn't passion that silenced me. I won't say my thoughts were on England, but neither were they (as Rita would have said) on the job. They weren't even focusing on this Tom Wilkes geezer, the entire contents of whose personnel file I nevertheless intended to wheedle out of Stephen in the course of the afternoon. I'd got nowhere so far. Not only was I shaken by Mac's little *coup de théâtre*, I'd had no chance to frame a pertinent question or ten because Stephen had pounced on me the minute I walked through his door. A brief hello, some hot-breathed gabble about a staff knees-up later in a wine bar, and here I was, flat on my back. My bra was off before my boots. Flattering really. If a crying waste of make-up.

Thunk . . . thunk . . . 'Am I hitting the spot?'

What spot? Bless the Lamb, he was always so conscientious. 'Yes, yes. Fabulous.'

'Oh aye,' Mac had confirmed, half an hour earlier. 'Yon Kevin's Frankie's son right enough. Dumped, along with his mammy, when the poor bairn was scarcely weaned. Such delinquency in parental duties appals me.'

Coming from a man who had never himself achieved more than twelve consecutive months of family life, this was pretty rich. But as Father Michael used to intone, we always hate worst the sin closest to our own black heart. Besides, in Mac's eyes, Frank Henderson had committed an offence far more heinous than quitting his family. He'd broken into television. 'Funny as a hysterectomy,' he growled. 'The lousiest vent ever to gargle a gottle of geer. So what do they do? They give him his own series, that's what. And of course it was goodbye Wakeborough, wife and babby, from that day onwards.'

I was sponging the lipstick off my shirt. Found myself thinking of a smear of blood . . .

'Frankie headed straight for the bright lights – and the dim broads,' said Mac, fixing an unpleasantly intent gaze on me. 'Or so I heard at the time.'

With steely composure, I rearranged my scarf to hide the stain. 'Oh really?'

'Can't imagine how he pulled them, mind. Fed choc drops to their guide dogs I shouldn't wonder.' He was still watching me closely. 'But perhaps you can enlighten me as to the little bastard's fugitive charms?'

Thunk . . . thunk . . . 'I'm nearly there, babe,' Stephen gasped. As if I hadn't noticed. 'Are you gonna come along with me?'

What is it about the act of copulation that makes perfectly sensible men babble the mid-Atlantic slang of sixties pop songs? Curious. Anyway, I thought it was probably more convincing not to answer and just gave an appropriate gasp or two. Dammit, I've never been able to keep up a running commentary through sex, even when I'm not deafened by the rattle of skeletons against the closet door.

First this so-called Tom Wilkes and now Frankie's ex-wife and child. Honestly, it was too much. Time was when I had occasionally wondered about Frankie's abandoned family, but as I'd never encountered a Mrs Henderson in all my years in Wakeborough, I'd comfortably concluded the woman must have quit the area once he'd quit her. It's a dangerous temptation, when you work in local radio, to assume you know everybody on your patch who has the remotest claim to being anybody. It hadn't crossed my mind she might not be Mrs Henderson any longer, but Mrs something else. *Lorna.* I'd never met her, to be sure, but I suddenly remembered the name through the mists of time . . .

'*Yeah*,' roared Stephen, for all the world like an Argentinian footballer scoring the winning goal, then flopped beside me. And, do you know, for the first time in years, I found myself wishing I'd got a cigarette to hand. The old post-coital fag. Mac's fault for winding me up. I settled firmly back into the pillow, reminding myself how much I hated the stink of smoke.

Then all at once I noticed the spider. It was dangling from the ceiling, right above my head. Spinning and spinning . . .

'You're not concerned?' Mac had demanded, jerking his head towards the window where the two anoraked figures, my daughter and Frankie's son, were doggedly trawling the stream. 'Them palling up like this?'

Well, I wasn't exactly thrilled, no, but I'd have died before admitting it. Mac might suspect Rita had shared more than the bill of an end-of-the-pier show with Frank Henderson, but he could stew as far as I was concerned. 'Why on earth should it worry me?'

Whereupon, for once in his combative life, Mac had fallen silent. He'd retreated into his crossword, grunting that he hoped I knew what I was about. Because he damn well didn't. And never had.

I knew what I was about all right, I thought now. Mac's revelation had been a shock, certainly, but there was nothing in a friendship between Polly and Kevin to disturb my peace of mind. The boy, as my nosy father had evidently gone to some trouble to establish, had only ever been acquainted with his renegade parent via a television screen. He couldn't even have seen much of him there for a good few years. Last time I spotted Frank Henderson, he was reading a maudlin verse on the Sunday teatime God slot. You can't sink much lower than that.

I looked up at my chum the spider, swaying perilously low on his long, invisible lifeline. Cling on tight to that thread you've spun, little friend, I was thinking. I know just how you feel.

'Rose? Rose, darling?' Stephen, whose recovery time after orgasm can be measured in micro-seconds, had hoicked himself up on one elbow and was helping himself to a bottle of mineral water from the bedside table. 'You're miles away.'

'Sorry. Half asleep.'

He looked oddly naked without his specs. Quite different really, although his hair was as neat as ever. I'd tried to ruffle it before now, but somehow it always twanged back into place. 'It was good?' he enquired anxiously. 'For you, I mean?'

Performance Review is the buzz-phrase in BBC management these days. I sometimes thought Steve carried the concept too far. I smiled, however. 'Amazing,' I said.

And I wasn't lying. Well, at least I *wished* I wasn't. Oh how I wished. Stephen was fine, as lovers go. No, better than fine. Brilliant. Terrific. Lovely body, hard-muscled and stocky as a footballer's. And the energy of a whole bloody team.

So why was it, I asked myself despairingly as I accepted the swig of designer water he offered, that the only times I'd felt *really* turned on by the Lamb were when he was out of reach? Not when he was sprawled here in his bed, but when he was crisply shirted and smartly suited in the office. Those were the rare occasions when lust had surged, and I'd felt a potty desire for him to throw me across his desk and ravish me.

'You do know Corporation folklore always held that to be one of the two instant sacking offences,' George had observed when, over a gin too many, I'd recently confided this fantasy.

'Having it away on the desk?'

'Being discovered *in flagrante* on the premises. That and being caught without a television licence. And frankly, if the co-flagrantee were Stainless Steve, I'd be more excited by the detector van.'

I was sorry I'd mentioned it. Sorrier still when, with a disquietingly alert little smile, she'd continued: 'Finding it hard to conjure passion, are we? Mind, I'm not surprised, in that concrete-and-chrome laboratory he calls home.'

Well, OK, I conceded now, looking round at his bedroom – the bare white walls, the steel-blinded window, the matt-black bedside shelf – maybe techno-minimalism wasn't my cup of tea either. The first time I'd visited Stephen's flat I was dumb enough to ask when the rest of his furniture was arriving. But this was a bachelor apartment and I'd long since determined that all the Lamb needed to sort him out was the loving guidance of a good woman. And women didn't come gooder than me, not these days.

All at once he sat up and swung his feet out of the bed. 'I'll take first shower then, shall I?'

I blinked and yawned. 'What's the big hurry?'

'Darling, I gave you the rundown as soon as you walked through the door. We're due at the Tipsy Fox. Or at least, I am.'

I sprang up from the pillow. 'Now?' I squawked. Hell, was this why he'd stampeded me into bed? Not rampant passion, just smart timetabling?

'You're welcome to string along, but we'll have to go in separate cars with –'

'I thought you meant this evening,' I gasped. 'God, Steve, I'm not here just to . . .' But I couldn't exactly tell him that I hadn't come round today just for a quick bonk, that what I far more urgently wanted from him was every scrap of information he possessed about the man who might or might not be taking over the Assistant Editor's job. 'I told you,' I said helplessly. 'I need to talk to you.'

He shrugged as he retrieved his spectacles. 'Blame Head of Centre. Howard's the one insisting on the kid-glove and red-carpet scenario.'

'What is all this?' I demanded. 'All you said was that a few of you were meeting for a swift half at the wine bar.'

'At two and it's nearly quarter to now. I'll have to shift because I've got to round the guy up from the Elms first. From the sound of his voice on the phone earlier on, he couldn't find his own way to the bathroom.'

'Who?' I wailed.

Stephen was already vanishing into the shower. 'This attaché Howard's settling on us,' he shouted exasperatedly. 'New Assistant Editor. Tom Wilkes, he's called. Jesus, babe, what on earth . . .?'

He pelted back in. Probably because I'd let out a shriek that would crack windows.

'Sorry,' I mumbled, holding out my hand, from which a leggy corpse hung forlornly. 'I just, um, trod on a spider.'

14

Rita shrieks, too, when her shoulder's grabbed. Heart hammering, lungs heaving, she's plummeted out on to the prom, casting round wildly for a phone box. 'Get your filthy hands off me,' she screams, then sees that it's only Thomas. Whereupon she collapses all over him, bawling her silly head off.

'I'm sorry, Rita, I'm sorry,' he stammers, wrapping his arms round her, pressing kisses into her hair, glueing his body to every available inch of hers. 'I was waiting. Hoping you'd come out. I didn't mean to upset you. I didn't mean it. Not any of it.'

Does the poor fool thinks it's only him that's upset her? Even as he hugs her, Rita glances fearfully up at the penthouse. If they think she's gone running off to the police . . . 'Got the car?'

''Course, right behind you.'

'Then let's go.'

'Wherever you like,' agrees Thomas fervently. 'Where's your stuff?'

'In the lobby, don't bother –' But he's already loping off. 'Hurry,' she shouts, and scrambles into his car where she cowers below the dashboard, pretending to fumble in her handbag.

'What's that on your T-shirt?' he asks, chucking her last bag on to the back seat.

'What? Oh – nothing. Lipstick.' She spits on a tissue and rubs furiously. 'Look, drive, will you?'

'Where to?'

'Anywhere. Just – just move.'

And so they cruise off along the promenade, south into St Anne's, Blackpool's staider sister down the coast. By which time Rita has got at least half a grip on her wits again, and tells Thomas he can stop now. *No!* God's sake, not in the middle of the road . . . Honestly, she begins to think he'd drive straight into the sea if she said so. 'This do?' He noses into a space behind an ice-cream van on the sandy, sunny front. 'What now?'

'I want some – fresh air,' says Rita. Oddly enough, that is the simple truth. I say oddly because most of her life Rita has approached the great outdoors like most people treat nuclear fall-out. At this moment, however, she feels as though slugs have been crawling over her. She wants a wind to blow every stinking breath of that flat out of her clothes and her hair, to blast the traces off her very skin.

Perhaps Thomas realizes there's something amiss, because he doesn't pester her with questions. They wander along the beach and into the dunes, where the sand is fine as talc, soft as powdered silk, warm as ashes. It's a glorious, golden, late-September afternoon and yet they have the place nearly to themselves. The summer holidays are ended, the buckets and spades are gone. A few pensioners, in the distance, parade their dogs at the water's edge. Thomas takes her hand and hauls her, slipping and sliding, up the hot, shingly face of a dune. They slither down the other side and the town, the dog-walkers and the sea are all lost. She and Thomas are marooned in a deep golden saucer, with only a blue sky arcing above. A breeze puffs sand into the fine blond hairs on Thomas's arms as they flop, full length, on the sun-scorched slope.

'You're not going back to him,' he says finally. Fact not question. 'Frankie whatever-he's-called.'

'No,' says Rita. She doesn't feel as though she's having this conversation at all. She feels she's one of those gulls, careering overhead, staring down. Seeing two people lying on the sand, alone in the whole wide universe, hands just touching. 'No, I'm not going back. No way.'

And there's no way she's going to explain why. To Thomas, least of all. She doesn't yet recognize why she feels this so strongly. She supposes she doesn't want to shock him, baby that he is. But it's deeper than that. At heart, she's ashamed of herself. Sick with shame and a black, self-loathing guilt that only a Catholic upbringing can nurture. If you ask me, it was this same guilt prompted her to urge the snivelling girl in the flat to run. It's as though being Frankie's girlfriend makes her a party to all the filth. Which she wasn't, and isn't, and never would be. Rita's a girl who likes a good time, that's all. Her cabaret act may not be exactly

Shirley Temple and she's never claimed (least of all to herself) that she gives a stuff about Frank Henderson, but that does *not* make her a whore or a slag. Whatever Thomas thinks.

'I just went up to fetch my dress,' she says flatly. (A few presents don't turn a girl into a tart.)

'Wasn't it there? I didn't –'

'Doesn't matter.' (How could she ever have so much as touched Frank Henderson? Creep, Pervert.) 'Getting tatty, anyhow. Maybe I'll rethink the routine.'

'You deserve better,' says Thomas softly.

'Too right,' says Rita. With feeling.

He rolls towards her, frames her face in his hands and kisses her. And he's – different. This isn't a kid, scrambling to devour her, this is a grown-up lover, purposeful and serious. Who doesn't snag her zip. Who's spread his shirt under her before she realizes what's happening. Whose tongue rasps her nipples with the same breath-stopping proficiency as his fingers feather apart her thighs. Who holds her gaze steadily, even as his naked body locks into hers. 'Chrissake,' Rita manages to croak. 'What if someone walks over the hill?'

'Hush,' he says. The golden eyes are fixed on hers. It's as though he belongs here, in the bleached sand and pampas grasses. The lion eyes, the tawny mane . . . 'Hush.' He's watching her intently as he thrusts. Kissing the pulse that ticks in her throat as she wriggles and gasps. Waiting for each choked whimper. Holding back until she's sobbing for him to let go and only then tightening his grip on her shoulders, and tearing into her like a real conquering hero. And both of them are laughing and squealing for sheer, exploding joy. Clinging together, until every last shudder has ebbed. And still he holds her. Carefully, so she's not crushed. He kisses her eyelids one after the other. Licks away a tear. A *tear*? 'I love you,' he says.

'Love you too, baby.'

'No. Say it properly. Tell me you love me.'

'I – love – you,' says Rita. And, in that dreadful instant, she realizes she might actually mean it.

'You'll write to me,' Thomas said as he loaded her bags on to the train. 'Every single day.'

'I hate writing letters.'

'Every other day then. God, I wish your mother had a phone. Still, you can ring me. I told you, I'm living out of college this year and there's bound to be a phone, but I'll have to let you know the number when –'

'Don't worry,' said Rita, climbing aboard.

He yanked down the window before slamming shut the carriage door. And then hauled her through to kiss her again. He didn't give a stuff that they were being observed with interest by a carriage full of elderly day-trippers. His face split into a cheeky grin. 'Hey, I never gave you your garter back. Ma wanted it returned to its rightful owner.'

Rita smiled sadly. 'Hang on to it. Keepsake.'

'But you've got nothing of mine. You should have something. To make you think of me. I want you to think about me every minute.' He was patting his pockets, as though expecting a gift to materialize. Little did he know she'd already got her keepsake tucked away. 'Well, I'll think of something and send it to you. With my first letter. Nineteen, Sandy Lane, Wakeborough. That's right isn't it?'

Wakeborough was the first town that had popped into her head, when she'd insisted he must go back to college tomorrow with his chum. However much he pleaded and argued, she'd stuck firm to her story. She was returning home to her mother for a while. Which, so help her, she was. Naturally, he'd demanded an address, a telephone number. And she'd had the wit to claim her mother wasn't on the phone. Probably Wakeborough had occurred to her because it was none other than Frankie's home town, where lived the wife and infant he'd so recently abandoned. Whether he visited them there, Rita knew not. All she knew was that Wakeborough was the last town on earth she herself was ever going to inhabit, just in case Frankie was in the habit of popping home. After that, the rest had been easy. Nineteen was Thomas's own age. Sandy Lane: well, it was a sandy beach . . .

He beamed up at her from the platform. 'And you'll come and see me? Soon?' At Maudlin College, Oxford. Only it was spelled, Thomas had shyly informed her (just in case, by any remote chance, she didn't know), *Magdalen*.

'As in Mary?' she'd said incredulously.

'You'll love it.'

'You bet.'

The guard was walking down the train, slamming doors. Thomas grabbed her hand. 'Our two souls, which are one, um . . . Oh God, what's the next line?'

'You what?'

A bright-eyed elderly gent behind her nudged his wife. 'Hey-up, he's on the poetry now. Must be serious.'

'No, no, listen,' shouted Thomas. '"Our two souls therefore, which are one . . ."'

But she lost half the rest as the guard blew his whistle. I wouldn't be surprised if he'd got it wrong, anyway: John Donne, 'A Valediction: Forbidding Mourning'. *Our two souls, therefore, which are one, Though I must go, endure not yet a breach, but an expansion . . .*

'Like – "Like gold to aery thinness beat",' he finished triumphantly above the noise. Funny, Rita hadn't understood a word, but that line, *gold to aery thinness beat*, would stick with her for years.

'Get away with you,' she muttered at the time, conscious of the grinning spectators.

'Proper old brief encounter,' sighed bright-eyes' fat wife as the train jerked into motion. 'Mind, it's not the same with diesels.' As her husband began whistling a soupily familiar tune, she winked at Rita and raised her voice. 'Go on, chuck. Give the lad a smacker.'

But the train was already trundling down the platform, Thomas trotting along beside. 'I love you,' he was shouting. For the millionth time. Not a conquering hero, not a lion in the sand dunes any more. Just an eager, laughing, silly boy. Looking so happy . . .

'Love you too, baby,' she whispered. Telling herself grandly that she loved him enough to get on to this train. To chug off out of his life. That she loved him enough to lie.

'And one day,' panted Thomas, 'One day, we'll get married.'

Even Rita couldn't manage a lie that big. 'Don't talk soft.'

He didn't hear. He was running faster, but he couldn't keep up. 'One day,' he called, a shrinking golden figure on the end of the platform, hands cupped round his mouth as he shouted. 'One day. You'll see . . .'

15

I was going to marry Stephen. I glared at myself in his shaving mirror. *I was going to marry Stephen.* No matter that our affair was mere weeks old, no matter that Stephen didn't yet know it, I was going to marry him. Dammit, I'd more than halfway decided this before ever I clapped eyes on the guy.

Sorry, does that shock you? I realize it must sound calculating. Or crazy. But put yourself in my position. I was, let us say, on the wrong side of thirty when Stephen Sharpe arrived in Wakeborough and, frankly, I'd begun to feel my life had been one long, sweated race. A successful race, to be sure. Like I said, I reckoned I'd got myself the perfect job, gorgeous house, teeming diary. I also had a good school for Polly, even a healthy bank account ... God, how self-satisfied I sound. Mac recently called me smug as a slug in a lettuce. Then changed it to a slug in radicchio because, he said, even if it didn't scan I'd be bound to choose the leaf with snob appeal.

It seemed to me, however, that the feverish rush had left no space for a love life – and if you've found out how to combine a tenderly blossoming affair with a precociously protective daughter, then tell me the trick. Sure, I'd been out with the odd man over the years. Most of them very odd, according to Polly. But it was as though I was forever searching for some elusive extra, and it was never there. I'd wake up in a strange bed – on those rare occasions when I could escape into one – look at the body sleeping beside mine, and want to weep for loneliness.

My father, quite unintentionally, had been the catalyst for reform. Once I'd installed him in his bungalow down the road last year, I suddenly realized I was an unsupported single mother no longer. I had got myself a resident child-minder. His spare bed-room was decorated for Polly before I'd hung his lounge curtains, and, at last, I could stand back and review my emotional life.

I was appalled. The job, the burgeoning committees, Polly: they were no more than excuses for my lousy emotional track record. The truth was that I'd wasted all these years hankering after a myth. A misty memory. A bonding of so-called twin souls – *gold to aery thinness beat* – instead of recognizing that a sensible woman will settle for Bacofoil. After that it was easy, because I realized exactly what I should be looking for. Not a twin soul, but a matching lifestyle. Not airy romance, but a rock-solid husband. And not just any old husband, you may be sure, but a shiny-bright husband to match my shiny-bright, hard-earned life. I was laughing at myself as I drew up my checklist, but that's not to say I didn't mean every word; presentable, conversable, smart, ambitious . . .

Whereupon, right on cue, we heard we were getting this new boss for Radio Ridings. On paper and gossip-vine, Stephen Sharpe might have dismayed my colleagues, but he fitted my own private job-spec miraculously. Right age, unattached, starry with prospects: here, surely, was my identikit other half. All that remained was to check he didn't have three legs or disgusting personal habits. Having ascertained this within a minute of clapping eyes on him, I refused to be dismayed that my heart didn't flip or skip or do whatever hearts are supposed to do. Great love, as a member of our local Sikh community assured me in an interview only the other day, often follows arranged marriages. I did realize, however, that there was the small matter of arranging Stephen Sharpe's own feelings.

Initially, this didn't seem to be a problem. In fact, he invited me out to dinner that very evening, on the pretext – for I naturally assumed it was a pretext – of mining my vast reserves of local knowledge, as our Head of Centre had so helpfully recommended he should. As a result, I was rather daunted, when, before the cork had been drawn at our candlelit table (I'd chosen the bistro with care), Stephen produced from his pocket a small tape-recorder which he placed on the table between us. 'Let's kick off with the interface between the station and the business community, shall we?'

That bloody pocket machine played chugging gooseberry on every subsequent table, too. And although there are barely two subjects closer to my heart than Wakeborough and Radio Ridings,

I'd had in mind a different sort of interfacing. It wasn't long before, as a mine of information, I was worked out. As a *femme fatale*, I reckoned I might as well trade in the Wonderbra for a woolly vest. However, even when Stephen pronounced himself, as he put it, up to speed, and our tape-recorded tête-à-tête conferences petered out, I couldn't *quite* bring myself to give up hope. There was something mysterious about the way he tried so hard *not* to touch me, if you know what I mean. If his knee even brushed mine under a table he would jump away as though I were electrically charged. He talked about listener motivation and audience dynamics and I (maybe I was kidding myself?) heard rampant lust.

The crunch, however, when it had eventually come eight weeks ago, took me by surprise. I was giving him a lift home after a particularly tedious civic banquet. Sober because I was driving, tired and frankly pissed off, I drew up outside his flat, opened my mouth to say I'd see him on Monday, and couldn't get a word out because he was kissing me. *Kissing* me? He was practically eating me alive. 'God, I'm sorry,' he gasped. 'It's the drink. Shouldn't do this.'

''Course you should,' I'd said enthusiastically. 'Just let me shift this seat belt and –'

'No – no.'

'Steve? What on earth's wrong?'

'Don't you see?' he roared. Truly the wail of a soul in torture. 'I'm your *line manager.*'

I laughed. I laughed so much I popped the waistband on my new skirt. Stephen, I admit, didn't quite get the joke. This was, he said crossly, the horniest of dilemma scenarios. And that, I fear, nearly gave me an apoplexy. Even he had to smile when he realized what he'd said. But he was right. I suppose I'd dimly known there were rules about this sort of thing. I now discovered the Corporation holds views on sexual relations between management and consenting underlings which make the Pope sound liberal. These dangerous liaisons are held to corrupt staff moral, undermine trust, rot the whole damn Corporate edifice. If the sinners come clean, Aunty expects one of you to Do the Decent Thing. Which, OK, is not quite to shut the Grams Library door and take out the revolver, it's just to change jobs. Fine in London. Impossible in a one-cell outpost like Radio Ridings, and neither Steve nor I was prepared to sacrifice our job. No wonder he'd kept his tape-recorder ticking so decorously between us. Forbidden fruit, however, was ever the most delicious, and you'd have thought the secrecy might at least have spiced the sex.

Maybe it did for Steve, but I craved the deep peace of a marital divan and I thought it was about time he recognized the need to, well, to formally contractualize the mutual benefit potentiality of an on-going partnership situation. I mean, *you* can see why he needed a good woman, can't you? Not to say an English graduate. There were still a few obstacles, yes: Polly, George, the BBC itself, come to that, because I'd been dismayed to learn that the Corporation is even tougher on marriage than it is on unshackled fornication. Marrying the boss, known as 'doing a Des and Esther', is not a legitimate career objective. But I'd been prepared to tackle all these. I'd seen my path clear and bright before me.

Until 12.08 last Monday morning when the name of Tom Wilkes had blundered across it.

'Of course it won't be *him*,' I told my reflection in the mirror as, for the second time that day, I brushed on my lipstick. Funny how long it takes to apply the kind of make-up which looks as though you're wearing none. Rita could paste on her lurid warpaint in five minutes flat. 'Hundred to one it isn't *Thomas* who even now is being shepherded into the Tipsy Fox. Oh God, even now. This very minute . . .'

Stephen had long since roared off, showered and cologned, to collect his new deputy from the Elms Hotel. To my intense frustration, I'd failed to extract from him any single fact which would positively prove or disprove the identity of the newcomer. That this Tom Wilkes had worked on the *Western Mail*, the *Guardian* and *Panorama* meant nothing. Where was he born? Where did he go to school? Did he have long legs and tawny eyes?

Of course I hadn't actually asked that. But blood gushes from stones compared with in-house gossip from the Lamb. He squared our unauthorized relationship with his managerial conscience by disclosing nothing over the pillow that he wouldn't over the desk. About work, I mean. I don't suppose he told my colleagues he had sensitive nipples. Such discretion is admirable, I grant. And maddening. Only after he was dressed and combing his damp but still orderly locks did he open up a bit. He muttered something about giving his word to Howard but, all the same, regarding this as a trial fixture, and if the guy couldn't make the grade . . .

'You don't like him,' I said swiftly.

'Never met him. Anyway, setting aside personalities, it's the principle of the thing. Offloading him on to us, just because he was too hot to handle in –' Steve broke off, biting his lip. 'Tom Wilkes is an experienced journalist. An asset, according to our Head of Centre.' Then he burst out: 'Even if, after a fortnight of stonewall silence, the bastard's just turned up, without so much as a fax.'

I pounced. 'How'd you know he was here then?'

'Fluke,' he snapped, and was ruffled enough to continue, unprompted. 'Howard rang his flat yesterday when we were winding up the working party. They're buddies from way back – old alma mater, I shouldn't wonder. Anyway, the man's cleaning woman said he'd just that minute left for Wakeborough. There were hotels scrawled on the phone pad and Howard wouldn't rest until he'd located a booking at The Elms. This welcome in the wine bar is all down to him. Still, given the guy's recent track record . . .'

'What track record?' I demanded, rather too eagerly.

Stephen paused for a moment, visibly assessing the confidentiality-classification. 'It's his wife. Supposedly.'

'I thought –' I moderated my shriek to a semblance of casual interest. 'I thought you said he wasn't married?'

'She died. Not recently, mark you, back in January, but it's only now he's cracked. Howard claims it's delayed reaction, but as I said to him, this is a tough kitchen and if you can't take the heat . . .' Just *occasionally* I could forgive George her obstinate conviction that a wolfish soul lurked under the Lamb's cuddly exterior. 'I'd better go and round him up,' he said, shrugging on his jacket. 'See you there?'

'Yes,' I said. 'I mean, no. Oh, I don't know. Maybe.'

'We could come back here later. Pick up where we left off?' And with an undoubtedly wolfish grin he was gone.

Pick up where we left off. The words were still echoing in my head now as I wrenched a comb through my hair. No chance, I sternly told my reflection. But I wasn't talking about Stephen – I was going to marry Stephen – I was toying with the dangerous idea of picking up very much older threads. To my horror, I saw that my face in the glass was bright with – yes, with excitement. Not just nervous apprehension. For Pete's sake, I looked like a kid about to embark on her first date. This was madness. Thomas Wilkes was a bastard, right? What's more, if by some crazy chance it *were* him, waiting even now in the Tipsy Fox, then I should be scared out of my wits. He could wreck everything I'd worked so hard to achieve. What about Stephen? What about *Polly*?

That sobered me. For a second or two I even considered flunking out. I refused to admit I might actually be less afraid of meeting Thomas than I was of discovering it wasn't him at all. Besides, I had to find out some time, if not today in the Fox, then tomorrow in work. Given the choice, I preferred the anonymous bustle of a wine bar to the twitching ears of the office. And I wasn't a coward, was I? *Whoever* was waiting in that bar, I'd hack it. One way or another.

I put away my comb like a hood pocketing his automatic.

The first face I saw, towering beakily over the smoky, golf-pullovered lunchtime crowd, was George's. No surprise, really, although I never for one moment supposed Stephen had invited her on to the welcoming committee. For all he acknowledged her dynamic creative input at Radio Ridings, Stephen inevitably saw my friend George as being something of a pony and trap on the Porsche-roaring information highway. She was, he feared, in the immortal words of our leaders, 'tainted by experience'. George, however ('Tainted? Dyed to the bloody core more like, and proud of it'), is a regular at the Tipsy Fox. Of a Friday evening, she's often to be found at the piano, entertaining the customers with a little civilized cocktail music. Just now, though, she was standing at the bar, ordering a large round. 'Chic,' she said, eyeing my outfit. 'If a touch *managerial*. What will you have?'

Large brandy, I was thinking. Now I was here, my heart was thudding like an overheated piston. I looked round wildly, trying to find the clump of familiar faces among the crowd. 'Better not, I'm supposed to be joining, um, Steve.'

'Don't worry. I've gatecrashed the works coven. We're through by the window. Concentrate, Rose. Drink?'

'Um, white. Chardonnay. Is he here?'

'Stainless? 'Fraid so. Will you be a character witness for me if I slip strychnine into his low-alcohol lager?'

'The new guy,' I burst out.

'Ah, you mean Tom Wilkes.' She looked at me rather oddly. 'Well, yes, I suppose you could say he is. In body, if not entirely in spirit. Poor sod.'

'What do you mean?'

'Take this tray would you, old love?'

I followed George round the bar to the bay window where the office pack was clustered round a trio of tables. I smiled, acknowledged the grunts of greeting, took off my jacket, accepted the stool someone unearthed for me and edged in. Then stared round. All the old familiar faces with – one stranger. And he was a stranger, surely? Sitting beside Stephen. Actually, *slumped* beside him, in the curve of the window seat. Staring at the unlit cigarette between his fingers. Long fingers, long legs, yes, but greyish hair . . .

George was passing a hefty amber tumbler over to him. God Almighty, was that whisky? 'Drinkie, old love?' she said with unusual gentleness.

'What? Oh, cheers,' he muttered.

I knew. In the very instant he spoke, in just three words, I recognized that voice. And a dam inside me cracked wide open; a floodtide of memory thundered out. I shut my eyes. I couldn't speak, I couldn't breathe. I felt I was drowning in the past, in another world. Terror made me open my eyes again and I found I was clutching the table like a lifebelt. What's more, everyone round me seemed to be talking artifically loudly, as though they were embarrassed. Stupidly, I thought it was because of me, that they'd seen the state I was in and were covering up. Only slowly did I realize no one was taking any notice of me at all.

I made myself look across the table. Another shock, because it was like looking at his father, old Sir Philip. He was so thin-faced, so ashen. Except I doubt his dad would ever have appeared in public with two days of stubble on his chin. He didn't even glance in my direction. He was lighting the fag, or trying to. He didn't seem able to unite flame and cigarette. He's drunk, I thought, dazedly. That's why they're twittering like demented budgies. Because he's paralytically pissed. And Stephen, beside him, looked as helpless and wood-faced as a puppet. The hubbub dwindled eventually into awkward silence. And everyone stared at one another. For God's sake, Steve, I thought, *do* something.

It was George who saved the day. Temporarily. 'Welcome, Tom,' she said, raising her glass. And everyone followed suit, one way or another. 'Now, have you finally met everyone? Harry, yet another reporter. Oh, and this is Rose Shawe, star of the mid-morning show.'

A gaunt face turned towards me. It was like the face of a corpse, a familiar lantern when the light has gone out. There seemed to be nothing inside. 'Hi, Rose,' he said with a caricature of a smile. For a minute, I was tempted to say nothing, to postpone the inevitable. But I was sitting facing the window with the full light on my face. And he did perform a sort of double-take. Uncertain. His brow creased, and his bleary eyes blinked at me a couple of times.

I managed a smile. 'We've met actually,' I said briskly. 'Although it was an *awfully* long time ago. How are you keeping, Thomas?'

I shouldn't have spoken. Because he hadn't recognized me, not really. He was too drunk to recognize his own mother. But his jaw dropped now. Slackly, as though the muscles had capsized. 'Rita . . .' he croaked. '*Rita?* Oh fucking hell.' And he crashed face-forward on to the table.

2 Radio Ridings News

At breakfast, lunchtime and drivetime every weekday, keeping you up to date with the latest news, locally, nationally and internationally.

Is this thing recording . . . ?

(A CLICK ON THE TAPE)

The wheels are turning again and — and a light flicks when I talk. Shit, I can't even see straight, let alone operate gadgets. Shouldn't mix pills and booze.

Uh, look, if it doesn't work, I'm sorry. Although I guess if it's not recording, you'll never hear this anyway. What the hell. I'm beyond pen and paper.

(PAUSE, WITH SOUND OF SWALLOWING)

The thing is, Rita — sorry, Rose. ROSE-ROSE-ROSE. Thing is, I'm only doing this because you might start thinking it's got something to do with you. Here I am, turning up out of the blue, and then . . .

Well, it hasn't, OK? If I'd had any clue you worked for this lousy outfit, I wouldn't have gone along with the half-baked scheme to ship me up here. But you know Howard, once he's got a do-gooding bee in his bonnet. Or do you know Howard? Your Head of Centre? My old friend, rot him. No, forget I said that. He was only trying to help.

But truly, if I'd known you were in Wakeborough, I swear I wouldn't have come within a hundred miles of the place . . .

16

'Thanks, Nigel. Well, hello again. BBC Radio Ridings, this is Rose Shawe with you until lunchtime, and a very good Monday morning to you . . .'

My voice, in my headphones, sounded remarkably bright, considering that at two a.m. I'd been brewing tea, wondering whether I could drive down to Mac's to steal a couple of his sleeping pills. I'd resisted – my tranquillizer days are behind me – but my brain felt as sludgy as if I'd swallowed a fistful. '. . . packed programme coming up today. I know we're all looking forward to some more memories of the war years in Wakeborough . . .'

Wakeborough at War, now into its second series, was one of George's epics. Craftily edited old codgers recalling the events of half a century ago were evocatively packaged with the twin wailings of sirens and Dame Vera Lynn, the thuddings of ack-ack guns and army boots, and the hissings of steam trains and tea-urns. Stephen might mutter that he wasn't convinced this sort of sepia-tinted nostalgia sat happily in what was, first and foremost, a news and current affairs station (blah-blah), but even he couldn't argue that it didn't sit very happily in the ears, and hearts, of our listeners. The fan mail thuds in by the sackful, and I'm talking literally now, not in figurative 'floods' of a dozen. George knows how to pull the punters.

And it was George, wise, great-hearted George, who had stepped into the ghastly breach in the Tipsy Fox yesterday. Thomas had been splayed nose-down in a dripping wreckage of glasses and ashtrays, and the rest of us were entranced like gawpers round a motorway pile-up. I was the glassiest-eyed of the lot, expecting the whole bar to point at me: *Rita?* Idiot. George, though, surged forward and, yanking Stephen out of the way, planted herself beside Thomas.

'Completely whacked, poor boy,' she said, wrapping an arm round his limp shoulders. 'He told me he didn't get a wink of sleep last night, what with a wedding reception discoing till dawn and the plumbing in his room.' Her steely glare challenged anyone to state the obvious. That the guy was paralytically drunk. She bent over him. 'Don't worry, old darling. Black coffee and a nice quiet snooze in my house, and you'll be a new man.' He grunted without stirring and she clucked at us. 'So what are you lot dangling round for like unplugged appliances?'

The others began retrieving coats, shuffling off to the bar. But not me. I was staring stupidly down at Thomas's bowed head and thinking that, of all the hundreds of reunions I'd dreamed up over the years, none had resembled this. I'd always imagined a Thomas looking much the same. Matured, yes, but not aged. And as often as not in these daydreams he would produce a frayed garter, now faded to a tasteful pink, and stutter some pretty speech of penitence. The wording varied, but the conclusion didn't. He would always end up asking if, after all that had passed, I could possibly still consider marrying a shit like him? Whereupon I, with the sad sweetness of a Madonna, would reply that those first few years had been tough and –

'Rose?' Stephen had said, breaking into my reverie. 'That, um, *report* you wanted?'

'Report?'

'Occurs to me I've a copy at the flat, if it's on your route home.' Only then did I recognize the clumsily disguised invitation.

'You're in my way, Rose,' said George exasperatedly. 'I need to shift this table. Don't worry, old love.' This was addressed to Thomas, who was stirring. 'My house is only a step round the corner. Well, Rose? Are you coming with us?'

I looked from her to Stephen and panicked. 'Sorry. Got to get to – Tesco's. Catfood.'

Smart excuse, if it hadn't been well known that my lovely ginger Persian was twelve months dead. I slithered out of the door before anyone could challenge me. Even before I reached the bypass, though, I was berating myself for cowardice. I should have gone. Oh, not to face Stephen's inevitable questions, although the spider in me was busily spinning explanations for Thomas yelping, 'Rita,' in that unfortunate way. He was drunk, it was a long time ago, hardly surprising he'd got the name wrong ... But there were a lot of other things about me, *Rose Shawe*, that Thomas was liable to misremember. I should have accompanied him back to George's and force-fed him a few facts along with the black coffee. On reaching home, I didn't even take off my coat before stabbing her number into the phone. 'It's me. How is he?'

'Rose? Well, thanks for all your help, poppet.'

'I'm sorry. But how is he?'

'Sleeping like a baby on my sofa. No, let's be honest. He's snoring like an adenoidal rhinoceros. I'm tempted to whip out a microphone and immortalize him for my effects library in glorious stereo. Truly the temple shaketh.'

'Has he – did he – mention me, at all?'

There was silence. George's silences are always significant, in life and on air. One of her dicta regarding the God-given music of language is that the most telling bits of speech are the silences. Windows into the soul, she says. The openings through which one hears the pulse of thought. She particularly abhors interviewers who feel compelled to leap in at the least hesitation and naturally I agree, but ... '*George?*'

At last she sighed. 'He could hardly utter two coherent syllables, poor soul, but I thought I caught the name "Rita" as I led him out of the bar. He breathed it,' she added pensively, 'rather as I'd imagine Macbeth in the later acts might "Banquo". Not *quite* sure he believed what he'd seen.'

'Oh God.'

'You didn't tell me you knew this man, Rose. In fact, you specifically –'

'I didn't know it was him, did I? Not for certain. Anyway,' I went on, anxiety making me belligerent, 'you don't know him from a bar of soap. How come you were so quick to take him under your wing?'

'Darling, there I was on my usual perch, enjoying a quiet Bloody Mary and a juicy scandal in the *Sunday Mirror*, when I saw this woebegone specimen being wheeled in on the prongs of the Great Dalek. Of course I toddled over. Any prisoner of Stephen Sharpe is a friend of mine, even if he is a television journalist.' George inflected these words with a colour appropriate to *recidivist paedophile*.

'Tight as a tick, too, but I'd never hold that against anyone. Strange that he seemed so amazed to see you, though.'

'Why shouldn't he?'

'Well, darling, given your melodramatic eruption into the proceedings, I naturally remembered the postcard.'

'Postcard?'

'From the enigmatic Mr Adorable?'

'Oh, *that*. No, not from him, can't be. You saw, he barely even recognized me.' My brain was cranking up again. Whatever Thomas might blurt out, he was in safe hands with George. Lord, I'd been within a hair's breadth of confiding the whole sorry saga to her myself long ago. Probably would have done, if I hadn't thought it would retell less as a Blackpool *Romeo and Juliet* and more as an end-of-the-pier farce. 'Look, George, when he surfaces, ask him to keep his mouth shut about, um, Rita, will you?'

'*Rita?* Oh for God's sake, spare me the silly games. Call yourself what you like, but stop trying to pretend you weren't once Rita Bagshawe. As I've told you times without number, who gives a twopenny fuck that you used to flash your tits in a nightclub?'

'*George!*' Even though I was alone in the house I glanced round guiltily. 'It's not just me. You don't know the full story.'

'Evidently,' she retorted, adding, with breathtaking disregard for the truth: 'And far be it from me to probe, but –'

'Quite,' I cut in. 'So I'd be grateful if you'd ask him to keep stumm, until I've had a word. He'll be coming into work, won't he?'

'If he's conscious by then,' said George.

He certainly hadn't appeared in Radio Ridings by the time I went on air. As I settled myself in studio, I'd despatched Amanda up to the news prospects meeting with instructions to report back soonest.

This meeting is convened at ten daily and its purpose, naturally enough, is to define the news agenda for the day. Or to invent one when, as is too often the case in a civilized town like Wakeborough, not a fat lot has happened. A big-city station like Leeds can take its pick from yesterday's juicy crop of murders, muggings, industrial closures and general mayhem; we've been known to lead on a new design of litter bin. Given this sparsity of raw material, everyone is expected to toss in ideas, whether they work on the, ahem, cutting edge of news proper – which comprises the breakfast, lunch and teatime sequences – or in the softer and (as I like to think) more agreeable byways of general programmes like mine. These meetings had got longer in recent months as Stephen, poor Lamb, strove to reorganize our news operations in line with the latest policy directives. Don't ask me what directives. Every so often, when the powers-that-be up the misty Corporate mountain have a bit of time on their mighty hands, they chuck down another set of tablets, redefining the entire purpose and philosophy of local radio. About which, take it from me, they know *zilch*.

Normally, stranded as I am on the airwaves between ten and one, I'm only too happy to miss the daily free-for-all. By a quarter to eleven that morning, though, with *Wakeborough at War* nostalgically sirening over the White Cliffs of Dover, I'd chewed off two nails and was contemplating a third when, at last, Amanda plummeted into the studio. I didn't even have to ask. 'He's here,' she panted. 'Sorry I'm late. We've been post-morting round the coffee machine. How long?' She nodded at the tape.

'Minute and a half. So he came to the meeting?'

'George shovelled him through the door. Didn't say much though. You could tell he'd got a king-sized hangover.'

'I'm not surprised. And?'

'And nothing, really. Well, like I said, he's only just arrived, so he couldn't add much to the meeting. But . . .'

My shoulders unknotted a bit. He obviously hadn't said anything about me. 'But what?'

'It's just . . .' She put her head on one side. 'Well, to be honest, Rose, I got the impression he couldn't give a stuff. I reckon Steve did, too, because he looked grim as a gasometer. You know,' she went on, warming to her novel metaphor, 'like you could see his patience level sinking by the minute. Any rate, when he suggested Helen stays acting-up in the job until Tom finds his feet, Tom just shrugged and said, fine. As though he was on a different planet and none of this mattered. We all clocked it, and we're laying odds he won't stick it out. He's had a look round, and that's enough. Breaks your heart really.' She caught my astounded eye and gave a self-conscious giggle. 'Well, he's dead sexy, isn't he? For an older man.'

Thomas? An *older* man? 'He's barely thirty-five,' I gasped. But then, Amanda was only a child.

'Same as you – is that all? Still, it doesn't matter so much for men, does it? He's got that sort of haggard look. Keith Richards-ish. As though he's really, you know, seen life. What's so funny? Don't you – ?' She stopped in mid-sentence, stiffening. 'Watch it, leader coming up.' By which she didn't mean the Director General, or even Stephen, but the red tape at the end of *Wakeborough at War*.

As I backlinked the item I wondered where, if Helen was still occupying the Assistant Editor's office, Tom Wilkes was to be found. Two hours later, I handed over to the lunchtime news, walked out into the corridor, and there he was. Waiting for me.

'Rita – *Rose*,' he said. 'You wanted to see me?'

OK, I freely and frankly admit it. When I saw that tall, tousled figure leaning against the wall, just for a second my innards flipped, and I wanted to fling my arms round him. I'd recovered even before he opened his mouth. Besides, a second glance showed me this wasn't Thomas, not *my* Thomas, my boisterous, golden cub. This was a mangy old lion who, by the look of him, had been shot and stuffed some time last century. And, like they always say, the taxidermist had got the eyes all wrong. I stared at him, and I could have wept.

'Sorry,' he muttered, looking away. 'Rather embarrassing, really.'

'Yes,' I said dazedly. 'Yes, I suppose so.'

'Wakeborough of all places. You haven't really been here all along, have you?'

For a minute I was bewildered. I'd forgotten my long-ago lie, my invented address. 'But for goodness' sake . . .'

He tried a smile. Clearly an effort. 'I was an idiot, wasn't I?'

Idiot wasn't the word I had in mind. 'Yes, well . . . Look, we need to talk, don't we?'

'We do?' Now he sounded wary.

'But not here.'

He peeled himself off the wall. 'Drink, then?'

I'm rarely at a loss for words. You don't get my kind of job unless you've a turbo-charged tongue. Nerves don't silence you, they just accelerate the engine. So, as I led him up to the office where I dumped my programme box and grabbed a coat, I chattered on about the rotten weather, the static in the carpet, the lino-cuts on the wall — Wakeborough's mills: magnificently Satanic, didn't he think? Local artist but hung in the Tate. Dated from the days when the BBC used to invest in art for its corridors instead of in-house publicity campaigns . . . I suppose I was trying to impress him with my erudition. Rita, after all, thought a lino-cut was where it fitted round the lav. I paused in Reception because I realized he was staring at me. 'Something wrong?'

'Oh . . . I can't quite believe it's you, that's all. You've changed so much.'

I glanced at Audrey, our receptionist, but she was deep into car stickers on the telephone. 'I certainly hope so.' The hennaed hay-stack was long tamed into a rusty bob, the scarlet talons were blunted and blanched, and the very thought of stiletto heels made me wince. This was not Rita Bagshawe shrugging into a Burberry. 'Don't you want a coat?'

He shook his head, then shuddered. The hangover, as Amanda had observed, was palpable. 'Even your voice is different.'

'My accent?' I could have told him my reconstructed vowels had once been even more drawlingly impressive, until George had taken me in hand, informing me that I wasn't going to get anywhere in local radio if I insisted on talking as though I'd got a finger stuck up my you-know-where. Nevertheless, I knew exactly how different I was — how different I'd *made* myself — and I thought he should've sounded a damn sight more complimentary. 'Well, you've changed, too.'

And how. What had Amanda said? Haggard? As though he'd *seen life*? Well, God knows what sort of life he'd seen because the word that sprang to my mind was ravaged. A ravaged angel. Handsome, but wrecked. Hard to imagine that anything could be shabbier than the boy I remembered, but this lanky figure managed it. He'd made an attempt at shaving — there was a raw scab on his chin — but the bones of his nose and jaw were painfully pronounced, with lines reamed across his forehead and round his mouth. His hair wasn't particularly grey, I now saw. It was fair still, but lustreless, like cheap jewellery left too long in a drawer. Strangely though, it was his eyes that aged him most. They were dead as pebbles.

He was barely through the door of our smoke-free citadel before he'd produced a fag packet and stuck a cigarette in his mouth. He then continued patting his pockets. Harry, a young reporter devouring his own cigarette on the pavement, hurried up with a lighter and a shy, no, dammit, almost worshipful smile. 'I think *Fulcrum*'s the best current affairs show on the box,' he offered.

Tom, bending over the lad's cupped hands, offered a sweet flicker of a smile. Which, for an instant, reminded me of my Thomas. Only for an instant. Snuffed quicker than the flame of the lighter. Because otherwise, I promise, this was beginning to seem like a complete stranger who turned back to me and asked if I minded going to the Elms for our drink – did I know it? 'I stayed there Saturday night. I need to check out and collect my gear.'

'George said something about an uncomfortable room,' I found myself answering as I led the way across the road. 'What a drag. It's supposed to be one of the best hotels in town.' This was surreal. Civil small talk when every nerve in my body was out on stalks and jangling so loud I was surprised he wasn't deafened. 'They've spent a fortune on renovation.'

'Should have put more fucking baths in.' He caught my look of astonishment and grunted something which might have been an apology. 'I crashed out at, um, George's last night.'

'So I gathered. We turn left here.'

'Actually, she's offered me a flat in her house, but –'

'She *what*?' In looking round at me, he stumbled on a kerb stone. I caught his elbow, and a whiff of stale tobacco and whisky. This man didn't even *smell* like Thomas. I let go.

'I tried to tell her I wouldn't need it, but she wouldn't listen. She's unstoppable, like a tidal wave. She'd swept me into work this morning before I knew what was happening. Or maybe I just didn't have the strength to fight.'

The stab of pain was so unexpected it halted me in mid-stride. Could he mean it? Was he so little anxious to see me that he wouldn't even have come into work without George's prompting? Reaching a junction, he halted and looked round enquiringly.

'Straight across,' I snapped, hurrying forward, telling myself angrily I was daft to expect anything else. After all, I'd spent years expunging every trace of Rita Bagshawe from my life: why should he feel differently? A boy who had ignored Rita's pathetic appeal all those years ago was unlikely to rush to embrace her now . . . 'So, um, are you going to accept George's offer?'

'It's terribly kind of her . . .' He suddenly seemed to shiver. 'I just wish she weren't so kind.'

What was that supposed to mean? 'It's quite nice, for a basement flat,' I felt obliged to say. 'She used to live down there before her parents died. I dare say you'd be comfortable.'

'As if it mattered,' said this shambling stranger, who spoke in a parody of Thomas's voice, like a computer simulation. The sound-waves were making the right patterns, but human life had been sucked out. He then fell silent, and didn't even look at me as I directed him across York Road. He didn't look at the traffic either, and only blinked when a taxi-driver leaned out of his window and swore. We reached the Elms having barely exchanged another word.

17

Before I'd even unbuttoned my mac, he'd ordered a pint of bitter and a double whisky, neat. 'And for you?'

'Tomato juice,' I said primly. 'It's not like, um, the old days of the BBC, is it? No one drinks at lunchtime now.'

'Too right,' he murmured. And knocked back the Scotch in a gulp. I supposed he needed a bracer. I could have done with a stiffy myself, but picked up my tomato juice and followed him. Fortunately the place was near-empty, with more potted palms than customers. A discreet chirp of Vivaldi camouflaged the glaring silence between us as we settled at a corner table. We were avoiding one another's eyes. I was toying with a beer mat. He lit a cigarette. In the end I couldn't stand it any longer. 'Look, Thomas –'

'Thomas?' He almost smiled. 'Years since anyone called me that.'

'Tom, then.'

'Call me what you like. Shawe's your married name, is it?'

'I'm not married.' No thanks to you, I could've added, but didn't. 'I changed it. Well, Bagshawe's pretty ghastly, isn't it?'

'Rose, too.' It was as though he were tasting the name, and found it didn't smell so sweet after all.

'I've always liked Rose,' I said defiantly. 'And anything's got to be better than Rita. Barmaids and bosomy aunts.'

'But I thought Rita suited you.'

'It doesn't now,' I said. I'd drafted my script in the long cold hours before dawn, and this wasn't going to plan. I drew a slow, calming breath. 'I was, um, thinking last night. It's been a long time. Sixteen years, almost to the day, since you put me on that train in Blackpool.' There. I couldn't give him a less contentious opening than that.

'Lord, is it so long?' He murmured this without so much as a flicker of – well, of anything. He might have been talking about some half-remembered dinner party. 'Of course, yes, I was just starting my third year at Oxford, wasn't I? Seems like another world.'

He sounded so utterly, so *unnaturally* detached, I was thrown off balance for a moment. I found myself saying: 'Look, you did go back to Magd –' I broke off. That damned name could trip me up still. Pronounced maudlin. 'You went back to Magdalen, didn't you? After you left me in Blackpool?' What was the point of asking this? I *knew* he'd gone back. He'd taken signed delivery of a Registered bloody Letter at Magdalen College, Oxford.

He blinked. 'Sure. Although I might as well not have bothered, because my last two years were a write-off academically. I came out with a lousy third.' A sour cough of laughter. 'I can't say you helped.'

'What's that supposed to mean?' He didn't answer. He was stubbing out his cigarette, and straightaway lighting another. I couldn't stand it. 'Well?'

'Well, what? I don't want to talk about all that.'

Suddenly, there were hot tears in the back of my throat. 'I think we should talk about it, actually.'

'Why?'

Why? Because you owe it to me, that's why. Because I want an apology. Because all my drafted scripts start with you, at least, saying you're sorry. To my shame, I heard myself stammer: 'I thought that . . . well, that you were quite fond of me. At the time.'

His head jerked up. '*Fond* of you?' He made a noise of contempt. 'Do me a favour.'

I wanted to run. I couldn't bear it. I *had* to bear it. 'Look, it's all a long time ago,' I said rapidly, 'and there's no point chucking blame around, not now, but –'

'What the hell are you doing here anyway?' I couldn't believe it when I saw you yesterday. The guilt's bad enough, without you stirring it up.'

'Is – is that your idea of an apology?'

'Why should I apologize to you? At least you knew exactly what you were playing at. I was just a stupid kid, testosterone on the rampage, fuck first, think later.'

'Thomas, please –'

'Look, I know I was a little shit, and I have to live with it.

Talking won't make a blind bit of difference. I'm up to my ears in people who seem to think I should be talking, and I don't want to, OK? So drop it or sod off and leave me in peace, will you?'

The Vivaldi had turned into Andrew Lloyd Webber. Tom Wilkes – not *Thomas*, this wasn't Thomas – barely seemed to notice as I stumbled to my feet, and crashed through the door labelled Cloakrooms. The place was deserted. I crumpled against the wall and howled. Silly cow.

'Sorry, I thought you'd gone,' he said, indicating his own refilled glass and my near-empty one. The dregs of tomato juice looked unpleasantly like blood. He paused, cigarette halfway to his mouth. 'Are you all right?'

'Trouble with – with a contact lens. No thanks, nothing more, I must get back. There were just a couple of, um, minor points I wanted to settle with you.'

'Oh? Look, I'm sorry about that outburst. Uncalled-for. Can we forget it?'

Forget it? That's what Rita would have screamed. *Wham, bam, forget it, ma'am? You bastard.* But I was not Rita. That's what I'd reminded myself as I'd dredged powder over my blazing nose. I was Rose Shawe, a civilized, middle-class pillar of Wakeborough life. A woman with a fine present, a dodgy past, and a lot to lose. And this was a public bar. 'Sure,' I snapped. 'You don't want to rake over old history; well, nor do I. You see, once I'd got to university, I decided –'

He was taking a mouthful of beer and nearly choked. 'You've been to *university*?'

'You needn't make it sound like the planet Jupiter.'

'Well, I'm sorry, but . . . which one? I mean, where?'

'York,' I said impatiently. I didn't want to be side-tracked.

'Good place, I hear.' He pulled a comical face which almost reminded me of Thomas. '*Educating Rita*?'

I was bored with that gag and told him so. 'I did a couple of A levels at night school,' I said, but couldn't resist adding: 'I got good grades. It was the tutor there who persuaded me to apply for a university place. I went as a mature student, Honours course, grant, the whole works.'

'Well done,' he said. Rather as though I'd performed a conjuring trick with the beer mat. And to think I'd once been foolish enough to imagine my going to university would narrow the gap between us. Make feasible between Rose and Tom what had been absurd between Rita and Thomas. 'What did you read?' he added.

In spite of myself, I remembered a similar exchange all those years ago. *What are you studying? Greats. Pardon?* I bit my lip. 'English.'

'Good?'

It wasn't even as though he sounded interested. Only polite. Besides, how are you supposed to answer a question like that? It's a standard dinner-party gambit over the starters. Did you enjoy university? The nearest I've ever come to summing it up is likening it to the summer when, as a child, I'd been given a pair of roller skates, which were too old, two sizes too big, and near-lethal. And for days – weeks – I'd strapped them on and launched myself across the pavement. And fallen flat on my face. Or on my bum. And on most flesh in between. I'd been a patchwork of grazes and plasters and, to this day, have the shadow of blue grit embedded in one knee to remind me. And then finally, one sunny evening, I'd got the hang of it. And it was like flying. Suddenly I could do it, and whizzed off exhilarated as a bird, the whole wide world under my skidding feet. Well, university was the same.

'It was OK.'

'Been long with the Beeb?' Another standard question. And it could have been anyone asking it. The longer we talked, the less I could believe that this dead-bored, dead-eyed man was Thomas. Actually, it made my task easier, because, as I'd reminded myself, I was going to have to work with this jerk. A local radio station is a very small place.

'Eight years,' I said chattily. 'I came in straight after graduating, thanks to George. She'd once interviewed me for a feature, centuries ago, and I wrote to her, saying how keen I was to work in radio. She'd moved from London to Wakeborough by then, and told me there was a job going in Radio Ridings. I admit I was a bit wary . . .' I paused, because I was manoeuvring on to my new script. The old one had been binned in the powder room along with half a mile of tear-soggy tissue. 'Wary of coming to Wakeborough, I mean, because I knew it was Frankie Henderson's home town.'

'Who? Oh, the creep who used to front that cruddy *Family Quiz* on Thames? Why on earth – ?'

'He owned that flat in Blackpool.'

That at least captured his full attention. 'It was *him* you used to shack up with? Frankie Henderson was the ageing Lothario with the sleazy décor?'

'Hush,' I said furiously, glancing round. Unnecessary. There were only two other drinkers in the bar: rotund-bellied businessmen spreading their brochures over a distant table. 'But that's what I wanted to say to you, Tom. Frank Henderson, all that.'

'Did you go back to him? Forgive the vulgar curiosity.'

''Course not,' I squawked, caught unawares. 'I've never seen him since and never want to. If I hadn't been assured he'd quit the town for good, I probably wouldn't have applied for the job, no matter how crazy I was to work in radio.'

'Were you really?' He looked amazed. 'The old steam wireless? Wouldn't you have preferred television?'

Coming from anyone, this kind of remark is like a match to a short fuse. Coming from *him* ... 'I realize it mystifies people like you, stuck up in the ivory transmitters of telly-land,' I said hotly, 'but there are still those of us who don't just prefer radio, but who are deeply and passionately and profoundly commmitted to the so-called steam wireless – glorious past, embattled present and digital bloody future. And what's more –' I checked myself. I hadn't forced myself back to this table to argue the case for radio. 'Sorry. I'll get off my soapbox.'

'Feel free,' he said. 'At least it sounded more like you.'

'What?'

'Forget it.' He stifled a yawn. 'So what's the next move? London?'

'What on earth for?'

'You can't mean to stay in local radio?'

Try as I might, my temper was frothing dangerously. 'And why not?'

'A tinpot set-up like Radio Ridings?'

'Have you heard any of our output?'

'George had the breakfast show on. Hell, I've found livelier news in a parish magazine.'

Never mind that I generally found our breakfast show about as riveting as the noise from the washing machine. 'It may sound parochial to – to an outsider like you, but people care about what happens locally.'

'Locally? But –'

'And you better learn that pretty damn quick, if you're going to run our news programmes.'

His face twisted into an ugly sneer. 'I'd rather be dead.'

I could have hit him. 'Oh really? Then what the *fuck* d'you think you're doing here?'

We glared at one another. His gaze fell first. He shifted in his chair. Suddenly he looked unutterably weary. 'Look, Rita –'

'Rose. Sorry, I shouldn't have sworn at you.'

'Don't be ridiculous. Truth is, I screwed up with a programme in London. Or hadn't you heard?'

'And that Radio Ridings is your punishment? Yes, we'd heard.' Was that what had soured him so horribly? But one little career setback couldn't have changed my bright, shiny, laughing Thomas into – into *this*. 'Given what you obviously think about local radio, I'm only surprised that you didn't take redundancy.'

'Couldn't face the paperwork.' If this was his idea of a joke, I wasn't amused. 'They were screaming for my head on a platter, sure, but I didn't care. I just wanted out – from London, the flat. So when Howard muscled down, saying he'd got this newsroom falling apart . . .'

'Howard Hemingway said *that*?'

'Oh, it was a bluff. At least, I thought so, but if that morning show's anything to go by . . .' He bit his lip. 'Anyway, he managed to keep the wolves off my back by claiming he needed me to come up and sort things out.'

'You reckon?' None of this was what I was supposed to be saying, but I was beyond caring. 'And no matter what poor Stephen might think about it?'

'Stephen? That the prat in the baggy suit who's supposed to running the place?'

'How *dare* you?' I hissed. 'Frankly, I'd have thought better of Howard. Although, God knows, he's not the only one in this organization who thinks that anyone who's so much as – as swept the floor of a television editing suite is capable of running a radio station. Do you know anything about radio? Do you even care?'

He shrugged. 'I guess I'd argue that news is news is news, what-ever the medium. Anyway, what's it matter?'

'It matters to me. It matters, let me tell you, to Howard Hemingway.'

'Oh, come on . . .'

'Did he tell you *his* bosses are trying to shut us down? Claiming Wakeborough doesn't need its own station, now Harrogate's on air? Did he tell you how hard he's been fighting to keep us in existence? Because he has, believe me. And if you've decided we're crap, on the basis of five whole minutes, then it beats me why he wanted you up here. You don't know anything, don't give a toss . . .'

I couldn't go on. The tears were back. Only this time they were tears of rage. I'd forgotten all about Thomas. This was a cynical, sneering jerk from television who thought he knew everything, and at that moment I hated him with a passion.

'You're upset,' he said in apparent bewilderment.

''Course I'm bloody upset,' I said thickly, groping for a tissue and blowing my nose. 'We care about this place. We don't want it shutting. And we can do without the likes of you sticking your oar in.'

'Howard said I was his last throw.'

'God help us then.'

'He really stuck his neck out to get me up here. He's been a good friend.'

'Obviously.'

'Don't,' he said suddenly. 'Oh Jesus, what kind of mess have I walked into now?' He shut his eyes.

And only then did I hear the change in his voice. 'Tom?'

He stood up. 'I need a drink. Don't pull faces. I tell you, I *need* a drink.' Only as an afterthought did he turn back and say: 'So do you, by the look of you. Scotch?'

By the time he returned, with two whiskies, I was quite calm. Eye-of-the-hurricane calm. 'I must go,' I said. 'But I still need to ask you this favour.'

He looked surprised. In so far as that blank face could look anything.

'Like it or not, we'll be working together.' I ignored his grimace. 'What happened between us was a long time ago, so – so we don't need to make it public round work, right?'

'You think I make a habit of discussing my juvenile sex romps over the morning coffee?'

I gritted my teeth. 'No, sure, but it's not just that. You see, I've kept it pretty quiet, my younger life. That I used to be a singer. That I, um, knew Frankie Henderson. All that kind of thing.'

'Your colleagues don't know you used to proffer your gartered thigh to impressionable boys?' He smiled faintly. 'More interesting than most people's early careers.'

'I'm sure they'd find it hilarious,' I hissed, 'but I also have to think of my family, the village where I live – oh, *everyone*. I sit on committees, I'm a governor of a Church of England school . . .'

'You're kidding.'

'And as far as they're all concerned, I'm . . . to be honest, I've knocked a few years off my age. I had to,' I went on rapidly. 'I couldn't bear being so much older than everyone else at university. And when I got to Wakeborough – oh, the staff in local radio seems to arrive fresh out of kindergarten. So, if you'd just bear in mind, for what it's worth, I'm supposed to be thirty-five.'

Tom put down his drink. 'Let me get this straight,' he said slowly. 'You're now my age. You're Rose not Rita, and the Bag's gone from Shawe. You wouldn't touch sleazy comedians with a barge-pole and you've never so much as seen the inside of a smoky nightclub, is that right? And I don't know you from Adam.' His mouth twisted into a mocking smile. 'Or maybe that should be Eve.'

'No, no.' I protested irritatedly. 'I've said we knew each other, once.'

The smile had gone. 'Did we?' he said, and drained his glass. 'Personally, I'm beginning to doubt it.'

Oh Rita, I wish hadn't seen you. You've got to understand, as far as I was concerned, Wakeborough was off the map of the known world. But here you were, sitting in that hotel bar, haranguing me about your poxy radio station. I'd thought my conscience was long since battered to death, but you managed to find the only bit still living — and put the boot in. Sure, you were only defending your patch. But you made it horribly clear this was Howard's patch as well.

(ANOTHER PAUSE. CLINK OF GLASS BEING REFILLED)

Did I actually regale you with my crime? The one that earned me banishment? Just for the record, you've got this bastard robbing his shareholders with an efficiency that makes Robert Maxwell look like Inspector Clouseau. The shit will hit the fan any day. Unfortunately we went on air without the evidence to make our preview of his charge sheet stick. Or that's what his lawyers said, and Management's so pusillanimous they were grovelling before the credits stopped rolling.

(SOUND OF SWALLOWING)

No, that's not fair. The show shouldn't have been broadcast. If I'd seen it beforehand, I admit I wouldn't have let it go out. But then, I didn't watch the cutting of that particular edition. Why? Because I was cross-eyed drunk on the floor of my office weeping over a book of poetry. Yes, 'fraid so. They nearly sent for the men in white coats, let alone my P 45.

Anyway, that was when Howard stepped in. I thought he was offering a dusty shelf for me to moulder on — it was you who made it so appallingly clear he wanted something in return. And that if I didn't deliver, I could be leaving him up the creek without the proverbial. D'you know, I even began to think maybe I owed you something as well, can you believe it? For my — what is it the French call it? My educash . . . Too pissed for foreign languages. My educa-tion sentimentale. And, my God, what a sentimental little whelp I was in those days . . .

18

It's as well I'm not superstitious. My Tuesday-morning show featured the usual ten minutes of tosh from our pet astrologer, who's bald, baby-faced and camp as a crocodile handbag. He murmured darkly about conjunctions between this planet and that, 'which all means, my love, that Cancerians like you should be prepared for a turbulent time. We all know how crabs like to look back, but you've got to fight that urge, dear, *fight*. You mustn't get tangled up in the past.'

'Too right,' I said gaily. Too damn right, I thought grimly. Twenty-four hours on, I was still as angry with Tom Wilkes as I had been when I'd left him amid the potted palms. I hadn't been this angry since the great and terrible row with Mac, and that had blown up only days after Polly's birth. In the intervening years, I thought I'd tamed Rita's blazing temper along with her blazing hair, but this wasn't even like one of her fire-cracker spats. This anger was flat and cold and obsessive. Since yesterday lunchtime, I'd been unable to eat, or sleep, or concentrate. I'd be functioning fine when suddenly my brain would be wiped clean, like a computer when the plug's pulled. All I could think about was what I *should* have said to Tom Wilkes.

I'd armoured myself in studio with twice my usual array of crib cards. I remembered a London disc jockey jocularly confiding that he didn't just write out his guests' names in the order they were sitting in front of him, he added his own as well, in case he forgot that too. I began to think he might not have been joking. By the time I strode into the office at the end of the show, instead of feeling the usual mild deflation, I was nauseous with relief at having got through without disaster. Amanda had been out all morning, recording a piece at a giant vegetable show, so I'd had no spy at the daily meeting. I glanced round the humming desks. No sign of Tom. 'How's our new Assistant Editor getting on?' I enquired.

'Haven't you heard?' muttered someone. 'Pissed off home.'

'Home?' I squawked, thinking they meant London. That he'd already shaken the despised dust of local radio from his feet and scuttled back to telly-land.

'Is he still at The Elms?' asked someone else. 'Must be costing a packet.' As they established amongst themselves that Tom Wilkes was, in fact, renting George's flat, I gathered, incredulously, that he'd retired back there for the rest of the week, armed with a radio, intending, apparently, to acquaint himself with our output.

'Unheard-of behaviour,' said one of the news producers, cackling. 'Management actually *listening* to the station.'

'And guess what?' said another wag, amid groans and a shower of paper darts: 'Yes, we hear rumours he's writing a *report*.'

'So it would appear,' confirmed George, when I promptly rang her on some pretext about a new series. 'What do you expect in a management culture dedicated to pulping the world's forests?'

'Why'd you have to take him in?'

'Because I'm an old woman rattling round in a huge house and I'm lonely.'

'Balls,' I snapped, before I could check myself. I really was losing my grip, swearing at poor George.

'Not that he's likely to provide much company,' she said. 'He's shut away downstairs with his wireless. I've warned him prolonged exposure to local radio news-babble can seriously damage the brain, but he appears to regard it as a sacred duty.'

'Excuse to drink himself comatose, more like,' said Stephen, when I bumped into him in the car park that evening, although he immediately felt obliged to retract this indiscretion, and put on record his keen anticipation of Tom's views, blah-blah.

'If the report ever materializes,' I snarled. I saw no reason to tell Stephen that this sneering, drink-sodden incomer had already pronounced our news service rubbish. Still less was I going to pass on his ridiculous claim that Head of Centre shared his views. After all, as Tom himself had admitted, slagging off Radio Ridings had been no more than a ploy to secure a job for an old chum in trouble. 'Head of Centre must be off his trolley,' I muttered.

I dare say Steve would have felt obliged to take issue with this (however much he agreed), but he didn't hear. After glancing round furtively, he was whispering something about Friday evening, a Thai takeaway at the flat, any chance?

'Friday? Afraid that's –' I broke off. Not only had I been about to invent an excuse, I'd actually felt myself recoiling from the idea of an evening alone with Stephen. This was my lover, the man I wanted to marry. It was all Tom Wilkes's fault. Well, he wasn't going to interfere with one more semi-quaver in my well-orchestrated life. 'Come round to my place instead,' I said. 'I'll cook dinner. And – and you can stay over.'

'Run that past me again?' Stephen might well look surprised.

'Polly can lump it.' It was anger talking. 'Or she can stay at her grandfather's.'

'Well – great. And before I forget –' Suddenly his face glassed over. 'Oh, hi, Helen.'

'Evening, you guys,' she said, with a knowing grin which, in my edgy state, irritated me immeasurably. She was almost past us when, suddenly, she looped back. 'By the way, Rose. Tom Wilkes. Where'd you know him from?'

Everyone was asking that, and I was firing back the same glib retort all round. Tom and I had once met socially, years back – long before either of us joined the Beeb. This was guaranteed to choke off interest. In our narcissistic industry, a pre-Corporate existence is less newsworthy than life within the womb.

What the gossip-hounds of Radio Ridings *were* interested in though – and my God were they interested – was the BBC career of Tom Wilkes. The story of his fiasco in *Fulcrum* was soon common currency, although there was dispute over the juicier de-tails. One school of thought had him acting as a buccaneer and deliberately running the programme, even though he knew he couldn't make the story stack up. The other, quoting a colleague in Radio York who had a mole in Television Centre, claimed he'd been found dead drunk on the office floor and hadn't even seen the show before the libel writs started flying. Neither revealed him in a creditable light. I couldn't have believed it of the idealistic boy I remembered. I could believe anything of this Tom Wilkes.

Opinion was also divided as to whether his arrival here was to be welcomed or not. You'd think, given the above, and the fact that he came to us from both television and the much loathed London, there would be no argument. Not so. There were plenty mouthing pious, shock-horror sentiments, but I was incensed to discern a certain solidarity rumbling round the news desks. The poor bugger's wife had died, hadn't she? And they pooh-poohed objections that the bereaved widower had been functioning normally for the best part of a year since. Grief took people funny ways, didn't it? This man, after all, was one of their own kind. No matter that he'd departed London under not so much a cloud as a nuclear mushroom, he was a paid-up, time-served, card-carrying hack.

When asked for my view, I generally managed to be non-committal, and was only once driven to asking whether anyone in this bloody office could talk about anything other than Tom bloody Wilkes.

They couldn't. Oh, and there was also a third camp, led by my chum Amanda. Several of the younger female staff, with a bold-eyed lustiness which would have landed a bloke in front of an industrial relations tribunal, were as one woman in pronouncing Tom Wilkes to be the most drop-dead gorgeous hunk ever to walk through the door. Didn't I think so? 'You must be joking,' I snapped. Remembering the shining boy, I resented this ravaged shadow, however handsome.

So, even though he never showed his face all week, Tom Wilkes loomed with Godot-like significance over the station. As much as anything this was because we knew he was down the road, listening to us. Supposedly listening, anyway. I personally doubted he was doing any such thing, but I compiled my programmes with a furious stuff-that-up-your-ears determination to prove the indispensability of local radio. Never had my shows been so charged with public-serving content. I wheeled out the whole community alphabet, from Alzheimer counselling to Zebra crossings.

'Bit short on jokes, my deario,' observed George as, resplendent in purple trouser suit, she planted one buttock on the corner of my desk on Friday afternoon. 'Touch of the old knit-yourself-a-hip-replacement and here's some music while you find the needles.'

'Tom say that?' I couldn't stop myself demanding.

She looked at me rather sadly. 'Tom says very little. Except, this morning, to ask whether I had a *word processor*, foolish child. I told him my trusty Remington was at his disposal, but for more complex technology, he'd have to come in here.'

'He's actually intending to honour us with his opinions then? You do surprise me.'

'What's wrong, Rose?'

'Wrong? Why should anything be wrong? I'm just amazed you're laying out the welcome mat for a clapped-out television hack.'

'I like him,' she said squarely. 'I admit I've seen little enough of him, but there's a sudden sweetness in his smile which quite melts the heart.' I knew all about that, but I was amazed she could see it these days. 'And I'm concerned about him.'

'Why? Drinking himself stupid?'

George clucked. 'Just because this organization has fallen into the hands of the New Temperance Army is no excuse for priggishness. Besides, it's not the drink.' She sighed. 'I have an instinct.' She settled herself more comfortably on my desk, sending a pile of papers fluttering.

No point in telling George that I didn't want to hear about Tom Wilkes. 'Forgive me,' I said as I scrambled to retrieve my scattered notes for Monday's programme, 'but I'm a bit pushed this afternoon.' Which I was, with Steve coming round for dinner. George, however, much as I love her, has no concept of urgency. If your natural working rhythm is the slow condensation of the meaning of life into a pearly thirty minutes, you can occasionally lose touch with the mundane exigencies of knocking out three action-packed hours daily.

'Many, many years ago,' she mused, 'on a trip out East for the World Service, I recorded an interview with a soldier. He was a young American GI about to return to Vietnam. Black and quite beautiful, with a Deep South drawl which twanged like a blues guitar. Oh, I could have listened to that boy for ever and a day. Except, the longer I listened to my tapes when I returned home, the more I found myself thinking that he didn't talk as though there was a for ever. He talked as though he had no future at all, as though those few days of leave were a kind of limbo. He can't have been more than twenty-five, and yet he gave the impression that all his life was in the past. Which,' she said, 'you may very well claim is just me being wise after the event. Because I later learned he'd blown his head off two days after returning to the field. Rose? Are you listening?'

'Just scribbling a note to pick up some mineral water.'

'And I was just trying to convey that there's something troubles me in Tom's voice, too. Only I can't quite decide what it is. But please don't let me interrupt your shopping list.'

I sighed and put my pencil down. 'Sorry, but I've a stack of work to finish and a dinner to cook at home tonight.'

George, acute as ever, glanced in the direction of Stephen's office and raised an enquiring eyebrow. I glared back at her stonily. 'Pity,' she sighed. 'Because there's something rather delicate I have to ask Tom to do with the arts programme, and I'd been wondering, since you and he are obviously such old friends . . .'

'We are not.'

'I might invite him up for supper this evening. I was hoping you could join us.'

I stared at her.

'However,' she continued, 'if you're otherwise engaged . . .'

'Believe me, it's just as well I am. Because if I had to share a table with Tom Wilkes, I'd probably end up sticking my dinner knife in him.'

'Good heavens,' said George, rising to her feet. She leaned forward to whisper in my ear: 'Must have been *quite* some affair you two had. TTFN.'

19

Imagine a candle-lit room. Oscar Peterson ripples from the speakers, garlic sings from the kitchen, a jug of roses billows on the table and a fire crackles companionably in the grate . . .

'Honestly, Mother,' said Polly, with the ineffable superiority of a fifteen-year-old observing the antics of geriatric romance, 'bit over the top, isn't it?' She was at least smiling, however, as I shoehorned her out of the door, overnight bag in hand. She'd been less indulgent, two days earlier, when I'd first broached my plans. 'I'll have a pizza in front of the telly,' she'd murmured, not raising her eyes from her book. 'Don't worry, I won't get in your way.' She wrinkled her nose. 'I'd sooner keep well out of his.'

Stephen, in the past, had not endeared himself to my daughter by offering a McDonald's (she's vegetarian), discussing rave culture (waste of head-banging time), praising her school (middle-class ghetto) and, worst of all, admiring her jacket. Which was one I had bought for her, at staggering expense, and into which I'd practically had to force-feed her outraged body.

'Look, darling,' I had said – and floundered. The crude facts of life, with which Polly had been unblushingly acquainted throughout her animal-rearing childhood, are a doddle compared with the delicate nuances of courtship. 'Stephen and I might like, you know, to have some time on our own.' Ironical, because I'd never felt less inclined to spend an evening alone with Stephen. But this, I firmly told myself, was only because I was edgy. 'So if you wouldn't mind staying at Grandpa's on Friday night . . .'

'*Sleep* there?' As though she didn't stay there whenever I went out or away. As though she hadn't been known, when annoyed with me, to threaten to roll up her endangered species posters and move in permanently. 'D'you want me to die in my teens from inhaling his airborne carcinogens?'

I held on to my temper – just. I'd told Steve he could stay the night. Dammit, he *was* going to stay. Tom Wilkes had fouled up enough of my life; he wasn't going to blight this relationship. I carefully explained to Polly that Steve didn't like to drink and drive, so . . . It was as though I'd admitted to bubonic plague. Red-faced, she bounced out of the room muttering, fine, she'd go, whatever I wanted.

Whereupon – can you believe it? – Mac entered the fray, informing me, when I rang him, that I was growing too cavalier in my maternal duties. 'I see now why you were so eager to imprison me in The Willows,' he growled. 'I'm your captive childminder.'

There was enough truth in this to sting me. 'Polly's not a child.'

'Exactly. She's a headstrong young woman, and she won't fritter away an evening cheating her Grandpa at draughts. Sure as death and taxes, she'll be skipping round to that Kevin Henderson's.'

'So what're you complaining about?' I retorted, stifling a twinge of anxiety and wondering what, if anything, was going on between Polly and the boy. 'She won't be troubling you.' I then had to wait for an explosion of tarry coughing to subside before he managed to declare, with many a theatrical wheeze and gasp, that the sooner he could sell up and move, the better. Polly needed a firm hand, and he was too old and too frail to act *in loco parentis*.

'Better brace your aged bones then,' I'd snarled. 'Because I'll be running her down at seven thirty. Stephen's arriving at eight.'

So here we now were, candles a-flicker, Oscar a-strumming, and most of the claret gone before I'd got a quarter of the way through my duck. I couldn't eat. The very idea of food revolted me. I had, however, accounted for nearly all the wine. I only wished I were drunk, but it was as though the alcohol had percolated straight into my body, melting my muscles but by-passing my brain which was still buzzing round like a wasp in a jam jar.

Steve sat across the table from me, mineral water in hand, candle-light glinting off his spectacles. Unless I was careful, I could see two of him. Not the drink, just eyes too tired to focus. He was bleating on about some football match or other. Since I spend half my working life interviewing people on topics about which I know nothing, it was no effort to keep him happy with the odd 'really?' or 'amazing!' I caught myself wondering what Tom Wilkes was talking about at George's dinner table, if she had indeed invited him up. And if I were with them? There was so much I *should* have said to him on Monday and I'd failed, miserably and humiliatingly. I realized I wanted to make him sorry, but I was too tired now to frame a single killer put-down. All I really wanted was to go to bed. Alone . . .

No way. I couldn't do that to poor Stephen. I'd invited him here. It wasn't his fault, this mess I was in. How could I explain?

'Great meal,' he was saying now, pushing aside his plate.

'Thanks,' I replied colourlessly. 'More wine? Sorry, I'm, um, a bit knackered. Long week.'

He grinned. 'I'll cheer you up. I've got a surprise for you.'

'Oh?'

He picked up my hand and kissed it. 'I'd planned to ask you last Sunday, actually, but what with one thing and another . . .'

'Ask me what?'

He released my hand and it clonked limply back on to the table. 'Hang on.' His jacket was hung over the chairback, and he twisted round to grope in the pockets. The inside pocket. 'Have to keep it under wraps at work . . .'

All of a sudden, quite irrationally, my buzzing brain could imagine only question he might be about to ask.

'Damn, where is it?' He let out a distinctly nervous laugh. 'Just hope you buy the idea, because it's a bit late to back out. But you've dropped enough hints, and I think it's what you want . . .'

'It is?' I croaked. It *was*, I told myself. It was, it was, it was. 'Look, Steve –'

And then the telephone rang.

'About time too,' growled Mac, spinning round in his chair as I opened the door on the smoky fug of his lounge. Suddenly, how-ever, his face split into a grin. The grin of an evil troll-roll-de-roll sighting a plump little billy goat setting hoof on his bridge. 'Mr Sharpe, I assume?'

'Correct,' said Stephen, striding manfully after me through the detritus of newspapers and bottles. 'Good to meet you, Mr Shawe.'

'Bagshawe.'

'Mac,' I snapped. 'Everyone calls him Mac.' I hadn't meant Stephen to come. I wouldn't have turned out myself, no matter what Mac roared down the phone, if I hadn't been panicked by Steve's lunge for his breast pocket. Of course, I *wanted* the Lamb to propose – I'd already drafted plans for the ceremony (civil), the guest list (minimal), and honeymoon destinations (exotic) – but not tonight, not with a week's lost sleep jazzing my nerves and gelling my limbs. So I'd seized on Mac's call as a delaying tactic: a family squall requiring my immediate presence down the road. Only for Steve to insist that I'd drunk too much to drive. Besides, he'd like to meet my father. 'I doubt it,' I'd sighed, feeling wearier by the minute. I'd only intended to postpone his proposal. A parent like mine could stretch the postponement to infinity.

'How are you, um, Mac?' Steve said now, briskly shaking hands.

'Legless,' responded my father. His favourite jest for discomfiting strangers. Poor Stephen blenched but, before I could intervene, Dad swept on: 'Metaphorically as well as literally, as it happens. The strain of a feckless daughter and a wayward grandchild has driven a poor old man to seek refuge in the bottle.'

'As if you needed an excuse,' I said. 'OK, where is she?'

'More to the point, where are *they*? Because, as I told you on the telephone, she vanished into the twilight to visit one Kevin Henderson. Promising to return by nine thirty at the latest.'

'It's not even ten,' I said, telling myself that there was nothing going on between them, that I would surely have spotted the signs. 'And it's Friday, half-term next week. Polly's a sensible girl.'

'Maybe, but she's running amok with the son of –'

'*Mac!*'

Stephen smiled helpfully. 'Out with her boyfriend?'

'No,' I snapped; then recollected myself. 'It's just a friend.'

'Are we sure of that?' enquired Mac.

'Oh, for God's sake. Have you rung this Kevin's?'

He met my eyes squarely. 'There's the phone. Why don't you?'

It was a challenge. I knew it. And if I hadn't been so dead-beat, I'd have called the nosy old devil's bluff and picked up the phone. Why should I worry about talking to Frankie's ex-wife? There was no earthly way she could connect me with the flame-haired fancy piece who'd shacked up with her husband. But I hesitated an instant too long and saw the change in Mac's face. Not triumph, exactly, just confirmation of his suspicions. What the hell. 'Marlowe, isn't it?' I sighed, opening the directory. 'Newsagent's?'

'Give the machine here,' Mac growled, rather to my surprise. 'Hello, Mr Marlowe? Oh, I'm speaking to Kevin, am I? Is Polly . . . Did she indeed? No, don't worry . . . Thank you.' He slammed down the receiver and swivelled back to face me. 'She's not there. It seems she only dropped off a book *en route* elsewhere. Destination unknown.'

Mac announced this with perfect complacency. Well, I'd never supposed he was actually worried about Polly. It was just an excuse to spoil my evening. To register a protest, in the most disruptive way he could devise, at my taking for granted his babysitting services. I, however, for the first time, felt a prickle of concern. 'Where's she got to?'

'What's the problem?' said Stephen. 'You know what teenagers are.'

I only just curbed myself from telling him he obviously didn't. Polly might be argumentative and rebellious, but she was dependable on gate hours. 'Give me back the phone book,' I said. 'I'll ring round her friends.'

As I was doing so, and being met with sympathy but no help, I had to listen, behind me, to Stephen's plucky attempts at conversing with my father. Admiring his bungalow. You can imagine Mac's reponse. Asking if Dad attended a Day Centre. The reply was unprintable. And I know, I *know*, there is nothing more despicable than to be ashamed of one's parents. We can none of choose 'em, still less trade them in along with the G-plan suite when they fail to match our vaulting aspirations. But when Stephen got on to facilities for the differently abled in Wakeborough and Mac launched into his call-a-cripple-a-cripple tirade against mealy-mouthed euphemisms . . .

I couldn't intervene, because Polly's chum Sophy was on the line, saying, sure, Polly had been round, but it was the rats . . . '*Rats?*'

'For our Town Fayre exhibit, you know.'

'No, Sophy,' I said. 'I don't know.'

'Polly's idea. Really brill. We thought we'd better catch them now to give them a week to, you know, get used to people. Jim told us how sensitive they are, that shock could kill them.'

I shut my eyes. 'Let me get this straight. Jim Rumbelow has been telling my daughter how to catch rats?'

'On the tip, you know, the nature park. We put the cages out with the bait after school today. Only with all this rain, she was a bit worried they might drown or something.'

'Sophy, you're not seriously suggesting Polly could be out on that tip chasing rats at this hour of night?'

There was a nervous giggle. 'You know Polly.'

I did. I strode across to the window, wrenching back the curtains.

'Aye, the view's better by night,' said Mac. 'Black as a puddle of ink.'

'Quiet. Oh, turn the light off, will you? I'm trying to see . . .' He was right. Black as ink, with – as my eyes adjusted to the gloom – a faint gilding of street lamps over the frowning mass of the tip. The rain was slashing against the window. I was just about to turn away when a flicker of light caught my eye. Yellow. Surely a torch beam? I strode to the back door. The rain was bouncing off the path. 'Polly?' I yelled, cupping my hands round my mouth. 'Polly, is that you over there?'

I could see the torch beam more clearly now, and it swung round to face me. 'Mum?' Her voice sounded a hundred miles away. Between us, the stream was oiling past like jet-propelled tarmac.

'What the hell d'you think you're doing?'

'No prob . . . Bit stuck . . .' Her words were stripped away on the gale. '. . . stream's right up and I lost my welly. Be back in . . .'

'Stay right where you are, you hear?' I shrieked. 'We'll bring the car. Five minutes. *Don't move.* Steve?'

It took rather longer than five minutes to drive round to the bridge and up the rutted track which had once been used by the tipping lorries. The route was familiar from Polly's mountain-biking days, but the mud depths were not. For the first time, it occurred to me that COSH might have a point. We had to stop the car after a few yards. I grabbed the torch I'd had the sense to borrow from Mac, hitched up my skirt and got out of the car. The mud oozed round my ankles like chocolate pudding. 'Jesus wept,' I hissed, stomping forward. But when I saw a puny light bobbing towards me, a pathetic figure, limping along in one wellington, I forgot my wrath and surged forward. 'Great steaming idiot,' I gasped, wrapping my arms round her shivering body. 'What on earth are you playing at?'

She was hugging me back, which shows she was a bit shaken

herself. 'Sorry. I came over on the stepping stones. But the stream's up, I tripped over and – and my lousy welly got sucked off . . .' There were tears in her voice.

'Oh, sweetheart,' I wailed. 'It's all right, don't cry. Come on, not far to the car. And look, Stephen's here.'

She stiffened and shook off my arm. 'Stephen?'

In that instant, I saw the answer to my dilemma: maternal duty. 'Don't worry, darling,' I cooed. 'I know you want to get home to your own bed.' So did I, I thought, and no longer felt guilty at wanting that bed to myself. I'd been mad to think I could cope with Stephen when I was in such a lather of rage over Tom Wilkes. I smiled radiantly at him. 'My poor Polly needs to come home. You're OK to drive yourself back to Wakeborough, aren't you?'

He agreed he was, even if he didn't seem nearly as pleased as Polly to learn that was the plan. And was even less enchanted when she doubled back a few limping paces and returned with a small cage and a polite request that he carry the rat. Her sole captive. It was scuttling round the wire mesh of what she assured me was a humane trap, glaring at us. 'I'm going to put them in the old rabbit hutch.'

'*Them?*'

'When I've got some more. Look after them for a few days, so they won't be scared by people.'

'What on earth for?' Maternal solicitude was melting fast.

'I *told* you, Mum,' she said, with that familiar inflexion which means she'd done her damnedest to mislead me. 'COSH. Our stand at the Town Fayre next Friday.'

'You told me you'd got a stand, yes . . .'

'Well, Sophy's brother's lending us this huge tank he used to keep a python in. And we were going to arrange it with all kinds of rubbish from here – you know, weeds, and cans, and mud and stuff – and then have the rats running round and –'

'No,' I said firmly. But I hadn't been arguing with my daughter all these years without acquiring a certain cunning. 'I mean, one rat would be terribly lonely in the hutch. Probably pine to death. They're social animals.'

'What do you know about it?'

Fortunately the rat chose that moment to stage a hissing, eye-bulging, tail-lashing assault on the mesh. I leaped back, and even

Polly recoiled. 'For God's sake,' I urged, 'let the poor thing go, and let's get home.'

Polly looked from the rat to me and back again; then began very reluctantly to unhook the door. The animal streaked out before she could lower the cage to the ground. 'Don't know what we'll do for the stand now,' she muttered.

'Look, babe,' said Stephen half an hour later, standing on the doorstep. I'd left Polly in the bathroom, with the tub filling and her muddy clothes strewn across the floor. I urgently wanted a bath myself, but he was pinning me against the doorframe. 'I've got to ask you –'

'What?' I squawked. But no one, surely, ever made a proposal of marriage on a rainy doorstep? With a truculent, shivery daughter within, and a howling storm without? Nevertheless, he was groping in his pocket again, grinning like a maniac. 'Surprise, surprise.'

I was surprised all right. Because what he produced from his pocket was a large and very flat envelope. 'How's the diary a week tomorrow?' he said. 'I managed to get two tickets for the match at Old Trafford.'

Well, for Howard's sake – and yours – I've written a report. God knows if it will help, but at least now I can go back to where I was when you jackbooted in. Although I hate doing this to George. Tell her I'm sorry, will you? This has nothing to do with her, nor with any of you, it's . . .

(LONG PAUSE, CLICK OF THE MACHINE BEING STOPPED AND RESTARTED)

I'd better tell you the rest. Otherwise people will jump to stupid conclusions, and I don't want to dish the guilt around. The guilt's all mine, OK?

(SOUND OF POURING)

Last of the Scotch. Enough there to see me under the table, let alone into the bath and this won't take much longer. You know my wife died? It's – what? – ten months back. January 13th. Sure, everyone will tell you how amazingly I've coped, what a saint I am and all that kind of crap. Let's leave it that I was ticking over – in work, at any rate. Until a month ago, when her publishers sent me an advance copy of some poems of hers. Early stuff, that she'd held back, only to be published after her death.

The crazy thing is, I'd already read the poems. She'd told me where to find them and of course I flipped through before sending them off, as I'd promised. But it was as if, first time round, the words didn't penetrate. Maybe I was still gaga after the funeral. Anyway, when I opened the copy that day, saw them all printed up, and began reading . . . This was the day I was supposed to be editing the programme but –

(HIS VOICE IS CRACKING)

Suddenly, I just couldn't take it any longer. The guilt. I suppose I've got to tell you, if you're going to make any sense of this . . . Oh shit, it was me killed her. I did it, your honour. I killed my wife.

20

'By the way, darling,' I said brightly as I steered through the scrum of Saturday traffic in the town centre. 'I'm, ah, going away next weekend.'

'Terrific,' grunted Polly.

'Steve's got tickets for a football match in Manchester so –'

She slewed round in her seat. 'You cannot be serious?'

I could understand her amazement. To be fair to the Lamb, even he hadn't expected me to be overjoyed at the prospect of two seats at Old Trafford. No, his big surprise was the two nights he'd booked in a smart hotel a few miles out of the city. Looked wonderful on the brochure he handed me. Oak-panelled, four-postered and deer-parked, it was just the thing, I'd told myself, to pep up my flabby libido.

I drew up outside the Central Library. 'Now, you're sure you're OK for getting home?'

Polly gathered up her bags. 'Can't I ring you in work if I need a lift back?'

'May not be by the phone the whole time,' I said smoothly. Because, although I had a little to finish at my desk, I'd no intention of wasting the afternoon in work – and even less of disclosing my real plans. The last thing I wanted was Polly pursuing me. 'Anyway, I thought you said you were going back to Sophy's?'

'Depends what we decide this afternoon, doesn't it?' she replied grumpily. 'Now you've put the kibosh on the rats, we've got to come up with another idea for the stand. Gotta dash. I said I'd meet them at three.'

I kissed air because she was already out of the car, and pulled out into the traffic again, smiling. I'd slept for eleven whole hours last night. Why? Because I knew what I had to do. As a stress therapist had explained on my show only the other day, stopperingup anger, or rather, 'internalizing negative emotions', as she put it, 'toxifies the soul and de-enhances spiritual flowering'. Or something like that. She was into hate-objects, whacking the stuffing out of pillows and so forth. At the time, I'd thought, well, *bullshit*. Like you do. Not any longer. Instead of fretting over all the things I *should* have said to Tom Wilkes, I was planning to, ahem, externalize these negative emotions, but this time, in the privacy of George's basement flat, with neither listening ears nor humiliating tears. Thus, although I parked behind Radio Ridings, I intended to spend only a few minutes there before walking round to George's. Gathering up my files, I hurried across the car park and out on to the pavement.

'You're looking very industrious,' said a quiet voice. I spun round. There was a convertible Bentley drawn up to the kerb and, standing beside it, the only man in Wakeborough to drive such a ritzy motor. His face was crumpled, with a nose so remarkable it might have been sculpted by the likes of Mike Tyson, but his great bull of a figure was packaged as immaculately as ever, in a buttery soft vicuna overcoat which matched the dull gold of his car and made my fingers itch with envy.

'Trevor,' I stammered. 'Hi, how are you?'

'Bruised, Rosie,' sighed Trevor Green, shaking his head. 'Battered, bruised and bewildered, after the duffing-up you gave my PR man on your show not so long ago.'

'What? Oh, the Willows thing?'

'Did we really need the dead frogs, Rosie?'

'Yes, well, I'm sorry if your guy was made to look a bit of a fool, but –'

'Look like a fool? He is a fool,' said Trevor, with no change in tone. 'Complete and total wanker. Seems to think PR is a brand of toothpaste. I've given his firm the push.'

'Good heavens,' I said faintly.

'Come straight to me next time, eh?'

'Actually,' I ventured, 'as it happens, I was out on that tip myself last night –'

'By "tip", do we mean The Willows' nature park?'

'Call it what you like, but it just seems to be a sea of mud.'

He was tutting reproachfully. 'You think I don't know? Don't worry, it's all in hand, as you can tell your listeners. Phase Two landscaping plans are drawn up for the residents' approval. These things take time, that's all.' He chuckled softly. 'Chatsworth wasn't built in a day, was it? And not for twopence, neither.'

I eyed him uncertainly. There's something about Trevor Green that always does rattle me a bit. It's not that I'm overawed by megabucks. In my job, I interview fish much bigger than him, sharks in the national ocean, whereas he's only the fattest goldfish in our local pond. Or pike, if you listen to Her Worship the Flo and her cronies – but they would say that, wouldn't they? Local lad getting too big for his Gucci loafers and so on. And yet Trevor didn't hide his humble origins. On the contrary, he was fond of reminiscing about his dad, Wakeborough's last rag-and-bone man. But from that background, with no education to speak of, he'd gone out into the world and made his pile before returning here with a Bentley and Savile Row suits. These days, he owned God-and-the-VATman only knew how many enterprises, and there was barely a civic or cultural function in the town ungraced with his bulky presence. Remarkable – the stuff of airport fiction – and I, more than most, recognized the heroic scale of his achievement. I felt I ought to *like* this fellow self-improver. He'd always been nice enough to me, and yet . . .

'We won't fall out over it, will we?' he was saying. 'I'm a big fan of yours, you know. You do a good job on that show. Great asset to the station. Very popular figure in the town.'

'Well, thanks.'

'And how're your Festival plans coming along? You know, I'd been expecting to hear from you.'

Thus it was that, two hours and half a dozen panicked phone calls to fellow committee members later, I was hunched over my desk in Radio Ridings, tapping into my computer the long-overdue draft schedule for the Dales Arts Festival. I could hardly tell our richest corporate sponsor that he couldn't choose the event he was going to cough up for this year because I hadn't yet got round to producing the menu.

Tom Wilkes's fault. Of course. If I hadn't been in such a state all week, I'd have had the thing typed days ago. Never mind, I said to myself, wondering how to spell Tchaikovsky, there'd still be plenty of time to go round to George's later and vent my spleen. In the meantime, I thought, dredging my purse for change, I'd have a coffee.

He was there. Squatting in front of the coffee machine at the top of the stairs. I nearly tripped over him.

'Oh, hi,' he said, with no particular interest. 'Is this contraption bust? I've put the money in.'

'You need to bash it,' I said, delivering an unnecessarily vicious clout. I don't know what it did for my spiritual flowering, but my hand hurt like hell.

'Thanks,' he said as the machine gurgled and spat inky liquid into a beaker. 'What're you doing in on a Saturday?'

'We work hard in local radio,' I retorted priggishly, which was not at all the tone I was aiming for. I bit my lip, and fed my own coins into the slot. Pressed the button, delivered a rather milder blow, composed a frosty smile and turned round ready to suggest we take our coffees to a quiet corner . . .

He'd gone. I was just in time to see the door closing on the broom cupboard which served as the Assistant Editor's office. I shut my eyes and cursed. Then told myself it didn't matter. Even on a Saturday it would be hard to find privacy here. Sport was going hell for leather in studio, there was a weekend editor and a duty news producer somewhere around, and any number of other bods might be wandering in and out before we finally went off air at six. No, better to bide my time.

As I walked past Helen's office – I couldn't think of it as Tom's, although I supposed technically it was – I heard the faint bleep a computer makes when you've pressed a wrong button. Was it possible he was writing his report? I also detected a thick aroma of tobacco. Maybe he thought rules didn't apply on a Saturday. I returned to my own computer.

In the end, he took me by surprise. It was close on six and the office was dark. I nearly jumped out of my skin when a soft voice behind me asked if, by any chance, I'd such a thing as a tape-recorder.

Fine question to ask in a radio station. I twirled round to face him and was shocked afresh by his appearance. In the eerie upward glare of my desk lamp, he looked like a corpse. 'Uher?' I said, naming the reel-to-reel juggernauts which the Corporation still favours over the nippy cassette jobs widely employed elsewhere – and which doubtless lend gravitas to our news coverage, in every sense of the word. A tip for would-be Sherlock Holmeses on the differentiation of BBC employees from our commercial competitors: we have one shoulder permanently dented. But I didn't want this television invader sneering at our stone-age gear. 'Of course we're also trying out the new digital machines and . . .'

He was shaking his head. 'I just meant some kind of dictating job. My writing's bad enough, even without the DTs.'

I assumed he was joking about the shakes, but if this telly-crat thought he could get away with dictating his report for some minion to type up, he was in for a shock. Secretaries are a near-extinct species here. Only Stephen retained one – and, to be sure, he had the dictating machine to match. The selfsame little gadget that had chaperoned us through our early encounters.

Tom was already turning away. 'Forget it.'

'Stay right where you are,' I said sharply. I wasn't going to let him escape twice. 'Back in a minute.' I didn't say that I was about to break into Stephen's office. Not that this was any big deal. We all knew how to do it. The boss's office has always been the stronghold to raid when you can't find a single pen that writes, a reel of editing tape, or a current *Radio Times*. Steve always locked up meticulously, of course – the door to the corridor, that is – but the cleaner tended to leave the connecting door to his secretary's room open. Sure enough, I found the machine in his top drawer. I didn't, however, hand it immediately to Tom when I returned. 'I'm finished here too,' I said. 'Ready for a drink?'

'Sorry?'

'I've a script for George,' I continued smartly, 'so maybe –'

'No.'

I blinked. I mean, people don't just say 'no', do they? They apologize, burble excuses . . . He leaned over and took the tape-recorder. For one bewildering moment it actually seemed he was about to kiss me. Then he drew back. 'Thanks,' he said quietly. 'Thanks for everything. Goodbye, Rita.'

And he was gone.

I sat at my desk, not so much vexed as stunned. How could he be so rude? No, not just rude, strange. Completely weird. That look on his face . . .

I stabbed a few buttons and set the computer printing extra copies of my schedule for the rest of the committee. Might as well finish the job, because I could hardly go and accost him at home now. Only as I bad-temperedly stuffed Trevor's copy into an envelope (with a note trusting that we would enjoy his generous support again this year) did my thoughts begin, dangerously, to stray. You see, it wasn't only I who'd been churning out words on the computer that afternoon. So, it seemed, had Tom. He'd actually produced a report. I'd seen it when I sneaked into Stephen's office. It had been lying on the carpet. A neatly paper-clipped bundle of A4, which he'd obviously slid under the door, was waiting for Stephen to find when he walked in Monday morning.

The building grew quieter. Sport had gone off the air and the last shouts of departing hearties echoed round the building. The computer winked conspiratorially at me. WHAT NEXT? the screen enquired.

I shouldn't have done it. I *knew* I shouldn't. I told myself I was going to get another coffee. That I only wanted to check I hadn't disturbed anything in Stephen's office when I filched the tape-recorder. Surely you can sympathize? I mean, had the report been sealed in an envelope, I couldn't have done it. But Tom hadn't been initiated into the esoteric secret of where, in this budget-conscious building, large envelopes were secreted. Besides, I told myself as I slunk back to my desk with the pages casually tucked under my arm, I only wanted to see what he had to say about me. Not that I cared, to be sure. He knew nothing about radio . . .

It was a disappointment. Maybe sneak-readers, like eavesdroppers, learn what they deserve. Right up top, Tom Wilkes made clear he was dealing only with the news output. Flipping through, I couldn't see a single mention of my show. It was all news, day-by-day, item-by-item. I didn't bother to study the text, but I couldn't help divining the general tenor. Words like 'stale', 'predictable' and 'irrelevant' leaped out. Along with phrases such as 'swamped in pseudo-interpretation' and 'stagnant amalgam of theoretical constructs, lacking any real response to local events'. What did he know about local events? By the time I turned over the last page I was spitting curses at this arrogant, ignorant invader . . . Then my eye alighted on the last page.

I don't know if this analysis will be useful. I can't claim experience of local radio even as a listener, let alone a journalist.

Then why bother writing? I hissed.

I have to say that a week's monitoring of the news service provided by Radio Ridings only confirms my long-held view that the resources committed to local broadcasting would be better used elsewhere, at a national level.

'Oh brilliant,' I cried aloud. It didn't matter, because I was alone in the building. 'He listens to us for four lousy days and cheerfully pronounces that the whole of local radio should be abolished.'

I also realize my own recent career gives me precious little authority to preach editorial ethics. However, since I won't be taking up this appointment . . .

What?

. . . which people have gone to some trouble to secure for me, I thought the least I could do for Radio Ridings was offer my honest – if necessarily subjective – appraisal of their news and current affairs coverage, and my suggestions for improving it.

I'm now about to cause inconvenience, if not embarrassment, to the station, for which, very sincerely, I apologize.

What embarrassment? What inconvenience?

He hadn't signed his name. Just typed it. 'Thomas Wilkes'. *Thomas* . . . And suddenly, I was seeing his gaunt face as he took the miniature recorder from me half an hour or more since. What'd he wanted it for anyway? He'd written his report. And he'd said 'goodbye', hadn't he? Not 'see you Monday'. Not 'thanks for the machine'. Just 'goodbye'. Final.

'Holy Mother of God,' I wailed and, stuffing the report into my desk drawer, I knocked chairs and bins flying as I scrambled across the office and ran out of the building.

21

'Where is he?' I screeched.

George, standing at her open front door, gaped at me. 'Who, Tom?'

'For pity's sake, is he here?'

'In the flat, so far as I'm aware,' she said, standing back – or rather, being shoved out of the way. 'Came in half an hour ago and . . . Well, I'm sure you can find your own way.'

I was already thundering down the stairs. But the little sitting room was empty. There was a suitcase, packed. An empty Scotch bottle. And a small fat envelope propped against it, labelled in tottering capitals: FOR ROSE, I didn't bother to open it. I could recognize the shape of a cassette tape at ten paces. And I'd lent him the means to record it. 'Thomas?' I yelled. '*Thomas!*'

I heard water running. The bathroom. I charged back into the little hallway, flung myself against the bathroom door. Can't have been locked because it flipped open and I staggered into the room. Relief made my head spin. Tom, still dressed – still alive – was sitting on the edge of the bath, which was nearly full. 'Oh, shit,' he sighed, screwing the tap shut. 'What now?'

Beside him, on the soap rack, was a near-empty tumbler of what looked like whisky. And two razor blades. Not the sort you shave with, which might not have been out of place in a bathroom. No, these were the square, single-edged blades we use for cutting recording tape. I pounced on them.

'Don't be melodramatic,' he said.

'You trying to tell me you weren't about to use these?' I gasped, shaking the blades under his nose before pocketing them.

'I can find another.'

I looked at the bathwater. White and clear and gently steaming. Imagined it slowly turning red.

'Supposed to be nearly painless in warm water. The Romans were fond of it as a way out.' His shoulders shook in a miserable travesty of amusement. 'Benefits of a classical education, eh? Anyway, take it from me, it's got to be more reliable than drugs. You'd be surprised how hard it can be to snuff out even the frailest little spark of life with chemicals.' He shuddered. 'Not many people know that. I'm an expert. Sorry, I'm a bit high. I've popped the odd pill too, Swiss courage. Take my advice, Rita, if you're going to top yourself, do it straight off. Hang around for a week or so, and it gets much harder to take the plunge.' He began, helplessly, to laugh again. 'Oh God, take the plunge . . .'

Relief at finding him before he succeeded was ripening into anger. I couldn't help myself. 'You should be *ashamed* of yourself.'

He stirred the water with one long finger. 'Oh yeah? It's my life. You telling me I haven't a right to do what I want with it?'

'No,' I snapped. 'No, you bloody well have not.'

He looked up. 'First time you've really sounded like yourself, you know that? *No, you bluddy well 'ave not.*' He was mimicking my accent.

That was all it took. I went off like a rocket. I told him exactly what I thought about spoilt upper-class boys who'd never had to work at anything, who'd had the entire world handed to them on a silver sodding salver, and just because their career hit one little setback, and they found themselves banished to the indignities of tinpot cruddy local radio, they thought the only answer was to slash their wrists. If they only knew how some people would give anything – *anything* – for a job like theirs . . . And more of the same. Totally unbridled and, under the circumstances, totally, *wickedly* unforgivable.

'Good heavens,' said George faintly, who had appeared in the doorway at the end of this tirade. 'I don't think I'm quite following the plot, but the dialogue's splendid. Even if the acoustic's a bit lively. Rose, forgive me, but why are you choosing to harangue Tom in the bathroom?'

I was too angry to answer. Tom, slumped on the edge of the tub, looked as though he couldn't be bothered.

'Was Tom about to take a bath?' enquired George. And although she spoke lightly enough, I could tell she'd a fairish clue what was afoot.

'No,' I said.

Tom shrugged. 'Not immediately, it seems.'

'Well, shall we all go upstairs and have a nice little drinky?' George spoke with the firmness of an old-style headmistress. 'Tom, is that whisky? But I dare say Rose would prefer a glass of wine. Plenty upstairs.'

So saying, she ushered us inexorably up into her own drawing room, and promptly whisked herself off to the kitchen.

'Well?' I said hotly.

'Well, what?' Tom slumped into a chair. 'Oh, just for the record, this has nothing to do with my so-called career.'

'Why then?'

'Please don't shout.' He shook his head despairingly. 'Know something? I'm not even drunk. Half a bottle of whisky, tranquillizers, and I can still see straight.'

'So maybe . . .' I was fighting for control of my temper. Dimly I knew I was behaving badly. That this man needed help – tact, sensitivity, all that – but whatever my better self knew, my worse self was bubbling with outrage. 'So maybe you'd better start talking straight.'

'What's the point? You – someone like you – won't understand.'

The anger of the whole week – of sixteen long years – was gathering inside me. 'Oh? Too stupid?'

'Not *stupid*,' he said with a flicker of irritation. 'Sensible, practical. God, I've been listening to you on the radio, babbling away, bright as a budgerigar. Dear, dear, brain rotting with Alzheimer's? Pop along to your nearest support group. Terminal cancer? Counselling can be *so* helpful. Talk about audio fucking Elastoplast. You think there's an answer to everything, don't you?'

My mouth worked helplessly. I couldn't speak for rage.

'Yeah, well, we're not all like you, Rita,' he went on flatly. 'Something doesn't suit you, you just shut the door on it, pretend it never happened, rewrite the past on prettier lines. Can you imagine what it's like to look at your life and see one black hole? Nothing left except guilt? Nothing worth living for?'

Any last vestige of self-control exploded. '*What?*'

'Exactly. I know –'

'You know *nothing*,' I roared. 'How do you think I felt when I found myself burying my mother one day, and giving birth the next? With my career gone, a bloody shop to run, howling post-

148

natal depression and a screaming premature baby, whose father refused to admit she existed?'

He shut his eyes, as if in pain. 'Oh, I'm sorry, but –'

'*Sorry?* I should hope you are sorry. For three years, let me tell you, I was putting back vodka like it was lemonade, I was *stiff* with valium, two stone overweight and – and smoking like a chimney.'

The bastard wasn't even listening. He was patting his pockets. 'Want one?'

'I don't smoke,' I shrieked. 'But it's no thanks to you, is it? I was on sixty a day after Polly was born. And you *dare* to sneer at me for shutting doors on the past, for refusing to face facts.'

Now he looked up. 'What are you talking about?' And his face was blank. Completely blank. 'Why should it be no thanks to me?'

I stared back at him, open-mouthed. The floodtide of rage was ebbing treacherously fast. 'Oh my God.' Suddenly the floor underneath me felt spongy as a mattress. I crumpled into a chair. 'Thomas, you're not saying – *claiming* – you don't know?'

'Know what?'

'I mean . . .'

That was when I heard the voices in the hall. The doorbell must have rung earlier, but Big Ben could have struck and, in that state, I wouldn't have noticed. Now, though, I could hear George apologizing for taking so long to answer. 'And your friend won't come in? No, angel, of course you're not disturbing me. She's in the drawing room, but I think perhaps you and I might be better in the . . . Ah, too late.' The door was flung open as she spoke.

And in walked Polly.

22

'Hi, Mum,' she said. 'Brill, you're still in town. I thought I was going to have to ring you at home and grovel for a lift. Still, it's George I came to see.' She turned a smile on George, gold and dazzling as a pair of Continental headlamps. 'Aunty George, I need to ask you a big, big favour.'

'But, my love,' said George distractedly, handing glasses to Tom and me, 'you know I don't have a car these days, and –'

'Professionally,' interrupted Polly.

'Oh?' She glanced from me to Tom. 'I'm, um, delighted, naturally. Would you like something to drink? If we went into the kitchen, I believe I could find some orange juice or –'

Polly shook her head, clearly bursting with purpose.

'Shall we go next door then, so we can, um, talk in comfort?'

'More comfortable in here,' replied my truthful daughter. 'Your house is freezing.'

George sighed. 'Come and sit at the table then, if we're to talk business. Have you met Tom Wilkes, by the way?' Polly flashed a cursory smile at him, but focused straight back on George who took a swig of gin and asked how she could be of service.

Polly proceeded to tell her, blithely unaware of Tom and me. He'd barely seemed to notice her at first. For an instant – only an instant – I thought I might get away with it. But almost at once, he looked up again, frowning, then turned to me. At least, I sensed his gaze, but I wouldn't meet it. Couldn't, not yet. I swallowed half my wine in one panicked gulp.

'. . . and we've got this stand at the Town Fayre next Friday. Actually, I'd had this amazing idea for a tank with rats and stuff.'

'Darling, I am not a faint-hearted woman, but if this has anything to do with rodents . . .'

'Oh, Mum wrecked that. Anyway, doesn't matter, we've got a

better idea now. Kevin's borrowing a video camera from his school.'

'A vid-e-o camera?' echoed George, in a tone which suggested rats were preferable.

'Uh – Polly?'

I jumped so violently I spilled my wine. It was Tom who'd spoken. But Polly was chattering on to George and he had to repeat the name before she heard. She twisted round enquiringly.

'How – ?' Then he stopped. I held my breath. God knows what he might be capable of saying. Why oh why did she have to turn up now? 'Could you, um, pass me an ashtray?' As if he didn't have one already. But Polly didn't see it. She was looking particularly pretty today, I thought irrelevantly. Well, except for the crumpled sweat shirt and filthy fingernails. Her face was flushed with excitement, and her hair had escaped from the rubber band and was waving wildly in the damp.

'There you go,' she said, thumping across the room.

'Polly,' he repeated wonderingly. And she looked at him, puzzled, as he took the ashtray. 'Nice name.'

'Better than the one I was christened,' she said, grimacing at me. '*Mary*, can you believe? After my sainted gran. But they've always called me Polly. For some bonkers reason, it's supposed to be short for Mary.'

Mary after Mary Bagshawe. Mary, also, as in the sainted Mary who gave her name to Magdalen College. But I was hardly likely to have told her that. She clumped back to the table and Tom leaned towards me. 'How old is she?' he whispered hoarsely. And this wasn't a polite social enquiry. Well, not unless he had spent his formative years without ever looking in a mirror.

'Fifteen,' I sighed. 'She was fifteen in June.'

And she was the living, glowing, golden image of her dad.

You hadn't guessed? Or maybe you had. I can only say I hope nothing else could have made me behave so wildly all week, and so – so *shockingly* tonight. A spitting virago, I'd unleashed the accumulated hurt of years on a man who didn't even know why I was so angry. Worse – and this was the unforgivable part – on a man I knew was in the blackest depths of despair, a man who'd been ready to end his life. And now he was confronted with Polly . . . '*Tom*,' I hissed.

He was staring blindly at her as she rattled on to George about the tip and their precious campaign. He looked – stunned. I mean literally stunned, as if he were concussed. He hadn't known about her. I could still hardly believe it. Sure, over the years I'd dreamed up fantastical plots where my letter was stolen and his signature forged – his mother had been my favourite culprit – but even at my loopiest, I hadn't believed them. Far more plausible that the nineteen-year-old Thomas had preferred not to face the awkward truth.

George caught my eye and twitched a quizzical eyebrow. For a dismayed instant, I thought she might have guessed too, but she was gesturing towards the wine. I shook my head, although, so help me, I could have downed the bottle. Besides, it wasn't as if Polly resembled Tom now, not so remarkably. It was his younger self I could see in her, had been watching unfold all these years. She had his eyes, chin, hair, lanky limbs – even her ear-lobes were the same shape as his. Sometimes, when she laughed, I could swear it was Thomas laughing. Who'd ever imagine such a detail would figure on the genetic blue-print? And yet resemblances are mysterious – must be, because Mac swore she was the image of my mother as a girl. But then he didn't even know who Polly's father was, let alone what he looked like.

I had to get Tom out of here. Only minutes ago I'd stopped him putting a blade to his wrists. This might unhinge him beyond help. Besides, I had to protect Polly. As far as she was concerned, her father was called Will Thomas, and had read Classics at York University. And was dead.

I've never felt so helpless. Tom seemed to have forgotten my existence. That terrifyingly blank gaze was fixed on Polly as she blathered on about their planned video. George's contribution, apparently, was to provide suitably gory effects and music track for this masterpiece of propaganda. 'Actually, Kevin said we should take the camera and go and bash on Trevor Green's door, you know, like they do on the telly, but –'

'Sorry, but can I get this straight?' Tom's intervention surprised them – and scared the wits out of me. 'There's, um, a defunct tip, and you claim it's both an eyesore and a potential hazard. But as things stand . . .' I could see the effort it took for him to articulate the words and hold his voice steady, 'you haven't any evidence for claiming what was dumped there is dangerous?'

'It *might* be dangerous,' said Polly pugnaciously, suspecting mockery. 'How'd you know, anyway?'

'I don't. That's why I'm asking.'

To my alarm, she upped her chair to face him. Polly has the zeal of any evangelist if she scents a possible convert. 'Since all this rain, it's got really horrible. There was a load of earth dumped over the tip years back, when they built the bungalows, but it's all washing away into mud now. We've already found bits of metal barrels, rusting away. We reckon there's loads more buried under there, probably all oozing vicious gunk. But how can we tell?'

'Get some scient –' He stumbled, cleared his throat, but managed to finish: 'get some tests done?'

Polly was nodding vigorously. 'We've been on to Friends of the Earth, but they weren't even interested. Well, they *say* they'll help, but they're tied up with Ackersley stupid Wood and the bypass.' This was said with disgust. No hint of her own (until recently, passionate) commitment to Ackersley Wood and its threatened bluebells. 'We can't just wait around. We want to – to *mobilize* public opinion, and that's why we need a video for our stand at the Fayre, so everyone can see what we're on about.'

'Surely what you need,' he said, 'is to get the press behind you.'

I can't bear this, I thought, I can't bear it. Sitting here, having to listen to them talking about bloody rubbish dumps: Polly blithe as a squirrel; Tom, drunk, drugged, shocked, suicidal . . .

'Trevor Green,' said Polly triumphantly, 'whose company owns the so-called nature park, also owns the local paper.'

'A media baron and a polluter to boot. Called, ironically enough' – bemusedly, I saw Tom's face lighten – '*Green*.' But what a wretched little smile.

Polly (was she blind?) chuckled appreciatively. 'You said it.'

I couldn't take any more. 'He is not,' I burst out. 'A polluter, I mean. The tip's nothing to do with Trevor, he built The Willows after it was closed.' I turned on my daughter. 'And what's more, Polly, I ran into Trevor this lunchtime, and he personally assured me they'd got plans for landscaping the damn site. And now, if you don't mind, Tom and I have something to discuss so –'

'Trevor Green'd promise anything,' she snorted. 'But he never does it. Honestly, Mum, you just creep to him because he gives you a load of dosh for your Arts Festival.'

'Polly!' I gasped.

'I begin to see,' murmured George, 'that the misery of a child-less life is not without its compensations. I'm only surprised poor Rose didn't strangle you at birth, you unnatural brat.'

Polly, not at all put out, blew a kiss and said she knew George loved her really.

Tom just ignored me. 'So your local paper's gagged by its, ah, villainous proprietor. But what about the other news organizations? Radio Ridings?'

'*Them*,' spat my daughter. 'They don't know the first thing about what's important in this town.'

He smiled faintly. 'It's taken me all week and thousands of sweated words to say just that. They don't, do they?'

I choked. Even George raised her eyebrows. But Polly laughed aloud. 'Although,' she added with the air of one making a great concession, 'Mum did do a discussion on her show.'

'I meant news,' he said. 'It's the news programmes you want. Have they covered it?'

'Oh, sure. I don't think they even open our press releases.'

'But if there really is anything in the story?'

''Course there is.'

He shrugged. 'Better get them interested then.'

'How?' she demanded. 'Who do we talk to?'

'For goodness' sake, child, you're talking to him now,' said George impatiently. 'This ungrateful specimen has been imported as our News Editor, if you please. Isn't that so, Tom?'

'Are you?' exclaimed Polly. 'Well, you might have let on. Will you do something about The Willows?'

'Me?' His eyes widened. Until that moment he'd seemed in com-mand of himself, fraying the odd consonant perhaps, but other-wise coherent. Now, though, speech seemed to desert him. He stared at Polly for a second or two, then dropped his head on to his hands.

'Tom?' she said, more amused than alarmed. Obviously thinking this despairing slump was some kind of joke. 'Is George having me on?'

The grandfather clock clanged the quarter-hour into the yawn-ing silence. 'Great heavens, *supper*,' cried George. 'Tom, I will brook no excuses this evening, you are dining with me. Polly, if I'm to contribute to your Cecil B. De Mille epic, then you're going to be an angel and skivvy for me in the kitchen for half an hour.'

Even George didn't understand. She knew something was dreadfully wrong, but didn't know what. Only I had read the final paragraphs of Tom's report, where he'd made clear he was not planning to take up the job at Radio Ridings. And if his plans ended in a bath with a razor blade . . .

'Tom?' said Polly again, but more doubtfully now. 'Tom, are you OK?'

It seemed like hours but I suppose it was only seconds before he lifted his head. If his eyes were wet then probably only I was near enough to see. 'Fine,' he said, blinking. 'Sorry, sure, I'm fine. George mixes a powerful whisky.' His glass was beside him, untouched. 'However, yes, she's, um, absolutely right. For my *sins* . . .' I wasn't imagining the wry emphasis he put on the word; and I wasn't imagining, either, the change in his face, as he looked at my daughter. There was a warmth I hadn't seen in sixteen years, not since the day we'd lain in the sand dunes, since the day – who knows? – she might even have been conceived. 'I'm taking over as News Editor of Radio Ridings. For a while, anyway. So, um, I guess you'd better bombard me with your press releases. I can't promise anything except that I'll check the story out. However . . .' He hauled himself to his feet, stumbled a little and grasped the mantelpiece. His voice was steady, though, as he finished: 'However, I can promise you I'll do that.'

Polly whooped innocent jubilation; George clicked her tongue and hustled her towards the door. I was dumb and dizzy with relief. With more than relief – with wonderment. I was realizing that, quite as accidentally as I'd initiated Polly's life all those years ago, I now seemed to have given her father a reason for not terminating his. And that reason was Polly herself.

'Rose?'

I didn't trust myself to look up. I stretched out a hand mutely, too dazed, too full of emotion to speak. Felt him grasp it – and yank me to my feet.

'Why?' he demanded savagely. 'Why the the fuck didn't you tell me?'

23

'Tom's OK, isn't he?' said Polly as we drove home through yet more sheeting rain. This was high praise, coming from her. And indeed, in case it went to my head, she added: 'Better than most of your other boring BBC friends, anyhow.'

I should have been pleased by this unsolicited – not to say unprecedented – approval of Thomas. No, not simply pleased. I should have been enchanted, elated and even moved to tears that Polly had taken such an immediate liking to ... her *father*. The car skidded on a waterlogged corner and I grappled with the steering wheel.

That was how I felt inwardly. Out of control.

'Keep your voice down, Thomas,' I'd hissed, twisting out of his grasp, hurrying across the room. In the distance I could hear Polly asking whether George had got any crisps. I slammed the door and slumped against it.

'She *is* mine?' he said. 'My – child?' There didn't seem any point in answering. 'So why didn't you tell me? Years ago?'

I spun round, about to shout back at him, but couldn't. He was looking as much baffled as angry. I didn't know what had driven him to this despair, but I wanted to spare him any more pain. 'I did tell you,' I said gently. 'I wrote to you.'

He tossed his head back. 'Don't lie.'

'I sent a Registered Letter,' I said. 'Addressed it to Thomas Edward Featherington Wilkes, care of Magdalen College, Oxford. I can't answer for the spelling inside, because Lord knows I was barely literate in those days, but I made sure I got the address right.'

'I never got it.'

I half smiled. I couldn't help it. He sounded so like Polly at her most fractious. 'No? Then I suppose it was signed for by some other Thomas Edward –'

'The porter? A friend? How on earth should I know? If you did write.'

'Why should I lie?'

'You lied about everything else, didn't you? Giving me an address in this town which didn't even exist, promising –'

'For goodness' sake, Thomas,' I said, catching hold of his shoulders. 'Surely you can see why I did all that?' He shook out of my grasp, his face crumpling. I ached to put my arms round him, to comfort him. But he shied away, so I walked over to the table and sloshed wine into my glass. 'I'm sorry,' I said. 'Sorry for all the terrible things I said. Sorry you had to find out like this. Tonight, when . . .' I couldn't bring myself to put it into words.

'When I was going to kill myself?'

'Don't. You mustn't even say it.'

He swung away from me. There's a huge fireplace in George's drawing room. Massively ornate, massively ugly. He grasped the mantelshelf with both fists, letting his head fall forward. There was no fire, just a dusty grate, and a withered basket of heather. 'I doubt I'd have done it. Shaming, isn't it? All this melodrama, and I'd probably have flunked it. I did a week ago in that hotel. Just drank myself stupid. And tonight I mucked around for hours, recording my excuses for posterity. I imagine if you truly mean to kill yourself you just do it. You don't pack a suitcase ready to disappear if you change your mind. I'd always known I might just take off instead, and lose myself somewhere.' He glanced over his shoulder. 'But it wasn't a cry for help, nothing as pathetic as that. I wasn't playing games, I never intended you to come barging in. God knows, it's pretty humiliating being found with your soul stripped naked.'

'Hush . . .'

'I'm sorry, too,' he said abruptly. 'I should be thanking you, all that. If I haven't, it's because . . . Oh, because I'm a worm and I don't think I'm worth the trouble. But don't worry. For what it matters, I shan't try again.'

'No,' I said. 'No, I know.'

'Do you?' He looked at me for a minute. 'Yes, you would, of course. You always did know exactly what I was thinking.'

'You were always so transparent,' I said. 'Just like . . .'

'Polly?'

I gulped. 'She – takes after you.'

He actually seemed surprised. 'Does she? You know what I thought when I saw her? I'd never have realized, if you hadn't been shouting that it was all my fault . . . No, don't keep apologizing. We can't go on saying sorry. It's just, when I saw her, my first thought was that I knew her, must have met her before. Then I realized I was thinking of a painting that used to hang in my father's dressing room at Ashburtley. Terrible, chocolate-boxy portrait of my mother, done when she came out. All pearls and curls.'

'Polly reminded you of that?' I exclaimed, in spite of myself.

He gave a cough of laughter. 'Not exactly a twinset and tweeds girl?'

'You could say that.'

He didn't speak. Just gazed down at me, as though he was seeing me for the first time. Then let out a long, weary sigh. He didn't so much sit down as topple back into the armchair. 'So tell me.'

'Tell you what?'

'How the hell I've come to spend all these years without knowing she existed.'

There are times, though, when even I am not sure what the real story is. When I don't know where the artful spinning ends and only truth remains.

Take that picture of Rita, chugging out of Blackpool Station, a tear glinting in her eye. She was, genuinely, telling herself she loved Thomas enough to clear out of his young life. Oh indeed, this was one tart lost in admiration of the goldenness of her own heart. Was that what she *truly* felt, though?

After all, in the general run of her twenty-four years, Rita had not been much given to self-sacrifice. In fact, I'm hard put to think of a single object of desire, animate or inanimate, she had ever willingly relinquished. Moreover, as I've already observed, she was no fool. Thomas, in her view, was a mere child. He might be all starry-eyes and soppy poems now, but he'd soon outgrow that. Once he discovered that her body didn't hold monopoly rights on the novel delights of sex, he'd forget the likes of her and revert to his own kind, wouldn't he?

Rita had her pride, plenty of it. She'd seen enough of the way her dad treated Mum to have resolved early in life that no man was going to leave her sobbing into the kitchen sink. And so, the minute she recognized that what she felt for Thomas might be more than mere liking, I reckon it was a smart instinct for self-preservation that decided her to give him the boot. She wasn't going to go pratting down to his Oxford college – where she knew she'd be made to feel like a tin bucket in a china cabinet – just to allow him the luxury of recovering from his infatuation in his own sweet time. Thus, the invented Wakeborough address and the lies about Mum not having a phone. She expected he'd moon around for a while, swearing his heart was broken. Well, she wouldn't be too chipper herself, would she? But they'd both recover soon enough. And that was that.

Only that, of course, was not to be that. Accidents will happen. Had, as she would eventually discover, happened. Still, it could have been dealt with and forgotten if it hadn't been for Mum. Rita, you see, had taxied home from the station late that sultry Sunday night to discover the house empty. Stupefied, she learned from a neighbour that Mum had been taken into hospital, to have a breast removed. Mrs Bagshawe might have been 'under the doctor' for some time but, a modest woman to the last, had been reluctant to draw his masculine eye to the long-standing lump behind her right nipple. The operation was radical, but too late. It was only the beginning of a prolonged, pain-racked and irreversible progress.

Which brings me to the undoubted truths I prefer not to face. I don't care to think what would have happened if my sick and pious mother had not opened the card from the hospital and found this particular out-patient appointment was not for her, but for her daughter. Rita, appalled to discover Thomas had indeed left her with a little keepsake, was briskly assuring herself that God would understand the exigencies of a showbiz career, even if his earthly lieutenants were less broad-minded. Her mother, of course, didn't see it like that. I don't even remember the scene that followed. Honestly. Some things, like the pains of childbirth itself, are so bad nature seems to blot them out afterwards. But I dare say you, as easily as I, can imagine the battle for this unborn soul. The only variant on the familiar arguments was Mum's tear-choked whisper that this infant would give her something to live for. That God –

no, seriously, she said this and she *believed* it – that God would spare her to care for her grandchild.

And for all Rita had sneered at her mother for years, modelling herself instead on her dashing, devil-may-care absent dad, that was the clincher. Because she was quite unable to grapple with the notion that her mother might actually be dying. She simply couldn't imagine a world where Mary Bagshawe wasn't there in the corner shop, ready with tea, scones and refuge whenever she deigned to sashay home.

I also remember, because Mum shrank pitiably even as she herself ballooned revoltingly, Rita raging at God for pulling this contrick. A cruel and total con, because Mum never did live to see her precious grandchild. Although, by the end, even Rita couldn't have wished her to endure longer.

'Believe it or not, I went into labour cutting the ham sandwiches at my mother's funeral,' was all I said to Tom, with the glib polish appropriate to this oft-produced one-liner. Wasn't even strictly true. I'd left the neighbours to it, and had been in the act of pouring myself a whacking drink. 'Within a week of registering one Mary Bagshawe dead, I was back in the same seedy office registering another born. You can see why I got post-natal depression.' The flippancy was defensive, but it sounded crass. 'Anyway, that's why I ended up writing to you.'

'Why not before?' he said. 'I mean . . . didn't you know it was mine?'

''Course I knew,' I retorted, stung. But I couldn't really answer his question, because I didn't know. I wish I could wholeheartedly claim Rita hadn't wanted to wreck a teenage boy's life with fatherhood. Maybe, dimly, she did feel that. But that isn't the whole story because she wrote to him in the end, didn't she? I think it was as much because she was wary of him seeing her in that disgusting state, in that crummy shop, which she reckoned would cure him of his infatuation for good and all. I even seem to recall she was daft enough to imagine, for a while anyway, that once she'd converted the ugly lump into a cuddly bundle of white knitting – and handed it over to her mother – she could convert herself back into fancy-free, glamorous, irresistible Rita. Then, maybe, she'd crook one scarlet-taloned finger, and he'd come running . . .

Reality was a fat, black-clad, grieving slattern with fingernails bitten to the quick and a bawling, red-faced monster in a borrowed pram, being ticked-off by a harassed civil servant.

'I wrote to you because they wouldn't let me register you as the father,' I said to Tom. 'Reasonable enough, although I can't say Rita saw it that way.'

'Rita? You talk as though she's someone else.'

'It *feels* like that.' I said with a flash of irritation. 'As though it was all in another life. Anyway, I was told the father of an illegitimate child has to sign for himself. Otherwise, as the clerk whined at me, unmarried mums could walk in off the street claiming they'd been having it away with Elvis bloody Presley. So I posted my letter. I was only asking for your signature on a document but ...' I bit my lip. Remembered Rita gushing crazy tears over her pathetic little missive. All the bloody-minded stubbornness which had carried her through to this point had expired along with her mother. There was no question I'd been hoping for more.

Tom winced. 'I feel a complete bastard.'

'You mustn't,' I said, assailed with guilt. I shouldn't be pouring this out now. 'I don't – *can't* – blame you for anything. Besides, even if you had got my letter, you were only a child yourself, I knew that. That's why I didn't write again. I was daft to imagine you cared twopence for the likes of Rita Bagshawe.'

He blinked. 'Oh, come on. I may have been a tiresome kid as far as you were concerned, but you can't claim I didn't care.'

I stared at him. 'But when we were talking, in The Elms ... I mean, I know we were misunderstanding each other, but when I said you'd been fond of me once, you –'

'Of course I wasn't bloody *fond* of you. I was as agonizingly, ludicrously besotted as only a nineteen-year-old boy can be. One word from you and I dare say I'd have jumped off a cliff. I was out of my tiny mind in love with you.' He didn't say this with passion. It was just a slightly mocking recital of historical fact. But it sent the blood pounding up to my head. Only now was it dawning on me what all this meant. He'd never received my letter. He'd never abandoned me. 'So what happened?'

'Sorry?' I said stupidly.

'What did you put on the certificate in the end?'

'Oh, nothing. Don't worry, it's fine. Polly knows her father isn't named, she's always known. I didn't want her getting a nasty shock in adult life. She thinks he was a boyfriend from my first year at university, who died in a car crash before she was born.' I wasn't thinking what I was saying. Blotting out every coherent thought was the idea that Thomas had been out of his mind with love for me. As if I hadn't always known . . . I realized, with a start, that he'd risen to his feet and was staring down at me. My dazed smile faded as I saw his face.

'You've invented – been living one huge lie? All these years?'

I flushed. 'It wasn't all lies. Every word I told her about her father was true. What you looked like, how we used to talk, how funny you were, that you read classics, everything.'

'Like that I'm dead?'

'For Pete's sake, I had to say something! It just grew. You see, she thinks I jacked out of university first time round because of her. That I was just going back later, starting again.'

'You've rewritten your entire life history. Chopped years out of it.'

I jumped to my feet. 'I had to.'

'Chopped me out of it.'

'You were never in it. Not when I needed you.'

'Christ, Rita!'

'I'm not Rita. At least . . .' He was turning away, and I grabbed his arm. 'Thomas, don't look at me like that, as though I'm some kind of monster.'

I don't know quite how it happened. We didn't embrace, so much as collide, but I found myself with my cheek squashed against his shoulder, and his arms clamped round me. And everything changed in that instant, because every inch of me remembered his body. It was as though a contour map had been locked away inside me all these years: his every muscle and bone was familiar. I felt I'd come home. And in that instant I knew I wanted him. That I'd always bloody wanted him. And that, what's more, I was going to get him back. Nothing else mattered. This was my every barmy daydream made flesh and blood. Total insanity. Total, transfiguring happiness.

'Why do we make such godawful messes?' he groaned.

'It's not a mess.' It's a miracle, I was thinking. I've been given another chance. It would never have worked all those years ago, anyway, not with Rita. But now, in my new life . . . 'I'll make it all right.' Could I dump Polly here for the night? Take him home with me? 'I'll make you happy again.'

I didn't catch his words, but I heard the sadness and locked my arms round him more fiercely. 'Tell me what was so bad? So awful you could want to die?'

I felt him stiffen, but thought it was because George was shouting something from the kitchen. 'Surely you know about Lucy?' He said this almost matter-of-factly. 'My wife?'

'Now then, my dearios,' called George loudly, kicking open the door. 'We have a crisis. Since Polly seems to regard lamb casserole as akin to eating one's cousins, do I raid my cupboards and rack my brains for ethically acceptable substitutes? Or are Tom and I to dine *à deux*?'

We'd sprung apart anyway, but now he was walking to the door. 'Tom?' Alarm sharpened my voice. 'Tom, where are you going?'

'Just getting something from downstairs.'

George flattened herself against the door as he strode out. 'Dear me,' she said interestedly. 'You look rather as I felt when, after travelling halfway across the world and recording a two-hour interview with Maria Callas, I discovered I'd been issued with a dud microphone.'

All I knew was that my face was hot with embarrassment. 'Has he mentioned his wife to you?' I hissed desperately. 'What's she called? Lucy?'

George glanced over her shoulder. But he could be heard clumping down to the flat. 'Well, I had to say something,' she whispered. 'When I found the publishers had sent me a review copy of her book, for *Artsround*.'

'Review copy?'

'Lucinda Flint. Tom was married to the poet Lucinda Flint. Surely you knew that?'

'No.' So he'd married a poet. How *appropriate*.

'Of course, modern poetry by young women is *not* my forte, as you know. And although this being a posthumous collection does, I concede, present problems on the author-interview front, I couldn't help feeling it might please Stainless, with his sudden yen for poetry. Poetry by a female (big tick), written when she was barely out of her teens (gold star), and – God forgive me for joking about such things – *disabled* to boot. Naturally, I wouldn't dream of it, if Tom –'

'Disabled?' I said. 'Lucinda – Flint?' The name had triggered a memory. Not of poetry but of a glossy magazine feature, half-read in a dentist's waiting room. 'Did she have some dreadful illness?'

'Tragic,' murmured George, and put her finger to her lips.

Tom reappeared, and held out a cassette to me. 'I don't know if it makes any sense, but it's the best explanation I can offer.' I took it numbly. 'Oh, and' – he fished from his pocket Stephen's little dictating machine – 'better have this, too. I used the tape, but I've replaced it with one I found lying around –'

'How dared you introduce that beastly little gadget into my house?' interrupted George, with a theatricality which showed she had a pretty exact notion what he'd been recording. 'Never let me see it again.'

'Are we off then, Mum?' enquired Polly, lounging in with her Parka flapping from her shoulders. 'I'm starving.' When, helplessly, I nodded, she turned to Tom, holding out her hand with the manners I'd drummed into her and which, generally, she affected to despise. 'I'm so glad,' she said, with a saucy sideways glance at me, 'to meet *someone* at Radio Ridings who cares about the things that matter.'

'Not half so knocked out as I am to meet you,' he responded. He spoke lightly enough, but there was something in his voice which sent George's eyebrows shooting up. Even Polly blushed and, rapidly disengaging her hand, turned away to zip up her Parka.

''Bye,' said Tom to me. 'Um, thanks.'

'Forget it,' I mumbled. And I managed a smile before I stepped out into the rain.

Sorry. It's cheap and melodramatic saying I killed my wife. She wanted to die, or she told me she did. I thought I believed her.

Anyway, I never could take the euphemisms, and neither could she. Euthanasia, mercy killing – assisted exit, which she said sounded like an automatic door. Everyone's so scared of the word 'death', but there's nothing terrible about death. When you actually have to face up to it, death's fine. Commonplace, even. In the midst of life, and all that.

Look, Rita, have you ever been with someone who's dying? I never had, not before. And yet – never mind what I've felt since – that night, the night she died, I can only say I felt as though the so-called Grim Reaper was an old and familiar friend. As though I'd been through this business a hundred times before. As though I already knew exactly what it was like to watch a human soul ebb away. It was . . . amazing. Not distressing, certainly not frightening. I think maybe it's the only time in my life I've had a sense of something beyond this world, something good. Call it God if you like.

I remember how I wanted to discuss it with Lucy, ask her if she felt the same, only of course I couldn't, because she was the one who was dead. Well, dying. Certainly beyond rational conversation, although not, as it turned out, quite dead.

That was the catch. The mechanics of killing someone aren't nearly as straightforward as they'd have you believe. That's why I'm not prepared to risk pills now, not again. But it was Lucy had read all the bumf.

Do you remember her by the way? Lucinda? You met her once. When you came home for lunch, all those years ago, in your other life. God, it seems like another life to me, too, a whole other world. I'd never have believed it if anyone had told me then that, within a year, Lucy and I would be married. That we'd be setting up home together like a pair of kids playing house, both of us still at college . . .

Anyway, that's neither here nor there. Where was I? Oh yeah, the pills. It was Lucy, you see, who'd been stacking up the Do-it-Yourself euthanasia literature for years, only, of course, she couldn't do it herself. By the end she couldn't even hold a cup, let alone mix the cocktail of pills she reckoned would do the trick.

Turned out even the medics don't know everything. The doc who'd been treating her for years was a kindly old bird. He'd prescribed the right stuff. And, on the night she finally decided she'd had enough, we said our goodbyes, I crushed the pills up in vodka, put her favourite record on and . . . Oh, never mind. You can imagine. And she was going. I knew she was going. Her pulse got tinier and tinier. And I thought she'd died. Given up the ghost, as they say. Which was exactly what it was like. As though her shell remained in the bed, but the real Lucy was a ghost, which gently dwindled away into the air . . .

(HIS VOICE IS CRACKING AGAIN)

I left the room. Rang her sister. Came back to sit with her . . . And that's when I realized her heart was still beating. I could feel it. So faint, but I could feel it. I mean, what could I do? I couldn't let her come back, probably, God knows, with some unspeakable brain damage. It was the last thing I could do for her. The only thing. So I got a big pillow and . . . Oh Jesus.

There was a long, long silence on the tape. Then a muttered word which might have been 'sorry'. Followed by a loud click of the machine being switched off. Suddenly, incongruously, I was hearing Stephen talking about audience statistics. So that was it. End of Tom's message. I snapped the machine off.

I crouched on the edge of my bed. Pathetic: a middle-aged woman, sobbing like a jilted teenager. Of course I remembered the thin, droopy girl at lunch, flicking her plait, fixing yearning eyes on him. And apparently she'd got him. Married him while they were still students together. She must have been so young when she died. It was tragic, unimaginably awful. But I wasn't weeping for her, I was weeping for Thomas. Worse, I was weeping for myself.

Even though I knew I should be pitying her, I was, God forgive me, racked with the blackest, most coruscating jealousy of Lucinda Flint. No matter that I might have foreseen it, I could not bear the idea that Thomas – however madly he'd once been in love with Rita – had nevertheless forgotten her so fast, he'd married his childhood sweetheart within a year.

Even less could I endure his loving this Lucinda so much, he still wanted to follow her ghost into the air.

3 Artsround

Whether you're a bookworm, a music lover, a theatre buff or just a square-eyed couch potato, there'll be something for you in our hour-long weekly round-up of all that's new in the arts world. Regular features include **Album of the Month** and **Poets' Corner.**

Draft Script/Lucinda Flint feature
Artsround/Week 44

Producer/writer: Georgiana Penistone
Presenter: to be confirmed

And so, as they say, to verse. In our poets' corner this evening, we turn to Lucinda Flint, who died in January this year, aged only thirty-four. She left a collection of early work to be published after her death, however, which comes out this week, under the intriguing title 'Strange Airs'.

DISC: Delius 'A Walk to the Paradise Garden'.
DIP MUSIC AT 18" AND LOSE UNDER:

Now you might wonder why, instead of celebrating home-grown talent, we're featuring a poet who was born in Cumbria and spent most of her life in London. Well, for a start, she was a marvellous wordsmith — clever, funny and touching. More to the point, Lucinda Flint is the only poet I know of ever to immortalize in verse our own dear town. 'Wakeborough', she wrote, 'shiny citadel of dreams . . .' Can she be serious?

Flint/transcript/BBC Archive recording/LP 5408, band 2

TAPE A, LUCINDA: *I think perhaps, if you want me to sum myself up in a single word, then that word is 'pig-headed', No, honestly. I seem to have spent my whole life reaching for goals which always remain beyond my grasp. Robert Browning, you know, claimed that that was what Heaven was for, 'Ah but a man's reach should exceed his grasp' . . . and all that,* (laughs) *I hope he was right.*

Lucinda Flint, in an interview she gave to the BBC a few years ago. What's so touching about the picture she draws of herself is that, towards the end of her life, Lucinda Flint couldn't even reach out a hand to pick up a cup of coffee.

Not long after she left St Anne's College, Oxford, Lucinda was diagnosed as suffering from a rare form of rheumatoid arthritis. By her late twenties, she could no longer hold a pen, but she still managed to tap her poetry into a word processor.

Flint/Archive interview/details as before

TAPE A, LUCINDA: *Well they say economy's a great virtue in a poet, don't they? And, I promise, the fact that it takes hours to bash out a single line is the most amazing incentive to keep my verse tight.*

cont. over

24

'Yes, it's just after ten, on yet another rainy Monday morning, and this is Rose Shawe, with you for three action-packed hours. Well, the half-term holiday's upon us, isn't it? And if you're anything like me, unnatural parent that I am, you're already praying for it to be over . . .'

I stabbed the 'play' button on my opening disc and leaned back. So far so good. Time was when I used to be really neurotic about the first few words of a programme. I'd be scribbling notes beforehand, desperate to avoid the same old clichés, morning after morning. After all, how many ways are there of saying 'hello, this is me, and this is what's coming up'? George eventually took me aside. 'Look, did you ever script the intro to your cabaret routine?'

'What's that to do with anything?' I had retorted indignantly.

'More than you seem to realize,' she sighed. 'Put it another way. If you drop into someone's house for coffee, you don't arrive with a speech rehearsed, do you? You say the first thing that comes into your head. Well, that's what local radio should sound like. A friend dropping in, not a bloody great public address system.'

So now I don't plan my opening link. I make myself think about something quite different – anything will do – until the moment I open the mike, and then I trust to the Almighty appropriate words will trip out. My mind had been only too ready to wander that Monday morning, however. Focusing it back on the programme was the problem. '"Money, money money", from Abba, and a riddle for you. What do you do with a lump of dough and a splash of Lucozade? Why, the housework, of course. At least, you do according to a book of hints compiled by fundraisers at St Peter's Church, Maltbury. The editor is Enid Hope . . .'

I beamed across the desk as I introduced her, hoping she'd remember my plea not to touch her notes. I've been known to confiscate such props from nervous guests. Paper, in the hands of an amateur, rustles on mike like a collapsing oak tree. Much worse, though, is the stubborn conviction of certain interviewees that they'd sound twenty times better if only, instead of chatting, they could read the little answers they'd prepared earlier. They never believe me when I swear, hand on heart, there is nothing more surely guaranteed to kill an interview stone-dead. As well claim a waxwork replica is an improvement on flesh and blood. The difference to the ear between ad-lib chat and the pre-written word is just as glaring.

However, although Enid eyed her papers wistfully, she was soon chatting away about dough cleaning roller blinds and yes, truly, someone put a dazzle on an old brass tray by spilling Lucozade.

'I could have done with your book yesterday,' I said smiling. 'It might be October, but I was doing a little spring cleaning . . .'

Therapy, that's what it was. Spiritual balm in a bottle of Ajax. God, Mac was right, I *was* getting like my mother. Whenever troubles had clustered in my childhood (generally after he'd breezed through) I would invariably find Mum on her hands and knees, scrubbing the floors as though her life depended on it. And, for all that the youthful me had sneered I'd never end up like her, the Marigolds had come straight out yesterday morning. Long before a cold dawn slithered over the moor top, the pictures had been off the walls and the dining chairs up-ended on the table. The air was soon sweet with beeswax, sharp with lemon windowspray, and dancing with dust. By ten o'clock, which seemed the earliest hour I could legitimately pick up the telephone on a Sunday, I'd even black-leaded the grate.

To my dismay, the minute I tapped in George's number, Polly sauntered into the sitting room, night-shirted and yawning. Just as I would have done, twenty-odd years earlier, she sniffed the air disgustedly, as though this disruption to Sunday morning had been undertaken specifically to inconvenience her, and picked a path to the kitchen. I heard a clash of kettle and tap and prayed she'd stay out of the way.

'George? Rose. Tom up yet?' I twisted a duster between my fingers. 'Tom, hi. Look, I just wanted to say . . .' I'd been polishing this graceful speech of condolence along with my dining table. I'd told myself that it was not just mad to resent his late wife, but downright *bad*. I should be grateful that Tom at least remembered how he'd once felt about me. That would have to suffice to start with, because I'd no intention of giving him up. My every instinct bawled that I *deserved* Thomas and if he couldn't see that, then I would just have to go right back to the beginning and build our relationship afresh. After all, even the worst grief must soften eventually. It would take time, to be sure, but during that time he would need an understanding friend, a sympathetic ear ... 'I listened to the tape when I got home last night. Now I know about your, um, your poor wife, I wanted to tell you how –'

'Don't,' he burst out. 'Please, Rose, spare me the polite condolences. I can't take any more of them.' Ten months after she died, and still he felt like this? So much for rehearsal, I thought, George was right, ad-lib intros are better. Already, though, Tom was apologizing, yawning. 'Hardly awake. I slept like the dead last night.' The yawn exploded into a hacking laugh.

'Not funny,' I said.

'No.'

'How are you?'

'Fine,' he said, so fast he obviously wasn't.

I smiled into the phone. 'Pillock.'

'Lord, that takes me back. Pillock. You were always calling me a pillock.'

'Probably because you were.'

'Very true,' he said flatly and it was like a door slamming in my face. There was an awkward silence, then we both began to speak at once: I was apologizing lamely for waking him; he, I'd swear, sighed something about hoping I'd understand if ...

'Go on,' I insisted.

'Oh –' Suddenly, in that very instant, his voice changed. I can only describe it as being like a light switching on, a brash, unnatural light. 'No, actually I'm terrifically glad you've got me out of bed. I have to go into work.'

'*Work?* It's Sunday.'

'I thought you said you worked hard in local radio?'

'Well, we do, but –'

'Joke. I need to retrieve a report I wrote yesterday. I've a feeling I

172

signed off with some farewell-to-the-world bullshit, and they really will send for the men in white coats if –'

'Oh, *that*.' I was bewildered. He sounded so much more like the merry boy I remembered, and yet . . . 'Don't worry, I've got it.'

'What?'

'Your report. I saw it lying on Stephen's carpet and . . .' I blushed, a kid caught jam-handed with the tart plate. 'Why'd you think I came hurtling round to George's last night? Anyway, not to worry, it's in my desk drawer.'

'Both copies?'

'There's more than one?'

'God's sake, I didn't sweat all week for the benefit of the idiot who's supposed to be running the place. I left Howard's copy in the out tray at Reception. They won't have emptied it yet, will they?'

'Well, no.' I barely noticed the cavalier dismissal of Stephen, the man whom, until mere hours ago, I'd been determined to marry. My head was spinning. I couldn't equate this breezy voice on the telephone with the desolate ramblings on the tape I'd wept over last night. 'No, not until tomorrow.'

'Fine. I only need to amend the last couple of paras and –'

'What?' In my horror I nearly dropped the phone. 'You surely weren't thinking of submitting it still?'

'Why not?' Typical. Thomas had always been just such a mixture of brilliance and downright stupidity, and while I was prepared to believe he might be brilliant at his own job, that didn't mean he knew anything about radio.

'Because,' I said carefully, 'your report struck me as being not so much an appraisal as a full-scale demolition job. Look, I realize you were in a wretched state, and I don't entirely blame you for taking your miseries out on us –'

'Balls,' he interrupted – very amiably, mind. Well-mannered as ever. Pig-headed as ever. 'I may've had a few screws loose on the personal front, but I knew what I was writing. Your news set-up's a joke.' He was wrong, of course, as he'd learn once he'd been with us another week. But if Stephen glimpsed so much as half a page of that blistering prose, Tom'd find himself on the train back to London within an hour, never mind a week, because Steve would tell our Head of Centre there was no way they could work together. With, what's more, perfect justification.

'Surely,' I said cunningly, 'you only felt obliged to write the report for Howard because you weren't planning to take up the job?'

'Perhaps, but –'

'So I'll rescue the other copy before the post goes tomorrow, OK?' Polly wandered in with a mug of coffee, stubbed her toe on the vacuum cleaner and hopped over to a chair, cursing. 'Because I honestly think we need to discuss this, Thomas, before you –'

'That Tom you're talking to?' she exclaimed, scrambling to her feet again and squeezing past the sofa towards me. 'Great. Can I have a word?' The receiver was wrested from me and I had to listen as she steam-rollered across whatever Tom was replying with assurances that she would call at George's later this morning with all the Willows gen. No, truly, no hassle, she was coming into town anyway ..

'I didn't know you were out today,' I said after she jubilantly clapped the phone down. And, in the typical way of mother/daughter exchanges, this had nothing to do with what was vexing me.

'Got a problem? Don't say homework, because it's half-term.'

I did have a problem, yes, but I couldn't define it to myself, still less to Polly. 'I'm not sure you should be pestering Tom with all this Willows' – just in time I stopped myself saying nonsense – 'business.'

'He's really interested. Unlike some people.'

'Maybe, but . . .' But what? My feelings made no sense. Polly was the single indissoluble link between me and Tom. If Tom and I were to build afresh, here, surely, was the obvious foundation. I should be thanking God she liked him. But it was all happening too fast, slipping out of my hands. Polly and Tom belonged to separate parts of my life and I wanted to keep them apart until I'd sorted out my own relationship with him. If then . . .

'I'd better shift,' she sighed, cutting across my tangled thoughts. 'Kev's picking me up in an hour.'

'Kevin?' I gasped unguardedly. 'You're not going out with Kevin Henderson?' That, I thought, was all I needed.

Polly flushed. 'Don't you start as well. I've had enough of Grandpa bending my ear on the subject. We're just friends, OK? He's the only one of us who's got a car, that's all. He said he'd run me up to see Uncle Jim about the campaign. I hope you haven't used all the hot water because I want a bath.'

If she hadn't spent so long in the bathroom, I've no doubt she would have scurried to the door when the bell rang, and had herself whisked away in Kevin's precious car before I so much as glimpsed the boy. Polly, who had once dragged home her every little chum like a proud kitten with captive mice, was now prone to resent the faintest glimmer of curiosity about her friends. She would never have believed how reluctant I was to open my front door that morning. 'Hello, um, Kevin, is it?'

'Mrs Shawe? How nice to meet you.'

I don't know what I'd been expecting, but it wasn't this. A fresh-faced, gangly youth with horn-rimmed spectacles and sober mackintosh, Kevin Henderson was nothing like his father and, in truth, looked a lot more respectable than my daughter usually did, let alone some of her nose-ringed, dreadlocked Green confederates. As I led him into the sitting room, where he bashfully confirmed he was indeed hoping for a place at Cambridge – 'King's, actually, yes, medicine' – I found myself, in spite of everything, warming to the boy. He even stammered his admiration for the arts show, which I occasionally presented for George. He must be keen on Polly, I thought, if he felt he had to sweet-talk her mother. Sure enough, the look he gave her as she thumped into the room, with all the grace of a charging bullock, was touchingly worshipful. Lord knows why. Except . . .

As she brushed past me, I caught a distinct whiff of scent. My scent. My *best* scent. I looked at her more closely. Was that excitement in her cheeks, I asked myself incredulously, or could it be just the teensiest dusting of blusher? Because her eyelashes were undoubtedly thick with mascara. She turned on me, daring me to notice. So, of course, I didn't. Just waved them off with a shouted reminder (which I knew she'd forget) to give my love to Tom.

Moments later, as I slumped in a chair, wondering dispiritedly why my daughter had chosen to discover the male sex just when my own emotional life was in such an adolescent mess, the doorbell trilled again. Assuming she'd forgotten something – along with her keys – I strode back into the hall and flung open the door. For an instant, I gazed, mystified and exasperated, into empty space. Then a shrill voice chirped: 'Wotcha, gorgeous.'

I looked down and saw the small green face leering round the doorframe. With its emerald pelt, red felt mouth and gold button eyes, this apparition might not immediately strike you as resembling a ferret – but I recognized it. And, as the green furry neck grew longer and merged into the leather-jacketed arm of a short, grinning man, I also, with dismayed incredulity, recognized Ferdy the Ferret's famous sidekick. Looking older, certainly, as he emerged from his hiding place round the corner. Ash-haired now rather than bottle-yellow, but unmistakable, nevertheless.

'My God,' I whispered. 'Frankie.'

25

'Got it in one, love,' he said, and winked at his ferret-gloved hand. Like all the ventriloquists I've ever known, Frank never travelled far without his doll. 'Say hello, Ferdy. You remember Rita, don't you?' He looked up at the house. They both did. And, honestly, the ferret's red felty mouth flapped: '*Hey-up, Frank, this village's changed a bit since we used to bike out here as lads, hasn't it?*' Frank's own mouth was far from motionless (he always was a lousy vent) as the puppet squeaked on: '*Houses were that damp in them days, they'd catch newts in the mousetraps, Boom-boom.*' Frankie laughed uproariously. He'd had his teeth fixed, I saw. 'Well, then? How's our kid?'

Cursing Mac for letting me believe Kevin never saw his father, I stammered: 'I'm afraid you've just missed him.' And I was thanking providence he had, because he'd thereby missed my daughter too, who thought my singing career was an ad-hoc madrigal group at university. Honestly, it seemed my long-buried past was exploding out of the ground wherever I turned.

'Pardon?'

'Your son, Kevin. He's gone.'

The ferret hand had flopped and Frankie gaped at me, seemingly aghast. Then he broke into another wheezy laugh. 'Oh, *Kevin* you mean? Lorna's lad? By gum, she really got us going then, eh, Ferdy? *Got you going more like, you dirty old man. You thought our Rita meant you'd got her in t'pudding club all them years ago, and –*'

'Put that ridiculous puppet away,' I snapped. My neighbour, Sarah Cooper-Hyde, was climbing into her car with her mother-in-law. They were both staring across at us.

'Lorna's boy, stone me,' said Frank, still spluttering. 'Have they moved out this way? Small world. And here's me thinking –'

'Get in off the doorstep,' I said desperately.

'Well, now,' he said as I slammed the door behind him. 'You don't sound very pleased to see us.'

Pleased? I couldn't believe that even Rita had stooped to consorting with this . . . this *clown*. Everything about him: the piano-toothed leer, the jangling bracelet, his very existence outraged me. I did not, however, scream at him to stuff his ferret up his Khyber and get lost, which is what Rita would have done. I barred his passage along the hall and, with glacial composure, suggested that since we had nothing to say to one another –

'Speak for yourelf, I've plenty,' he interrupted, with the rhinoceros plating of any third-rate club comic who's ever competed with the pies. 'Didn't you get my postcard then?'

'Postcard? That was from *you*?'

'Mr Adorable, remember? Eh, that were a routine and a half that garter business were, real bit of class for a stag do. Nowadays, you know, it's all these blinking strippergrams. Tat, I call it.'

'I *don't* know,' I said, 'and I don't want to. I've left all that behind me. So –'

' 'Course you have, *Rose*, why'd you think I'm here?' And he pushed past me into the sitting room. 'I heard you on the wireless, didn't I, when I were up here, couple of weeks back. Yacking on about some tree, you was, with a right barmy old Doris and I'm thinking, Rose Shawe, Rose Shawe, know the voice, can't place the name. Then suddenly you goes shouting it's your dad pulling a stunt. Well, MacBagshawe, old MacMisery himself. Laugh? I nearly had a rupture.'

Oh, thanks a bunch, Mac, I thought furiously. Not content with humiliating me on air . . . 'Out,' I barked.

'Anyroad, next thing I know, my partner's saying – last night this was – how's about we ask this Rose . . . *Pardon*?'

'I'm asking you to leave.'

'Come again?'

I looked at him. Never mind the ludicrous trappings, I was seeing the perverted little creep inside. 'I want you out of my house,' I said, 'because the thought of that – that disgraceful party in your flat in Blackpool turns me sick to this day.'

'Party? What party?' he demanded. But he sounded uneasy. 'Look, you must've got the wrong end of the stick. I –'

'It wasn't me getting the wrong end of any stick that afternoon, it was some poor bloody under-age tart in a gymslip. You deserved locking up, the lot of you.'

His eyes bulged. 'You don't think I were in on owt like that? I'm a family entertainer, clean as a whistle. Nothing blue about Frankie Henderson.'

'Get out.'

'No, I flaming won't,' he said, with an indignation that surprised me. 'I'll not have muck like that thrown at me. I don't know about no party, but I can tell you one thing for definite: I wasn't at it. Have we got that straight?'

He met my gaze squarely. He might even have been telling the truth. Frankie's notion of sexual high jinks had been pinching a chorus girl's bum with the ferret arm. Mac, in philosophical vein, had claimed the puppet was a phallic alter ego. He hadn't even pounced on Rita so much as stumbled into her gold-digging clutches. Contempt for him mingled sourly with shame at myself.

'It was in your flat.'

'That's as may be, but . . .' He rolled his eyes resignedly. 'By, you always was a stubborn bunny. Look, if you must know, I had a deal on that place. Pal of mine, old schoolfriend, he used to lend it off me when I were away for, like, business entertaining, clients and such. Anyway . . .' The wizened grin returned. 'Long time ago, and I can see you don't want to talk about the old days. So how's about we get down to our own business?'

'Oh for God's sake,' I snapped, assuming that, for Frankie Henderson, there could be only one sort of business. 'I told you, I've long quit show business, so will you please just –'

'Are you deaf or what? I *know* that. It's the blooming wireless I've come about.'

'Hey, Rose,' said one of the reporters, dodging into studio with a yard of tape strung round his neck and a distracted frown. 'Heard the latest?'

A disc was pulsing out of the speakers. I was drumming my fingers and watching the clock. 'Have you seen Amanda?' I demanded. 'Surely the news meeting ended ages ago?'

'Search me.' Alistair, that was his name, was riffling through a pile of tapes, with a chinagraph pencil tucked behind his ear. 'I've had to miss it.'

I scowled. Once again, I was trapped in my padded cell, waiting for Amanda. Funny: with quilted sound-proofing on the walls, triple-glazed windows and a door the thickness of a mattress, you'd think you could sit in a studio like this and miss World War Three breaking outside, but I swear I could physically *feel* the buzz of trouble that morning. It was as if the very bricks and mortar had begun to hum when the meeting upstairs got under way. With Tom Wilkes in the chair. If I didn't find out soon what'd been happening, I would go mad.

'Well?' Alistair demanded, having found an empty spool.

'Well what?'

'The ILR franchise. We've found out who's fronting one of the bids.'

'Do me a favour,' I snorted. 'Who'd you think got the story? Me. I told Stephen about it first thing this morning.'

I'd had to say *something*.

Stephen had bounced into his office, a good half-hour earlier than he'd any right to, and found me frozen, scarlet-faced, beside his desk. Feeling like a bomb-disposal operative, I'd already filched Tom's report from Reception and now – fortunately – had just completed my covert duties by slamming Steve's dictating machine back into his drawer. However, it wasn't that which made me blush, jealously though he guarded his toys. No, it was rampant guilt over the Lamb himself. Ever since Saturday night I'd been thrusting aside the problem of Stephen. Now here he was, in the too, too solid, grinning, aftershave-scented flesh. Closing in with the very evident intention of sneaking a quick snog.

'I've identified one of the runners in the great franchise race,' I squawked. 'I knew you'd want to know.'

As a diversionary tactic, it wasn't bad. I don't know if you're acquainted with the procedure by which the Independant Local Radio Authority dishes out a franchise to launch a commercial station, but it's conducted with a cloak-and-dagger secrecy which makes Freemasonry look like the Tufty Club. They announce a slice of the airwaves is up for grabs. Interested parties scuttle around and form themselves into consortia to bid for it. Money, of course, is the real qualification for participation; radio expertise comes way down the list, although they always include some biro-in-the-breast-pocket engineering cove to handle the pluggery and kilo-hertz. Additionally, the men-in-suits like to add gloss by recruiting a home-grown celebrity to front their consortium. What spices the business is that these bids are submitted in sealed envelopes and no one – officially – need ever know who's competing. This, as you can imagine, provides rich ore for speculation and gossip. And, indeed, Stephen immediately ditched any amorous designs and demanded details.

'It's a consortium called Veridian, or something like that,' I said, as he walked over to the desk and shrugged off his jacket. 'And,' I continued, warming to my theme, 'you'll never in a thousand years guess who they've got on board as the celebrity window-dressing.'

'Sock it to me.'

'*Frankie Henderson.*'

Stephen blinked, 'Who?'

'Frankie Henderson,' echoed a soft voice behind me, and I spun round. Thomas walked in, twitched an enquiring eyebrow in my direction, then turned to Steve. 'Sorry to butt in, but I thought you'd like to know I'm here at last. Present, correct and, well, ready for duty.'

Correct? Ready for duty? He looked like he'd been dragged through a hedge backwards. His shirt was creased, his jeans were frayed and his shoelaces didn't match; he was jacketless, tieless, hopelessly styleless and . . . Oh, who did I think I was kidding? To my besotted eyes, he was utterly, irresistibly, wit-shattering gorgeous. Everything I'd ever wanted was embodied in that tall, shaggy man, standing there, with mere inches separating us. Mere inches, the last sixteen years and a dead wife. My heart was thumping somewhere in my throat and I looked helplessly from him to Stephen. Stephen, who was bright-eyed, shinily shod and immaculately pressed; Stephen who was sensible, presentable, marriageable . . . Everything I *should* want, and knew I didn't want any more. Worse still, that I had never really wanted, even as I'd so industriously set about snaring him. What was I going to do? I began edging towards the door. Eight thirty on a Monday morning is no time to play tortured heroine in this kind of drama.

'With you in a minute, Tom,' said Stephen and, even in my disordered state, I recognized this as a snub. 'Oh, I've got you, Rose. Funny little ventriloquist. Sort of green snake?'

'Ferret.'

'You sure?' he said doubtfully.

'Ferdy the . . . Oh, sorry, you meant am I sure he's in the running? Yes,' I said, uncomfortably aware of Tom behind me. Frank Henderson epitomized everything about my past I wanted buried for good and all. 'Absolutely positive. He actually called round to offer me a job if this Veridian bunch wins.'

'He surely can't be running the show though,' said Steve. 'Who's behind him? Where's the financial muscle?'

'Sorry. Didn't find out.' I couldn't tell Steve I was too busy ejecting the little toad from my house to ask intelligent questions. I risked glancing round at Tom, then wished I hadn't because I caught him staring into space with stony misery. Worse, the instant he sensed my gaze, he very visibly forced his features into a smile. Then turned to Steve and said cheerfully: 'You're obviously tied up. Shall I come back?'

'Now's fine. I've a heavy diary later. So . . .' I barely heard Steve's welcome-aboard spiel. I was still watching Tom. That polite smile might fool other people into thinking he was OK, but not me. I'd forgotten how tall he was. He loomed over Stephen like a telegraph pole, and I soon realized it was rattling the Lamb. He pattered though his small-team/young-team/dynamic-team routine (management-speak for understaffed, underpaid and overworked) and declared, unconvincingly, that he was sure Tom would relish the challenges of –

Suddenly Tom laughed. 'Shall we cut all this crap?' Steve gaped at him, and I nearly fainted. Surely he wasn't going to throw up the job and walk out now? 'Look, we all know why I'm here. I ballsed up in London. Howard's foisted me on to you and I can see you resent it. You've every right, particularly since the last time we met I was dead drunk, face down in an ashtray.' His smile was rueful. 'I can only grovel for my loutish behaviour, and promise to mend my ways. You didn't want me here any more than I, to be honest, wanted to come. Still, here I am, and I can only say I'll try to fill this job to the best of my, um, rather tarnished abilities.'

I breathed again. And I thought Steve could have offered more in response to this handsome speech than an embarrassed mutter (typical man) about appreciating Tom's frankness. However, relief that he wasn't quitting mingled in me with the recognition that working in the same building as the two of them was likely to give me a nervous breakdown unless I got something sorted out. Suddenly I realized Tom was gazing at me enquiringly. 'Sorry?' I said.

'I was just asking Tom how his report was shaping up,' explained Stephen.

I flushed crimson and, before I could gather my wits, Tom was shrugging and telling Steve that, um, on balance, he thought he'd rather decided against committing his ideas to paper.

'Oh really?' In those two grim words, I heard the Lamb concluding he'd been right all along, that Tom had been drinking himself into a stupor all week and had probably never so much as switched on the radio.

'My fault,' I felt obliged to stammer. 'I suggested to Tom he should wait. Until he'd settled in. Got the hang of the place.'

'Oh was *that* the idea?' asked Tom innocently. 'I got the impression it was because nothing an ignorant telly pillock like me could produce would be worth the paper it was written on.'

Stephen nearly fell over his desk. Tom grinned at me. 'Don't be silly,' I hissed. I could hardly explain to either of them I'd seized his stupid report because it would blow sky high his chances of staying here. Staring at my feet, I burbled something about local radio being very different from television.

'Quite,' Stephen agreed, shooting me, nevertheless, a distinctly *et tu Brute* look. He likes his reports, does the Lamb. Amanda swore he'd once requested one on the watering of office plants.

'I can see it's a different culture,' said Tom equably, 'and I'll do my best to learn. But I can't help thinking that, at root, news is news, wherever you are and whatever the medium. You know the old cliché, the story that someone, somewhere, doesn't want told.'

He said this with a particularly sweet smile. Just such an expression does Polly wear when she's at her most dangerous. Angelic, abstracted – and stubborn as hell. I began to realize that confiscating his report might not, by any means, have defused the bomb. 'I'm looking forward to getting down to work,' he added. 'What time does this news prospects meeting start?'

26

'Gotta talk,' panted Amanda, crashing through the studio door. Or she would have crashed through if the door weren't so padded and pneumatically restrained a faint wheeze was its loudest protest.

'Where've you *been*?' I wailed. Rhetorical question. I could guess exactly where she'd been; clustered with her coven round the coffee machine, just as she always was if anything remotely gossip-worthy had occurred in the prospects meeting. 'Look, one minute and I want to hear *everything*. End of this disc. I'm putting Rambling Jim on and then –'

'No,' she yelped, brandishing a reel of tape. 'That's just it. Jim hurtled in, in a real lather; he wants to change his piece.'

'He *what*? But I've got it all lined up, sweet little story about a tame pheasant in his garden.'

'Which got splatted under a milk lorry this morning. Jim said it'd break his heart if we put it out now. Good thing he'd already got next week's ready.'

I ripped the old tape off the machine and laced in the new, barely had time to line it up before the music was fading and I backlinked, gave a station ident and read, straight off the cue sheet, 'Time for our regular outing with Jim Rumbelow, who ventures down to the waterside this week, in search of a very fishy story . . .'

SPLOSH! echoed in my headphones, followed by a glugging, which suggested I might, in my haste, have laced the tape inside-out. I twiddled the levels until I heard Jim rumbling that there was surely nothing lovelier on the ear than the babble of an English brook. Whereupon I pushed the cans back from my ears, mopped the sweat from my brow and slumped over the desk. This morning, as I said to Amanda, was proving too damned eventful all round.

'Why?' she enquired innocently.

But I couldn't tell Amanda about my predicament: how miserably I was torn between guilt over Stephen and hopeless longing for Thomas. I'd felt a real cow when Steve caught my arm as I left his office, whispering (*apologetically*) that he'd be grateful for any help I could give Tom while he was finding his feet. Mind, that hadn't stopped me hurrying out to catch up with Tom and breathlessly offering just that. Foolishly, though, I also went on to offer a sympathetic ear whenever he needed one. He'd stiffened. 'Shit, Rose, don't worry. I won't be inflicting any more maudlin twaddle on you. I'm OK.'

'No you're not.'

He looked at me, then shrugged. 'So I'm not. But hard work and soft drinks will soon sort me out. Stop pulling faces, will you? Burying the battered soul in work may be a hackneyed remedy, but there's nothing wrong with it. By the way, your leader's a bit of a comedian, isn't he? I tried to catch your eye when he got on to – what was it? – vectoring the critical productivity performance paths? Honestly, I –'

'Sorry,' I muttered. 'Must dash.' I can't even claim it was loyalty to the Lamb which prompted my abrupt exit. It was this game Tom was playing I couldn't bear. This over-bright, joking camaraderie when I knew, inside, he was as wretched as all hell.

'I got a bit caught up earlier on,' I explained lamely to Amanda. 'With, um, Stephen and Tom Wilkes.'

'Were they at each other's throats even then?'

I winced. 'They are now?'

'You should have been at the meeting.'

Oh God. 'Lively?'

'*Explosive.*' She shook her head in wonderment. 'Tom really picks his moments. He just sat there at first, as we ran through the diary, with that gloomy, dead sexy scowl he has, like he's lost in a world of his own . . .'

The next world, I thought blackly, with his wife. But I could cure him, if only he'd let me.

'. . . and I was beginning to think he wasn't going to open his mouth again when suddenly, right out of the blue, he asked whether anyone had looked into the tip at The Willows. You remember? The story about –'

'Do me a favour. My dad lives there and my daughter's practically spear-heading the campaign.' And all the time Jim's voice was rumbling on in the speakers behind us, comforting as cocoa, and we didn't hear a blessed word.

'Polly is? Good on her. Yeah, well, Tom said he thought it should be checked out. And old Stainless said . . .' Whereupon Amanda produced what I had to concede was a smart impersonation of the Lamb: '"Good point, Tom, but we haven't the budget flexibility you're used to in television. We have to prioritize," blah-diddly-blah, you know, the usual leaner-meaner-cleaner rubbish. "We can't resource speculative investigation when our remit is comprehensive coverage of all local news." And that's when Tom said, "What news?" Just like that. Because he claimed he couldn't see a single decent news story – what he'd consider a story – on the day's agenda so far.'

'We're a small and civilized town,' I snapped. If Tom was going to carry on like this, Steve would have him out within a week – and I wouldn't blame him. 'What does he think we should do? Commit a few murders to spice up the bulletins?'

'Our agenda read to him,' persisted Amanda gleefully, 'like a cobbled-up patchwork of PR handouts, network hand-me-downs and diary fillers. God, Rose, it was *electric.*'

'I can imagine.'

'And then he gave a huge smile – the guy has got the most fabulous smile – and said this had to be his fault as much as anyone's. After all, he'd been dossing all last week, hadn't he? But if there was anyone interested, he'd appreciate seeing press cuttings and scripts of anything we'd done in the past about The Willows or Trevor Green. I nearly got trampled under the rush. Mind you,' she added, 'he already seemed pretty clued-up. Can't imagine what's got him on to this one.'

I didn't enlighten her. Polly's good humour last night had been incandescent. I'd put it down to young love and Kevin Henderson, but maybe it was the triumph of enlisting Tom to her cause. She'd even been moved, sunnily, to assure me that, this being half-term, she'd be listening to my show this morning.

'That's funny,' said Amanda suddenly.

'What is?' And I swear it was only at that moment I began to reflect how uncharacteristic it was of Polly to show any interest in my programme. With that very particular abstracted smile on her face, so like Tom's . . .

'Nothing, really,' said Amanda. 'When I said "The Willows" just now, it was as though old Jim echoed me.' She stopped laughing. I slammed up the volume on the studio speakers.

'. . . be a babbling brook, but the residents of The Willows, in what should be the peaceful twilight of their years, have had to put up with something smelling more like the outflow from a chemical works . . .'

'Oh my God,' I gasped. 'How *could* Jim? I told him to keep his politics off the air.'

'. . . Now they'll be asked to foot the bill to clear it up. Yes, a little bird tells me Mr Green's fancy landscaping plans will likely cost these poor old folk more than two thousand pounds a head, on top of their regular service bills. Now in my book, this is blackmail. Because what Mr Green is saying is pay up or shut up.'

Amanda's face was as horrified as my own. 'What does the old fool think he's doing?'

But I had seen the light. Where had Polly been yesterday afternoon, after visiting Tom? At Uncle Jim's, that's where. 'He knows exactly what he's doing. So does Polly. Probably half of COSH too. He deliberately sneaked this tape past us. I bet you a tenner that bloody pheasant is still wandering round his garden. Hush, I'll look for a pot-cut.' The tape was nearly finished, however. The most I could do was try to limit the damage with my backlink. 'A very *personal* point of view from Jim Rumbelow. And for the other side of the story, I will of course be inviting a spokesman from Lime Holdings on to the show, who I'm sure will be anxious to answer Jim's, um, comments.'

They evidently were. The phone was flashing even before I'd put the next disc on. I let Amanda answer it and just sat there, head in hands, composing grovelling apologies to Trevor Green. I was furiously angry – with Jim, with Polly and, most of all, with myself. Because it was I who'd committed the biggest crime of the lot. I'd broadcast a tape without checking it first. Worse, I hadn't even listened as it went out because I'd been too busy gossiping with Amanda. I may have been conned, but I'm producer as well as presenter of the show and the responsibility for what goes out rests with me. *Mea* no question *culpa*.

'Actually,' said Amanda, covering the mouthpiece with her hand, 'it's George.'

I grabbed the phone. Expecting instant advice on my predicament or, at the very least, commiseration, I heard instead: 'Sorry to intrude while you're on air, old love. I'd have left a message but Amanda said you could talk. Won't take a sec. Thing is, about this feature for the arts prog, *marvellous* news, there's a full half-hour interview with the woman in Archives down in London, and I wondered if you'd be a darling and –'

'Not now, George,' I wailed. 'Anything you like, but not now. I gotta go.' I'd seen Tom flashing past the cubicle window. He burst through the door and halted, mouth open, a volcano awaiting permission to erupt. 'Go ahead,' I said miserably. 'Mike's shut.'

'Tell me I haven't heard what I think I heard.'

'But it's a short disc. Only twenty-odd –'

'What're you playing at?' he roared, striding over to the desk. 'Give me the tape, for God's sake. Has a lawyer heard it?'

'Are you kidding?' I muttered. '*I* bloody well hadn't heard it until –'

'Christ, I do not believe this place. You're broadcasting allegations of blackmail and you haven't even listened to the tape?'

Guilt sparked me into shouting back that he was a fine one to talk. 'You put out a whole television programme without bothering to watch it. At least I . . . Oh hell. *Quiet!* Five to twelve, here on Radio Ridings. Our Good Neighbours phone-in coming up after the news headlines, but now we're going over to Claire Small in AA roadwatch for the latest travel reports . . .' I couldn't even explain to Tom, let alone apologize. I had to listen to the breathless babble of broken gas mains and temporary traffic lights as he grabbed the offending tape and stalked out of the studio.

I don't know how I got through that phone-in. We would have been taking end-to-end calls about The Willows if Tom, apparently, had not ruled that we were to do nothing – but *nothing* – more about the issue. All this Amanda explained in whispered bursts over talkback. News had taken over. Stephen was listening to the tape upstairs. Tom was bracing himself for an onslaught of libel lawyers. They were all running round like crazy, trying to put together a package for the lunchtime news. Eventually I reached the safe haven of a long piece of music and stabbed the talkback button. 'I promised on air I'd give right of reply,' I said. 'Can't I just get Trevor on the phone now? Let him give his side?'

Amanda, framed in the cubicle window, looked as despondent as I felt. 'I tried to tell Tom how Jim swung a ringer on us. But he just said news was handling it.'

'He doesn't understand local radio,' I wailed. 'It's not like the national stations, broadcasting into the great anonymous ether. We *know* our listeners personally. I know Trevor. And if he's been insulted on my programme, then the least I can do . . .'

She shrugged and shook her head.

Tom doesn't trust me, I thought. He doesn't believe I'm up to dealing with serious issues. So much for building our relationship afresh. He obviously still sees me as some daffy ex-nightclub singer, only fit for spinning a few discs and chattering about community support groups. He doesn't realize I'm a professional broadcaster, used to interviewing government ministers as well as housewives.

The talkback clicked in my headphones again. 'By the way, he's said he's sorry,' Amanda's voice crackled. 'Left a note at Reception.'

I slewed round to look at her behind the glass. 'Tom?'

'Jim, of course. Apologized for leading us up the garden path.'

'Great.'

'Yeah, yeah, I know, but it's sad really, because he says he knows he'll get the push after this –'

'What's his phone number?' I interrupted. 'I want a word with Polly's favourite uncle, and it won't wait until I'm off air.' But the call rang unanswered. Still fuming, I picked up my pen and a pad of paper. 'Dear Jim,' I scribbled, only to have to thrust it aside, and open my mike again. By the time the programme was finished, however, so was my letter.

It's all very well writing apologetic notes now, but the damage is done. I warned you, you can't use this station as a soapbox. And as for chucking round accusations of blackmail . . . Our new Assistant Editor is shouting about lawyers and libel writs. For Heaven's sake, Jim, you're supposed to be taking us on gentle stroll through the hedgerows, not a headlong gallop into the civil courts. What's more, it was a mean trick to pull on me, because I've been made to look a complete idiot.

> You're sorry – well, so am I.
> Yours, Rose

WILDTRACK/FX COMPUTER OPERATION

TAPE A, LUCINDA: *I always wanted to be able to sing. Unfortu-nately, when I open my mouth, the noise I make is like the screech of a rusty hinge. Or so kind friends tell me. This has nothing to do with my stupid illness, by the way. It's always been the same and it used to break my heart when I was younger and, you know, cherished these dreams of driving men wild with desire with my siren songs, only to be told I was the next worst thing to tone deaf. (LAUGHS) No, I won't demonstrate, just take my word for it. But I've sometimes wondered, if this doesn't sound too utterly potty, whether I haven't always been trying to sing in words because I couldn't sing in musical notes. As though my poems are my songs . . .*

DISC: Ralph Vaughan Williams 'A Lark Ascending'. CD, band 2
DIP MUSIC AT 15" AND HOLD UNDER:

TAPE A, LUCINDA: *I do love the actual music of words. And these days when I tend to be cooped up in one room most of the time, it's only too easy, if I'm in a particularly path-etic mood, to picture myself as a rather scrawny little caged bird, singing for the sky and trees I can't fly in any longer. Gosh, you know people are terribly ready to tell me how brave I am but – look – I can be quite nauseatingly self-pitying.*

TAKE CRESCENDO IN MUSIC THEN FADE AND LOSE UNDER:

Lucinda Flint called this collection of her early work 'Strange Airs', and there's a pun behind the title. Some of the poems are wry and witty parodies of well-known songs. 'Are you going to Wakeborough Fair?' for example. Yes, I told you we got our five seconds of fame in this book. And do you re-member this hoary old ballad?

DISC: Harry Belafonte 'Scarlet Ribbons'. CD band 3
TAKE HALF CHORUS THEN FADE UNDER:

TAPE B: Poem, Page 17, 'My Love at Prayer'
In words: 'I looked in, to pick a fight . . .
Out words: . . . it's his affair.'
Duration: ? (not yet recorded)

cont. over

27

'It's a poetry book, what else?' said Polly as she clambered into the car beside me that evening, shiny paperback in her hand. 'By Lucinda Flint. You know, Tom's wife. Kevin bought it for me. Sweet of him, wasn't it?' Even in the dim glow of the car's interior light, I saw she was pink-faced as she continued: 'Love poems and stuff, but it's not bad. Not soppy or anything. Quite funny actually.'

My fingers itched to take it from her, but I set them firmly back on the steering wheel and restarted the engine. I didn't *want* to read Lucinda Flint's love poems, funny or not. Besides, I'd other matters to raise with my daughter. 'Polly . . .'

'I know,' she said. 'I know exactly what you're going to say and I'm sorry, OK? Uncle Jim thought if he sneaked the tape in, no one could blame you.'

'Oh yes, they could blame me,' I retorted, although Steve couldn't really bollock me, not as he would anyone else. After ten squirm-making minutes of him expressing pained surprise I'd finally understood why there were rules about sleeping with the boss. Sheepishly, we'd concluded by agreeing he would pass my apologies to Trevor, along with his own. 'It's my show,' I said, 'and –'

'Yeah, yeah, I realize that now. I've, uh, compromised your professional integrity, haven't I?'

I nearly missed the turning on to the dual carriageway. 'Come again?'

' 'S what Tom said this afternoon. Didn't he tell you?'

'I've been out. Recording an interview.'

'Oh, well, I rang him to see if he'd heard Uncle Jim, but when he sussed Kevin and me were in on it, he was but *seriously* pissed off. Had a real go at me.'

'He did?' Because she sounded perfectly cheerful.

'Totally ballistic. And I see now he's right, it was a dumb trick.

As he says, campaigning's like journalism, it's all about facts, not opinions. You don't get anywhere just by shouting your views louder. You have to dig out evidence to back them up.'

'Yes,' I said stupidly. 'I mean . . . Yes.'

'So that's what we're going to do. Literally. We're organizing a mass dig on the tip for Saturday. We'll publicize it with the video at the Town Fayre, invite everyone to bring a spade, and get whatever we uncover analysed.'

'Analysed where? By whom?'

'We're working on that,' said Polly loftily, adding: 'Tom thinks it's a great idea.'

Relief that Tom realized I wasn't devoid of editorial ethics was spiked with dismay at this swift-burgeoning friendship between him and Polly. Wonderful, if Tom and I were to get back together, if the day ever came to tell her the truth, but otherwise? What if Tom didn't want me, but did want to hang on to this newly discovered daughter? The idea was unendurable. I *had* to wrest him back from Lucinda. As we were going into the house, I asked Polly if I could, um, take a look at the poetry book Kevin had so kindly given her.

'Some other time, OK? I'm taking it up to the bath. By the way, have you got any of that hair-removing stuff? I want to have a go at my legs.'

Poetry in the bath? Stripping her legs? My God, I thought, torn between amusement with her and dismay at myself, I'm not the only one who's got it bad.

'I shouldn't have lost my temper,' Tom insisted when he came to find me early the next morning. I wasn't in the best of tempers myself, as it happens, because I'd just slammed the phone down on my dad, but that didn't stop me beaming soupily and admitting my carelessness. I also said I was sorry for throwing his débâcle on *Fulcrum* back at him.

'Fair comment. After all, I really did give the lawyers a field day.' He laughed, but I wasn't taken in. There was a bleakness behind the bright smile. 'Whereas we're in the clear, have you heard?'

'What?' He was perched on the edge of my desk. I ached to touch him with a longing so intense I couldn't believe it wasn't mutual. But then I'd felt the same at thirteen about John Lennon. For all he was locked in the telly, I'd been convinced he shared my feelings. I anchored my hands on a pen. 'Oh, you mean about The Willows? Yes, Steve said he was going to ring Trevor and grovel.'

'You're joking. I hope.'

'You think I should've apologized myself? Surely it's better coming from the boss?'

'We've nothing to apologize for,' he said exasperatedly. 'That's the whole point. Your friend Jim was pushing his luck calling it blackmail, but he got his facts right. That bastard Green really is planning to offload the clear-up costs on to the residents. I wouldn't let him loose on your show yesterday, because I was afraid he'd try and flannel his way out, but they can't deny it now. Turns out the letters'd already been posted, thank God.'

That at least snapped me out of my lovesick trance. 'Who's thanking God?' I squawked, seizing my bag and rummaging furiously. 'Not me, for sure. I'll have you know my dad lives at The Willows and I pay his service charges.' I thrust at him the large envelope which had plopped on to my doormat that morning. Across four pages of tasteful pistachio green were listed Lime Holdings' alternative schemes for landscaping the nature reserve – with price-tags which suggested the stream might become Lower Mill's answer to Canary Wharf. If Polly had been within reach, I'd have throttled her. So much for her campaigning. Mac's response, when I'd rung him, was only to complain that this would scupper his plans of a quick sale. Not a word about what it would do to my bank balance. I remembered Trevor on Saturday, assuring me plans for The Willows were in hand, smiling as he said Chatsworth wasn't built for twopence. 'You've got to hand it to Trevor Green,' I said as Tom gave me back the letter, 'he's one hell of a smooth operator.'

'Crook, you mean?'

'God, you don't change, do you? I remember you . . .' But a buzzing office was no place for recalling a much younger Tom, ranting about fat-cat landlords. 'No, I don't mean crook. You think I haven't checked the lease? Lime Holdings fulfilled their contractual obligations by spreading some topsoil. Further cosmetic improvements are subject to residents' approval and willingness to bear two-thirds of the costs. Et cetera, et bloody cetera. Trevor

Green hasn't got where he is today by planting free tulips for senior citizens. He's a hard-headed businessman who –'

'Who stinks,' interrupted Tom cheerfully. 'Everything I hear confirms it. I spent yesterday evening on the phone, tracking down every friend-of-a-friend I could in newsrooms up here. Plenty told me Green was well known as a twenty-two-carat shit, and warned me to watch my step. But there was one chap, a television reporter in Leeds, who nearly jumped down the phone trying to find out what I'd got on Green, and then swore blind he'd never heard of him. That's when I knew I really was on to something.'

'Give me strength.'

His mouth twitched. 'Go on. Tell me I'm a pillock.'

'Don't tempt me.'

'Still, you're right. On the face of it, Green isn't the villain of this particular piece.'

'Thanks very much,' I said. 'I wish you'd tell my daughter that, because . . .' But the words 'my daughter' somehow tripped me up. She was his daughter too.

Tom saw my stricken look, and sprang to his feet as though a fire alarm had gone off. 'Yeah, well, you're busy. I'll fill you in some other time. As I've said to Polly, unless it can be proved there's something seriously nasty festering under that tip, there's no villain at all, and no story.'

I was beginning to twig. He was happy to talk about work, but scared witless of anything more intimate. Hell's teeth, what did he think I was likely to say in a crowded office, with phones trilling, tape-machines screeching and Amanda watching us beadily from the far side of the desk? What's more, I was due in studio any minute. But I found myself babbling that, if there were indeed tadpole-endangering substances buried on the site, then I supposed responsibility would rest with whoever had owned and run it as a tip. Not that I gave a stuff. I just wanted to keep him here.

'Sure,' he agreed, relaxing against the desk again. 'It was a company called Vertco; I've established that much. I'll have to see what else I can turn up in the cuttings files, but it's an uphill struggle.'

'Oh?' I said. In that instant a plan began to form.

'Well, your boss's right about one thing, if nothing else.' He shrugged. 'There isn't the manpower for speculative investigation. He's got the place rotated up so tight, you let one reporter loose and you're five stories short of a bulletin. It's crazy. Everybody's correspondent for something, no one's a straightforward honest-to-God hack. Still, I'll have a bash this evening but as I don't know the first thing about this town, who's who, what's what . . .'

Bingo. 'Can I help? Polly's staying at a friend's. I've got a meeting after work, but it won't take long.'

'Would you?' He beamed. 'Thanks. It'd be absolutely terrific if you could spare an hour or so in here.'

'Here?' I squawked. 'I was thinking you might like to come round to supper.' A mistake. I knew it, the minute I'd spoken. His face clamped shut, and he muttered something about needing the cuttings files, wanting to chase up a few leads on Trevor Green . . . I wasn't fooled. This wasn't Trevor Green coming between us, this was the wife. I could almost see Lucinda's ghost, twining icy, jealous hands round him. I jumped to my feet, grabbing running order and discs. 'Sorry, due in studio,' I snapped. And couldn't stop myself adding: 'If you want to waste your evenings chasing Trevor Green, fine. Personally, I'd be happy if I never heard his bloody name again.'

'Rose,' said Trevor Green. 'We can't go on meeting like this.'

'Good heavens,' I stammered. 'I didn't know you were here.' Here was a conference chamber in the Town Hall. A meeting to agree the final details of the Town Fayre was due to start, and I dare say I'd have spotted Trevor long since if my gaze hadn't been riveted to item three on the agenda. The Rotary Club raffle, I'd read, was now to be drawn by well-loved family entertainer Frankie Henderson . . .

The annual Fayre, I should explain, is an ancient civic tradition invented all of eight years ago, when the heritage brigade got their hands on the old Market Hall. To be sure, the market square had once been the site of a Michaelmas horse-and-hiring gathering, but that had long ago long dwindled into dodgem cars and toffee-apples in Meadow Park. When, however, a benevolent European Community grant restored our Market Hall to its Victorian glory, there was an embarrassing need to find something to fill it. The glass-canopied, iron-curlicued pavilion was obviously too splendid for mere market stalls. So, with much grumbling, the cheese, knickers and pork-pies were banished to a hangar behind

Woolworth's, and the Market Hall was redesignated a *venue*, for concerts, craft fairs, conferences and the like. The Fayre was a cocktail of all these and more besides. It encompassed everything from home-made jam to steel bands, along with stands for local societies and, indeed, local pressure groups. Which was how Polly and her chums had secured a patch for COSH.

Such a motley jamboree took some organizing. I, you may be surprised to hear, was not actually on the committee. I was here at the meeting only because my show was to be broadcast live from the event. The *Gazette*, however, had a big stake in the Fayre, so it wasn't surprising the proprietor had shown up. The very person whom, in the light of yesterday's disaster, I least wished to meet.

'I'm sorry,' I said baldly. All very well for Tom to claim we didn't need to apologize. He didn't understand local radio, didn't live in Wakeborough, didn't realize Trevor was a seriously big cheese round here ... And for all I wasn't happy at the prospect of shelling out my deposit account to improve the view from Mac's window, I was a fair-minded woman. I couldn't blame Trevor for demanding his legal dues. I was just praying the residents would opt for the cheapest scheme.

'Shush, shush,' he murmured. 'Your boss explained it all, very civilly. This Mr Rumbelow spun you some cock-and-bull ...' He chuckled, 'Sorry, no pun intended. He spun you a yarn about his pet pheasant, and you'd no idea what the old so-and-so was springing on you, right?'

'I hadn't,' I said. 'Honestly. It won't happen again.'

'I'm sure it won't.' Something about the way he said this chilled me for an instant. Silly. In the light of my conversation with Tom this morning, though, I couldn't help but appraise Trevor afresh. A broken-nosed thug in Savile Row suits? A soft-voiced, smiling, twenty-two-carat shit? He was graciously pressing on me a coffee he'd rescued from a passing tray, smiling rather oddly, I thought. As though he were amused by some rich private joke. 'By the way, thank you for your letter, Rose.'

'Letter?' Stupidly, I was thinking of the stinging missive I'd sent Jim. I made a mental note to ring him.

'The Arts Festival. The list of events for sponsorship looks very interesting.'

'Oh that. Oh, um, good.' I was amazed, and impressed. I would never have dared bring it up. Pretty tactless to ask the guy for money the day after he'd been, if not strictly speaking libelled on my show, then pretty comprehensively insulted. I only wished Tom Wilkes were here to witness the fruits of a civil apology. This was what local radio was all about, I thought. Neighbourly give and take. 'I was rather hoping the string quartet series would suit you.'

'Ah, well, that's up to you, isn't it?'

I blinked. 'Surely you'd prefer to choose for yourself?'

Trevor's smile didn't waver. 'I don't think I want to go putting my hard-earned pennies into some festival when the organizer's trashing me on her radio show, do I?'

I gulped. So much for neighbourliness. 'I'm sorry you see it that way. It seems rather hard that the Festival should be penalized for what I admit was my mistake.'

'Now, now. I didn't say I wasn't going to sponsor you, did I? Take a look at this.' He'd thrust out a hand which, for all it was pinkly manicured and expensively be-watched, looked as though it could have smashed through a few planks without bruising.

'Sorry?'

'The cufflink. Designed them myself. You see?'

The cufflink was plain gold, engraved with what looked like crossed swords. On inspection these proved to be . . . 'A carrot?'

'Correct, a carrot crossed with a stick, in memory of my old man, driving his rag-and-bone cart round this town.' Trevor winked. 'Wily old devil, Dad was. He'd wave the stick to make the kids feel sorry for the nag, then flog 'em the carrots so's they could feed it. I learned a lot from him.' He chuckled. 'Get as much as you can for the carrots, but keep a stick on the cart, just in case.'

I began to feel dizzy. Call me naïve but I was sure I was misunderstanding the drift of this conversation. I said as much.

He opened his eyes wide. 'We're talking public relations, right?'

'Sponsorship? Well, yes, I suppose so.'

'My name on a concert, my name on the radio. But I'm not one of those silly buggers believes all publicity's good publicity.' He leaned towards me, so close I could smell his cologne. Givenchy Gentleman. But there was nothing gentlemanly about the way his hand closed on my wrist. My coffee cup rattled in its saucer. Dammit, my *teeth* were suddenly rattling. The crumpled potato nose loomed inches from my own. 'We all like to choose what we tell the world, right? Well, I hope I'll be tipped off if there's any more surprises about The Willows brewing in Radio Ridings. Because it'd be bound to change my other PR plans, wouldn't it? I've carrots to give out, but I always keep a stick, remember.' A final squeeze and a friendly smile. 'No need for that, though, eh? Ah, looks like the meeting's getting under way. Always nice to talk to you, Rose.'

28

'He tried to do what?' exclaimed Tom. He was swinging back on his chair and nearly toppled off.

'I know it sounds bonkers,' I said. 'But it was as though he actually thought he could hold me hostage. If Radio Ridings did anything more on The Willows, and I hadn't tipped him off, goodbye sponsorship.'

'Amazing.' He gave a shout of laughter. 'Absolutely bloody amazing.'

'It amazed me all right,' I retorted, feeling my wrist. Trevor hadn't actually hurt me, there wasn't a shadow of a bruise, but . . .

'Told you he was a crook.'

'Hardly,' I said irritably. I didn't exactly want to be cosseted and comforted – I'm not that much of a wimp – but I was in no mood for glee. 'He's a bully, that's all, used to getting his own way. Bloody stupid, really, thinking he could lean on us, a BBC station.'

'Hark this incorruptible daughter of Reith. What did you do? Incant the Charter, let the shadow of your microphone fall on him, and watch him frizzle?'

'Very funny.' I wished he would stop all this, drop the relentless wisecracks, because I knew it was only an act. I wanted to talk to the real Thomas, lurking inside the shiny-bright joke-studded armour. No chance. He was already raising his voice. 'I say, you chaps, come and hear this . . .'

He was not alone. It must have been well past eight by the time I returned to Radio Ridings, but instead of finding Tom hacking a solitary path through our cuttings cabinets, I'd stepped into a building ablaze with lights and hopping with industry. Unpaid volunteer industry because, as Tom bemusedly explained, he'd been overwhelmed with offers of help. I noticed two of those eager volunteers were young and female, including my own programme assistant Amanda. Chalk-faced and coal-eyed, this Goth-haired Bride of Dracula winked happily at me before tucking a mug of coffee on to the desk beside Tom. Mind, naked lust didn't explain why Pimply Pete was ambling over to listen, nor his two male cronies, a reporter and a sports producer respectively.

They all exclaimed and chortled delightedly at my account of Trevor and his cufflinks – well, to be sure, I recounted our conversation as a good joke. I wasn't going to confess it had taken a full quarter of an hour for my knees to stop trembling. I felt a bit of a fool now, in truth. What, after all, had I imagined anyone – let alone this respected citizen of Wakeborough – could do to me in a crowded Town Hall? Nevertheless, I couldn't help feeling I wouldn't want to bump into him in a dark alley. I'd stuck out the meeting to the bitter end, and exited in a thick crowd.

'Even so I don't get it,' said Pete. 'Everything about The Willows seems above board, as far as Green's concerned. Why should he care what we put out? It's not great for his image, us telling the world he's screwing money out of pensioners . . .'

'Not just pensioners,' I muttered.

'Nah,' chipped in his reporter chum, Harry, who was as fat as Pete was thin, with a straggly pony-tail and wire-rimmed glasses, 'Trev hasn't got to where he is today by worrying about a few hurt feelings. There's got to be more to it than that.'

'Point it, he *is* worrying,' said Tom. 'Ergo, the bastard's got something to worry about.'

'Reckon he's got the wind up The Willows?' Pete had to dodge a shower of missiles, as they all groaned. Honestly, they were like over-excited toddlers, with Tom a glamorous big brother, winding them up to fever pitch.

'It's got to be Vertco, hasn't it?' said Amanda, and turned to me. 'You haven't heard this, Rose.' They none of them doubted I wanted to hear, that I was as excited as they by the chase. And so, perforce, I learned that Vertco Ltd, former owners and operators of the Willows tip, had offered a waste-disposal service to companies too small for on-site arrangements. They would lorry away anything from broken-up buildings to old sheep dip, and were duly licensed to deal with toxic substances. 'Except,' said Amanda, triumphantly, 'one of their landfill sites up in Middlesbrough, which was supposed to be strictly low-level waste, got turned over by a television programme last year –'

'Great piece, I saw it,' chipped in Pete. 'This reporter turns up driving a lorry, right? He's got a load of drums on the back with danger signs and words like "acid" plastered all over them in red letters a foot high, but he waves a wodge of tenners, asks if he can dump them, nudge-nudge, wink-wink, and they wave him right in. Turned out the place was already stiff with toxic gunk, most of it benzene – benzo – shit, some by-product of oil anyhow, which is pretty grisly, and can't be disposed of without a licence and God knows what safeguards, here it was, leaking out of a stack of unmarked barrels.'

'Got the site shut down, anyway,' resumed Amanda. 'But it makes you wonder what's under The Willows, doesn't it? Right next door to your dad, too. I mean, it could be poisoning him.'

'Chance'd be a fine thing,' I murmured, sneaking a sideways glance at Tom. But he was watching his pack of young newshounds with lazy amusement. 'Anyway,' I said, wishing them all a million miles away, 'what's all this to do with Trevor Green?'

'Fuck all,' said Tom promptly, and grinned as he tossed this bone into their seething midst. 'Unless there's a link between him and Vertco. And what have we turned up?'

'Family business,' offered Amanda. 'In a way. I mean, like Rose said, Trev's dad was a rag-and-bone man – that's waste disposal, isn't it?' She ignored the hoots of mockery. 'Well, I bet you it turns out he's behind Vertco, somewhere along the line.'

'*Was* behind it,' chipped in Pete. 'I told you, Vertco's folded. I found that piece in the *Yorkshire Post*. Where is it? Harry?'

'Hang on a sec,' murmured Harry, who was poring over a sheaf of photocopies. 'Yeah, look. Here. Vertco goes into liquidation, managing director . . . never heard of him. Parent company, blah-blah.'

'Parent company,' said Pete eagerly. 'See? Who owned the parent company?'

'One thing at a time,' said Harry. 'Yup, here we are . . . Former environmental consultant to the board, *Harold Buckerill*.'

Pete snorted. 'Well, it's too late to get anything out of him.' He turned his laugh into an embarrassed cough. 'Sorry,' he said, for Tom's benefit – the rest of us knew the story, the biggest scandal to rock our civilized town for years. 'This was a local councillor who got caught with his trousers down. Lay preacher, JP, you name it, and it was all over the paper. Poor bugger ended up sticking a hosepipe on his exhaust and shutting the garage doors.'

Tom sat up suddenly. 'When you say this was in the paper, do you mean the *Gazette*? As owned by Trevor Green?'

'Sure,' said Pete. 'I mean – sure. They broke the story. Why, do you think that's a connection?' He looked round. 'Anyone know if Buckerill was a mate of Trevor's? I'd only been here a couple of months when he topped himself, I never even met the geezer.'

All eyes turned, inevitably, to me. Eight years in one station gives you Methuselah status. 'No idea,' I said. 'Yes, I knew Harold Buckerill . . .' I wasn't about to add that my most vivid memory of the said councillor, JP, and lay preacher was of his determinedly fondling my knee through an interminable carol service. I was sorry for him, ending up as he had, but I wasn't as amazed as some to learn he had an appetite for for blonde nymphettes in rubber underwear. 'I'd be surprised if he were mixed up with Trevor Green, though, because he was an old-style Labour lad, one of Flo's chums, and you know what Her Worship thinks of Trev.'

'There's got to be a tie-up between Vertco and Trevor somewhere,' persisted Amanda. 'Why else would he corner Rose?'

I stood up. I'd had enough. Tom was obviously stuck in for the night with this lot. To my surprise, however, and gratification, he immediately stretched and yawned and let his legs clunk from desk to floor. 'Yeah, home time for all of us. No, be sensible, you chaps,' he said, over an indignant clamour. 'We've a day's programmes to fill tomorrow, and Stainless will probably have me arraigned under some Euro-reg for allowing antisocial working hours. Besides, if I don't have a fag soon, I'll start climbing walls.'

A few minutes later he was following me down the stairs. 'They're a bright bunch,' he said, flattening himself against the handrail as Pete and Harry galloped past. I was unwise enough to murmur smugly that maybe our news set-up wasn't as awful as he thought.

'God no, much worse. Beats me how so much talent and energy can be mangled into the drivel that's been coming over the air, even by a cerebrally challenged toady like Stephen Sharpe.' That silenced me. Tom glanced round at we reached the door. 'Oh Lord, Assistant Editors aren't supposed to slag off the boss, are they?

Well, I dare say I never was management material. Don't worry, though, I'm guarding my tongue *heroically* on the shop floor.'

He refused their entreaties to join them in the pub. Said he'd drunk enough in recent weeks to see him through to Christmas. No, honestly, he was drying out for a few days. I was daft enough to hope this might be an excuse. Particularly since he waited until they'd all gambolled off down the street before turning back to me. 'Did you say Polly's away for the night?'

I nearly let out a whoop of triumph. 'Yes.'

'Damn.' It was probably too dark under the streetlights for him to catch my look of chagrin, because he continued calmly: 'I promised I'd keep her informed, and she'll be ecstatic to hear this Vertco outfit was done for illegal dumping. It means I'm justified in sending a reporter up to cover her massed dig on Saturday. Never mind, I dare say she'll ring me tomorrow.' He pulled a face. 'She's hardly been off the phone these past two days.'

'I'm sorry,' I said flatly. 'It's half-term. Besides, once Polly's in crusading mode there's no stopping her.'

'Like the kids here. They'd have been at it all night if I hadn't thrown them out. I tell you, Rose, the worst thing about coming to local radio is it makes me feel about ninety-seven.'

'You think I don't know? I live with it daily.'

He laughed. 'Sure, but when I quit London, I was still playing *enfant terrible*. Rude shock to arrive here and find myself recast overnight as wizened old sage. And as for Polly . . .' He shook his head. 'This afternoon she was pelting questions down the phone about this video they're making – oh, camera angles, all kinds of technical stuff – and I found myself thinking, I just don't believe this. She is the most astonishing infant.' We were strolling idly along towards the car park, but that made me halt. I recognized sickly that I was jealous. Not only was I jealous of his late wife, I was jealous of the kids at work, I was jealous of my own daughter. Tom, realizing he'd left me behind, turned. 'She *dazzles* me. It's the only word I can find.'

'She's – like you,' I managed to say. 'Always was. A golden child.'

'Tarnished, in my case. Do you think you'll ever . . .' He broke off, with a brusque shake of the head. But I knew exactly what he'd been on the brink of asking. He'd been about to ask if I would ever tell Polly the truth about her parentage. A question which had been obsessing me, because I knew exactly the mean and green-eyed answer my soul was spitting; if he didn't want me, he could forget Polly . . . Shameful. All I should have been worrying about was my poor daughter herself. How would she feel? 'Look, Thomas . . .'

'This your car?' he interrupted determinedly. 'D'you want me to check one of Trevor's heavies isn't lurking in the back?'

'Christ, stop it, will you?'

'Stop what?'

'Fobbing me off with jokes.'

'Prefer me to cry?'

'If that's what you want.' I grasped his shoulders. 'I just want you to be honest with me. You might kid everyone else into thinking you're batting along fine, but I know different.'

'Give me credit for trying.' He unpeeled my hand from his shoulder and, to my surprise, touched it to his mouth. 'See how splendidly stiff the upper lip is?'

'For God's sake . . . Come home with me, for a drink.'

'Told you, I'm on the wagon.'

'You don't have to bloody drink.'

He gave a cough of laughter. 'I think I would. I always do, these days. Only the bottle never fails.'

'What's that supposed to mean?'

He looked down at me. He released my hand to cup my face between his own. The orange glow of the street lamp was behind him, his face was in shadow, but I could see the misery in his eyes now. Dreadful, heart-wrenching despair. 'Rose, don't. You don't realize. It's no good pretending that anything could be like it was. We're different people.'

'Are we? At least . . .'

He was brushing a thumb across my cheek. My voice tailed away because he was going to kiss me. I knew he was. Giddy with anticipation, I stretched up on tip-toe. But he just stared blindly into my face, as though he was searching for something. 'You're different, of course you are. Just look at you. Anyway – anyway, you don't want to get tangled up in all this. I'm a mess, don't you see?'

'But I understand,' I said passionately. 'About grief, I mean.

When –' His hands dropped abruptly and he twisted away. 'Thomas? What is it?'

'Ignore me,' he said. 'Shit, don't look at me like that. I know you want to help, but you can't, OK? You of all people, I'll see you tomorrow. Thanks for coming in with the news about Trev. Terrific spur to the juvenile sleuths.' He was backing away down the street. 'Tell Polly I'll ring her.'

Anyone else would have seen a lone, lanky figure vanishing round the corner. Me, I was seeing the ghost at his side, with an arm locked tightly into his. And it was my fault. I'd conjured Lucinda up this time, talking about grief. Would I never learn to curb my hyperactive mouth? An empty crisp packet fluttered across the road in the slipstream of a bus and smacked wetly into my leg. I felt pretty much like a discarded bit of litter myself.

29

'Come in, lass, come in,' said Florence Rowbottom, Mayor of Wake-borough and proprietress of the Cheery Chip Café. The place was doing a bustling trade at six thirty that Wednesday evening. She hustled me through the miasma of hot newsprint and vinegar, up a staircase and into a warm and cluttered living room. 'You look proper buggered,' she said. 'No, 'course you're not disturbing me, I hate nights off. It's only that gormless lout down there' – her middle-aged and much loved eldest son – 'makes me tek 'em. Sit yourself down, I've just brewed up. Or would you sooner have a glass?'

Being well acquainted with the brain-numbing scale of Flo's hospitality, I accepted the tea. I'd first called round here yesterday evening, actually. Well, you didn't think I'd just limped off home, did you? Consigning Thomas to Lucinda's deathly clutches without a fight? Even before plugging in my ignition key, I'd resolved that, if the way to Tom's heart (or at least the way to get to talk to him) lay through a rubbish dump, then I'd just have to haul on my wellies and wade right in. I lay no claims to being an investigative journalist, but I've a web of contacts in this town second to none. Having found Flo downstairs and up to her arms in batter, I'd arranged to return tonight when, she assured me, she would be neither frying nor mayoring and thus free for a quiet chat. Eyeing me shrewdly now as she handed me a mug of treacle-coloured tea, she settled her bulk into the chair opposite mine, crossed her slip-pered feet on a footstool and asked if young Stephen was giving me the runaround.

'Steve?' I spluttered, because I'd just taken a mouthful of her tooth-stripping brew.

'Well, don't tell me there isn't a bit of summat going on between you and him,' she said. 'I'm not daft.'

She wasn't. Not much happened in Wakeborough without her knowing. A fellow councillor swore he had only to sneeze in the privacy of his own lavatory for Flo to be on the phone offering aspirin. That's why I was here. 'Whatever there might have been between me and Stephen,' I said carefully, 'it's finished now.' Only problem was, Steve didn't know yet. As far as he was concerned, we were off to Manchester on Friday. He'd been tied up in work with some community liaison initiative, and every time I'd dredged up the courage to ring him at home, his machine had answered.

'Glad to hear it,' grunted Flo. 'You can do better for yourself than that bag of wind. So what's getting you down?'

'Oh, you know, busy at work.' But I wasn't half so busy as Tom, whose constant presence round the general office – joking one minute, arguing passionately the next, firing questions continually – was fraying my nerves raw. Everyone else thought he was a hoot. Wilko, they said, seemed to have forgotten he'd an office of his own. You would never have found Stephen hi-jacking your desk, scribbling phone numbers on your pad, and absent-mindedly helping himself to your coffee while he was about it. How could I concentrate when my pulses blipped like a radar scanner every time he wandered within range? But never too close, never close enough. Still, I was here to ask the questions, not answer them. 'I'm doing a bit of investigation, Flo. Off the record, OK? I want to know about Harold Buckerill.'

She's a wily old so-and-so. Her eyes never flickered. 'God rest his soul. What about him?'

'I've looked up the cuttings. You know, the big scandal.'

'Silly sod. Here, have a biscuit.' She chewed one thoughtfully herself. 'I blame Sheila, his missus. Did you know her? No, likely you wouldn't. She's back in Huddersfield now, and not before time. Ideas above her station, that were her problem, always on at him for bigger houses, bigger cars, Caribbean holidays and what not. Well, he couldn't keep up. Not on what he earned down the tech, let alone after he took early retirement.'

'I'm not following, Flo. What's that to do with him picking up tarts?'

'It's plenty to do with him sticking the pipe on his exhaust,' she retorted fiercely. 'And what's more it were Sheila's fault he couldn't keep his trousers up. I had the old bugger in here many a night, sitting where you are now, knocking back the rum and pep – and he'd no head for booze, hadn't Harold – telling me she'd shut the bedroom door in 1976 and that were th'end of that. You can't blame him for getting a bit frisky. By heck, though, he were a menace round the council chamber with any woman under fifty, more hands than an octopus. He should've divorced her, I told him straight. But you know how soft men are. Reckoned he loved her. And that's what got him into all the trouble –' She broke off. She'd been about to say something, but thought better of it. 'Still, we don't want to rake up old ashes. He's dead, and there's an end of it.'

But I wasn't giving up. 'Did he know Trevor well? Trevor Green, I mean?'

She stared at me. 'Not that I know of.' This wasn't fencing. She was genuinely surprised. 'I mean, we all know Trevor, but . . .'

'Vertco. A waste-disposal company. Harold was some kind of adviser, wasn't he?'

Now I'd hit the target. Not that Florence said anything. She studied her rings. Having buried three husbands, she had plenty. 'So I heard.'

'Oh, come on, Flo. I'm not just prying for the fun of it. You were the one pushed me into doing something about The Willows. Well, Vertco ran the tip there.'

'Did they now?' She let out a soundless whistle. 'You're sure of that? And the old bugger promised me, hand on heart, there were nowt going on round here . . . Mind, now I think on, that tip shut – what? – five years or more back, when Trev built his bungalows. Aye, it'd be before Harold got himself tied up in all that lark.'

'All what lark?'

She met my gaze squarely. 'Harold Buckerill,' she said, 'was a silly old fool, and he's paid for it. In spades. What's more he was a good party man, one of the old breed, more heart than sense – but at least he had a heart. That's why I've said nothing. The firm's folded, and I don't want this coming out unless . . .' She sighed. 'Well, not unless it has to.'

I didn't immediately hurtle back to Radio Ridings with my findings that Wednesday evening. I'd no doubt Tom would still have been there, but so would his yapping hack pack because, in meticulous deference to Stephen's orders, he'd decreed that no working hours could be spent on Trevor Green or The Willows until there was a realistic chance of a story stacking up. Besides, I cunningly calculated that the prospect of a quiet pub sandwich at lunchtime might alarm him less than another attempt to lure him home of an evening. So, as soon as I was off air on Thursday, I hurried away to suggest this. Only to run him to earth eventually, back in the cubicle I'd so recently quit, observing the lunchtime news. 'Rose, hi, were you looking for me?' He grinned. 'I'm learning to drive a live show. Supposedly.'

'Doesn't matter,' I muttered. So much for my cosy sandwich. 'Something I've found out about Vertco, that's all.'

'Really? Terrific.' But at once he'd turned away, asking the producer who was running operations from the control desk beside him what had happened to the court report.

'Search me,' she hissed, stabbing a button and telling the presenter to take the line to Westminster next, OK? Producing a live news programme is like co-ordinating a major rail terminal in rush hour, composing the timetable as you go. There are tapes chattering on air and more tapes screeching behind you as they're edited. One contributor is being trundled in and soothed while another is wheeled out and thanked. There may be an anguished plea crackling into your headphones from an interviewee in an unattended studio miles away, sure you're forgotten him. Plus there are phone lines to raise and plug through, a constant traffic of staff and a presenter through the glass who must be kept apprised and reassured because he or she has to ringmaster this madhouse in a voice of measured authority. Ho ho. What's more, news, unlike my show, has no slabs of music to give a breathing space. The whole thing hurtles along at breakneck pace – or it was doing that lunchtime.

But it wasn't only the pace that was different today. As I stood with my hand on the cubicle door, I realized, with a start, that I was hanging around because I was *interested* in the story being broadcast. This forced me to consider the embarrassing proposition that, generally speaking, I'd taken very little interest in the news output of my own beloved station. By the time I'd caught a dutiful half-hour of the breakfast show, I generally reckoned I'd heard all I needed, and more than I wanted. I'd always assumed the fault for this indifference was mine because, as I say, I'm not a news animal. Now, though, listening to a report about a children's home down the east end of town – which was, as they say, news to me – I began to wonder. In fact, watching Tom as he queried the cue to a tape, I began, rather self-consciously, to ask myself whether his views on the station had been quite as adrift from the gritty realities of local radio as I'd thought. His report was still locked away in my desk. Maybe I ought to read it more carefully.

I'd probably have gone upstairs and done just that had I not collided in the doorway with Harry. Uher over his shoulder, gasping for breath, he hurtled across to Tom like a podgy Labrador pup who's retrieved a particularly tricky bone. 'Got it,' he panted. 'Only the bloody thing wouldn't talk.' He was so breathless, I laced up his tape on one of the studio machines for him, and handed Tom a pair of cans. It's odd watching someone listen to a tape on headphones. They don't twitch to the beat and croon tunelessly like people do with a Walkman, but their face contorts, they smile, frown . . . Tom clapped a hand over his face. Next thing I knew, he slumped forward, as if in pain.

'I'm sorry,' stuttered Harry, his plump cheeks blazing. 'I did my best.'

'Sorry?' gasped Tom, and I saw he was laughing. Laughing? He was nearly apoplectic. Just so had he laughed when he'd first seen his face goggling down from the mirror over that huge circular bed . . . I was smiling too, even though I'd no idea what the joke was. 'Oh, Rose, come and hear this. Listen, you chaps, we can drop that lousy story about the leisure centre. We've got ourselves a cracking new tailpiece.'

'I don't understand,' said Stephen. This was an hour later, back in a swarming general office. Harry's report had already been replayed twice on a machine up here for those who'd missed it live on air. People were reciting the choicer lines from memory. 'The bird hardly said a word.'

Well, that was the point, wasn't it? It's a well-known tenet that not only should you never work with children and animals, but the animal to be avoided above all others on radio is the talking parrot. This particular bird had been the star exhibit in a court case over alleged thefts from a pet shop. It had been reclaimed by its owner because, in the courtroom at least, it had shrieked its own name, loudly and often. 'Is this some kind of a wind-up?' our fearless reporter, Harry, was heard to ask the owner, after failing utterly to lure the fowl into conversation. 'A parrot called *Rover*?' The owner retorted indignantly that Rover had originally been acquired as a present for their daughter, who wasn't expecting a parrot.

'Let me guess, she wanted a dog?'

'No, a horse.'

As Tom said, the exchange thereafter took on a surreal quality. Finally, after a desperate Harry tried to bribe the creature with some apple, it bit a chunk out of his thumb and, as he yelped, squawked triumphantly, 'Cobblers to you and all, mate.'

I know, I know, classic local radio fare, and never as funny in the retelling. I regale you with it only because it had consequences beyond a good joke. You see, while the office guffawed, Stephen didn't find the piece at all funny, and was unwise enough to say so. I can only say it felt as though someone had opened the door of a giant fridge. A damp chill rolled over a room which, seconds earlier, had been warm and noisy with laughter. Worse, the silly chump ploughed straight on to ask why he hadn't been kept informed about The Willows. What was this about a reporter being sent up there on Saturday?

I wasn't a part of all this. I was sitting at my desk, eating a lonely sandwich and waiting for my chance to corner Tom, but that ill-timed mention of The Willows reminded me that I still hadn't spoken to Jim Rumbelow. I owed Uncle Jim an apology for my letter. Within minutes of slamming it into the letter box, I'd repented my harshness, and Flo's disclosures last night only increased my guilt. If she was right, then his campaign wasn't half as crackpot as I'd believed. However, as I swallowed a mouthful of tuna, wedged the phone on my shoulder and tapped in his number, I became aware of a muttering and a rustling around me reminiscent of the crew on the HMS *Bounty*. Tom (a natural for Fletcher Christian) was politely but determinedly justifying the reporter for Saturday. Steve was about to reiterate his ojections when someone pressed a button on a tape-machine. Accidentally of course. Just as it was accidental that the tape was aligned at precisely the right cue, and that the speakers were turned to full volume when the parrot squawked: *Cobblers to you and all, mate.*

The hilarity was unbounded. Cruel too, in the way a herd is cruel when it turns on one of its own. Except Stephen had never been one of their own. Tom, on the other hand – who was already shouting exasperatedly for someone to turn that bloody machine off – had very evidently been clasped to the collective bosom. I winced, stuck a finger in my ear, and listened to Jim's phone ringing.

'Rose?' I glanced up and, to my dismay, saw Stephen. He cleared his throat self-consciously. 'I got your message on my answering machine last night. You wanted a word?'

At that moment, I wanted nothing less but I couldn't help feeling sorry for him. He might be smiling with his usual composure as he suggested I step up to his office, but he must surely have been feeling miserable as hell. Worse, he was probably turning to me, thinking I was his only chum on board this mutinous ship. Little did he know I was the meanest turncoat of the lot. The only thing I had to say to him was that I would not, after all, be joining him in his smart hotel this weekend. 'I'll be along in a minute,' I mumbled, clutching my telephone like a lifebelt. 'I simply must talk to Rambling Jim. I've been ringing him for the past two days.'

Amanda leaped to her feet at the desk opposite mine. 'God, *Jim*,' she gasped. 'I'm so sorry, Rose. I haven't told you yet. George came in specially to let us know. He's had another heart attack. It's OK,' she went on hastily. 'I mean, it's not OK, but at least he's not dead. Luckily he wasn't on his own, and they whizzed him straight into the Infirmary. George's going to see him tonight, after she's finished editing some feature or other for *Artsround*. I told her to buy a bunch of flowers from us all.'

I let the receiver plop back on to the rest. 'No wonder he's not been answering his phone,' I said, in the daft way you do when you hear bad news. 'Oh Lord, poor old Jim. I wanted to apologize for writing him that stinking letter. When did it happen, do you know?'

All at once she looked uneasy. Horror-struck wouldn't be putting it too strongly.

'Amanda?'

'I'm – sure it's not connected,' she stuttered. 'I mean, it doesn't really happen like that, does it? Heart attacks come out of the blue, particularly when you've got a dicky ticker like Jim. It could happen any time.'

'I don't understand. What's not connected?'

Amanda looked rather as though she'd like to crawl under her desk. 'It was, um, Tuesday morning,' she said. 'According to what George heard from his sister-in-law, he collapsed while . . . Well, it was while he was opening his mail. Apparently it was the postman called the ambulance.'

Artsround/Flint feature cont.

Dr Susan Griffiths is a lecturer in the English Department at Wakeborough University, who specalizes in contemporary poetry by women.

TAPE B: Susan Griffiths/Interview by GP/no fee

You know, what always strikes me is the feeling of yearning in Flint's poems.

Actually, I don't think there's an English expression which fully describes this quality. I need the Welsh word hiraeth. *Ask a Welsh speaker to translate that, and they're always stumped. It's often mistranslated as some kind of nostalgia, but that's not true. You can feel hir-aeth for the future as well as the past. The nearest I can come to conveying the meaning is to say that it's a kind of longing. An aching, inchoate desire for something out of reach.*

And it's this, I think, which speaks so very powerfully to younger readers. Because it's remarkable that, in an age when, to be sure, certain kinds of performance poetry are enjoying a vogue — you know, rap and so forth — Lucinda Flint who, to my knowledge, never gave a public reading in her life and, indeed, towards the end of her days wasn't capable of doing so, is so very widely bought and enjoyed by the under-twenties.

I think what she puts so eloquently into words is the kind of dumb anguish of young love. The sort of painful obses-sion which tears you apart in your teens because you know — oh, God, how painfully you know — that you'll only ever love this one person in your whole life, but they're never going to love you in return, not like you love them. So there's nothing in the world worth living for and, you know, you think you'd as soon end it all . . .

Except you might just wait until tomorrow because there's chips for tea and Lethal Weapon III *on the telly. Well, that's what she catches. All the angst and over-wrought emotion is there, but she always chucks a twist of lemon into the syrupy slush.*

I think she's wonderful.

cont. over

30

'She's terrific,' said Polly that evening. Not without difficulty, because her features were encased in a fast solidifying face-pack. 'Best poems I've ever read. You know George is doing something about her on the arts programme?'

'Apparently,' I said, lifting my iron off a sleeve in imminent danger of scorching.

'She was a bit dubious about suggesting it to Tom but he's really keen.'

'Oh?' I smacked the iron down again so hard it spat scalding steam over my hand.

'We think it's therapeutic, George and me. Like, this book is the last bit of Lucinda he's got, so he wants it to do really well. Although,' continued my worldly-wise daughter, having subjected this last claim to further consideration, 'he won't let George interview him. Maybe he's afraid of getting emotional.'

'Probably.'

'He just needs time. As I was saying to George –'

'When was all this?'

'Yesterday afternoon, when Kev and I went round to mix the soundtrack. She's got some fantastic squelching effects. Did it with cake-mixture, can you believe? Anyway, we got talking about Tom. The way he looks so tragic when he doesn't know you're watching him. He must have really loved her. Although . . .'

I hid my scowl by bending low over the ironing board. 'Although what?'

'Oh, don't be dense, Mum. She was ill for ages. Awful, all knotted up and helpless. George says he's a hero. I think she meant, well, they can't have been – like husband and wife.'

I strove for the nonchalance appropriate to a modern, no-holds-barred mother. 'There's more to love than sex, if that's what you mean.'

Bristling with embarrassment Polly retorted she knew *that*. So much for modern parenthood. She added, in a tone which implied a sad old specimen like me couldn't hope to understand, 'Anyway, the spiritual side is a million times more important than all that stuff.'

Out of the mouths of babes, I thought. The spiritual bond Tom had forged with his poet was only too obviously more important than the rampant sex he'd enjoyed with Rita. But was that really all I'd shared with Thomas? A fortnight of lust and laughs?

Polly picked a flake of mud off her chin and studied it thoughtfully. 'Lucinda must have been pretty amazing, wouldn't you say, to keep him loving her all those years?'

The stab of jealousy I felt was so intense, so physical, it knocked the breath out of me. 'Tom's a warm-hearted man,' I gasped. 'You know it's funny, but in some ways he's very like your father.' Pathetic. I was just staking my own little claim – my flesh-and-blood claim – to Tom's love.

'You're kidding.' She sounded appalled. Surprising, given her blatant admiration of Tom Wilkes. Fortunately for my peace of mind, she didn't pursue the matter, and asked instead what time I was leaving for Manchester tomorrow. I felt a terrible urge to chuck the iron at my best gilt-framed mirror. I didn't, of course. Just went on pressing the shirt I thought appropriate to a deer-parked, four-postered hotel . . .

Well, could you have sprung it on Stephen? In those circumstances? Never mind that his secretary was clattering in and out, I'd crawled along to his office awash with remorse, haunted by a vision of Uncle Jim. I imagined him opening my letter, smiling, beginning to frown, clutching his chest . . . I'd only written so angrily because he'd made me quarrel with Tom. That same blind obsession was compelling me now, not just to pull out of a weekend, but to finish the whole affair. And it wasn't Stephen's fault. He surely deserved more than ten gabbled seconds of apology in the office.

'I'm down at the Fayre all morning,' I told Polly miserably. 'I guess we'll be leaving mid-afternoon.' At least the hotel would guarantee uninterrupted privacy. I would give Stephen a zonking drink; break the news; gallantly offer to foot the bill; and get the hell out. 'Plans are, um, fluid, though. I might be back on Saturday.' Friday night if I could contrive it. 'I'll ring you at Grandpa's.'

'Don't hurry back on my account,' she said. 'Stay till Monday if you like.'

Typical. The one weekend I *didn't* want to escape would have to be the one time she chose to spare me the child-neglect routine. I heard a car draw up outside. 'That'll be George. She promised she'd drive out after she'd seen Jim, if she could borrow wheels.' I went to the front door. But there were two figures climbing out of the car. George and . . . 'Tom!' I shouted happily.

Polly clapped her hands to her mud-caked face and thundered up the stairs.

'It seems she's in love,' I explained, stifling a qualm at the thought of her chosen love object. 'Anyway, she's discovered uses for the hitherto despised contents of my bathroom cabinet. She'll be down in a minute. Coffee? Drink?' I was painfully aware of Tom standing in the middle of my sitting room, just as I had so often imagined him. He was gazing round. Impressed? Or just surprised?

George said they mustn't linger but, since Tom was kindly chauffeuring her, she'd have a whisky. 'Oh darling, *don't.*' This was addressed to Tom, who had murmured something polite about my house. 'Once on the subject of her nest, Rose is unbearable.'

He grinned at me. I grinned foolishly back, apologizing in one jumbled breath for the ironing board, the lack of a fire, Polly's debris – 'You'll be glad to hear Jim's out of danger,' interrupted George tartly. 'Sitting up, drinking tea.'

I handed her a whisky and waved the bottle towards Tom who was folding his long limbs down on to the sofa. He shook his head, pulled a face – rueful, conspiratorial. As though he wanted to talk to me. As though he, too, were wishing George a million miles away. With an effort I dragged my gaze from his. 'Jim got my letter though? You did tell him –'

'Darling, I honestly don't think you can blame yourself,' said George. 'He certainly didn't seem to think you'd anything to apologize for. He was a bit confused actually, worrying on about his pheasant – the famously un-dead fowl, one assumes – and his houseplants. Drugs making him woozy, I dare say, but I took a key and promised I'd drop into his cottage at the weekend, if I can get transport.'

'I must go and visit him myself,' I said. 'He'll soon perk up when he hears what I've unearthed about Vertco.'

Tom catapulted forward. 'Well, go on. Why'd you think I'm here?'

To see me? Was I crazy? 'Vertco?' echoed Polly, appearing in the doorway, pinkly freed from her mask. 'What've I been missing?' She flopped on to the sofa beside Tom. Side by side, two identical pairs of eyes fixed on me. The effect was mesmeric. On second thoughts, I poured myself a whisky as well. A large one. 'Yes, well, I asked a few questions yesterday evening.'

'About The Willows?' said Polly. 'You never told me.'

'I'm telling you now. OK?'

'Oh, I remember Harold Buckerill,' she interrupted after a minute. 'Councillor Fuck-'em-all? That's what they were calling him at school, anyway.'

'So much for the benefits of private education,' sighed George.

'The point is,' I said, 'Florence Rowbottom reckoned the sex scandal was only the final straw. Yes, it tipped him over the edge, but she told me he was near-suicidal before ever the bonking story broke. Because of Vertco.'

'He was some kind of environment consultant, right?' said Tom.

'And they'd approached him, obviously, because of his glowing reputation on green issues. He told Flo he'd felt obliged to take it to keep the wife in fancy holidays, but he soon twigged Vertco didn't want environmental advice. All they wanted was a respectable mouthpiece to spout the company line, and he found himself doing it. He kidded himself it was all above board and took the money, until that television programme Pete told us about blew the lid off. That finally forced Harold to open the blind eye. He toured a few of the sites and found they were all stinking. He washed up on Flo's doorstep distraught because, as she said, he hadn't just built a political career on the environment ticket, he did actually care. So she told him . . .' I broke off, only now considering the implications. 'She told him the only decent thing he could do was resign, and see if he couldn't lever Vertco into cleaning up their act by threatening to go to the press himself. And if that meant admitting his own part, well, he'd just have to bear it. And he said he could – and would.'

'Whereupon,' said Tom wonderingly, 'his sex life's blazoned all over the newspaper. Trevor Green's newspaper.'

'Wow,' whistled Polly. 'Excellent.'

'The man's dead, you heartless brat,' said George.

'I'm just saying it was pretty smart of Mum.'

'Certainly is,' said Tom. 'I'm knocked out.'

'Except,' I said modestly, 'Flo knew nothing to connect Vertco with Trevor Green. What about you?'

'All we've done is trace it back to a holding company, registered offshore.' He shrugged. 'The kids at Radio Ridings are great but, honestly, you need professional expertise to hack through the financial jungle. We're like boy scouts with a home-made compass and a pen-knife. And you know me, I can't add up a milk bill, let alone interpret balance sheets.'

'Can I help?' offered Polly.

He smiled faintly. 'Good at maths, are you?'

She pulled a face. 'Not bad.'

'She's already got an A in her GCSE,' I chipped in. Just occasionally the mother instinct *will* out.

'Takes after you then?' he said softly.

I began to feel glad I'd poured myself a whisky. Not that it wasn't a harmless remark, and Polly didn't query it. But seeing them side by side on the sofa was churning up dangerous feelings. Just as, on a cliff edge, with not the remotest wish to end my life, I'm beset by a crazy temptation to jump, I was aware now of a reckless urge to shout: *This is your father.*

He was telling her about a conversation with some of the *Gazette* journalists earlier this evening. 'I'd been told they drank at the Brown Cow. On the basis that no one hates a newspaper proprietor more than the hacks he employs, I dropped in while George was at the hospital.' He grinned at me. 'The office jokes are all about boat trips and pension funds. They're scared witless he's going to do a Maxwell because word in the business community is he's dangerously over-extended. Instead of sticking to what he knows, which is property, he's been doing daft things like buying newspapers. They say it's a house of cards. Pull out the right one and the whole empire could tumble.' Tom snorted. 'He's certainly got the authentic megalomaniac ego. You'd be amazed how many of his companies have a sneaky reference to his own name – Lime Holdings, for one, as in lime green. Then there's Emerald Investments, Forest something or other –'

'Vertco,' cried Polly. '*Vert*'s French for green.'

'Yeah, quite, that's what Pete said.'

'You'd already guessed?' She looked rather crestfallen.

'Well, it's cheering, but it could be coincidence.'

'Rose, my old darling,' said George, 'if you've a minute, there's something I need to discuss.'

I didn't answer. I'd scrambled to my feet and was dragging a dictionary down from the bookshelf. 'Veridian,' I muttered, tracing down the column. 'Veridian . . . shit. Doesn't exist.'

'Are we talking colours?' she sighed. 'Because, if so, the shade is called, I believe, *viridian*. With an "i".'

She was right. 'Blimey,' I breathed, staring at the definition. '"A green pigment consisting of a hydrated form of chromic oxide". Frankie's partner with the money . . .' They all stared at me. 'Don't you remember, Tom? My telling Steve I'd been approached by a consortium bidding for the commercial franchise? Honestly, I'm amazed I didn't guess. Trevor always used to bang on about admiring my show. At least, he did before . . .' Remembering my last exchange with Trevor Green, that ugly nose thrusting into my face, I stifled a shudder and ploughed on. 'Thing is, these small commercial stations often have a tie-up with a local paper. It saves them hiring journalists. They're legally obliged to carry a news service, but they're not interested. All they care about is big-audience music, end-to-end adverts and raking in the dosh.'

You'll notice, by the way, there's not much comradely doffing of caps to our colleagues in the commercial sector. We know where we stand in local radio. We are the British Broadcasting Corporation. They are crap.

'So,' I continued, 'if they can swing it, they'll take their statutory dose of headlines from the local paper. There's a limit on how much of a radio service a newspaper can own, but' – I smiled triumphantly – 'I bet you anything Trevor Green's behind this Viridian consortium that's bidding for the Wakeborough station. Along with Frankie Henderson.'

'Fascinating,' said George, rolling her eyes. From her lofty

Reithian perch, the machinations of ILR are about as interesting as the sex life of newts.

'Frankie Henderson who used to do the cruddy family quiz show?' exclaimed Polly. 'That's my friend Kevin's father, did you know that? God, has he been in Wakeborough?'

'And for some unaccountable reason,' murmured Tom, glancing mischievously at me, 'offering your mother a job.'

Polly's face curled with disgust. 'Well, I just hope he's not thinking of coming back up here to live. It'd be *awful* for poor Kevin. Honestly, it's enough to make you glad your own dad's safely dead. At least he can't suddenly pop up to embarrass you.'

Tom flinched. I choked on my whisky. And George's jaw sagged. Infinitesimally, but unmistakably. The next minute she was declaring briskly that they must toddle, but she would appreciate a quick word with me first. A *quiet* word.

31

Outside Broadcasts are among the more dare-devil stunts we feel obliged to perform from time to time. A presenter like me quits her orderly (well, semi-orderly) studio, sticks a mini-transmitter in her back pocket, grabs a roving microphone the size of a stun baton and charges out to waylay innocent citizens as they try to get on with their normal lives.

Not that there was much normal about the Town Fayre. It was bedlam down there that Friday morning, even before we went on air. Amanda and I had plotted a meticulous running order of people to interview, stalls to visit, events to catch on mike. The chances of the show working to plan were lottery-winning slim. My friend George, it must be admitted, hates these exercises with a passion. Listeners, in her view, are conservative souls. 'Their daily programme is like their daily pinta. They expect it to be delivered same time, same flavour, same packaging. Imagine your listener, quietly peeling her spuds. She doesn't want to be plunged into some noisy jamboree, where her pet presenter's bouncing around like a ball in a bagatelle, too breathless to frame an intelligible sentence . . .' And so on.

I know what she means – kind of. But I have to confess I love Outside Broadcasts. Love them? I'm totally hooked on 'em. The buzz of adrenalin when, in my little earpiece, I hear that the airwaves are now being handed over live to Rose Shawe at . . . Well, I can only say it operates on me like a surge of rocket fuel. Lord knows, a studio-based show can be hairy, but an OB is somersaulting on the high wire with no safety net. And you can see, touch, *smell* your audience. Normally, no matter how vivid, my listener is an imaginary construct. Out on the road, I'm eyeball-to-eyeball; they're laughing at the jokes, and roaring at the cock-ups.

These are all part of the fun. You can plan till you're addled, but you never really know who you're going to talk to or what they're going to come out with; whether the producer in the van outside will feed the right cues into your earphone; whether they'll play in the music back in the studio; whether some idiot won't unplug the wrong cable . . . We once managed to fuse the power supply to an entire folk festival, but you can bet I talked right on. In pitch black. This morning, at a couple of minutes to ten, I was poised at the Market Hall entrance, gripping the sleeve of the organizer while Amanda whipped up the crowds, ready to cheer when we went on air. In spite of everything, I felt as happy, as charged up, as intensely *alive* as I think it's possible to feel.

When I say 'in spite of everything', I don't mean just the prospect of driving away with Stephen that afternoon, although an awareness of the suitcase in my car lurked like a little black cloud. No, I mean the row I'd had with George last night. Well, perhaps 'row' is an exaggeration. George doesn't stoop to rows. She floats as majestic as a Zeppelin while I buzz around like a maddened wasp. I'd followed her into the kitchen fearfully braced for questions about Tom and Polly, because I could have sworn she'd guessed. I know George too well. Not a word, however. She just asked, matter-of-factly, when I'd be able to voice her feature on Lucinda Flint.

'I don't like to talk about it too much in front of Tom, poor child,' she explained, 'but it's ready for studio. All I need is your mellifluous larynx, and maybe your inimitable personal polish on the script I've drafted. I've a feeling it's a tidge Radio Four-ish, but I'm sure you can render it more, ah, *listener-friendly* for a local audience. I've no real qualms because the interview with Lucinda I found in Archives is a jewel – that woman would charm worms out of a compost heap. The only thing I haven't yet secured is someone to read the actual poems. Not a word to Equity, but I hope to bribe a needy thespette from the University Drama department with a few gins. Not to worry, I'll mix them in afterwards if needs be. So, if we can find a spare studio tomorrow evening, say . . .'

'I'm – going away tomorrow,' I stammered.

'Oh really? No matter, no hurry. Transmission isn't for another week. After the weekend perhaps?'

'George, you can't seriously be asking me to present a feature about Lucinda Flint?'

'And why not?'

'No,' I said. 'No. I'm sorry. But no.'

'Yes,' she said flatly.

'What do you mean, yes?'

'I've put a great deal of love and labour into this feature. I don't quite know what it's saying, but I know it's *right*.' (Typical George-ism: cut faithfully the little truths you hear, and trust the listener to discern great zonking philosophies you never dreamed of, Horatio.) 'But me no buts. It matters to me very much that you should present it for me. Anyone else could ruin it.'

She was implacable. As I say, she didn't argue. Just murmured I would do it for her, one way or another, swept out of the kitchen, wished Polly a rapturous reception for her video at the Fayre, and told Tom she was ready to go. And that annoyed me too because I'd barely had a chance to talk to him.

'Maybe see you in the morning,' he said to my surprise. 'Stephen seems to think I should catch an Outside Broadcast.'

'Yes, it's two minutes past ten, I'm Rose Shawe and, as you can hear from the cheers – thank you very much – the show this morning is coming to you live from the annual Town Fayre, in Wakeborough's Market Hall. If you're in the area and want to drop in and join the fun, the doors opened half an hour ago, and the place will be bustling until late this evening – or so William Gregory tells me. He's coordinating the event and he's with me now. So, what's in store . . .?'

We were launched and, although the clock had seemed to doze off several times in the excruciating seconds before we went on air, it was hurtling along now. Literally, as it happens, because Amanda was carrying a battery-powered timepiece the size of a dinner plate as we cavorted round the hall, which she held up behind whomever I was addressing so I could wrap the interview on time. It doesn't matter where the show's coming from, whatever excitements are fizzing around us, we still have to break off to supply the listeners with news headlines, road-traffic warnings, all the familiar staples at their appointed times.

I won't say I forgot Tom was due to appear – that would be impossible – but I'd a lot on my mind. Not least Amanda's bright suggestion of fixing a quick chat with Frankie Henderson. 'He'll be down at the *Gazette* stand, signing copies of his book called – get this, Rose – *One Man and his Ferret*, so I thought –'

'No,' I said. Seems I was destined to stamp on everyone's pet projects this week. 'I'm not having that man on the show. Can't explain now, disc's finishing. Gotta move.' I hurried on to taste Yorkshire Pudding Bolognese (honestly) and Elderflower Cordial – but not at the same stall; I had my palm read; discussed job opportunities for the town's youth; conducted a burst of Souza from the silver band; and learned from a cocky little member of the local history society that the going rate for a wench like me in the old hiring fairs would be fifty pounds a year. To which I'd replied, predictably enough, that if you worked for Aunty, times hadn't changed much. I was settling into my appointed chair in the Age Concern tea enclosure when I finally spotted Tom amongst the crowds.

'Ten past twelve here on Radio Ridings, and I'm sitting next to a rather special birthday boy . . .' With a dazzlingly dentured grin, Joe agreed he was indeed ninety-one years young today, so naturally I led his pals in a vigorous if variably pitched chorus of 'Happy Birthday'. As I nodded encouragement to Joe and his wife ('Her's nobbut a lass, not passed eighty-nine, herself hasn't') I was intensely aware of Tom watching me. Herself was keen to tell me about her dad's tripe stall, which had stood on this very spot before the war. There was lusty nostalgia all round the table for the good old days when you could buy proper honeycomb tripe, decent black puddings (not all great Northern myths are mythical) and, oh, the trotters . . .

'Trotters?' I exclaimed, with the appropriate yuck-factor. 'Pigs' feet?'

'We loved 'em and all,' chirped up a bright-eyed crone opposite. 'My mam reckoned they was an aphro – what d'you call it? Gets you frisky?'

'Aphrodisiac? Pigs' trotters?'

'Well, my dad allus asked for 'em Friday tea, and I'd eleven brothers and sisters by th'end.'

'How did you cook them?' I asked, laughing. And as they told me – with some dispute over the finer points of breadcrumb coating – I saw Tom's face. He was smiling, yes. And I was about to smile back until I realized he was looking absolutely dumbfounded, as though he couldn't believe all this. And suddenly I saw myself as he must be seeing me: giggling away about tripe and aphrodisiac trotters; God, it was no different from Rita, was it? How often had she sat at a table like this, waving round a mike, chatting up the punters, leading the singing? So the clothes had changed, so I flashed my teeth instead of my tits – I'd grown older along with my audience – but at heart, somehow, it was the same old act. And Thomas, with his pure and airy poet wife, was palpably agog at the vulgarity of it all.

Amanda distracted me by waggling the clock and the next time I looked round he'd gone. How typical he should roll up now, not when I was grilling a local MP about investment in the town, not when I was pursuing an intelligent exploration of Pennine folklore . . . I shoved these bitter reflections aside and ploughed on.

Only as I reached my last stopping place did I spot Frank Henderson's ashen Beatle cut. It was, fortunately, at the far side of the hall. He was grinning, gesticulating, talking to . . . Heavens, Trevor Green. Whose face swivelled this way. And where was I standing, microphone in hand? Why, right under the banner advertising Polly's massed dig at The Willows tomorrow. Trevor wasn't to know I was here to talk, not about green politics, but about the thrills and spills of junior film-making. I told myself I didn't care. Thugs like him had to learn they couldn't dictate editorial policy to the BBC. Or me. Shit, he was pointing me out to Frankie, who was raising a hand . . . I spun away, and collided with the thin, bespectacled figure of Kevin Henderson. My last interviewee. 'Must be you he's waving at,' he commented, 'because he wouldn't know me from Adam.' To my surprise, he smiled wryly. 'Don't look so worried, Mrs Shawe, it doesn't bug me. My father's not even history as far as I'm concerned.'

What an *excellent* young man, I thought. Because those few words banished my every last trace of unease about this would-be Cambridge doctor. He was assuredly in no position to enlighten my daughter about my own disreputable history. I was just resolving to inform Polly her romance enjoyed my warmest blessing (as if she cared) when I realized the music in my earpiece was ticking to a cadence. 'Standby,' I hissed, and pinioned him with a smile more hopeful than confident. Thing is, the interviewability of the human race rises in direct line with age. Take a table full of crumblies like the trotters crowd and it's all you can do to shut them up. Your average child on the other hand, no matter how precocious, needs to be painstakingly milked for every lisped syllable. Worst of all, usually, is the self-conscious teenager who regards the very idea of participating in your sad middle-aged show as a terminal affront to his cool.

The excellently sensible Kevin Henderson, however, for all he flushed darker than the beetroot chutney on the next stand, managed to gargle a few jokes about the making of their video. I held the mike close enough to the television screen to pick up a snatch of George's sound effects and music (noticing that the final product, of which, thus far, I'd glimpsed only a rough cut, looked surprisingly polished), and then was in the process of wrapping when I heard a noisy voice near by. An all-too-familiar voice.

'. . . just savouring my first lung-restoring bolt of nicotine, when I sense a *trrrrembling* in the very ground beneath my feet. I speak of feet in a metaphorical sense, you understand.' Out of the corner of my eye, I could see him holding forth to Polly, to assorted bystanders, to *Tom* . . . 'The next minute the air is rent with the roars and bellows of these mechanical monsters . . .'

'Well, thanks for talking to us, Kevin, and I think before we have the last traffic round-up, we've just time for some more music.'

Nothing. No music. Not even an apologetic voice in my earpiece to tell me why.

'. . . a prancing, dancing chorus line of bulldozers and giant lorries. But Rose needs to hear this!'

I raised my voice and moved away a couple of paces. Kevin, I noted, took one look in Mac's direction, grimaced apologetically, and bolted. Would I could have done likewise. 'Looks like we've got a slight technical hitch on the record-deck.' There was a tug on my sleeve. 'I thought it was too good to be true, a whole three hours on the hoof down here, and everything running as smoothly as clockwork.'

'Rose? Look at me when I'm talking to you, woman.'

I looked at him all right, a look that would have halted a battalion of bulldozers. It had sod-all impact on my father. 'However, it's nearly ten to one. This is BBC Radio Ridings and I'm talking to you live from the Town Fayre . . .'

'Fiddling while Rome burns, more like,' snorted Mac, who was fast increasing his own audience. He was just opening his mouth to continue when Tom and Polly, as one, surged forward and yanked his wheelchair out of microphone range. He yelped, the crowd roared and I could happily have burst into tears.

32

'Ungrateful hussy,' growled Mac when, off air and ripe for patricide, I returned to find him. Clad in a suit of shrieking checks with a trilby jauntily askew, he'd been holding forth to the variously amused and bemused passers-by at the COSH stand about his morning's adventures. 'No entertainer worth his salt is thrown by a little heckling from the floor. He should thrive on it, blossom, be inspired to give of –'

'I'm not an entertainer,' I snarled, bitterly aware of Tom's lazy grin as he leaned on the stand beside Polly. 'I'm a broadcaster. Besides, you're not a heckler, you're my father.' And how, at that moment, I wished he were not. 'For God's sake, shift yourself out of the aisle. You're holding up the traffic.'

'And what is the wireless, pray, if not entertainment?' demanded Mac, bowling rapidly after me. 'You revel in an audience, girl, don't deny it. It's in your blood. Your genes were programmed with an unquenchable thirst for applause.' He glanced round at Polly who, with Tom in tow, was squeezing after us into the alley between the stands. 'Sad that it has failed to transmit to the next generation. However' – he crossed his hands piously in his lap – 'we mustn't inflict our family squabbles on strangers. Even a stranger who did not hesitate to lay violent hands on my wheelchair without so much as a how'd-ye-do.'

Tom started forward with a smile. 'Gosh, I'm terribly sorry. I rather thought –'

'Tewwibly?' echoed Mac, his face suddenly alight. 'My word, what dulcet accents are these? Who is this overgrown Hoowway Henry?'

'This is Tom Wilkes,' said Polly. Which was just as well because I don't think I could have trusted myself to speak. 'Tom, Mac. My grandfather.'

Tom thrust out a hand. 'I should have introduced myself. How are you?'

Mac smiled back. 'Legless.'

I shut my eyes.

'I can see that,' said Tom politely. 'But otherwise?'

'I'm really sorry, Mum,' sighed Polly, cutting across the civilities. 'I didn't see him charging over to you. Thing is, I was so gob-smacked when he told us –'

'Tom,' I said hastily, 'I'm sure you want to get back to the office. Don't let us keep you.'

'Have we met before?' demanded Mac, removing his trilby in order to peer up at Tom's towering figure more closely. 'There's something curiously familiar about your long-nosed features. Or is it just the famous predilection for incest among the ruling classes makes you all look alike?'

'Leave Tom alone, Grandpa,' interrupted Polly. 'Tell Mum what's been going on.'

'Can't I fill Rose in on the way back to work?' said Tom with a touch of impatience. I wasn't surprised he was keen to escape, only that he asked me for a lift. 'One of the reporters dropped me here.'

'Dear me, chauffeur's day off?' murmured Mac.

'Pack it in, can't you?' said Polly. 'You were bad enough, persecuting poor Kevin. What've you got against him?'

'Maybe,' said Mac darkly, 'you should ask your mother.'

I could have strangled him. 'Kevin Henderson strikes me as a charming young man. In fact, I meant to say to you, Polly –'

'Never mind that,' she snapped. 'What're we going to do? Trevor lousy Green's ruined *everything*. He sent a load of workmen in this morning. He's wired off the tip, and he's got lorries just dumping earth everywhere.'

Anxious as I was to get away – to get Tom away – that halted me. 'He can't do it,' I gasped. 'Not without the residents' consent, not if we're supposed to be paying for it.'

'Honestly, don't you care about anything except money? He's done it to stop us digging tomorrow, that's all, and to bury whatever's there even deeper.'

'Without a word to us,' said Mac, 'let alone any nonsense about consent. We just looked out of our windows and saw the ballet of the bulldozers being staged across the stream. The old tabbies are hopping round like fleas in a bucket.'

I stared at Tom. 'He's going to these lengths? Just to stop a few kids sticking their spades into the tip?'

'Mum!' yelped my outraged child.

'Don't worry, sweetheart,' said Tom. The endearment was unthinking, but it stung me. 'I promise I'll chase Lime Holdings as soon as I get back to a desk.'

'Confront Trevor himself, if you like,' I said bad-temperedly. 'He was over by the *Gazette* stand.'

'He's gone,' said Polly. 'I saw him leaving. And so's Kevin, thanks to you,' she added, turning on her grandfather. 'So if you want a lift home now, you'd better sweet-talk Mum.' This would have put a final seal on my misery if Mac hadn't immediately refused.

'Having put myself to the ruinous expense of a taxi-cab into town, I intend to enjoy a few civilized metropolitan pleasures. A turn around the hall here, because' – his eyes flickered towards me – 'I'd swear I've spotted a few old acquaintances. Then perhaps a drink, and a look-in at a turf accountant's. There's a nag running in the three fifteen at York by name of Campdown Belle which –'

'Save your money,' said Tom briefly.

We all stared at him. Or rather, Polly and I did. Mac was glaring. 'I beg your pardon?'

'I'll lay you a tenner it won't be placed. Try Bonny Sky Boat. With luck, you might still get seven to one. Nice to meet you, Mac. Shall we go, Rose?'

'You've got to hand it to this Trevor Green.' Tom had dodged away to a newspaper stand on the way to the car park and now, as he clambered into the passenger seat beside me, tossed a copy of the *Gazette* into my lap. He let out a crack of laughter. 'Hot off his own press. Look, bottom right corner: "IN MEMORY OF DAD".'

I picked up the paper which, if not actually hot, was still loose with ink. '"Millionaire local businessman Trevor Green today launched work to landscape a park in Lower Mill, to be dedicated to the memory of his father, Mr Sydney Green,"' I murmured. '"The site, adjacent to" et cetera . . . "previously uncultivated to conserve wildlife habitats . . ." What?'

'No, no, it gets better,' said Tom, wresting the paper from my hands. '"'Conservation remains a priority,' said Mr Green. 'We will take the project step by step to see how best we can safeguard the rich variety of local flora and fauna . . .'"' For which read, he intends to do as little as possible for as long as possible. Oh, but he's also quoted as admitting there's been controversy over the site, "the scars of our great industrial heritage". One way of describing a slag heap and a waste tip, I suppose. This is the best bit, though. After the inevitable drivel about an amenity for the whole area, he reminds us that his dad was a rag-and-bone man, making a living from rubbish, so what better place for a park to his memory than atop an old tip? Fantastic. This guy really takes the biscuit. No wonder he bought himself a newspaper, it's a ready-made PR machine. Continued, we are told, with pictures on page seven.'

I flopped back in my seat, shutting my eyes. 'Just as long as the bastard doesn't expect us to pay for whatever he's up to.'

'Shouldn't think he's intending to do more than erect his fence and bulldoze a bit of earth around to keep COSH and their inquisitive spades out. Still . . .' He broke off, casting the paper aside. 'Rose? Something the matter?'

'I'm whacked,' I sighed. Which was true. You always are after an OB. The adrenalin suddenly ebbs and leaves you stranded, limp as a bit of seaweed on the shore. But there was more to my deflation than that.

'I'm not surprised, the energy you put into the job,' he said. 'I was watching you.'

'I noticed.'

'Astonishing. It was like, oh, years being stripped away. You've changed so enormously, but today I was reminded of what you used to be like when I knew you, and –'

'Don't,' I burst out.

'Sorry?'

'Just don't say it. I saw the look in your face. Silly, vulgar local radio, jokes about tripe and black puddings, me working the crowd just like Rita used to, only –'

'But you were brilliant.'

'– only now it's pensioners' tea parties instead of stag – What?' I slewed round to stare at him.

'It was a revelation. God knows why, because you're great on your regular programme, but this was something again.'

'I'm not hearing this,' I said faintly. 'You said my show was audio *fucking* Elastoplast.'

'Oh for Christ's sake, no need to take it personally.'

I gasped. 'How else was I supposed to take it?'

'Yeah, well.' He pulled a wry face. 'I've had it up to here with the caring, counselling classes recently. Didn't stop me recognizing a bloody good journalist.'

'You're calling *me* a journalist?'

'What else? At the softer end of the spectrum from hacks like me, maybe, but if your show isn't reflecting life as it's lived in Wakeborough then I don't know what is.'

I was silent, digesting this extraordinary notion. Says everything for what I felt about Tom Wilkes that, for the first time in my life, I was *flattered* to be called a journalist. 'But you despise local radio.'

'So I've seen the light. No, truly, you were right. As ever. I was an ignorant, bigoted jerk from television, and I shouldn't have let the balls-up Stephen Sharpe was making of news reinforce all my blinkered metropolitan prejudices. Behold, I'm grovelling at your talented feet. And just what's so funny about that?'

'Pillock.'

He grinned back at me. 'Ungracious cow. Here I am, holding you up, in these benighted times, as a model Reithian, and –'

'Oh yeah? Discussing tripe?'

'Did I know before this morning how to cook a trotter? Exactly. Information, education – and as for entertainment value . . . Your papa may not know one end of a racehorse from another, but he was absolutely right about that, you're a born entertainer. You've that gift, always had, of getting through to people, making them open up to you. I watched the faces – oh, how can I say it? – *blossoming*. Lord, that sounds fatuous, but . . .'

'Are you kidding?' I breathed. I felt dizzy. Drunk. Wondered if he was. 'But what?'

Suddenly he wasn't laughing. 'I suppose what I really meant, if this isn't too utterly ludicrous, is that I was suddenly seeing again the you I used to know and . . .' He grimaced. 'Look, don't misunderstand me, I admire terrifically everything you've achieved, everything you've done with your life. But this was the first time the woman you've become merged back into the one I remembered. And it knocked me for six. Absolutely. I felt like some wet-behind-the-ears nineteen-year-old again.'

Now I *really* couldn't believe I was hearing this. I stretched out a tentative hand. Touched his cheek. 'But I thought you wanted to forget all that. You've seemed so wary of me.'

It wasn't that he withdrew. He was still smiling. But it had hardened into that self-mocking, defensive smile. 'Be grateful I have. You've sorted your life splendidly. I've fucked mine. Believe me, you don't want to get tangled in the wreckage.'

And this time, for once, I didn't leap in. Didn't tell him I understood grief, that I wanted to help. No, just this once I had the sense to keep my hyperactive mouth shut. I'd like to think I finally began to suspect his afflictions might be more complicated than simple bereavement – why should a man whose wife has died talk as though he himself has wrecked his life? – but I'd probably be flattering myself. Whatever, I held my peace. Also my breath. And it worked.

'What about this evening?' he said abruptly. 'Drink? Dinner, maybe? Anywhere we can escape George and Polly. I warn you, you'll probably regret it, because if I break my week's abstinence, God knows, I may end up blubbing into your shoulder and –'

'Oh shit.' I flopped forward over the steering wheel.

'Rose?'

'I can't,' I wailed. 'Come out this evening. I'd *love* to, but . . . Thing is, I'm going away. Only for the night, and not very far, just over to Manchester as it happens, so I'm hoping to be back by –'

'Manchester?' said Tom with sudden frosty politeness. 'Popular place. It's where Stephen Sharpe's headed, or so I gather.'

If I'd had any sense I'd have assumed a look of amazement and invented an ailing aunt in Salford. But I was tired and, besides, there'd been too many lies.

'I'm sorry, how crass of me,' he said tightly. 'Steve felt obliged to give me the number of his hotel because the weekend editor's sloping off to a wedding reception. If civil war breaks out in Yorkshire, I gather I'm supposed to rush in and assume command of the bridge. God, I've been dim, haven't I? Considering you went to such lengths to protect the bastard – Sorry, I shouldn't insult your chum. I'm sure there's a truly warm and wonderful person lurking somewhere inside the Armani-plating, but there's no point pretending what I think about him, I've already said too much. Besides, you read my report. As you pointed out at the time, I did a pretty comprehensive demolition job on Stephen Sharpe. I'm not surprised you persuaded me to drop it.'

'It wasn't *that*,' I gasped. 'I only wanted –'

'Christ's sake, you don't have to explain anything,' he snapped, 'least of all to me. Tricky, I should think, working together in a small outfit like Radio Ridings. Well, I hope you have a wonderful weekend, both of you. Shall we get back to work?'

33

It was one of the more unpleasant journeys of my life. Barely a mile, but it felt like halfway round the globe. Via the Pole. The only sound was the click and swish of the windscreen wipers. I concentrated on the traffic; Tom studied the newspaper with matching ferocity. Only after I'd nosed into my space behind Radio Ridings and jerked the handbrake up with a savagery which made it squeal did he speak. 'Rose? This photo of Trevor Green . . .'

'No more about that bloody man,' I wailed. '*Please*. Listen, Thomas, about Stephen, I won't lie to you, but –'

'Forget it. Just look at this, will you?'

I tugged the keys out of the ignition and turned, reluctantly, to study the picture he was thrusting at me. It was a full-colour head-and-shoulders of Trev clad in one of those yellow helmets so beloved of PR men. He appeared to be in the cab of a bulldozer. 'No wonder it's a close-up,' I muttered, 'because they can't have shot it at The Willows, not for today's paper.'

'That's Trevor Green?'

'It's captioned clearly enough, isn't it? Surely you've seen other pictures?'

'Small ones. Photocopies. Whereas this . . . Oh, never mind.'

'What?'

As he took the newspaper back, he was excruciatingly careful not to touch me. 'You'll say it only crossed my mind because you linked them in the radio bid. Anyway, you've had enough of Trevor.'

I stifled an exasperated snort. 'I'm listening, OK?'

He twisted towards me. 'Remember at your flat in Blackpool – Henderson's flat, rather – that strange bloke turning up? Claiming he owned the place?' I stiffened, but he misunderstood. 'No, sure, now I think about it, you weren't there. You went crazy when I told you, though, convinced it was Frank Henderson.'

'Lincoln.'

'*Lincoln.* Absolutely. How on earth did you remember that?'

I shuddered. 'What about him?'

'This photo of Green suddenly reminded me of him. Yeah, I know, mad. It was the extraordinary nose, that's all. Still, he isn't the only thug in the world with a rearranged phiz.'

There were goosebumps prickling up and down my arms. 'You reckon?'

'Mind, there's the name too, I guess.' He began to laugh. 'Lincoln as in Green? You don't suppose the bastard operates under as many names as his dodgy companies?'

I suppose I made some noise of dismay. Tom thought I was just sick of the subject and snapped that he was sorry he'd mentioned it. 'Besides, you've wiped the memory banks clean of the Frankie-Henderson-flat days, haven't you? Let's get inside.'

He was already halfway out of the car. I caught his arm. 'I saw . . .' I hardly knew where to start. I didn't even *want* to embark on this. 'I saw Frank and Trevor together today.'

'Oh?'

'In the Market Hall, talking. Look, do you think we could find out whether they went to the same school? They're much of an age, both Wakeborough lads, both from the poorer end of town.'

Tom frowned. 'Why? Easy to establish, I imagine, but –'

'And then there's the flat,' I went on doggedly. Even though half of me was screaming that I should shut up. 'Bella Plaza, the block was called then, New South Promenade, I forget the number. Could we find out who owned the freehold? After all these years?'

Now he shut the car door again. 'Go on.'

'That – that man, who turned up, calling himself Lincoln. You wondered whether he might have meant he owned the whole block, don't you remember? You'd heard a sob story from a couple downstairs who were being bullied by the property company. You were ranting about fat-cat landlords, screwing a fortune out of helpless tenants.'

He pulled a face. 'Sounds like me.'

'Yeah, well, suppose you were right? Where did Trevor Green make his pile? In property.' I smiled bitterly. 'What's more, I wouldn't put it beyond him to throttle the odd budgie.'

'Blimey, the budgie,' he said, surprised into a snort of laughter. 'I'd forgotten that.'

'You didn't think it was funny at the time. And you can take it from me, Trevor Green levies astronomical service charges on his current properties. He hasn't changed much.'

'Oh, come on. This is fun, but it's totally off the wall. Lincoln equals Blackpool landlord equals Trevor Green? We haven't even established he and Frank Henderson are cronies. They could have met for the first time at the Fayre for all we know. And why would he be swanning proprietorially round that flat?'

I bit my lip. I hadn't wanted Thomas to know sixteen years ago. Even less did I want to dredge all this up now, with everything between us hanging so nerve-rackingly in the balance. But I'd come too far to stop. 'Suppose Lincoln was landlord of the block. And that he'd flogged his penthouse showflat – with mirrors, sunken bath and all the rest – to an old friend. With a few strings attached.'

'I'm not following. Do you know something I don't?'

I didn't answer directly. 'When he turned up on my doorstep last Sunday, Frank Henderson actually told me he had a deal on that flat with an old schoolfriend. Exactly, *schoolfriend*. Has to be a Wakeborough boy. When Frank was away, the friend would occasionally borrow the place to host – to host a party.'

'What sort of party?'

'What sort do you bloody think, in a flat like that? Business entertaining was how Frankie delicately put it. What he meant was fat drunken old men slobbering over underage tarts in gym-slips.'

'My God,' breathed Tom. 'This isn't guesswork, is it?'

'One thing's for sure. Those girls knew the man who was hiring them as Lincoln. Although it seemed he never showed up in person. I'm not surprised. Not surprised he used a pseudonym, either.' I was clutching the car key so hard it had dug a hole into my palm. 'No, it isn't guesswork. On that last day in Blackpool, I walked into one of Lincoln's parties. Which, take it from me, was a roaring, no-holds-barred orgy. And if you're about to ask whether I had anything to do with that kind of entertainment,' I shrieked, 'then bloody well don't, because the answer's no.'

I'll say one thing. It cracked the constraint between us. Tom shouted indignantly that he would never dream of suggesting such a thing. I snapped back that he'd probably every right to. And – after a glaring instant of silence – we both began to laugh.

'Why didn't you tell me about it at the time?' he said.

'You'd have been shocked rigid. Even *I* was shocked.'

'Good Catholic girl.'

'Heathen.'

'No, no. Only a heretic these days. In your book.'

'I don't have a book,' I said. 'Not any longer.'

We sat in the car with the rain beating down, and the windows steaming over as we pieced together our Byzantine mosaic of villainy. We never doubted that lonely, sex-starved Councillor Buckerill had enjoyed some business entertainment, courtesy of Trevor Green. Nor that details of his cavorting had reached the public courtesy of the same source. Very juicy carrots, one hell of a big stick.

'But it's still wild,' insisted Tom. 'We haven't a shred to link Trevor to Vertco. Nor to Frank Henderson, come to that. And the thing is, even if we make the big leap and assume, yes, Vertco was in Green's empire, I don't honestly see why he's running so scared now.'

'What?'

'Seriously. OK, we know what Vertco was up to. Unregulated waste-dumping's an offence, but they weren't exactly dealing in live plutonium. Even if the tip at The Willows were turned over, and they found the same dodgy practices had been going on there as elsewhere, what of it? A fine? Besides, the actual company's gone bust. I don't even know if he'd personally be liable. And yet he's spending a fortune shifting mountains of earth, just to stop Polly and her cronies digging around. Why? Being publicly identified as a reckless polluter may be bad for your image, but it's hardly life-threatening.'

'His image . . .' I let out a long whistle. I understood at last, even if Tom didn't. 'Remember you laughed at me for saying I was crazy to get into radio? Well, even I wasn't prepared to move mountains . . .' 'Course it wasn't the aesthetics of wireless that had attracted Trevor. Commercial stations, as I said to Tom, made money. Competition between bidding groups was intense, and the all-powerful Radio Authority didn't have to answer to anyone. In a fortnight's time, they would simply emerge from a locked room with the name of the winner. Secretive as the Vatican Council, and even squeakier clean. 'They're bloody careful who they let loose on the airwaves,' I said. 'Any scandal, and Trevor's consortium would be out. If you ask me, he's brought in the bulldozers to buy time. Couple of weeks from now, I shouldn't think he'll give a damn what COSH get up to. In the meantime, he's guarding his good name like a Victorian virgin. Look at the way he jumped on me.'

'Bloody hell,' murmured Tom. 'You're a genius, you know that?'

'Yup.'

'All we've got to do is prove it.'

I smirked. 'I leave the legwork to lesser intellects.'

'Anyone ever dropped you head first in a puddle, Rita Bagshawe? Because when we get out of this car . . .'

We were still spluttering and squabbling when we collided with Stephen at the door of the general office. Tom, who'd let out a triumphant whoop and was gesticulating wildly at Pete and Amanda, sobered up enough to say that he needed to find a way of taking a couple of journalists off the rota for a week, maybe two.

'Run that past me again?' said Stephen.

'I realize it will take some organizing,' responded Tom promptly. 'But we can hire casuals to cover. We've a huge story on our hands, and I need a team, with overtime budgets, the works.'

'I'm sorry,' said the Lamb. 'Out of the question.'

Tom wasn't going to argue in public, not with his bright-eyed crew massing mutinously at his back. 'Hang on, you chaps, tell you in a minute,' he said, and politely suggested they should talk in Stephen's office. 'Coming, Rose?'

I suppose I was surprised he invited me, but the door had shut behind us before it occurred to me that a wiser woman would have retreated. Steve, ushering me into a chair, gave my shoulder a sly squeeze as I sat down, only it wasn't sly enough. God knows why, after weeks of zealous discretion, he chose that moment to weaken, but Tom clocked it. Then looked away. I wanted to shake him. Tell him, yes, I'd had an affair with Stephen, but it had been a mistake, and it was finished now, even if the poor Lamb didn't know. Which led me to ponder, dejectedly, just how I was going to break the news tonight. I hardly heard Tom's brisk proposals for staff shuffling.

'All to resource an investigation into Green?' interrupted Stephen, looking bewildered. Not so much a lamb as a myopic sheep. 'I don't think you've joined up the dots on this one, Tom. Radio Ridings is threatened with shutdown, right? It's only solid local support that's keeping us afloat, and you're suggesting we take on, not just a prominent citizen, but the local *newspaper proprietor*? I'd need rock-solid grounds to agree this.'

'I want to go out and find the bloody grounds,' said Tom impatiently. 'Call me old-fashioned, but I've always thought that's what journalists were for.' Anyone who claims women always fall for the same type must be crackers, I thought. These two came from different planets. Stephen, stocky, grey and dapper as ever, was perched on the edge of his desk, bemusedly watching Tom who was striding the carpet, hair flying, arms flailing, gold eyes ablaze. 'Don't tell me this station gets a million-whatever quid a year just to reinterpret the unemployment statistics? Nor to dream up the Wakeborough angle on – on the economies of the Pacific fucking Rim? Surely we should be more interested in the dodgy economics of the wide boy up the road?'

Stephen frowned. 'What's dodgy about the man offering to landscape a former tip?'

'Plenty, if he wants to stop a local pressure group digging up whatever was dumped there.'

'But,' said Stephen, rather plaintively, 'you admit there's no proven connection between him and the company which operated the tip.'

'Well, not on the face of it, perhaps. But . . .' Only then, far too late, did I begin to assimilate that Tom hadn't invited me along as spectator. Nor even as collaborating genius. What was sinking in on my oh-so-brilliant brain was that all our wilder theories about Trevor Green were rooted in my past – in the flat in Blackpool – in Frankie Henderson. 'If I tell you,' continued Tom with strenuous calm, 'that I've had it from an unimpeachable source Green's past was tangled in any manner of shady dealings . . .'

I was shrinking into my chair.

'What source?' enquired Stephen politely.

Tom turned to me. Only for a second. He didn't need longer to read the sick panic in my face. I couldn't – simply couldn't – expose all of that here, now, to *Stephen*. He swung away from me. 'Sorry, I, um, can't tell you that.'

'Well, you'd better if you expect funding,' retorted Stephen, hopping to his feet. Suddenly he didn't sound plaintive or bewildered any longer. He sounded absolutely sure of himself.

Tom threw back his head, like a great caged lion about to roar. Stephen dodged smartly behind his desk, but all that emerged was a weary sigh. Tom was looking at the door and I knew what he was thinking. He was thinking of Pete, Amanda, Harry and the others out there, who deserved a crack at the juiciest story to come this station's way in a decade. For their sakes, he was striving – oh how transparently was he striving – to keep his temper. 'You're absolutely right,' he said at length. 'Everything I've got is unsubstantiated – so far. But I'm prepared to stake my career we can stand this story up. You've a bright staff, bursting to get to work. So . . .' He stuck out his chin. 'I can only ask you to trust me, as an experienced journalist, when I say Radio Ridings has to do it.'

Stephen, very slowly, shook his head.

'You realize what you're saying?' said Tom.

'I do. And let me put this one hundred per cent on the line. I'm vetoing all investigation. Green's a high-profile local citizen. I can't risk a cold-war scenario with him or his newspaper on the basis of some half-baked hunch.'

I shut my eyes, because I expected Tom to explode. In fact I wouldn't have been surprised if he had grabbed Steve by the scruff of the neck and shaken him. I wouldn't have blamed him, although I could sympathize with Steve's reluctance too, under the circumstances. It was all my fault for not backing Tom up. *Everything* was my fault, and now there was going to be the almightiest row, and I would have to drive off with Stephen in an hour and . . .

The explosion didn't come. I opened my eyes again to see Tom looking very weary, very much older – and every bit as bleak-faced as when he'd first arrived here. 'You're wrong,' he said. 'And if that's the way you choose to run Radio Ridings, then it might as well be axed now. Still, that's not my concern, is it?'

At first, believe it or not, I didn't quite grasp what he meant. But Stephen did. Like a shot. 'Would you like to put it in writing? I'll copy to Howard Hemingway and Personnel.'

'Oh for fuck's sake, I'll tell Howard myself,' said Tom tiredly. 'I'm not hanging around to compose letters. I'll clear my desk and get the hell out.'

34

'You can't do this,' I squawked, grabbing Tom's arm once we were outside in the corridor.

'Come on, Rose,' he said. 'That wanker gave me no choice, did he?'

'I'll talk him out of it,' I stammered. 'I'm sorry, I was an abysmal coward. I'll tell him everything. About Blackpool, about –'

He shook his head. 'Too late. Oh, don't look so bloody tragic. It probably wouldn't have made any difference. He wanted me out, has done since the day I arrived. Be glad you've kept your nice shiny façade intact. Don't want to shock lover boy, do we?'

'No!' I gasped. 'Oh Thomas –'

But he'd already bashed through the doors into the general office. They were waiting for him. They'd smelled trouble and they were all poised. Not a telephone was in use and every eye was fixed on the door. I shrank miserably into a rack of coats against the wall as Thomas squared his shoulders and strode into the room. 'Bit of a shock for you chaps,' he said cheerfully.

'You can't let this happen,' I said furiously to Stephen. I'd burst into his office to find him squatting beside his hi-fi tower.

'Who's this?' he demanded, and pressed a button.

'What?'

An elderly voice trickled out of the speakers, recalling an outside lav buried in a ten-foot snowdrift. 'There,' he said, 'the interviewer, whispering some question about the Moors Road.'

'George, who'd you think? Pretending she's a stereophonic fly on the bloody wall.'

'George,' he said, tapping his fingers thoughtfully on the fascia of the machine. 'I might have known.'

'Listen to me, Stephen,' I said fiercely, striding round the desk and grabbing his shoulder. 'Tom Wilkes has just left the building. He made a speech in the office –'

That at least made him look round. So sharply he overbalanced from his squatting position and thudded into me. And at that precise moment, with Stephen wrapped round my thighs, his secretary put her head round the door. She took in the whole scene and giggled coyly. 'Whoops, do I intrude?'

I could have screamed with vexation. An eye-witness report of this undignified clinch would be round the building faster than e-mail. I couldn't even struggle free immediately, because Stephen's specs were snagged in my sweater.

'Just wanted to say I can't raise Howard Hemingway,' she carolled. 'He's in a meeting, but I'll keep trying, shall I?'

'Get Georgiana Penistone in the meantime, would you?' Stephen snapped, clambering to his feet and snatching his glasses off me. 'I want a word with her, too. What did he have to say?'

I realized he was addressing me. 'Sorry?'

'Tom Wilkes. Just now. You said –'

'Oh, don't worry,' I answered bitterly. 'He behaved like the proverbial officer and gent. There was palace revolution brewing out there, Steve, and it was Tom calmed them down. He told them not to be so bloody silly.'

'And he's gone?' said Stephen.

'But we can still catch up with him at George's. Look, I blame myself for all this. We've more on Trevor Green than Tom admitted, much more. He couldn't tell you because –'

'Oh, bent as a corkscrew,' Steve said impatiently, and with such matter-of-factness I thought I must be misunderstanding him.

'*Tom?*'

'Green. At least, if the buzz round the business community is anything to go by. He's one dangerous son-of-a-bitch, for sure. Gives me the creeps.'

I gaped at him. 'But you said . . .'

Steve, who was just settling himself in his desk chair, blinked up at me. 'But that's no argument for bankrupting ourselves, just to be first to blow the whistle. Let a bigger outfit with a bigger budget fund the legwork. Soon as the story cracks, Radio Ridings will be in there.'

'My God, Steve, you've let Tom resign, and all the time –'

'Can I say something, Rose?' He leaned forward earnestly. 'Strictly non-sexist, OK? But the workplace should be a no-go area emotionally. Don't get me wrong, nothing to do with the situation between you and me, this is a general point.' And he was warming, visibly, to his little management pep-talk. 'You're headed nowhere fast, career-wise, if you let feelings take over. Tom Wilkes, textbook case. I rattle his cage, show him the cliff, stand aside – and the silly bastard's over like a lemming.' He was actually smiling.

'You *wanted* him to go,' I gasped incredulously. 'You deliberately goaded him to –'

'Which proves my point. He's dangerously unstable. Look at the rumpus he kicked up in London.' The phone was ringing. He picked it up, but clamped one hand over the mouthpiece and continued rapidly. 'We can't afford to have loose cannon like him blundering round the decks of a modern organization. As it is, I've saved the Corporation a sizeable redundancy package, as I'm about to tell Howard. Oh, sorry, it's George you've got for me is it, Monica? Yes, put her through.' He replaced the hand over the mouthpiece for an instant. 'Shut the door after you, would you? See you in, say, half an hour?'

Facsimile machines are dangerous toys. If we still relied on the postal services I would never have done it. The letter would have lingered in the out-tray, positively inviting second thoughts. Even if I'd ventured down to the post box, I'd have had to face the prospect of a weekend haunted by a vision of my envelope winging invisibly along mysterious channels of delivery.

As it was, within minutes of quitting Stephen's office, I was feeding Tom's report on Radio Ridings, page by careful page, into the fax machine, along with a covering sheet addressing the document to Howard Hemingway, Head of Centre. And, for good measure, I'd emblazoned the word URGENT across the top, in giant capitals. As I'd read Tom's views this time, instead of cursing as I had a week ago, I found myself nodding fiercely. Our news coverage had been every bit as dull and irrelevant as he claimed. And probably more so. I'd had the Tipp-Ex ready to obliterate anything which might embarrass him, but in the end hadn't needed to change a word. All the apologies for causing inconvenience to the station sounded perfectly appropriate. I was tempted to paste out his views on local radio in general – given his magnificent change of heart – but I stayed my brush even there. With the likes of Stephen Sharpe in charge, he was probably justified in every bitter word. All I blotted out was the date.

I watched with grim satisfaction as the pages peeled out of the machine, one after another. And then, just for good measure, in case any single word might have been scrambled along the way, I fed the whole lot through again. Tom, I had no doubt, was planning to be idiotically noble about the affair when he got round to contacting Howard, just as he had been when he made his little speech in the general office.

He'd insisted he was going for personal reasons. No, strictly personal, OK? They probably knew he'd had a rocky year in his private life. Well, there was, um, a spot of bad news from home and he thought he needed a spell away from work altogether to sort himself out. 'It's been a pleasure and an education working with you chaps,' he'd said, grinning. 'Even if I never did learn to work a fucking tape-machine. Keep the faith . . .'

'Don't,' he'd said to me as I blocked the door to his office. 'Whatever you're going to say, don't. Not now. Tell Polly . . . oh, that I'll be in touch.'

When I'd tried to argue with him, he'd just said that he could afford to play fast and loose with his salary, but these kids couldn't, and he wasn't going to stir them up, because revolutions always ended with the poor bloody foot soldiers piled high on the pavements before ever the generals got a whiff of gunpowder. And that, what's more, the laboratory where they cloned the likes of Stainless Steve had a stack of pre-programmed replicas waiting to glide into the gap if he fell and, oh Christ, before he said anything he really regretted, would I *please* let him go?

'Rose?' said Amanda, rolling up behind me, looking as dejected as everybody else in the office. 'George just rang for you.'

'Not now,' I snapped, yanking the last sheet from the fax machine. 'Anyway, I'm going round there almost immediately.' And please God, I was thinking, don't let Tom have left yet. 'Just got to give something to Stephen first.'

'Another quick snog behind the desk?'

I didn't deign to answer. Nor did I bother to knock before stomping into Stephen's office. He was tapping something into his computer, and looked up with a frown. 'Not quite ready for off yet, I'm afraid.'

'Nor am I,' I said. 'Nor will I ever be, at least, not with you.'

Even then, he carefully stabbed the 'save' button before swivelling his chair round to face me. 'Sorry?'

'We're through, Stephen. Or should I say, I'm unilaterally terminating our ex-officio inter-personal shagging scenario forthwith, heretofore and for good and all. Are you reading me?'

'Are you crazy?'

'I think I must have been. Insanity's about the only justification I could offer for wasting so much as five minutes of my life on a –' I planted my fists on his desk and leaned forward – 'on an intellectually stunted, verbally challenged, ethically defunct skunk like you.'

'My God.'

'I don't think the Director General can hear you.' I tossed a fat envelope on to his desk. 'I've just faxed this to Howard Hemingway. I thought you should see it. No, no,' I said cheerfully, 'it's not a letter of resignation, although believe me, I seriously contemplated putting my notice in. I refrained, however.'

I strode back to the door, and beamed at him.

'Frankly, it seemed to me, with a moron like you in charge of the joint, Radio Ridings needed me.'

Artsround/Flint feature cont.

TAPE A, LUCINDA: *I've been very lucky. And that isn't quivering-lip martyrdom speaking. My disease – notice the way I speak so proprietorially about it – my disease is, in many ways, just as horrible as you would imagine. It's my cage, my prison cell. My – let's be honest – my condemned cell.*

But what's hard for other people, outsiders, to realize is that a cage isn't just a trap. It's also a kind of security. If you're inside, no one can get at you. And it even represents a sort of freedom: I've never had to worry about the things other women have to worry about. Children, earning a living, rushing round the world doing all the clever things expected of us these days. Even putting make-up on, for heaven's sake – I gave that up years ago. My mind is freer than most people could ever begin to imagine. And, materially, I am lucky. It's no good pretending money doesn't make any difference. Illness is more bearable with all the little luxuries and gadgets and full-time care – I owe more than I can say to the people around me. Every caged bird should have a kind owner. To fill up the seed tray, change the millet and rattle the toys. I . . . well, I've been very blessed.

Lucinda was married to a television jouna~~li~~
Childhood friends, they married w~~h~~

'I can't read *this*,' I howled, ripping the page across and hurling the script away. 'Oh for pity's sake, George, no. No, no, NO!'

35

I pelted round to George's the minute I left Stephen's office. Didn't even grab a coat, which was stupid because the rain might have stopped, but clouds the colour of pewter were massing for a fresh onslaught. There was an ominously dry patch on the tarmac outside Brook House, as though a car had recently pulled out. Surely, I wailed, George wasn't about to tell me Tom had left?

'Yes – no,' she said, disjointedly. 'Or rather, he was calling me a few minutes ago. I – I said I couldn't come downstairs, that I was in the bath. Which I wasn't, of course. He shouted something about a note on the kitchen table.' She was leading the way down the dark hall to the kitchen as she spoke. 'Oh yes, there it is. Tea?' Without looking at me, she shuffled over to the ancient battleship of a gas cooker.

I suppose I noticed there was something odd about her, as though age had suddenly sagged her splendid frame, but my attention was riveted on the note, a scrawl on a torn half-sheet of paper. I couldn't *not* read it.

> Thanks a million, George. Sorry to do a bunk, but Rose will fill you in. Rent herewith. I'll be in touch.
> Much love, Tom.

There was a cheque, too. 'Five hundred?' I gasped.

'What?' said George, in the strangest voice. 'Oh, the foolish boy . . .' She hadn't turned round. She was hunched over the cooker, kettle in hand. Only then did I realize that she was crying.

'George?' George never cried. Well, except perhaps when listening to a particularly exquisite mix in one of her productions, and that wasn't *crying* crying. It wasn't the ugly sobs that were now making her shoulders flap like the wings of a very old and weary bird. I hurried across. 'George, love, whatever's the matter?'

She shook off my arm. 'What do you think? Stephen *bloody* Sharpe, that's what. Oh, who wants tea at this hour of the afternoon? Get me a gin.'

'Ignore me,' she said, blowing her nose with vigour. 'I'm a stupid old woman who should have hung up her microphone years ago.' She emerged from her handkerchief, briefly, to glare at me. 'Is that supposed to be a drink? Wouldn't give a flea a footbath. Pour away, woman. And leave the bottle. Help yourself to whatever you want.'

'Gin'll do fine,' I said dismally, pulling up a chair. I was still holding Tom's note. I'd just have to track him down. Personnel would have his address in London. *Their* address. Dared I turn up at the marital home? Would he even want to see me? With a mighty effort, I shoved my own problems aside along with Tom's scrap of a note. 'So what's Stainless done to offend you?'

George didn't so much drink, as fling the contents of her glass down her throat. She shut her eyes for a second, then shook herself like a dog emerging from water. 'He sacked me.'

'*What?*'

'Well, not in so many words. It appears he's considering putting weekend and ad-hoc programming out to competitive tender.'

'For the peanuts he pays you? Fat chance.'

'In the meantime, he wished to remind me I am not a member of staff, and cannot expect to rape and pillage Corporate facilities as though they were my own.'

'What's he been doing? Counting paperclips?'

'Worse than that.' She sighed. 'It seems he pressed the button on his dictaphone this afternoon, expecting the sacred chanting of audience statistics, but was treated to some recollections of the snows of '48 instead. He identified the interviewer as myself.'

'Oh shit,' I gasped. 'It was me. He played me the tape, I told him who it was.'

'If he didn't have tin ears,' she retorted with asperity, 'he should recognize any recording of mine from the very music of the words. However, this naturally led him to conclude I was in the habit of burgling his office.'

'But it was me. I lent the damn thing to Tom.'

'Quite. But I could hardly explain that Tom Wilkes had taped a farewell to the world over his precious statistics, could I? Nor did I think you'd be pleased if I, ah, grassed you up as the culprit.'

'I wouldn't have given a stuff. In fact, I'll ring the bastard and tell him myself.'

George shook her head. 'No matter. I told him I wouldn't employ a tinpot toy like that were it the only tape-machine to hand when Gabriel blew the last trump live. And even he had to concede my stereophonic gem could not actually have been recorded on his office gadget. Indeed, he was obliged to agree that, since my used cassettes litter the station like autumn leaves, anyone could have picked one up and plugged it into his lousy machine. But . . .' She sighed. 'I'd lost my temper by then, and offered one or two unwise aspersions on his style of management. Which was when he declared he'd long been considering restructuring the referral practices of . . . Oh I can't be twisting my tonsils with this Birt-babble. The crux is that, after forty-eight years in the BBC, my work now needs the beady-eared supervision of a senior producer young enough to be my grandson. Probably, had I been precociously prolific, my great-grandson.'

'Oh, George . . .'

'No, no. There's more. I am to be barred from the building outside scheduled working hours; I can no longer drive the works jalopies without multiply signed chits; programme ideas must be submitted with costings of merchant bank complexity; my . . . Oh, what does it matter?' A fat tear squeezed out of her eye. 'It's over. Half a century near as dammit working for this Corporation and it ends with Stephen Sharpe. I'm sorry, Rose. I've put up with a lot from that little toad, but I can't, I simply can't continue under those conditions. I'm too old to scramble through a new set of hoops, and he knows it.'

'Oh George . . .' I said again. Even more helplessly.

She blasted afresh into her handkerchief. 'Of course, I responded in the only way a civilized professional woman could.'

'What do you mean?'

'I told him to stuff his bleeding rationalization plans up his arse and fuck off.'

My mouth fell open. 'You didn't.'

'With a few animadversions on his parentage.'

'My God, George, I only told him he was – wait a minute, I've got to get this right – he was an intellectually stunted, verbally challenged, ethically defunct skunk.'

George had picked up the gin bottle, but she now paused in mid-air. 'You came out with all that *off the cuff*?'

I shook my head. 'Drafted the script before I went in. The only good ad-lib line was telling him I wouldn't go . . .' I began, help-lessly, to giggle. 'I said I wouldn't quit because – because Radio Ridings needed me. To – to save it from the likes of him.'

She hooted. 'Very true, old love.'

'But it's – it's not funny. The bastard's pushed Tom out, 's well as you.' The gin was hitting a stomach which hadn't seen food since last night and the laughter was very like sobs. 'George,' I wailed, 'what are we going to do?'

'Get drunk, what else? Except . . .' All at once, she was eyeing me thoughtfully. Next thing I knew, she'd screwed the cap back on the gin bottle.

'George?'

'Drinkies later,' she said, deftly removing the glass from my nerveless hand. Square-shouldered and steely-eyed with purpose, she rose from the table. 'First of all, my old fruit, you're going to record the links of the last feature I shall ever create. No, no, on your feet. You can't possibly refuse the last request of a dying producer . . .'

Which is how I ended up in George's dark and chilly dining room – her so-called Studio One – reading through that damned script.

We weren't recording, just giving it a dry run, but George in-sisted on playing me every word of her insert tapes, every laughing, heart-breaking syllable of Lucinda bloody Flint and her fan club. The only bits missing were the poetry readings. George was now gleefully planning – screw the budget – to hire an actress at full Equity rates to perform the poems. Nay, why be constrained by mere Equity rates? Was Dame Judi Dench free perhaps? Emma Thompson? It would give her exquisite pleasure to leave such a signed contract on Stephen's desk as a parting gesture. I was in no mood for frivolity. No, I muttered, I didn't want to see the printed copies of the poems. I just wanted to get the job over with. I sat in a dark corner, hunched over the script, striking out lines savagely, scribbling alternatives, flipping pages on to the floor, trying to block out the noise from George's huge speakers. But I couldn't. Lucinda's ethereal voice was echoing in my head, piercing my very soul. Only when I got to the stuff about Tom, though, did I crack. Flung the remaining script at George and told her no. No, no, NO!

'Why?' she said calmly.

'Because he's *mine*,' I howled. 'Not hers. And he's gone away and left me and I'm sorry, George, I know it means a lot to you but I can't, I truly can't bear it.'

'Pooh, silly girl. He'll be back.'

'Oh yeah?'

'Dear little Polly's going to be upset, though,' she said thoughtfully. 'Her father and what have you. How do you intend to break it to her?'

That halted me in mid-sob. 'You *did* guess.'

'It took me long enough. Heavens, from the moment he tottered into that wine bar, I'd been wondering of whom it was he reminded me. I even interrogated him about his family, to see if that was the link, but his papa was a diplomat so it seemed unlikely. And although I've interviewed the odd dippy wife in my time, I couldn't recall a Lady Wilkes. From the little Tom let slip, Mama sounds rather ghastly. Still, I gather that once she was widowed, she –'

'He's dead?' I cut in, momentarily distracted from my own concerns. 'I'm sorry, I liked Tom's father.'

'Look on the bright side. It means Mama has retired up a mountain in Chiantishire, where else? So at least she won't be troubling you.'

'Whaddya mean, troubling *me*?' I said thickly. 'Tom doesn't want anything to to with me, only Polly. He's in love with his wife, a bloody ghost, always was, and whatever I do I'll never –'

'Rita Bagshawe,' roared George, rising to her feet. A towering, glowering, six-foot column of wrath loomed over me. 'Have you listened to a single *word* of these tapes? Or has my work been washing past your ears like so much muzak?'

'How can I concentrate on sodding radio programmes,' I yelled, 'when my heart is breaking?'

'I wash my hands of you,' she snapped, stabbing buttons on all her machines and striding towards the door. 'The pair of you. All of you. Do what you like.'

'George?' I yelped, scrambling after her. 'Where're you going?'

'To the Fox, of course,' she said, yanking a cloak of marquee dimensions down from its peg on a stag's antler. 'Friday night is music night at the Tipsy Fox. Who knows?' She flexed her fingers. 'Now I'm bereft of other paid employment, I may yet become a full-time fixture at the cocktail piano. Kindly turn off the light when you go.'

'Not bloody likely,' I snarled, grabbing at random a mackintosh which terminated somewhere below my ankles. 'I'm coming with you.'

And so, a couple of hours on, here I am. Giving '*Mr Adorable*' the real old con-belto treatment. Except I'm sitting on a piano and not on some panting stranger's lap. Nor am I stripped to a couple of spangles and a G-string, although I'm dimly aware my skirt is rucked inelegantly high up my thighs. What the hell. I'm just wailing my broken heart across a smoky room and a sea of faces. Strange faces but also, so help me, *familiar* faces as well. Those are the faces which keep heaving into grinning close-up, telling me they'd no idea I could sing like this, had I ever thought of turning pro? And look, what am I drinking? And, as the evening winds on, and the place gets ever fuller, and are redder faces, shinier faces, matching, seen-in-double faces, but I don't care. As I wail my last high C and George ripples a sleazy arpeggio up the keyboard, there's a storm of clapping and whistling. Raucous demands for encores. Just like old times.

'Berra shtop,' I mumble, blinking. Funny, I can still sing syllables in some kind of order, but speaking them is another matter. Besides, there's the problem of getting off the piano. At this moment the floor looks several storeys down, and my head swims horribly when I peer over the edge. I hear a loud hiccup, realize it came from me. Maybe I'd better keep singing. I look round at George – both of her – but she's waving to someone.

'Woshhall we do nesht?' I ask exasperatedly. Because I'm stranded up here on the piano like a wally, with four, maybe five glasses next to me and – here's a funny thing – they're all empty. Before I can ask someone to fill 'em up, George's playing again and I don't know the tune. At least, 'course I know the tune, but it's not a song, is it? Rachmallin – Rachmangin – *Brief Encounter*, that's what. That's what she's playing. Piano sodding concerto from *Brief En*-sodding-*counter*. Which, far as I'm concerned, is just about as tactless as you can get. Like thumping out 'Too Darn Hot' in the crematorium. Because all I've been thinking about is Thomas on that station. Day I left him. And he was spouting poetry, silly pillock. And that old couple in the carriage were watching, laughing their heads off, saying it was just like the movie. 'Cept there wasn't any steam. Might've been a long, long time ago, but it wasn't *that* long. Rotten diesel chugger, wasn't it? But the old codger was whistling the tune. This exact same tune. And I don't *care* if George doesn't know all that. She could guess, couldn't she? That I'm in a senstiff condish. Sodding heart-broken, more like. And this kind of stuff'd make anyone bawl their eyes out. Most partic'ly me. Remembering Thomas that day, a little golden figure, end of the platform, grinning, waving, getting littler and littler . . .

Except he's not getting littler. His face is getting a whole lot bigger. Oh God, it'll be pink rats next. And what does George think she's doing? This piano's rocking like a boat in a thunderstorm. I'm the only one aboard, and I'm getting seasick. I look round, and she's grinning like a maniac, hurling herself on the keys like she's sodding Liberace. With twenty fingers on her hands – all of her hands. I close my eyes for a minute – much worse, going to throw up – flip them open again, and Thomas is in front of me.

'No,' I moan. 'I know I'm – bit drunk. I mean, very drunk. But I didn't think I was *that* drunk.'

And that, I'm told, was when I passed out.

Fortunately Thomas caught me.

4 Round-the-clock Service

Snow? Floods? Elections? If the need arises, you can be sure **Radio Ridings** will stay on air, keeping you in touch with the news as it happens.

36

'Well, hello, and a very good *evening* to you. Yes, this is BBC Radio Ridings, I'm Rose Shawe and I'm popping up this Saturday night because, as you've probably heard on the news throughout the day, there's some flooding in and around the town. Worst affected are the Cromwell Road and Blackthorn Estate areas, where the emergency services are evacuating some of the inhabitants. I'm afraid the police tell us the river's still rising – although not so fast as earlier. Hardly surprising, I guess, with all the rain recently, but that's no consolation if you live in one of those parts of the town which always suffer at times like this. I don't know if it's still raining now, but it was certainly pelting down as I drove in.

'Anyway, we've reporters heading out to the affected areas' – out of the corner of my eye, I see Tom throw up his hands in mock despair – 'and we'll be staying on air to keep you posted with the latest news, advice from the emergency services and, of course, any more flood alerts, if and when they come in. I hope to be talking, in a minute, to the man coordinating relief operations but, in the meantime, some music from Barry Manilow . . .'

'*Barry* fucking *Manilow?*' yelps Tom's voice in my headphones.

'We've got to fill with *something*,' I retort, 'until you line me up someone to talk to. It was the first disc came to hand. And you can tell whichever joker it was got "Singing in the Rain" out for me, I'm not amused.'

'Spoilsport,' he whispers.

'"And now good morrow to our waking souls . . .,"' had whispered that same voice into my ear rather earlier in the day.

'No,' I mumbled, face down in the pillow. 'No, not poetry.' I stretched a tentative arm to the other side of the bed. Nothing. Wiggled my arm around a bit. That side of the bed was definitely empty. Empty and cold. With immense care I raised my head and opened an eye. The daylight smote my brain like a stun gun. I whimpered, blinked, and finally made out Tom's face in foreground. 'Stay well clear,' I croaked. 'My breath'll kill at twenty paces if the taste in my mouth's anything to go by.'

'Want to drink this?'

'Drink?' I echoed feebly. 'Don't even say that word.'

Only very slowly was I piecing my situation together. That I was home, I knew. Even when you're three parts unconscious, there's an instinct that tunes into the very air, telling you this is your house, your bed. Whether Tom had shared the bed with me last night was less clear. I dimly recollected locking my arms round his neck as he carried me – yes, carried me – up the stairs. In fact I remembered being not entirely sure through which door to direct him. We had nearly ended up in the bathroom. But after that . . .

He was fully dressed now. Not what you'd call up-and-about, washed-and-shaved, bright-eyed-and-et-cetera dressed, just packaged in clothes. They looked like he'd slept in them. But then, his clothes generally did. He was holding both a glass and a mug. 'This one first,' he murmured, proffering the glass. 'Can you sit up a bit?'

I twisted on to my back, feeling my brain roll in my skull like a delinquent blancmange, and realized I was naked. I'd undressed then? But not got as far as finding a nightshirt? Or did it mean . . .? I shuffled a few inches up the bed, clamping the quilt primly across my chest.

'Well done,' said Thomas. 'Here you go.'

I took the glass. Murky concoction. 'What is it?'

'Little recipe of my own. Tastes filthy, but that isn't the point. No, no, don't sip it. Knock it all back.' I was too weak to argue. Whatever it was rampaged down my gullet like napalm. I choked. He smiled. 'Now some tea?'

But my head was clearing. 'What time is it?'

'Eight thirty or so. Why?'

'Very dark.'

'Yeah, well, we're in a lull now, but there've been tempests blasting half the night. At two o'clock this morning I was watching the lightning crack the skies over the reservoir. The view from your sitting-room window was spectacular.'

'Sitting room,' I said slowly. Contemplating the coldness of the

260

other half of the bed. His crumpled clothes. My condition last night. 'Thomas, does this mean . . . That's to say . . .' I took a deep breath which made the room lurch. 'What exactly were you doing in my sitting room? In the middle of the night?'

'Reading,' he said. 'Thinking. Listening to music. Finishing a bottle of wine I found open. I hope you don't mind. I thought I should, um, avoid the hard stuff.'

More memories were filtering back, in random spurts. Feelings first. My giddy bliss at discovering it really was Tom leading me – no, half carrying me – out of the Tipsy Fox. He'd come from Leeds, that's right, because he said he'd walked into Head of Centre's office, found Howard reading his report, realized it must've been me faxed it . . . I also remembered, wincing, the cheers from the regulars as I exited. And nearly passing out again as the cold air and rain hit me. But I felt dizzier still with the delight of Tom hoisting me up in his arms. And I wouldn't let him load me into his car because I was too busy kissing him – or trying to, surprised to find myself nuzzling his ear. I also remembered wrapping myself ferociously round him, telling him how much I loved him, how much I'd always loved him and . . . 'Oh, lumme,' I whimpered.

'You'll feel better in a minute. Drink your tea.'

'It's not *that*. I feel such a fool. Last night, I was so drunk, and you had to carry me and . . .'

His face creased into a smile. 'You were wonderful. Totally irrepressible. You seemed to think the whole of Wakeborough needed to know how you felt about me. And, take it from me, with a foghorn voice like yours, they probably do.'

The warmth in his face reassured me, but I still couldn't *remember*. I mean, it's so embarrassing, isn't it? Waking up the next morning, and not actually knowing if . . . I took a sip of tea. He was right about that cocktail he'd mixed. It was having a powerfully restorative effect. I can't say I was feeling well, but the fogs were uncoiling. And I suddenly remembered the buckle on his belt. Remembered it because it had nearly gouged a chunk from my thigh as we'd tumbled – yes, definitely, both of us – had tumbled on to this bed. And, one way or another, had shed our clothes, but . . . 'We didn't, did we?' I whispered awkwardly. 'In the end?'

Tom looked away. 'I'm sorry.'

'God, what've you got to be sorry for? *I'm* sorry. I'm amazed I wasn't comatose even before you managed to cart me up here.'

He shook his head. 'That wasn't the problem.' He'd been crouching at the bedside but he stood up now and walked over to the window. 'It was me. My fault. I couldn't make love to you.'

It took every ounce of courage I possessed. The tea was trembling in the mug because I was gripping it so hard. 'Did you, um . . . Did you, by any chance, want to?'

'Oh, Rita,' he said. 'What kind of a dumb question is that? I've never wanted anything more in my entire bloody life.'

The skies outside the window might have been the colour of day-old bruises, but as far as I was concerned, the sun beamed out at that moment, flooding my entire being. 'That's all right, then,' I said, grinning idiotically. 'Heavens, why are you looking so grim? Happens to everyone once in a while.'

'It's happened to me consistently for the past ten months. Whenever I've been stupid enough to make the attempt.'

That made me pause. 'Ten months?' I said cautiously. 'Are we talking – since Lucinda died?'

'Got it in one.'

I put down my tea. Held out my hand imperatively towards him. Very slowly he walked back towards the bed and let my fingers close round his. 'It's all right, Thomas,' I said passionately. 'I know you're grieving for her, that you still love her very much, but –'

'Bullshit.'

In my surprise, I let go of his hand. 'Sorry?'

''Course it's not because I'm in love with poor Lucy. That's the whole point, don't you see? I thought I'd made that much clear on that tape I gave you. I'm only in this mess because I didn't love her – and I never had.'

We talked in that bedroom for nearly three hours. The clock downstairs had long struck eleven when I finally sneaked away, leaving him sprawled across the bed, asleep. In the whole of that time, we barely touched, let alone tried making love, but I think we were more intimately locked in the end than ever we could have been after sex – even after the best sex imaginable. Which, Thomas assured me, was what he remembered with me. Nothing since, he insisted – to my smirking satisfaction – had ever, quite, matched up.

'First love,' I mocked. 'Rose-tinted memories.'

'Ungrateful sod. Don't you remember it as good?'

'Only total, soul-melting, wit-shattering paradise.'

'Can't you sound a bit more enthusiastic?'

But that is to leap ahead. At first it was all I could do to assimilate this astonishing revelation of his feelings for Lucinda. The oddest thing was that not just could I not quite believe him, but I realized, in some obscure way, I didn't *want* to believe him. Mad. I should have been jubilant, but I felt disturbed. Particularly when he went on to say, quite matter-of-factly: 'I was never faithful to her.' He had moved away and was toying with the debris on my dressing table. 'Ironical, isn't it? I've been screwing away adulterously for years, and it's only when I'm free to do what the fuck I like, I find, suddenly, I can't.'

I gulped. 'Is it guilt then?'

'Not about that,' he said impatiently. 'I was always honest. I made it clear to anyone I was involved with that, well, I *couldn't* get involved. That I was married to Lucy and I was never going to leave her. And Luce knew that, of course.'

I was desperately trying to shuffle these revelations into a pattern I could understand. After all, the woman had been chronically ill. Tom was neither a saint nor a eunuch. 'She knew that you were sleeping with other women?'

'Lord, yes. We didn't talk about it, that would have been crass, but she wasn't stupid. She was terrifyingly clever, right up to the day she died. That was the worst thing about her foul disease. Her body twisted into a husk, all her organs packing up – except her brain. That stayed as supple as ever. Besides, I wouldn't have lied to her. I only ever told Lucy one big lie in my whole life and that taught me how dangerous a lie can be, how it can fester away for years . . .' He broke off and glanced over his shoulder. 'Sorry. That sounds as if I'm getting at you. I'm not.'

'I don't understand,' I said. I didn't. Probably the hangover wasn't helping, but neither was Tom. When I asked him to stop pacing the room like a caged animal and, please, sit down and explain, he took refuge in that brighter-than-bright grin, said he was damned if he was going to bore me with his hang-ups, he'd work them out one way or another, and, for now, wouldn't I prefer a bacon sandwich? With a shudder I assured him there was nothing I would like less. All I wanted was for him to talk to me. Surely talking would help?

'It's a myth,' he said. But he did at least settle on the corner of the bed. 'The great sixties con trick. Let it all hang out and everything will be solved.'

'It helped me,' I said, so vehemently he started. 'Talking instead of gulping back the tranquillizers, which is what I did after my mother died and Polly was born.' That potion of his must have packed a powerful punch because I was waxing more articulate by the minute. Didn't even feel too deathly, provided I kept my head still. 'And I know this is no time to argue the merits of local radio, but that's what guided me out of the pit: an item on a show much like mine, about a helpline for women on prescription drugs. What's more, I found out about adult education classes from the same show. Do you see now why I wanted this job so passionately? But,' I went on firmly, 'that's beside the point. What I'm saying is that I talked my way out of the pit. It can work.'

He still looked unconvinced. But if there's one thing I'm good at, that I've spent the last however many years practising, it's the craft of making people talk. And you always start with a nice, easy, specific question. 'If nothing else,' I said, 'can't you at least explain how you came to marry Lucinda in the first place?'

'Pig-headedness,' he said. 'Remember me at nineteen? Well, try and imagine that starry-eyed little pillock returning to Oxford from Blackpool and, bit by bit, realizing he'd been given the bum's rush. The woman I loved – the only woman I was ever going to love, naturally – had vanished, and the whole world was going to know my life was ruined. I never did anything by half in those days. Believe me, sweetheart, I *wallowed* in it.'

I smiled faintly. 'Oh, Thomas.'

He laughed. 'No, seriously. And I took myself deeply, *deeply* seriously. I stopped shaving, took to drink, cigarettes – doubtless it would have been drugs if I weren't such an innocent. I swore I was through with women, through with education; I hardly went to a tutorial for weeks; I talked about joining the army – if not the Foreign bloody Legion.'

'Don't make me laugh, it makes my head hurt.'

'Serves you right, you heartless harpy. But I'm sure I was a huge joke to just about everybody who knew me at the time. Well . . .' The laughter petered out. 'Apart from Luce.'

'Ah,' I said. 'No, I don't suppose she'd find it funny.'

'She played ministering angel: pampered me, fed me black coffee and aspirins, listened to all my ravings and, in the end, climbed into bed with me. Which was much the best remedy, far as I was concerned. By the summer I was shaved, intelligent, re-enrolled in the human race and beginning, rather too late, to wonder what I was going to do about this sweet girl who was, by now, living in my room down the Iffley Road, cooking my meals, supervising my essays, and virtually running my life.'

'So what did you do?'

'The meanest thing of all: I let it drift. The long vac was coming up, I thought that would bring the affair to a painless end. Then I got back to my room one day after a cricket match – I remember it so clearly, because it was a gorgeous afternoon, brilliantly hot – and she was curled in front of the gas fire. At first I thought, how odd when the weather's so warm; then I realized. Oh, she didn't do herself any harm. We didn't have the kind of gas you *could* damage yourself with, not unless you lit a fag – which I bloody nearly did when I realized what she was up to. Lucinda never stopped apologizing for that afternoon, for years afterwards. You see, she went completely crazy. I couldn't believe it. Sweet, cheerful Lucy, screaming that I'd just been using her, shagging myself senseless every night when I didn't give a toss about her, had I ever even wondered what might happen if she got pregnant? Which, I promise, nearly gave me a heart attack. No, she wasn't pregnant, she yelled, but it was no thanks to me. I'd fucked up her work, her social life, her whole Oxford career. She loved me so much she just wanted to die.'

'My God,' I breathed.

'Quite,' he said, but he was misunderstanding me. He'd no idea what I was suddenly wondering. 'I felt an absolute shit. No, more than that, I *was* a shit, knew full well I'd been behaving like a king-sized bastard for months. And after all the song and dance I'd made about the miseries of unrequited love.'

'So?'

'So that's when I told the big lie,' he said. 'The whopper. I said of course I loved her. Maybe I didn't really know it was a lie, because, dammit, I *did* love her. She was my second cousin, play-mate, sister, friend; in a way, I'd always loved her. But not in the right way. Once you're launched down that track, though, there's no stopping. You find yourself protesting louder and faster and, the next thing I knew, we were on the phone to our families, telling them we were engaged, even though, somewhere, I knew it was mad.' He grimaced. 'You really want to hear this? Surely you've got the gist.'

'Go on,' I said fiercely. 'Why did you end up actually getting married? Did your parents push you into it?'

'Sure, but not in the way I imagine you mean. I say, I realize this is your bedroom, and it's a filthy habit . . .'

'Goodness sake, help yourself,' I said. 'Use that saucer. I'd prob-ably cadge a drag myself if I weren't terminally ill –' I broke off aghast. 'God, how tactless.'

He grinned at me as he lit his cigarette. 'You know you've got mascara halfway down your cheeks? You look like a sad clown.'

'Thanks. So what did your parents say?'

'All the sensible things you'd expect. That we shouldn't rush, that we were too young. My father was reasonable; he was fond of Luce, they both were, but he said I was only just finding my feet – his diplomatic way of suggesting she was only the second woman I'd been to bed with – and he recognized I'd been in a fair old stew over you. Said he understood that too, he rather took to you himself.'

'He *what?*'

'He seemed to think you were destined to carve an interesting path through the world. Said that, if he had to be stranded on a desert island with one woman and it was a choice of you or Luce, it would be you every time. And he wasn't speaking carnally. He said you were a survivor and a fighter with a great warmth of soul.'

'Jesus,' I mumbled, blushing so ferociously I felt my shoulders burning.

'Ma, however, made the mistake of throwing you back in my teeth. Claimed I wouldn't be in this mess if I hadn't got mixed up with that – that . . .'

'Whore? Tart?'

It was his turn to blush. 'I dare say. Anyway, she told me it was no excuse for hurtling into marriage, so, naturally, that's what decided me. Parental opposition was all I needed. We did the deed with a couple of friends as witnesses in a register office in Oxford. It actually seemed quite cool, getting married when everyone else was getting themselves laid as often and as variously as they could. Disastrous, of course. The parents were right. Once finals were out of the way, I was ripe for straying. Did, in fact, in the cold grey dawn following some ball or other. Luce didn't know – at least I don't think she did – but we were at each other's throats half the time. Before we actually reached the divorce courts, though, she was in the hands of the medics. She'd been suffering odd symptoms for ages, but students get all kinds of peculiar complaints under exam stress. Once the awful truth began to emerge . . .' He smiled sadly. 'Well, I suppose you could say everything changed.'

'My poor Thomas,' I whispered. Only then, at last, did I begin to understand. And found myself saying, with real feeling: 'Oh, God, poor Lucinda.'

37

'She told me to leave her,' he said evenly. 'Insisted I must go off and make my own life, have a family, all that kind of stuff. She meant it, too.'

'Yes,' I said. 'Yes, I can imagine she would.' I was remembering that brave, merry voice in George's feature. And I listened now to Thomas telling me he'd kidded himself a cure could be found. That his job was to look after her in the meantime, chase specialists, trundle her round hospitals. But as the truth emerged, that the best Lucinda could hope for was a slowing of her physical deterioration, the key, he said, had turned in the lock of his marriage.

'Recognizing that was a relief, actually. The dilemma was solved, I had no choice. Besides, she insisted she didn't expect sexual fidelity. She said the promise would crush her. In one of her poems, she claimed infidelity happened in the soul, not under the duvet, which I think is true, but . . .' He shrugged. 'Anyway, you may find this hard to believe, but I used to think we had quite a good marriage. In our own odd way.'

'I do believe it,' I said.

'I worked, she wrote, and with help from the families we had money to keep her looked after. And when things got bad, at least I knew she had me, that she could rely on me. Right to the bitter end. We'd agreed for years that, when her life became intolerable, I would . . .' He shrugged. 'But I've told you this.'

'She knew you would help her to die,' I said. 'And you did.'

Leaning against the bed head, he was turned away from me, staring out of the window at the iron clouds thudding across the sky. There was something wrong, but I didn't know what. Just the memory of Lucinda's death? But *why*? For the first time – the only time – he'd made any move to touch me – his hand locked over mine. 'God, I'm tired,' he said. 'Suddenly I'm so tired I can hardly speak.'

'Didn't you sleep at all last night? I know you weren't in here with me, but . . .'

'Know what I was doing? I was reading your house. Looking through your bookshelves, records; studying photographs, of you, of Polly. Trying to catch up with your life. Find out about you.'

'Oh, love.'

'The little woman with the spotted dress, sitting in a deck chair, that's your mother?'

'Sure. The first Mary Bagshawe.'

'But no old pictures of you, not as I remember you.'

'Of Rita, you mean?'

'Don't,' he said fiercely. 'Don't talk as if Rita is some stranger, someone you don't even like. I *loved* Rita, can't you see?'

'But . . . For God's sake, Thomas, you've got to admit it would never have worked. A relationship between us, then.'

'Wouldn't it?'

'I didn't think so, even at the time. I knew you'd grow out of me. Sex isn't everything.'

His face jerked round towards me. 'Sex wasn't everything we had,' he said, with an indignation which made him look so like the boy I remembered, I laughed. So did he, but he went on passionately: 'We didn't just screw. I've never talked as much in my whole goddamn life. I know you probably thought I was a pillock, spouting cock-eyed politics and loopy poetry . . .'

'You were off the known map for me, honey.'

'But we had something, didn't we?'

'I suppose so,' I said. 'I mean, yes, of course we did. But . . .' But nothing. I *had* loved Thomas. Suddenly I knew with absolute certainty that I truly had loved him enough to let him go, even if I'd finally been driven to break that great, unselfish resolve. Besides, if I'd wanted, I could have tracked him down. And I never had. I actually found myself admiring Rita — myself — because I doubted I'd ever have her sort of reckless bravado again. I might be prepared happily to scale mountains and forge rivers and what have you for Thomas Wilkes, but I would never again let him go. And what's more, it was only because Rita had been great-hearted enough to release him that I could gather him back now, with so much more chance of enduring happiness. 'Because it wouldn't have lasted, all those years ago,' I insisted. 'No, be realistic,

269

Thomas. You were at Oxford while I was working the Flaming Flamingo. Home for you was Ashburtley Hall, for me it was a corner shop in –'

'Anyone ever tell you you're an appalling snob?'

'Polly, frequently. Listen, will you? I'm not denying that, in spite of everything, you loved Rita. Like I loved the loopy kid spouting poems.'

He grinned. '"Our two souls which are one, um . . ."'

'"Our two souls, therefore, which are one . . ."'

'"Like airy –"'

'"Like gold to aery thinness beat". And you've missed out two lines in the middle, you pillock.'

'How'd you know?'

'I did a paper on Donne. You're talking to an Eng. Lit. graduate here, sunshine. First-class Honours.'

'You got a First?' he yelled. 'You jammy bugger.' He caught my shoulders. And then we both stiffened. I was just miserably conscious of my reeking breath. He – well, it was something more profound holding him back. 'I see Polly's into poetry, too,' he said abruptly. 'Or at least, into Lucinda. The new collection was tucked down the side of an armchair. I thought it was yours at first, but I read the inscription inside. *To Polly from Kevin.* Not *love from*, so he's obviously potty about her.'

I smiled faintly. 'Is that how it works?'

'Sure. The famous inarticulacy of young lovers. Well, not garrulous little pricks like I was, but normal self-respecting young lovers. Lucinda's home patch. Polly must have been reading it closely, too, judging by the spine. How bloody ironical.'

'Why?'

I sensed I was, at last, getting to the truth. The root of it all. 'I wonder what Polly would think,' he said flippantly, 'if she knew it was her own mother inspired the whole damn book?'

In the end, an hour or so later, he fell asleep while we were still talking. I didn't try to rouse him. Just slid out from under the quilt, tucked it over him as best I could, grabbed a dressing gown and pattered off downstairs. I urgently wanted a bath, but I wanted to see that poetry book first.

Thomas had exaggerated, I realized as I pored over the pages, although I knew what he meant. It seemed my ghost had stalked Lucinda's life as vividly as hers had mine, and for very much longer. There were, however, only three poems which could be said, indisputably, to refer to me, and of those, I was very sure Thomas hadn't deciphered the reference in the third. Had I only listened to George's feature yesterday evening, I would have known about the first two. Unmistakable. 'Wakeborough Fair' was not a hymn to a town, but to a girl from that town, a tarty, hearty wench whose memory obsessed the poet's beloved. And then there was her acid little parody of 'Scarlet Ribbons'. *I looked in to pick a fight* . . . Only her man doesn't have scarlet ribbons on his pillow, he has a tatty scarlet garter tucked underneath it. Poor Lucinda, I murmured. You'd have been well within your rights to strangle Thomas with that garter.

I almost rang George, to apologize, to tell her she had indeed cut to the very quick of the truth on this feature. As I studied the poems, curled in a corner of my sofa that grey blustery afternoon, I remembered Lucinda describing herself as pig-headed, forever striving for something out of reach. The unhappy child even joked about wanting to sing, to lure men with her siren voice. The academic had summed it up, though. Too many of these witty little verses were spiked with the yearning anguish of a love Lucinda knew would never be returned, or not in the way she wanted.

And this, I now knew, was the revelation which had so devastated Thomas when, months after his wife's death, he opened the shiny, fresh-from-the-publishers copy of *Strange Airs*, the collection of poems she'd written in the first months of their marriage, and then hidden away for the rest of her life. It didn't matter that their marriage had, by mutual agreement, settled into a sturdily platonic bond. What these poems glaringly revealed was that Lucinda had known all along that he'd never loved her. That his great big kindly lie had not fooled her for one wretched second.

'Which is what finally cracked me up,' he had said to me. 'Realizing why she'd kept the poems from me all these years. And I found myself wondering whether she had, truly, wanted to die. Or whether she'd felt obliged to do it, just to release me. The medics could have kept her going, maybe for years, but she'd always told me that, when the pain and the indignity got too much, she wanted to quit. And I'd believed her. We'd talked about it for years; she'd done her research, made her plans. I still believed it, 'course I did, when I fed her the drugs, when I ended up clamping the pillow over her face.'

'But now you don't?'

'I don't know,' he'd burst out. 'Can anyone really want to die? While their brain is still bright? And if there wasn't a part of me, somewhere, which hadn't wanted to break free, could I have done it? Shouldn't I have been persuading her there was something worth living for? Know what the last thing she said to me was? *I'm so sorry*. As though she was apologizing for hanging around so long.'

I'd let out a sigh. For the first time in fifteen-odd years, I was aware that in some dusty corner of my soul I was actually offering thanks to that cruel bastard in the sky I'd cursed for so long. I still choked on the memory of Father Michael's pious claim that all suffering has a purpose, because no one, surely, should ever have to suffer as Mum had, but I recognized that a frail blessing was, after all these years, emerging from her death.

I'd grabbed Tom's hand. 'If I could have done for my mother what you did for Lucinda,' I said, 'I would have. I know she longed for a quick overdose of something, although she couldn't say so, still less take one. Suicide, wouldn't you know, is just about as mortal as a sin can be, an express trapdoor down to the other place. But I'd have helped her, bet your life I would, only there were no kindly, worldly doctors like yours in her ward. And the nuns were stingy with even the puniest of painkillers because, they said, it wasn't up to them to prejudge Divine intentions. There might be a holy miracle. Mum might turn the corner, begorrah they mustn't risk turning my mammy into a drug addict, must they now? No,' I insisted, as he tried to speak, 'it's true, every word. I had blazing rows with all of them, priests, nurses, doctors, begging them to give her something, anything, to stop the pain. I sneaked whisky into her tea, crushed up aspirins; if I could have got my hands on poison, I'd have fed it to her like a shot. She wanted to die. Even though her brain was fine, even though she'd got *everything* to live for, because she was desperate to see her grandchild, it was still so bad in the end that she wanted out. And what's more, even though I passionately wanted her to live, because I was scared stiff of being left alone, for her sake I'd have killed her if I could. I was stupid enough to plead with the bloody doctors to give her a big dose of something. Fat chance. I only wish I'd had the sense – and the courage – to pick up a pillow.'

He didn't speak. Just looked at me, wanting to believe me, not quite able to, not yet. But he would. Because I *knew*. I too had watched someone I loved die, had felt the soul quitting the shell, and I'd known, just as he had, that it was right and good, and that they'd wanted to go. As Mum had said, she was ready to be gathered. Only difference was, Thomas had found some sense of God in the process, I'd lost any I ever had. Now I wasn't so sure.

'I love you,' he said at length. 'Always did.'

'And I love you,' I answered. 'And I always did. But . . .' I paused to think about this, because the time for lies, kindly or otherwise, was gone. I wanted to be sure this was the truth. 'But I'm glad you never got my letter. Maybe it would have worked between us, maybe not. What I do know is that I didn't deserve you all those years ago. And Lucinda needed you, in life, and in death. And I am, truly, thankful that she had you.'

I think he was asleep before I finished the sentence.

Now I was staring at the third poem; the last poem in the book, as it happened. The jaunty, silly little verse which, more than any other, was about me. Only no one except me would ever suspect. 'Male Mail', it was called. Reading it gave me the oddest sensation. As though this woman who'd been dead almost a year was actually sitting beside me, talking to me, confessing the last big secret. Barely twenty lines long, it began:

> How'd you get your kicks?
> Gazing in his eyes?
> Unzipping his flies?
> Or teasing your nail
> Through a hot and steamy veil
> Underneath the flap
> Of his confidential mail?

Poor, lovelorn Lucinda, who had so tenderly cosseted Thomas through his miseries, who had long since moved into his room outside college. As he'd said, she was running his life, cooking his meals, supervising his work . . . Well, it didn't take much of an imaginative leap to suppose that she'd regularly call in to collect his post from the college lodge, did it? That the porter would know full well she was Mr Wilkes's longstanding girlfriend? Of course he'd hand over even a Registered Letter. And she would see the Yorkshire postmark, the painfully awkward printing on the envelope, the words PRIVATE AND CONFIDENTIAL marching across the top. On that gloriously hot, summer's day, when Thomas was safely out of the way playing cricket . . .

It wasn't just Thomas who'd lived all these years under the weight of a long-ago lie. So had Lucinda. No wonder her last words were that she was sorry. She'd known not just that Thomas could have refound his tarty temptress, but also that he had a daughter. And she hadn't told him. Instead, she had turned on the gas to frighten him, screamed at him, and, finally, shamed him into marrying her.

I wasn't just guessing all this. The last line of the poem, surely, gave the game away:

> my sweet,
> Your witch may enchant, but she can't bloody spell.

The last piece of the jigsaw had finally fallen into place.

'Thanks very much. Wakeborough's Chief Fire Officer there,' I chirp, plugging a button to disconnect the line. 'Nearly half past seven here on BBC Radio Ridings, I'm Rose Shawe with a special programme, keeping you in touch with the latest about the floods affecting parts of Wakeborough this evening. Good news is, reports are coming in that the river level has stopped rising. I'll be talking to the police soon, hoping for confirmation of this, but in the meantime, I'm going to hand you over to our reporter Harry Sturrocks, who's down at the Community Centre on the Blackthorn Estate. Are you there, Harry?'

'Yes, hello, thanks, Rose. Well . . .'

I heave a sigh of relief and lean back in my chair as Harry ('Parrot' as he's now known) rattles into a breathless situation report. Tom, on the other side of the glass, looks even happier than I that we have at least one correspondent roving in the right place, with his backpack transmitter up and running. He leans forward to press the talkback switch. 'You must be mad letting me loose through here. It's like entrusting a nuclear reactor to a washing-machine mechanic.'

'You're in safe hands,' I say. And plenty of them, now. The first half-hour of this unscheduled flood special was a bit hairy. We had to pad with music because there was only me behind the mike, Pimply Pete driving the desk, and two bleary-eyed members of the sports team, who'd already been on air all afternoon, operating the phones. Now, though, we've raised reserve troops, including Amanda who, in full and breathtaking ready-to-club gear, is womanning the phone lines with black talons and a staggeringly cantilevered cleavage. Well, it is Saturday night. But she assured us she wouldn't miss a programme like this for the hottest dance music in town.

'I really get off on flood specials,' she said, then looked conscience-stricken. 'Sorry, I know it's tough on the poor sods with carpets floating round their knees, but . . .' Her face brightened again. 'Well, it's always the same houses get hit, isn't it? You'd think they'd have the sense to move. Besides, there's nothing like the buzz of a crisis special.'

I know what she means. I too sympathize with the poor old folks shivering in blankets down at the Blackthorn Community Centre who are even now, in my headphones, singing 'Keep the Home Fires Burning' with a little prompting from the enterprising Harry. But, if I'm honest, I can only say I'm having a ball. Would be, even if I didn't have Thomas meeting my giddy grin through the glass and, when he thinks no one's looking, mouthing a kiss. Pillock. Amanda's noticed, all right, and I can tell she's viewing me in a whole new light. So is my daughter Polly. God, *Polly*.

I'll have to sort her out. *We* will have to sort her out, Tom and I, but there's no time to fret over her troubles now, because this kind of programme is even more of a white-knuckle ride than an Outside Broadcast. I may be sitting pretty in studio, but I'm flying blind. We all are. By definition, with an emergency special – snow, floods, elections or whatever – all you can do is react. Sure, since Wakeborough's in a flood plain and the river surges beyond its banks every so often, we have certain fixed procedures, and a permanent studio-quality line to the Emergency Ops room. Beyond that, though, we can only respond to events. We equip as many staff as we can muster, post them out, press the button which puts the studio live on air and hope for the best. No time thereafter to worry about a hysterical daughter. Still less to ring an aged parent with whom you've had a screaming row. A parent you actually told you never wanted to speak to again. Ever.

'Call from the police station,' crackles Tom's voice in my ear. 'Unconfirmed report of fresh flooding in . . . I say, isn't this up your way? Lower Mill?'

I pause before replying, just to check Harry is still going strong at the Community Centre. He is. I press my talkback switch. 'No, you've got it wrong. Lower Mill's way above the risk zones. Doesn't flood up there. Never has.'

'Willows Close,' exclaims Tom. 'But that's The Willows, where your dad lives, surely?'

'Can't be,' I say, but with a fraction less certainty. 'I mean, it simply *can't* be. Look, will someone ring my dad? The number's pinned to the wall through there, top of the blacklist of callers not to be let on to the air under any circs . . .'

38

Mac had telephoned me at home three times during the course of the day. The answering machine had silently soaked up all the calls. I'd been in no condition to switch it off last night, and in no mood to do so today. Having left Tom sleeping, I bathed and rehydrated myself with several pints of weak tea, and a nap on the sofa fortified me sufficiently to bustle around and sort out the house. Only when darkness was drawing in did my conscience finally nudge me across to the machine to see if anyone had been ringing me. Judging by the tape used, it seemed half the world had.

I'd listen in a moment, I thought. First, I poured myself a modest glass of wine – hair of the dog would set the seal on my recovery – and, hearing a stirring upstairs at last, shouted: 'Masses of hot water, help yourself to a bath, whatever you want. Drink and supper down here when you're ready.'

Frankly, I didn't care who'd been ringing. After all, no one knew I was here. Officially, I was away for the weekend. Polly and Mac would assume I hadn't returned early from Manchester after all, and that suited me fine. I wanted to keep them and everyone else shut out until tomorrow at least. I'd drawn the curtains on a blasting storm without, lit the lamps within and built up the fire to furious warmth. I had champagne chilling, Burgundy warming, a casserole thawing, and a string quartet sawing. I slipped off a shoe and held out a bare foot to the fire. I felt as blessedly at peace as it's only possible to feel when your whole being is focused on a single simple goal. Which was to seduce Thomas. I never doubted I could do it.

I heard taps and the babble of a radio echoing down from the bathroom, then silence as the door shut. I took another gulp of wine, and wandered back to the answering machine. Better get the job over with. Nothing vital, it turned out. Three calls from Mac, increasingly testy, demanding I ring him the minute I returned. I paused, then spun the tape back over his final message. Listened again. Yup, I thought, he's been hitting the bottle. His blasts of invective were interspersed with two messages from George, equally astringent if more sober, saying much the same: would I please ring her? Finally, exasperatedly, demanding to know where the hell I thought I was if I wasn't at home? Only the last message caused me momentary disquiet. No, not disquiet, irritation. I'd actually heard the call click in, a few minutes ago, while I was opening the wine in the kitchen. Turned out to be Pete, ringing from work. Sounding quite uncharacteristically diffident, he asked whether, by any chance, not that he was suggesting anything, but did I happen to know where, um, Steve was to be found this weekend? He'd tried Steve's mobile but it was switched off. You see, he was doing a Saturday stint to help out, the weekend editor had gone to his wedding, Helen was away and none of the sports staff seemed to know where the boss could be contacted. Well, I was obviously out, too, so, not to worry, sorry to disturb me and all that. Then a buzz of dialling tone.

'No,' I said to the machine, flipping it off with satisfaction, 'I've no idea where Stephen bloody Sharpe is. At least, quite likely emerging from a football match in Manchester, so there's not a fat lot of use my telling you that. Besides, I've supper to cook.'

I suppose it was quarter of an hour later – I'd prepared some vegetables anyway – when I heard the sitting-room door slam. I re-emerged from the kitchen, glass in hand, beaming. 'Ready for a . . .' *Drink, darling?* was what I was about to say. But didn't. Because it wasn't Thomas standing in front of the fire. It was Polly. My daughter, dripping wet and thunder-faced. 'You *are* back,' she said. 'Why didn't you ring me? Honestly, Grandpa's just about driving me crazy. He's senile, you know that? Sick.'

'What are you doing here?' I said, stupidly.

'Getting away from him. And I don't care what he says, I'm going out with them tonight. You don't mind, do you?'

'Mind what? For goodness' sake, love, do you have to trample your great muddy boots all over the rug?'

'We're going out to cut the wire late tonight,' she said. 'Kevin, me, some of the others. The fence Trevor Green's put round the tip, I mean. So we can dig tomorrow. He won't have anyone working there on a Sunday. That's OK by you, isn't it?'

Almost anything which would have got Polly out of the house that night would have been OK by me, but even so . . . 'That's, um, illegal surely? Damaging property?'

She rolled her eyes. 'You're so *bourgeois*, Mum. So narrow-minded. Honestly, if it'd been left to people like you, women wouldn't even have the vote. What does Trevor Green care about a bit of barbed wire, anyhow? Is there anything for supper?'

'But you're staying at your grandpa's,' I squawked. 'I gave you a mushroom quiche, a risotto and a load of pasta to take down there, and –'

'I'm not going back to him,' she snapped, and there was an odd note in her voice. It wasn't just temper. There were bright spots of colour in her cheeks, and she was staring at the wall, as though she didn't want to meet my eyes. 'He's a filthy-minded old man. I've *told* him Kevin and I are just friends, but he keeps going on and on. As though I'm making all this up about the wire-cutting, as though it's some kind of cruddy excuse to stay out late with Kevin. I mean, how can he be so moronic? Like I told him, if I wanted to get up to anything with Kevin it'd be just as easy at four o'clock in the afternoon as midnight. Which I don't want to, anyway. I wouldn't touch Kevin with a bargepole.' She was beginning to sound hysterical. My heart was sinking. I suppose I assumed she'd had a row with the boy, but I was beginning to realize I couldn't throw her out now, not in this state. 'He's fixated on sex, that's his problem.'

I blinked. 'Kevin?'

'Don't be stupid,' she spat at me. 'Grandpa. You know what he said to me just now? Well, hinted. He said . . .' Her chest was heaving, as though she couldn't bring herself to utter the words.

'What, love?' I said, mystified.

'That you used to – used to go out with Kevin's dad. And babies didn't come out with a label attached, so I shouldn't go running round with Kev because . . . Well, he didn't say it, but it was almost like he meant, you know . . .'

'My God,' I gasped. 'How *could* he?'

She was blushing furiously. 'Sorry. Probably got the wrong end of the stick. But he was being so foul.'

'That *monster*,' I snarled. 'How *dare* he? How could he even think such a thing, let alone, let alone . . .? Where's the phone?'

Polly looked straight at me. Her father's clear, golden gaze. 'Did you know Frankie Henderson?'

I turned my back on her and seized the telephone. 'Met him, yes. Oh, for God's sake, your grandfather used to work the same bill with him sometimes, years ago. But to suggest . . .'

An uncertain giggle escaped her. 'Wow, Mum, the look on your face.' I lowered the phone and turned. 'I mean, I knew it was rubbish really,' she said. 'Just Grandpa going off his rocker. You know what he's like when he's been drinking, saying anything to stop you going out, just because he's pissed off, but –' She broke off, because the bathroom door had opened upstairs. There was a burst of radio. Then the thump of footsteps across the landing. 'Mum? Someone here?'

I could feel myself flushing now. I dropped the phone back on to the windowsill, bracing myself, telling myself, well, at the very least, she *liked* Thomas. I wouldn't get the hassle she used to give me with Stephen. 'Ah, yes, there is actually.'

She was looking round now. Clocking the bottle of wine, the music. 'Uh-huh,' she said, suddenly looking much older and wiser. 'No, no, it's cool, I can handle it. I was pretty stupid before, but I've grown up, OK? Don't worry, I'll, um, make myself scarce. Give Sophy a ring, see if I can go round there.' The footsteps were tramping down the stairs now. 'You won't want me around if you've got Steve in.'

'Know something Rita?' bellowed a joyful, laughing, masculine voice. 'I'm thirsty, hungry, and randy as all hell.'

The door swung open and there, dripping wet and naked, stood Thomas.

Well, not actually naked. He had a hand towel knotted round his loins, but that was all. He took in the pair of us, and blinked. 'Shit,' he said, with a bashful cough of laughter. 'Sorry, Polly. Didn't know you were home. I'll, um . . .'

'Tom,' she gasped. Until then, my gaze had been riveted on Thomas, but there was something in her voice made me spin round. She was staring at me, white-faced and wide-eyed. 'How could you?' she hissed. Her voice swelled into a howl of outrage.

'You – you – God, Mum, you're *disgusting*. How could you do this to me?' And with a shuddering sob, she charged past Thomas and I heard the front door slam. By the time I reached the doorstep, she was pedalling off down the hill, hair streaming, shoulders hunched over the handlebars, vanishing into the rainy night.

'I'll kill him,' I raged, striding back into the sitting room. 'This time, truly, I'm going to kill him.'

'I don't get it,' said Thomas. He was standing by the fire. 'I'm desperately sorry, Rose, crass of me, bursting in, but . . . why did she explode like that? I thought she liked me.'

'Don't ask me to unravel the mysteries of the adolescent psyche,' I panted, seizing the telephone. 'She's always been funny about my friends – men friends. Besides, she was in a state when she got here. Her grandfather's been winding her up, the evil-minded, interfering old . . . Oh, Tom, don't.' He'd moved in behind me and was wrapping his arms round me, pressing his naked body against mine.

'Sorry, I'm wet.'

'It's not that,' I said, wriggling free to tap in Mac's number. 'It's my bloody father's fault she came charging home, and I want to blow his head off while I'm still good and mad and you're mellowing me fast.'

'Why are you cross with him?' he murmured, nibbling the side of my neck in a way which made my knees buckle. 'Oh, I say, I meant to ask, what's all this about floods in Wakeborough?'

I lifted the receiver away from my ear. 'Sorry?'

'I had the radio on in the bath. Radio Ridings, I mean. They were talking about flood alerts all over the place, but it sounded a bit disjointed. As though they weren't quite sure how they should be handling it.'

But the other phone had been picked up. 'Mac?' I snapped. 'What's this – this *unspeakable* rubbish you've been telling Polly?'

'Rubbish, is it? I may be old, but I'm not senile, woman. Don't try and deny you used to shack up with that pathetic little ferret-keeper, I always had my suspicions and it was written all over your face the other night.' He was drunk, I could hear. Drink, however, doesn't render him inarticulate. It just speeds up the flow of words to machine-gun rapidity. I was shouting back but he wouldn't stop. 'So tight-lipped as you were, all those years ago, about which particular gooseberry bush you'd found your little bastard under. Well, considering with whom you'd been consorting, I'm not at all surprised you wanted to keep your murky philanderings secret, but –'

'How dare you?'

'But you can't play fast and loose with your daughter. When were you going to tell her? When the pair of them got engaged? Because I've got eyes in my head and that boy is as pottily besotted as ever a – Polly? Is that you, girl?'

'*Mac?*'

There was no answer. Only a noisy crashing of doors at the other end of the phone. Some muffled shouting. Mac snapping that, oh, she'd deigned to return, had she? 'She's locked herself into her bedroom,' his voice suddenly snarled in my ear. 'The tears streaming down her poor wee face. I hope you're proud of yourself, Rita.'

'Me?' I yelled. '*Me*? I've got only two things to say to you, Mac. One is that Frankie Henderson is no more Polly's father than he's King of Siam.' I heard an exclamation from Tom but just swept on: 'The other is that I never want to – to speak to you, or to see you – or to hear your bloody name ever again. And this time I bloody well mean it, for good and ever.' I slammed the phone down. Then flung myself against Tom and burst into tears.

'Hell, sweetheart, that was a bit ferocious, wasn't it?'

'He asked for it. You don't know him. He's – he's a monster.'

'What was all that about Frank Henderson?'

I couldn't even explain. Just shook my head dumbly against his shoulder. 'I should . . .' I gulped. 'I should never've made it up with him.'

'Made what up?' said Tom softly, stroking my hair.

'He was a pig to my mother, all her life. Never even came to see her when she was ill. Not once. So he was working away – on the boats. But when he got back, after she was dead . . .' I could hardly get the words out. 'He accused me of being responsible – for her death. Yelled at me that it was the shock of – of a little bastard in the family, that's what had killed her. Wouldn't listen – when I said Mum made me do it, made me have Polly. I – I didn't speak to him for three years. And I know it was just because he felt guilty – he always shouts when he knows he's wrong – just like now, and he's drunk as a skunk but . . . Oh, Thomas,' I wailed. 'I'm so miserable now, and it's all a mess, and I was so happy before.'

He cradled my wet face in his hands. 'It's going to be all right.'

I hiccuped. 'It is?'

''Course it is. Just because you've got a hysterical daughter, a delinquent, drunken father and an incompetent, unemployed and probably unemployable lover to support . . . I mean, what's your problem?'

'Pillock,' I said, halfway between tears and laughter.

'But before you tell me what Frank Henderson has to do with anything, can I ask you again about these flood alerts? Knowing your boss's mania for efficiency, this is probably a daft question, but after I'd walked out, he did leave someone minding the shop, didn't he?'

'. . . and, by the way, Sergeant Kitson,' I say, although I'm looking only into the unblinking eye of the microphone, because Sergeant Kitson is a couple of miles away in the Emergency Ops Room. 'Can you confirm this report of flooding up at Lower Mill? The Willows?'

'I'm afraid, at this moment in time, we haven't any more details than you've already given out, Rose.' (Where do they get these spokesmen? I sometimes suspect there's a secret Dock Green school of broadcasting, because I promise, this kindly rumbling voice is a dead ringer for PC George *Evenin'*, *all* Dixon. Except with a Yorkshire accent). 'We received a rather confused telephone call from one of the residents in The Willows, reporting water up to back-doorstep level, and one of our vehicles will be arriving on the scene as soon as they can be spared elsewhere. I can only ask residents of The Willows, if they're listening, to bear with us. As I'm sure everybody realizes, our resources are fully stretched, and most likely this is only a blocked drain backing up under the pressure. We certainly don't anticipate any actual flooding at The Willows. It's in a valley, but well clear of the flood zone. We will, of course, let you know when we have any more news.'

Mind how you go . . . I don't actually say that, but it's on the tip of my tongue. No, I just thank the good sergeant and link over to a reporter who's managed to get the radio car out with a fire crew down at the East End of town where the waters, I gather, are definitely subsiding, and they're bringing pumps into noisy operation. This isn't an interview the poor reporter is conducting, it's a shouting match. Oh well, highly atmospheric. I shut my microphone and press the talkback switch. 'D'you get through to my dad?'

Pete shakes his head. 'Still engaged.'

Suddenly Amanda's head jerks up. 'Frig-a-pig,' I hear her say. Whereupon the talkback goes dead, and I have to watch a mime show beyond the glass of her hopping up and down beside Thomas, mouth flapping, arms flailing, bosom heaving. I'm not *worried* exactly, more bewildered, as well as exasperated with Mac for gabbing on so long. And I wish someone in that cubicle would bloody talk to me. Tom does, at length, locate the talkback switch. 'Amanda seems to think your dad might actually have rung us. About ten minutes ago.'

I see her shove Tom aside. 'I'm so sorry, Rose. But you know what he's like – I mean, you did warn us. The number's up on the blacklist and I just thought he was having us on again.'

Only then does a tiny anxiety begin to nibble. 'Having us on about what? And be quick. I can hear Rob winding his report before he loses his voice in that din.'

'I thought he might be a bit, um, pissed actually.'

I don't waste time interrupting. I just grimace and nod.

'He was laughing, saying had we thought about offering DIY tips on ark-building. And I said, what? And he said he'd warned you about that, um, that bloody walking tree and maybe now you'd listen to reason and could he talk to you, and I said, no, you were on air, and then I heard shouting and – well – he just went.'

A girl who usually works on the teatime show pops into view behind Thomas and thrusts a piece of paper over his shoulder. 'Report in from an elderly woman taking her dog out,' he hisses, very fast because he, like me, can hear Rob is about to hand back to studio. 'Don't worry. It's *not serious*. Hear me? Not serious. There seems to have been a kind of small landslip. The tip, The Willows. A bit's peeled off and blocked the stream. That's why The Willows is under water. Few inches *maximum*, and –'

'Thanks, Rob,' I say smoothly, opening my microphone. And some devil takes possession of me. I listen, aghast, to the words tripping out of my own mouth. 'Back to The Willows, where we've now heard the flood has been caused by subsidence from an old tip blocking the stream. Funnily enough, I happened to be reading in yesterday's *Gazette* that local businessman Trevor Green has just launched work to landscape that tip into a park.' I can see Tom's jaw dropping. I smile grimly at him. Why shouldn't I rattle the bastard's cage a bit? After what he's done to Uncle Jim, he bloody deserves it. Besides, didn't he once urge me to come straight to him if there were any problems with The Willows? Well, that's exactly what I'm doing. 'The bulldozers and earth-dumpers moved in yesterday, and there seems to be a possibility that this might have triggered the landslip. If anyone up there in Lower Mill can tell us exactly what's going on, we'd like to hear from them. And, of course, if Mr Green himself happens to be listening, and would like to ring in with his views, then I'd be delighted to talk to him, too. In the meantime . . .'

In the meantime, I'm tapping a message into my computer: WILL SOMEONE PLEASE TRY TO GET HOLD OF GEORGE?

39

We had encountered George in the car park here. To my intense frustration, we'd had to come into work. I'd felt obliged to tell Thomas about Pete's garbled message on my answering machine and he'd rung the station only to find them bouncing round like panicked rabbits over the flood alerts, not sure whether to stay on air or not.

Thing is, on a normal Saturday, at six o'clock we throw a switch, opting into the evening programmes shared by stations in the region, turn off our lights and toddle home. Unless, of course, we have a particular reason for staying on air locally – such as floods. But only *serious* floods, as I said to Tom. Not the river-up-a-bit, sandbags-in-a-few-doorways sort of floods which happen every month in a wet winter. It has to be the real property-threatening McCoy. The decision whether or not to opt into emergency programming rests with the Managing Editor, but Stephen had evidently gone to his football match. Failing that, it falls to the Assistant Editor. Who had, as Tom flatly pointed out, flung in his resignation late yesterday afternoon. The weekend editor was tripping the light fantastic at a wedding reception in an unnamed hotel, Helen was away . . .

Thomas, with a noble squareness of jawline which made me want to punch him, had pronounced himself duty bound to drive into Radio Ridings and see if he could lend a hand. I meanly found myself wondering if he found the prospect of a chaotic radio station less daunting than my bed. I accompanied him not just because I couldn't bear to let him out of my sight, but because my car was still parked at work from yesterday. If I intended to go down and make peace with my father and daughter, I needed transport.

Worst of all, I nearly had a row with Tom as we drove in. As the radio chattered in the background, I was telling him what Mac had been up to. How he'd behaved oddly about young Kevin Henderson from the outset, how the inquisitive old devil had been needling me about Frankie, how he'd held forth darkly about Frank's irresponsibility as a father, but that I'd never in a million years guessed his real suspicions. 'I still can't believe it. And then even to *hint* such a thing to Polly? I told her it was rubbish, and she hadn't really taken him seriously, thank God, but the *shock*. It's no wonder she got hysterical. I'm sorry, I know he's old, and unhappy, and drunk and – and all that, but I can't forgive him this.'

'Can't you?' said Tom. 'Sorry, which way is it to get round into the car park?'

'Left at the lights. No, I can't.'

'Isn't it – forgive me – but isn't it partly your own fault? If only you'd told everyone the truth from the start, then we wouldn't be in this mess.'

'What?' I shrieked. Well, I was in a seriously overwrought condition. Plucked from my cosily seductive nest, plunged into family screaming matches, dragged out into a stormy night – God knows what I might not have said. But Tom had parked the car and, without even turning off the engine, twisted round in his seat and grabbed me. 'Sorry,' he was mumbling. Indistinctly, because he was kissing every bit of me he could reach. 'Priggish – thing to say. God, Rose – I need you, want you – so *desperately*.'

Our ardent wrestling amid coats, seatbelts, gearsticks and what have you was interrupted by a sharp bash on the roof, followed by the flinging open of the rear door. A package thudded on to the back seat, followed by George, who heaved herself in and slammed the door behind her. 'Very touching, I'm sure, children,' she snapped. 'But if you could curb your passion for a moment, I wish to have words with you.'

'George,' I gasped, sinking below the level of the seat and clutching my gaping shirt. 'What brings you here?'

'The Radio Ridings Fiesta. Which I borrowed in order to spite Stephen Sharpe and to visit Jim Rumbelow's cottage. I now feel obliged to return the damn thing, however, because, to judge by the increasingly hysterical tone of the flood alerts, I suspect every vehicle is about to be commandeered into use. That, I assume, is what brings the pair of you out of hiding?'

'Unfortunately,' I muttered and, restored to respectability, twisted round to look at her. Only then did a subtle and not at all pleasant aroma assail my nostrils. 'George? Can I smell something?'

'A present for you,' she replied. 'A pheasant. Whether it's fit for consumption is another matter. Game, I believe, should be hung in an airy larder, not left to rot on a front-door mat.'

'Sorry?'

'I thought you'd be interested to know that, on letting myself into Jim Rumbelow's cottage just now to inspect his geraniums, I found, inside the door, this letter, addressed to him in your own distinctive fist. The envelope, you will doubtless be glad to observe, is unopened.'

'He never read my grotty letter, then? It wasn't that made him . . .? Oh, thank goodness.'

'I dare say he was too busy opening this very much larger package,' continued George. 'Containing said bird, which had a luggage label tied with strangulatory vigour around its neck saying something to the effect — forgive me if I quote from memory rather than groping with the corpse to retrieve the text — that Jim would be wise to stop poking his nose into matters which didn't concern him.'

'I don't believe it,' I gasped, looking at Tom.

'It's the fucking budgie,' he breathed. 'All over again.'

'No it's a pheasant,' said George. 'Not, incidentally, Jim's pet pheasant. At least, there seemed to be a fowl pecking round his greenhouse so —'

'That *bastard*,' I hissed. 'Trying to put the frighteners on a harmless old man. If he thinks —'

'I suppose you may know what you're talking about,' interrupted George, 'but that's not all I wished to say to you. I have been cultivating a relationship of singularly redundant intimacy with your answering machine, Rose, because I need to be told what I'm supposed to do about your daughter. At a conservative estimate, I should say Polly has rung me half a dozen times in the course of the day, demanding to know where Tom is, whether he has yet reappeared, and where, if anywhere, she can contact him. To be sure, if I'd had my wits about me at dawn this morning, rather than being lost in a gin-sodden haze, I would have told her he'd emigrated. Failing that, I did at least retain sense enough not to disclose that the last time I'd clapped eyes on her idol, he was carrying her inebriated mother –'

'Idol?' exclaimed Tom.

'Don't tell me you hadn't noticed the poor lovelorn infant thinks the sun shines out of your you-know-where!'

'No,' I cried, flopping back in my seat. 'I mean . . . ' I let out a groan. 'Lord, how could I be so dim?'

'Quite easily, it appears,' retorted George.

'I don't understand,' protested Tom. 'What's all this about?'

I ignored him, twisting round to George again. 'Polly charged home after a row with her grandpa half an hour ago, not actually expecting to find me there, and certainly not expecting Thomas to wander downstairs. Wearing a soppy smile and a very small handtowel.'

A small cough of laughter escaped George. 'Oh dear,' she murmured. 'Oh my *dears*. What complicated lives you do lead.'

She hadn't wanted to go. Chekhovian family dramas, she declared – nay, Sophoclean tragedies, given the Oedipal overtones – were not her style. She was, she said, more at home in your light romantic comedy.

'All I'm asking,' I pleaded, 'is for you to go and calm Polly down.' My poor baby. The make-up, the baths, the poetry: they had nothing to do with Kevin. When Polly had claimed she and Kev were no more than friends she was, as far as she was concerned, telling the exact truth. No, along with half the junior staff in Radio Ridings, my daughter had developed a whopping crush on Thomas. 'Just let her talk to you, George. She likes you, you can comfort her. I mean, I can't, can I? Under the circs?'

'I have to visit Jim,' she said obstinately, 'and reassure him about his geraniums.'

'So go on to my dad's afterwards. It looks like we might be in work for a while.'

Tom started. 'Shit, yes, I'd better get in there, hadn't I?'

'I'm coming too,' I said firmly. 'If you're opting for a flood special, you'll need me. Unless you want it presented by a sports reporter. George, *please*.'

'I haven't a car,' she said in a feeble last-ditch protest. 'I couldn't take a BBC vehicle now, not in this hour of crisis.'

'Have this one,' I said instantly. 'Mine's here to get us home. Leave your key in the ignition, Thomas. And, George, look, there's a mobile phone under the dashboard, see it? Don't wait until you get home. Ring me the minute you've talked to her.'

40

So here I am. Live on air, with the station pulsating, every car in use, every reporter we can rustle up on a Saturday night out on the road, and I'm throwing down challenges to Trevor Green. Well, he deserves it. Sending threats and dead birds to Uncle Jim . . .

Thomas dodges into studio during a rumbustious report from the Old Ship Inn. Lifting the buzzing headphone off my ear, I express weary surprise we didn't instal a permanent line to the Ship along with the one to the Emergency Ops room because, whenever the river rises, the bar is always swimming, we always roll along and the regulars are *always* there, swearing a bit of water won't interfere with their drinking.

'Want a break, love?' says Tom. 'Pete's lining up the other studio so you can do a straight handover.'

'Fine for now. Not got through to Dad?'

'Still engaged. I can only assume he's left the phone off the hook.' Don't ask me why, but this provokes my first real twinge of worry. I have a vision of a receiver dangling at the end of its cord. Amanda said she heard shouting, that he vanished off the line . . . Daft, I tell myself. A few inches of water won't harm him, even if it's reached his bungalow. After all, wet feet never . . . I flinch, because, whatever else is afflicting my father, it's certainly not wet feet.

'George?' I say. 'You've tried raising her on your car phone?'

'Not answering. Would she recognize the ringing tone?'

Amanda waves from the cubicle. I hastily clamp my cans back into place, and hear her gabbling that George has phoned on Tom's mobile, should she switch it through?

'I hope you realize I nearly caused a major traffic accident as I entered Lower Mill,' barks George in my ear, 'with this ridiculous little contraption bleeping away under the dashboard.'

'George, where are you?'

Thomas drops to a crouch beside me, his head pressed to my shoulder to listen. 'Parked round the corner from The Willows, where total pandemonium reigns because of a few puddles.'

'Puddles? That's all?'

'You'd barely wet your chillblains crossing the road, although it is. I grant, highly picturesque, waves lapping round the waists of the garden gnomes and so forth. However, from what I gather, the entire population has decamped up the road in massed panic to some church hall or other. Those that haven't are standing at the water's edge here, gawping like trippers on Brighton Beach.'

'Is Polly there? Dad?'

'Haven't seen them so far, but I've only just arrived. Wait a minute . . . No, it seems they're the only ones with the sense to stay indoors. I can see a light in your father's window. I don't think the water's anywhere near the top of his doorstep.'

'Hold on, George,' I say, clamping the phone to my shoulder. 'Should we put her on air? On the phone, eyewitness report?' Tom nods, scrambles to his feet and lopes out of the studio. George is less than pleased to learn she is expected to contribute to the programme. No, I understate it. She is *outraged*. 'I have worked nearly half a century for this Corporation,' she roars, 'and I am a creator of features, a weaver of aural magic, not a sweaty-necked, tin-hatted hack, gasping despatches from the front.'

'Think James Cameron,' I retort. 'Think René Cutforth and Wynford Vaughan Thomas. I'll give you a couple of minutes to find out what's happening from the locals, then we'll ring you back and come to you live, OK? Oh, and when we're through, can you slip along and see what Mac's up to? He seems to have left his phone off the hook.'

'I have not got any wellingtons,' bellows George. 'And –' The line's cut off by Pete. I adjust my cans and concentrate on the output. The customers at the Ship are full of the old Blitz spirit and – by the raucous sound of it – several other brands of spirit, too, as the reporter hands back to me. 'The Ship crowd in their customary good voice,' I say. And then, for an instant, I flounder.

I've glanced across at the cubicle and seen to my dismay Stephen Sharpe's trim figure. What's more, he's holding open the door for – oh, my giddy aunt – for Trevor Green. In person. In *persons*, because, as if that weren't bad enough, Trevor has, trailing in his wake, Frankie Henderson. It's beginning to look like a tube train in rush hour, that side of the glass. Amanda, phone clasped to her ear, gapes round, visibly agog with excitement. Pete is hunched over the desk, twiddling knobs, ignoring the lot of them. And Stephen, who, it will transpire, skipped the extra night in the four-poster and tuned into the show as he drove back across the Pennines, is strutting around like a bantam whose farmyard is rioting. 'We return now to Sergeant Kitson in the Ops room,' I manage to croak, 'for an update on flood alerts. How are things going?'

'Basically good news, I'm happy to say, Rose . . .' As he chunters on in his Dixonish way, my gaze is fixed on the window. I feel like a goldfish trapped in a bowl. Pete is scowling, Amanda's laughing, Stephen is gesticulating and Tom is very ostentatiously ignoring him and monitoring the output. And Frank – Frankie's looking at me. For Heaven's sake, he's pale as a ghost, sweating . . . What's worrying him? He's mouthing something at me. That he's *sorry*? Trevor blocks him from my view, turns, catches my eye, and lifts his hand in a little salute. I can't help but think of a duellist at the start of a contest. Well, it's my own fault. I challenged him to respond, but I never expected the bastard to turn up in the flesh. Nor did a suddenly grim-featured Tom. He can't press the talkback and tell me this is the intruder who once introduced himself as Lincoln, but he doesn't need to. It's written all over his face. Trevor's talking to Stephen now who, in turn, gabbles at Tom. The pantomime seems to last for hours and no one says a bloody word to me. Sergeant Kitson rumbles away in my ears all the while and, somehow or other, I'm framing questions and parroting helpline numbers on cue. Suddenly Tom, with an impatient wave of the hand, silences Steve, and begins to tap words into the computer: TREV WANTS TO BE INTERVIEWED. STEVE SAYS WE SHOULD. I HOPE YOU KNOW WHAT YOU'RE DOING, KID, BECAUSE I DON'T.

I manage a wavering smile. 'Thank you, Sergeant Arnold Kitson of the North Yorkshire Constabulary.' I plug in a jingle, the longest we have. It's an operatic fantasy of ethereal voices and Wagnerian tedium, promising music and entertainment, news and views, all for you . . . I've slammed my microphone shut on the first note, and stabbed the talkback. 'Trevor Green first? Or have we got George yet?'

Trevor, however, is already shouldering across the crowded cubicle and appears in my doorway with a smile. The hypocritical, blackmailing, bullying thug. I wish I could yell at him to explain why a dead pheasant thunked on to a poor old man's doormat but, of course, this interview has to be played by the rules. The only angle I can legitimately pursue is whether his bulldozers and earth-dumpers destabilized the tip. Wouldn't he agree he sent them in precipitately? And, he'll doubtless claim, no, he's had the plans drawn up for months, with reports from structural engineers, et cetera, you name it. And *then* what do I ask? I'm not surprised Tom's looking apprehensive on the other side of the glass. I'm going to have to do some fancy footwork if I'm to stop Trevor twisting this whole thing into a further PR exercise.

'Not on air?' he mouths, creeping round to my side of the desk. For a big man, he's light on his feet.

'Jingle's running. If, um, you'd like to sit over there?'

'Let's go easy in this interview, shall we?' He's still smiling confidentially as he leans over me. Too close.

'I beg your –'

'I don't want to hear the word Vertco, right? You don't either, if you know what's fucking good for you.'

My mouth sags. I know he's a crook and a thug and all the rest, yet I can't believe I'm hearing this, now, in my own studio. I reach for the talkback. He catches my hand, pretends he's shaking it in greeting. 'You don't embarrass me, I won't embarrass you. OK by you, *Rita*?'

I try to speak. Find, shamefully, I can't. I glance into cubicle hoping someone, anyone, will come and rescue me. But Steve and Tom seem to be having some kind of shouting match; the sods aren't even looking this way.

Trevor straightens up again and moves away to the chair opposite mine. 'Sorry I couldn't persuade Frankie in to say hello himself,' he observes conversationally. So that's it, I think numbly. Christ, I should've been worrying from the moment I worked out the two of them were in business together. And that's why he's dragged Frankie along. Living proof he knows plenty to embarrass me. As though reading my thoughts Trevor adds: 'Being as the two of you turn out to be such *very* old friends. But he's still upset from the Fayre yesterday. Very sensitive soul.'

What? What about the Fayre? And I'm missing what Tom's saying in my headphones. '. . . give you a breather before you take on the Blackpool budgie-strangler, I've got George lined up. Go to her first, will you, sweetheart?' He says this with a warmth which sends Stephen's eyebrows soaring.

I can only nod because the heavenly Kilohertz are warbling to a cadence. Then I take a deep breath and beam radiantly at the microphone. Well-known tip. When all the world's collapsing around you, smile. It magically inflects the voice with confidence. 'And now we can go over live to Lower Mill,' I carol, averting my eyes from Trevor's scowl. (*It's crazy. What does he think he can do? Throw all this at me on air? I'll shut the mike; have him chucked out. Or will it be, Christ, like Harold Buckerill, a story in the* Gazette?) '. . . where a close of retirement bungalows has been hit. Our reporter' – there's an audible intake of breath from George at this undignified labelling – 'Georgiana Penistone is at The Willows. George, can you tell us what's going on?'

'Thank you, Rose.' Pause of symphony concert length. 'Well, this is a most extraordinary scene. I am standing at the edge of what appears to be a lake but is in truth a road.' Her dignified cadences remind me of nothing so much as Richard Dimbleby in Coronation mode. 'In the distance glowers the black mass of a former slag heap, some small corner of which slithered down earlier, blocking the stream which meanders around the gardens here. The rain has stopped falling now, and a vast sheet of water glistens under the orange orbs of the street lighting . . .'

In spite of everything, I almost laugh when I catch sight of Tom's face. I gather this isn't quite the style of hot-from-the-scene reportage he's used to. Even Trevor, who's picked up some headphones and is holding one to his ear, looks more stunned than enraged.

'. . . sprouting out of the shallow lake are fences, rose bushes, street lights and – like a flotilla of great barges afloat on the water – twelve bungalows, waves nibbling at their foundations. Only one still shows a light, however. Most of the elderly residents have taken refuge in the mighty stronghold of the Wesleyan Chapel a few yards up the hill . . .'

I notice, belatedly, that words are flickering up on my computer screen: STAINLESS ABOUT TO HAVE CORONARY, writes Thomas.

WE'VE MUTINIED AND WON'T LET HIM TAKE OVER. BE BLOODY CAREFUL WITH LINCOLN GREEN. HE´S ALREADY THREATENING LAWYERS. I LOVE YOU.

'. . . helped to safety before the water was more than an inch or so deep by a local schoolgirl, Polly Shawe . . .' I gasp and look at Thomas. He's leaped from his chair, waving a jubilant fist in the air. So's Amanda. '. . . who raised the alarm and assisted them, one by one, from their houses across to dry land. I gather –'

All at once, she shuts up. So abruptly I think the line is lost. I'm about to open my microphone when I hear the noise. It's a sound I will never be able to forget. Not that it's very loud. It's like, like a great exhalation of breath. As though the very ground is yawning. Next there's a distant thump and splintering, and an instant of silence so absolute it's uncanny. Then the screaming starts. 'George? George, what's happening?'

But I've forgotten to open the mike, and by the time I've slid up the fader, she's talking again. 'There's – there's . . . another slip.' Completely different voice. No majestic Coronation cadences. She's breathless, and frightened. Frightened to tell me.

'Another landslip? Where?' But I already know. I know exactly which bungalow is closest to the tip, to the slag heap. The bungalow which sticks out on a corner all by itself. The bungalow which, alone in the close, was showing a light in the window. I can hear panic breaking round George's phone; people shouting; a distant siren wailing.

'The tip's come down. Part of it. Swept down over two – perhaps three – bungalows at the far end. Rose, honestly, I don't think they were in there. All the residents got out ages ago.' She's talking direct to me now, giving up any pretence of reporting. 'You heard me say Polly was the one knocking on the doors, taking them to the chapel . . .'

Trevor's leaning forward, grim-faced. I ignore him. *Where is she now?* I want to scream. *Where's my daughter? Where's my dad?* But I'm on air. There are people out there listening. Maybe people as terrified as me. Other people whose elderly mum or dad live in The Willows. 'Can I – can I confirm the, um, rather alarming news we've heard?' I hear myself reiterating the facts, checking with George, forcing her to answer coherently, though she's distraught, sounds terrible. Only two bungalows seriously affected – No, not submerged exactly, but damaged, collapsed, walls pushed in – Actually it's hard to see. There are policemen here now, urging people back, someone's going to investigate, they have to be careful in case of further slippage . . .

You always wonder how you'll cope if something truly dreadful happens live on air. How you would have reacted if you were the one behind the microphone, blithely describing Jackie's pink suit when the bullet was fired. You never think it will happen to you, though. And never, in your worst nightmares, would you imagine a disaster involving not strangers, but . . . I find I can't stop talking. Because I know, if I do, I'll just scream and scream. So I thank George for her report, and say how terrible this is, that our prayers are with those at the scene, that we're anxiously awaiting reassurance about casualties. 'And I'm sure you'd like to leave us for the moment, George,' I say rapidly, only this isn't a suggestion, it's an order, 'to go up to the Wesleyan Chapel where the residents have taken refuge, and you can report back from there.'

DARLING, I'M SURE THEY'RE OK, says my screen. SIGN OFF. WE'RE PUTTING PETE IN THE OTHER STUDIO. THIRTY SECS AND HAND OVER.

I shake my head fiercely. And with immense care I recapitulate once again for the listeners exactly what we've just heard. Find myself repeating, a plaintively stuck record, that there are no reports of casualties, no reports of casualties, no reports of casualties . . . Shake myself out of it. 'So, um, we're waiting, and will pass on news as soon as we have any.' What now? My brain's blanked out. I stab a button at random and the operatic jingle starts warbling away again. Oh God . . .

Trevor's risen. I'd forgotten all about him. He's planted his fat fists on the desk and is leaning towards me. 'Don't even think about trying to pin this one on me,' he hisses. 'Not unless you want to read an exclusive on Monday about Frankie's teenage love-child.'

'What?' At first I don't understand what he's saying. Then I remember the Fayre, and Mac, Mac and his stupid ideas . . .

'You heard.' He's moving towards the door. At that moment I want to kill him.

Instead I kill the jingle. Bang, in mid-note. Open my mike. And his. 'And with me now,' I snarl, 'I have Mr Trevor Green. It's his company, Lime Holdings, which owns The Willows. And it's one of his former companies, Vertco Limited, which used to own and operate the tip which has just collapsed. I wonder if you'd like to comment, Mr Green?'

He doesn't speak. He just mouths the words: *I've warned you.*

'In case anyone didn't catch that,' I say, steadfastly ignoring the horror-struck faces through the glass, 'Trevor Green has just whispered: "I've warned you."' Mr Green, can you elucidate?'

Trevor is about to slide out through the door, but Tom has crashed in and glares at him every bit as murderously as I'm doing. When he draws his finger across his throat, though, this isn't a threat to Trevor, but a message to me, to shut up. Trevor misinterprets it. 'No comment,' he grunts.

'Really?' I say. There's a voice in my ear, but I realize I'm not supposed to hear it. Someone's pressed the wrong button. I will learn later that Stephen, who's never operated a desk in his life, is scrabbling around trying to take my studio off air and switch Pete's on. Anyway, I hear Amanda's voice gasping: 'Oh Christ, they're not in the church with the others. Rose's dad, Polly . . .' And then I don't care about anything any more.

'You bastard, Trevor Green,' I roar, rising to my feet. 'You were so anxious to cover up your sleazy activities on that tip, you sent a load of bulldozers and earth-dumpers ploughing in. And you *haven't* got a comment to make? Now that the whole filthy lot has come thundering down on my dad's bungalow? You didn't realize that, did you? That it's *my father*'s bungalow under there? With my dad and my – and my fifteen-year-old daughter inside? No – no, I'm not finished yet . . .' This is to Tom, who's on my side of the desk now, wrapping his arms round me. 'Yes, Polly Shawe's my daughter. The selfsame daughter you've just been talking about, muscling into my studio with your pathetic little threats to try and silence me. Well, for your information Polly is not Frank Henderson's so-called love-child. This is her father, standing right here beside me, Tom Wilkes. You've met before, by the way – in that Blackpool flat you used to borrow for your parties. Personally I'd have thought that was the story for your squalid rag: "Millionaire businessman arranges spanking schoolgirl sex romps." Much more interesting than me. After all, what else is there to say? That I used to be called Rita Bagshawe? That I used to strip off in nightclubs? Sure, I did. Big deal. And I was dumb enough to have a fling with your weaselly little partner, Frankie Henderson – well, who bloody cares? I screwed a lot of men, some of them even creepier than him, but it wasn't a crime, wasn't wicked. Not in the way you're criminal and wicked, Trevor *Lincoln* Green. You've made a fortune bullying, and blackmailing, and freebooting over anybody who gets in your way. Now you might actually have added murder to the list. And' – I catch my breath on a sob – 'and I hope you rot in hell. And if, by any chance, I'm still on air,' I gasp, 'this is Rose Shawe, handing over – handing over – to . . .'

I can't go on. There's a voice in my headphones. 'Mum?' it's shouting. With a fearful, ethereal echo, as from another world. '*Mum?*'

Epilogue

Several Months Later

41

'My Lord High Sheriff, my Lords and Lady Mayors, Fellow Guild Members, Ladies and Gentleman . . .' intones a fat little man in a rusty dinner jacket.

We're in the ballroom of the Imperial Hydro Hotel, Harrogate; chandeliers are glittering, candles are flickering, and nerves everywhere are quivering. The annual awards ceremony of the Northern Press Guild may not be the Oscars exactly, but, having received generous sponsorship from a Taiwanese manufacturer of television and audio equipment, the hitherto resolutely inky pressmen of the Guild have been moved to include a galaxy of extra awards for the broadcast media this year, radio and television. More immediately, since Samino Corporation is cannily keen to encourage the use of hi-tech equipment in schools, they have also created a special category for outstanding youth journalism. We have a nominee twitching anxiously at our very table. Polly.

Well, you surely don't imagine she'd waste her time at a middle-aged wake like this just in order to please her parents? No, Polly's here as co-producer of 'The Willows: the Movie'. And she was not amused by her grandfather's observation that no extraordinary talent was required to reach a shortlist of five when there were but five entries. This is not the Polly of last October, though. This bigshot movie producer is shrink-wrapped in gold satin, with glossy black tights, vertiginous heels, inch-thick but tear-proof mascara (just in case) and a hairstyle evocative of the after-effects of a bomb blast.

'Reminds me of you,' whispers her fond father in my ear as the chairman of proceedings, having meandered through fulsome thanks to sponsors and caterers, finally gets down to business. The awards.

Polly has certainly changed. Mellowed, even. This is not, I

should add, as a consequence of a brush with death. Polly never came anywhere near death. Had not a clue she was even believed to be in peril. With typical honesty, even though it's possible she might actually have saved the odd life, she briskly disclaims heroism. As she puts it, all she was trying to do was stage-manage a bit of smart propaganda. Staring, with tear-drenched eyes, through her bedroom window at Mac's, she didn't see merely the splosh of slag heap slipping into stream and the black surge of water snaking across the gardens and smacking into the adjoining bungalow, she saw her Big Chance. And seized it.

Realizing that nothing could embarrass Trevor Green more than the emergency evacuation of an estate of old people, she rushed out to raise the alarm before ever the water reached mown-lawn height, and frogmarched the bewildered residents up the hill to the Wesleyan Chapel. One can only be grateful this building had a modern and well-heated vestry attached, otherwise the night's events might indeed have produced a casualty toll. Naturally, the marshalling of the exodus, the unlocking of the chapel and the unearthing of the essential tea-urn required her undivided efforts, but she left comprehensive instructions with her grandfather that he was to notify the emergency services, the media, *everybody*. All was progressing smoothly, with every other bungalow evacuated, until she returned to collect Mac, her last refugee. She says she then learned an important lesson. You should always ensure sobriety in your press spokesman. Mac had spent rather more time rescuing precious memorabilia of his stage career from the bottom of the wardrobe than he had alerting the nation's media. He had, moreover, been prudently stocking the pockets of his wheelchair with the whisky and cigarettes necessary to sustain him through the crisis. Most infuriating of all, as she grabbed his chair – in mid ark-building call to Amanda – and dragged him out of the door into the ever-deepening lake, he had flatly refused to be taken to the Wesleyan Chapel.

Not bloody likely, he roared. Go and shiver in a chapel? Where they wouldn't let him smoke, and probably confiscate his bottle to boot? If the old biddies didn't steal it to lace their tea, because he was prepared to bet no one else would've had the wit to come prepared. No, thank you very much, he'd rather sit this one out at home. Which Polly most certainly would not permit. After all, setting aside the consideration that this would fatally undermine her scenario of massed panic and peril, the water was, genuinely, rising. So, she yelled, did he intend to sit out in the rain, then? No, he damn well did not. And as soon as she let go of his chair, his hands were on the wheels and he was sploshing straight back in a homeward direction. OK, she said, seizing the chair again, how about if he went up to Mum's? He was old and frail and knackered, he retorted. Quite incapable of ascending that long hill. He would probably die in the attempt. Be found halfway up in the grey light of dawn, blue-faced, with rigor-frozen fingers clamped round his fag-end.

You've got to hand it to my daughter. She's not easily daunted. She would shove him up the hill herself, she snarled. After all, as she explained to me, she would at least have a telephone there, so she could capitalize on her propaganda coup. It was a long climb, during every step of which her grandfather sang at the top of his voice, between fortifying swigs from his bottle. First thing they did, on letting themselves into my house, was switch on the radio. 'To hear,' as Mac put it, 'obsequies being pronounced over us. Touching, if a trifle premature.'

Thus it was that, when I heard the voice gasping, 'Mum?' in my headphones, it was underlaid by that fearful howling echo. This is known in the trade, descriptively enough, as howl-round. Howl-round is the reason – if ever you've happened to take part in a phone-in show – that you're instructed to turn off your radio. Otherwise the broadcast programme feeds back down the phone and on to the air in just such a dizzying spiral.

I stood there in studio with this cacophony whistling in my ear, and Tom frozen beside me. I was staring through the glass, not even daring to hope. Amanda was grinning and yelling into her telephone so loudly I could have sworn I was actually hearing the words and not just lipreading them: '*Turn that bloody radio off!*' I also noticed that she was physically restraining Stephen from intervening. Truly, she was practically lying across the desk so he couldn't yank any more switches. As she said apologetically to me later, she thought the least the punters deserved, having heard that tearful little earful from me, was to cop in for the happy ending. And so, with Polly's radio safely switched off, I'd heard another click in my headphones, and then Mac's voice. 'Didn't I tell you I'd get rid of that bloody bungalow, one way or another?' he hooted. 'Didn't I always say – my very words, woman – didn't I say it was like being buried alive? Oh Jehoshaphat, *buried alive* . . .'

'Give the phone to me, Grandpa,' snapped an indignant voice. 'Honestly, you're a disgrace. Mum? Mum, you there?' Listening to the recording-off-transmission tape later, I would hear only a faint, answering gargle.

'Yeah, well, is it true all that? Like, you and Frankie Henderson, all the other men, nightclubs?'

'Your mam in her day,' roared Mac's voice, off-mike, 'made Madonna look like a member of the Townswomen's Guild.'

'Shut up, Grandpa. I mean, *stripping*?'

I still couldn't speak. I thought I was offering up my prayers of thanks silently, but the gabble would later prove to be perfectly audible.

'And – *Tom*?'

'All of it,' I choked at last, tears dripping off my chin. 'Every damn word.' I didn't care. Just as long as she was alive, they were both alive.

'Shit, Mum,' she breathed. 'That's the last time I call you narrow-minded and bourgeois.'

Thomas and I have long since ruefully agreed that, as a tactful way of breaking the shock of her paternity to Polly, this all left something to be desired. On the other hand, the realization that she had come within a whisker, to so speak, of being confronted with a ferret-flaunting comedy ventriloquist as her sire might have helped reconcile Polly to the news. Even to mend her broken heart – not, of course, that we breathed a word about that. Still, the speed with which she adapted to her acquisition of a second parent has been startling. After a period of surreptitious checking that Thomas fitted everything she already knew about her father (save, to be sure, his name, university and extant status), she seemed prepared to take him for granted. As if, he bemusedly said, he were just a new sofa. Since she now insults him as cordially as she does me, I'm hopeful no lasting damage was done by my on-air soul-baring.

You can see why, though, when it came to putting forward pro-grammes for awards, George claimed our flood special could almost have qualified in the radio drama category. It packed a punch, she said, many a soap opera would envy. She is, of course, also sitting at our table, resplendent in ruby velvet. 'Human Interest Documentary?' she'd mused jokingly, studying the entry form. 'Or is it just to be boring old News and Current Affairs?'

The show might even, if you were feeling broad-minded, have made a bid for the investigative journalism award. My terror-charged outburst, or so Thomas claims, was the catalyst which yanked out the crucial card and brought the house of Green tumbling down. Unfortunate metaphor, considering the state of my dad's bungalow.

Nevertheless, within days every paper and television station up here was rushing out Trevor Green exposés. As Tom said, if there were an award for the man who'd inspired the most journalistic activity locally this year, Green would be on a shortlist of one. He's been likened to Rachman, Maxwell, J. Edgar Hoover ... You'll have to forgive the hyperbole. Financial scandals, even those with a hint of sex and violence, may be no great shakes in London, but it's not often we grow a crook of such interesting proportions in our cosy patch. Whether he'll end up in any court other than the bankruptcy variety is another matter. The empire may have crumbled with debts in strings of computer digits, but Trev is still, so I understand, running his Bentley. In Spain. What he is most certainly not running is a commercial radio station in Wakeborough. The winners of the bid, produced from a sealed envelope last November, turned out to be a cheap and shiny little bunch called Great North Sound. They launched themselves on the unsuspecting airwaves a fortnight ago. Crap, of course. Radio Ridings has nothing to fear there. Nothing to fear anywhere, at least for the time being. If our flood special achieved nothing else, it dramatically illustrated Wakeborough's need for its own BBC station.

And indeed, eight months on from the night of the flood, here we all are in the steamily hot ballroom of the Imperial with – hang the expense – three whole tables flying the Radio Ridings logo. How times have changed. We'd have been lucky to get a single ticket if Stephen were still running the joint. He isn't. Having earned his bi-media credentials with his stint in Radio Ridings, he was forcefully encouraged by Howard Hemingway to thrust his career onwards, upwards, and as far away as possible. Latest news is he's been head-hunted by a satellite television company – to run the catering, but that's probably a myth. Even I don't believe the stories about standardized pea-counts per spoon.

Our new Managing Editor (strictly temporary, given Corporation policy on in-house marriages) is looking ineffably handsome in his dinner jacket (bought by me), dicky bow (tied by me), and whiter-than-white shirt (no need to mention who bought, pressed, and buttoned and cuff-linked his unenthusiastic body into it). Still, he's now grinning, golden and gorgeous as ever. We will not, however, look under the starched damask cloth crumpling to the carpet round our table, because only as we were actually entering the pillared precincts of the Imperial did I observe that my husband was still, absent-mindedly, wearing *trainers*. At least they were black, he protested. I can only pray no one's foolish enough to dish out any awards in his direction.

My own dress – over which I lavished even more time, effort and money than I did over his – is of a staggering respectability. High-necked, long-sleeved and ankle-skirted in black voile, it makes me look, growled Mac, like I'm auditioning for *The Sound of Music*. For the role, he added – in case I was flattering myself with Julie Andrews-ish notions – of Mother Superior. I retorted frostily that at least I didn't look like a fairground barker. Mac's waistcoat is a gold-buttoned symphony of tartan. Sequinned tartan.

'Honestly, George,' I said, as we met up in the foyer, 'can't you control him?'

Mac is now her lodger, tenant of the basement flat. What began as a post-flood emergency measure has settled into a permanent arrangement, to their mutual satisfaction. The insurance on the bungalow paid for chair-lifts and ramps and Dad can now bowl himself round pubs, clubs and bookies to his heart's content. I'm not surprised he's happy, it's George I worry about. She, however, claims his company is a source of enduring entertainment. After all, as she says, when he becomes cantankerous, she can always banish him down to the underworld again. 'It's rather like keeping one's own pet demon.'

'I think he looks sweet,' she declared in the foyer tonight.

'I'm a showman,' was his smug explanation. 'It behoves me to dazzle my public. Besides, I'm damned if I'm going to be outshone by my granddaughter.'

I notice Polly's sneakily adjusting her chandelier-sized earrings because the youth award is about to be announced. I can't claim the ballroom is agog. The *sotto voce* buzz continues. Well, it's always the way with these ceremonies, isn't it? They get the unimportant prizes out of the way first and build up to the biggies. Which means, incidentally, that all the radio categories come early. It goes without saying telly ranks higher and, since this is a pressman's do, so do the print awards. I don't mind. Once we know who has to totter up there and grab the bit of hardware, we can all stop sipping prudent Perriers and hit the bottle.

'And the Samino Special award for Young Journalists goes to . . .' The compère beams, and I see Polly and her co-producer, Kevin Henderson, exchange excited glances. '. . . the St Mary's Youth Group magazine, *Strumpet*.'

'Oh, *terrific*,' hisses Polly, sloshing wine into Kevin's glass and her own. She is now, as she reminds me, sixteen, which is quite old enough to consume a little alcohol. And to think, so recently, I was complaining that she never went out, never wore make-up, never took any interest in men . . . Poor Kevin hasn't a hope. I'm having a second bathroom installed next month.

I'm just hissing commiserations across the table when I have to break off, because this is the award we're all waiting for. Local Radio Personality of the Year. Of course I don't care. These things mean nothing. The fact that I've been rehearsing my wittily modest acceptance speech for a fortnight is neither here nor there. This category is, at least, deemed important enough for them to play a clip of each of us nominees. Mine makes my toes curl because it is, inevitably, taken from the flood special: my last, official, words on air that night, immediately after Polly's phone call, when I announced, with very audible tears in my voice, that it had just been confirmed there were no casualties from the disaster at The Willows, that I was grateful to the listeners for bearing with my personal traumas and that I was, finally, handing over to Pete Crockett who would be continuing Radio Ridings' coverage of flood-relief operations.

It gets a round of applause, at any rate, which makes my father glower into his glass. But I notice he's drunk very little tonight and that his fag is already stubbed out. The shiny-faced compère up on the stage takes at least an hour and a half to open his envelope, to announce that the winner, this year's Northern Press Guild's Local Radio Personality of the Year, is . . .

'Mac Bagshawe, for *Mac Sez.*'

George's face is incandescent. As well it might be. *Mac Sez* is her own creation, her celebratory gesture on having her programmes restored to her after Stephen's departure. 'With his wit and gift for language,' she had said when launching this eclectic mixture of jokes, invective and big band music, 'I simply cannot understand how I never came to employ him before.'

Thomas grins at me as she trundles Dad up to the stage. I grin back. Polly sees our soppy faces and rolls her eyes skywards.

'Mind, I reckon you should have won,' he whispers. Fibber. He thinks Mac's terrific. They have a mutual admiration society, which is to say that Mac, who is now accepting his award ('Speaking as a humble, geriatric shock jock . . .'), describes his son-in-law as over-bred, oversized, oversexed and one spoon short of a silver canteen to be marrying me, but not entirely to be despised when it comes to horses. I can't claim to enjoy an equally warm relationship with Tom's Mama, although her instant discernment of the family nose in Polly helped. We should be OK, just so long as I keep half Europe between her and Mac. Mind you, now he's Radio Personality of the Year, there'll be no stopping him . . .

'It's all your fault,' I whisper to Thomas, in between clapping and stamping and whistling for the old devil. Who is revelling – oh, isn't he just revelling? – in his audience. He *lives* for his weekly Sunday programme. 'George reckons the broadcast confession of my colourful past only added an interesting lustre to my, ahem, public persona. But when it came to the live actuality . . .'

I was through, you see. Signed off, finished, high as a helium balloon and limp as a stringless puppet. My studio was off the air – or it should have been. Pete was certainly nattering away in the other, giving a round-up of reports. Stephen – well, Stephen was sitting at the control panel with fractured spectacles and a bloody handkerchief clamped to his nose. The poor Lamb had only wanted to *apologize* to Trevor, certainly not to block his furious exit.

Everyone else had exited, too, rather pointedly. The news guys had vanished upstairs to file reports to the networks, Amanda and chums had decamped to the coffee machine. So Stephen, having defiantly resumed captaincy of a ship which was beginning to look like the *Marie Celeste*, sat alone with his back to us, eyes glued to the brightly lit window of Pete's studio opposite. Thomas snapped off the overhead light our side. 'My darling love,' he growled, grabbing me in an embrace so savage I nearly toppled over. Fell back against the desk anyhow. Gave, it seems, just a teensy-weensy nudge to a fader.

'. . . reports are continuing to come in of flood waters generally subsiding,' declared Pete. 'On the Blackthorn Estate . . .'

Citizens of Wakeborough with acute hearing, however, might have detected a faint, gasping obbligato.

For goodness' sake, Thomas, Steve might look round.

He can't see anything, not with the lights off in here.

'. . . councillors are already calling for action to stop this kind of thing happening again . . .'

Besides, gotta get home. Polly, Mac. . . .

Exactly: Polly, Mac. I want you all to myself.

Blimey, Thomas!

'. . . the need is now urgent, declared the leader of the Labour group . . .'

God, Rita, I haven't felt like this in months. Years. I want to make love to you so much I . . .

Stephen did find the right switch in the end.

Well, you know what they say. Never trust a dead mike in a live studio.